I0699768

# KIDNAPPING THEIR THIRD

**Disclaimer**
This is a work of fiction. Names, characters, businesses, places, events and incidents are either the products of the author's imagination or used in a fictitious manner. Any resemblance to actual persons, living or dead, or actual events is purely coincidental.

**All rights reserved:**
No part of this book may be reproduced or transmitted in any form or by any means, electronic or mechanical, including photocopying, recording, or by any information storage and retrieval system, without prior permission in writing from the author.


**Copyright:** RK Munin, 2024
**Cover Illustration**: Ryn Katryn Book Covers
**Profession Editing:** Jenny Sliger, Owl Eyes Proofs and Edits
**ISBN-13**: 978-1-962699-19-8


**Warning:** Author is dyslexic as hell.

**The editing and beta reading team:** Martha Collins and Lauren Meghoo

Want to get some free novellas or find links to my social media? Everything's on my website: **www.RK-Munin.com**

## Content Warning

- Dysfunctional family dynamic with a verbally abusive father
- Drug addiction
- Several scenes of physical violence
- Talk of death of a parent - nothing on page
- Talk of an abusive and manipulative partner - nothing on page
- Scenes with explicit sexual content, all consensual - this novel is MMF so there will be crossed swords.

## Cora

"I'm going to end you!" Cora shouted at the mostly closed bedroom door. It was an empty threat, but she felt better for having stated her intentions.

She'd already searched the sparse bedroom for weapons but came up with nothing. Who didn't at least keep a baseball bat next to the bed or a knife in the nightstand drawer? But no, there wasn't even an en suite bathroom where she'd be able to use the heavy ceramic toilet tank lid as a bludgeoning tool.

Creeping up to the door, she peeked out the sliver-sized opening. The hulking shadow beyond hadn't moved since the last time she looked. If she didn't know better, she'd think he was a statue. The only thing that moved at all were those blood-red eyes. They slid over to meet hers without his head shifting. The guy's absolute stillness was freakish.

Considering what was going on, she wished his ability to be perfectly stationary was the strangest thing he did. Unfortunately, both the odd eye color and preternatural stillness ranked low on the list of inexplicable things. Much higher was the man's ability to shift into a griffin and fly away with her clutched in his claws!

"No one's going to believe me," she muttered, thinking about her father and brothers. If she had her cell, she'd call them, and they'd come in with guns blazing. Even if they thought she was crazy to talk about vampires and shape changers, they wouldn't hesitate. Not that she should need rescuing—she was a badass bitch who wasn't afraid of anyone.

Except that wasn't exactly true anymore. After watching a vampire rip a man in half with his bare hands as easily as she'd tear a sheet of paper, she was scared. Even worse, that same vampire was the one standing in the living room.

Running her fingers through her black hair, she tugged hard at the ends. At least Imani knew she'd been abducted by the red-eyed vampire. Imani was her best friend and a vampire too, so she could stand up to him, right?

Except Imani was a young vampire, and this guy was obviously old and powerful. Even if Imani found this apartment, she could end up getting seriously hurt trying to rescue Cora. Maybe even killed.

Cora pulled her hair forward, covering her vision with black and purple strands. "This is a fucking mess."

For a full minute she let self-pity take over. The bedroom window was boarded up. Even if she could get a board free, she was on the third or fourth story. Despite what action movies might have audiences believe, climbing down the side of an apartment building wasn't an option, not even if she tied the bed sheets together to make a rope.

Another wave of hopelessness hit her hard. This was not how she wanted to die. "There's nothing I can do."

No sooner did that thought cross her mind than she got angry. Yes, anger was much better than fear or self-pity.

"What am I doing, standing around feeling sorry for myself and waiting to be rescued?" she asked the empty room, squaring her shoulders and dropping her hands to her hips. Lifting her head, she swung her hair out of her face and looked at the door.

"I'm going to walk out that door and leave," she stated, as if she hadn't already tried to do that multiple times.

Taking a deep breath, she pushed the door open. This time, she didn't edge around the vampire or walk past pretending not to see him; she sprinted. The figure followed her with his eyes but didn't move otherwise. She couldn't be sure he was even breathing. Maybe she could take him by surprise and be out of the apartment before he had a chance to act.

Her hopefulness did nothing and this attempt at escape ended the same way as the previous one.

She was almost to the front door when he was suddenly a blur of movement. One moment he was standing in the center of the room like a red-eyed statue, and the next he was in front of her with no change of expression at all. He picked her up, effortlessly carrying her back into the apartment's only bedroom. After setting her down, he took up his same position in the living room.

Once again, she was back in the bedroom with the door wide open and those red eyes trained on her.

"Fuck!" she screamed and punched the wall. Her fist went through the paper-thin drywall and scraped against a stud. Pulling her hand free, she saw blood flowing from her knuckles. Flexing her fingers, she noted nothing was broken, but now her knuckles hurt.

She was still looking at her bleeding skin when two larger hands went around hers. She watched as the vampire's big hands cradled her hand like a wounded bird.

Looking up, she found his expression had finally changed. He looked worried.

"No hurt," he whispered. "Please."

Maybe he wasn't waiting to make a snack out of her. Could he even care about her? She needed to leverage that.

"Will you let me leave?" she asked.

His expression went from worried to desolate. He looked like he might cry. "No leave me. No leave us."

"Us?" she murmured, transfixed by his expressive face. "Who else lives here?"

"Me." Both of them looked up to see David Pike, known as only Pike to his friends, standing in the open door of the apartment. Standing at six-foot-all-the-inches, the black hair on Pike's head brushed the top of the doorway as he stepped through. His broad shoulders forced him to turn slightly to avoid bumping the sides of the doorway.

She'd gone out on a few dates with the giant man and found him gentle, kind, and unbelievably sexy. There had been instant sparks between the two of them and for the first time in years, she considered sleeping with someone. Maybe even risking a relationship.

"Pike!" Cora said, excited to see potential rescue. Her relief was short-lived as she remembered that the man gently holding her hand was capable of astonishing violence. "Run! Find Imani and get help!"

To her horror, Pike finished stepping into the apartment and closed the door as if there wasn't a red-eyed monster standing between them exuding menace. "What are you doing?" Cora screeched and grabbed hold of the vampire's hands to keep him with her instead of attacking Pike.

"Do you have no sense of self-preservation? You saw what this creature is capable of! Run!"

Pike held up both hands palms out and made a soothing sound. His hazel eyes were bright with calm concern. The weird part was he was trying to soothe her, not the vampire.

"It's going to be okay."

She couldn't believe what she was seeing. "We're all dead," she whispered.

"We're safe with Kimble, I promise," he said, crossing the room into the bedroom. "He'd rather die than hurt either of us. If anything, he's probably going to need our help very soon."

Cora went from raging fear to absolute confusion. "What?"

Pike didn't stop until he was close enough to put his hands over Kimble's. Standing at only five foot three, Cora was used to having to look up at everyone, but Pike's hulking body towered over both her and the vampire. Letting go of Kimble's hands, she rubbed her face, then met Pike's eyes.

Frowning, Pike stared at Cora's bloody knuckles. "What did you do?"

He was worried about a few scrapes while holding hands with Death? This was surreal.

Cora nodded to the wall. "Me vs the wall. Of all the luck, I hit a stud."

Pike blinked at her a few times, then a slow grin spread across his face. "You punched the wall?"

Either she was lightheaded, or Pike's grin was infectious. She found herself smiling up at him and shrugged. "Maybe."

"You're like a swan, gorgeous but surprisingly aggressive and scary. I bet you tried to hit Kimble first, didn't you?"

She'd been compared to a lot of animals in her life, including a New York rat, but never a swan. No one ever called her something that was the symbol of grace and poise. Pike was like that, always finding ways to compliment her.

"I didn't hit him," she said, rolling her eyes up to take in Kimble's look of concentration. It seemed like he was trying to follow their conversation but wasn't getting all the words.

"Don't lie," Pike pressed.

"I didn't hit him more than two or three times," Cora confessed.

Pike chuckled, then abruptly stopped when Kimble started swaying. "Damn it!"

Letting go of his hands, Pike swept Kimble up in his arms. The vampire seemed to deflate before her eyes. It wasn't only because Pike was so much bigger compared to Kimble; he looked suddenly gaunt and exhausted.

Cora followed as Pike carried Kimble to the bed. After Pike's words, she had mixed feelings about the vampire's sudden weakness.

He might be a brutal murderer, but he'd done that to protect her and Imani. He'd carried her off without permission, but even after they were alone, he hadn't done anything to hurt her. He hadn't even retaliated when one of her blows got him full in the face.

Pike drew the covers up over Kimble, covering his bare feet and old, too big clothing. Leaning in close, he gave the red-eyed man a kiss on the forehead. Jealousy raged through Cora, but confusion kept her quiet. She wanted to accuse Pike of cheating on her or making her his side chick, but she also felt moved by his display of gentleness.

A kiss on the forehead didn't mean lovers. Maybe they were brothers or cousins?

Pike drew back so he could smile at the vampire. "Rest, I'll get you food. I promise both Cora and I are safe."

"No leave," the vampire whispered, his voice fearful and hoarse.

"We won't leave until you're back on your feet," Pike promised, then straightened up. "Cora and I need to talk. After you've fed, you need to do better. You can't carry her off or restrain her like you did."

Kimble's brows wrinkled. "Kept safe."

"You did great by killing Vincent, but you shouldn't have flown here," Pike admonished. He sounded like he was talking to a five-year-old and not a deadly mythical creature! "If you'd waited, I could have driven us all home."

Kimble's expression turned stubborn, and he tugged the blanket higher as he repeated, "Kept safe!"

He was so weak, Pike had to help him get the blanket to his shoulders. "I know that's what you meant to do," Pike agreed with a sigh. "We can talk about it later."

Kimble made a grumpy sound, rolled on his side and closed his eyes. Cora got the distinct impression the vampire was pouting.

Turning to face her, Pike pointed to the living room. Walking ahead of him, she came to a stop in the center and eyed the front door.

She could run. The door was right there. Everything she knew about Pike told her that he wouldn't try to stop her.

"Please don't leave. Give me a chance to explain."

Cora turned to face Pike. He was standing with his back to the closed bedroom door, hands in his pockets, and looking at her with his typical sincere expression. He was such a big guy that most people would be intimidated by him, but it had taken Cora all of five minutes to realize he was a gentle soul wrapped in a hulking body.

"If I let you talk, can I leave after?"

"You can leave at any time," he started to say, and she snorted derisively, making Pike wince. "I mean, you can leave now that Kimble is so weak. I won't try and stop you, but I really hope you'll give me and Kimble a chance."

She must've taken a blow to the head because she wasn't turning tail and running. Instead, she looked at the ancient couch next to her. At one time, it had probably been a light tan color, but grime and stains had turned it into a dirty Rorschach test.

"I'm not sitting on that. I might catch something."

Pike grinned. "I don't blame you. It came with the apartment."

He pointed to the kitchenette area where there was a small round table with two chairs. "Are you hungry or thirsty?"

His question made Cora realize she was dying of thirst. "I could use a drink."

With a nod, he walked to the fridge. She followed him to the kitchen area and sat. Both the table and chair were sturdy but battered. She knew Pike worked three jobs and made decent money, but everything he owned looked like it should be taking up space in a landfill. Where was all the money going?

"Do you have any of those Coca-Cola's? The ones in the glass bottle that have the cane sugar in them?" she asked as he rummaged around in the fridge. How had she gone from being afraid for her life to asking for a sweet drink? If she didn't know better, she'd think she was stuck in a bizarre fever dream.

Pike emerged from the fridge with a glass bottle held in each hand. Nudging the door closed with his hip, he flicked the caps off the bottles with his thumbs. Huh, neat trick. A single stride brought him to the table, and he handed her a drink as he sat down on the opposite side.

Neither talked as both took long swallows. The sweet flavor tasted good, and the cold carbonation was soothing on her throat, sore from screaming and cursing at Kimble. The sugar hit her empty stomach, making her instantly feel better. She drank half the bottle in one go, then set it down on the table with a clink.

"Time to explain to me what the fuck is going on."

**Pike**

Pike hadn't cried since he was young, but then Kimble had come into his life and tearing up became a more common thing. This moment was only one in many evenings where he felt the urge to weep.

The last nine months had been stressful and turbulent, but things had finally started looking up. Kimble was starting to talk, giving Pike hope the vampire was finally getting better. Then Pike met Cora and his inner bear went ecstatic because she was their mate.

Knowing Cora was human and didn't know anything about the magical world that existed alongside her own, he'd planned to introduce her slowly. It helped that he'd found out her best friend wasn't only a vampire but had claimed one of Pike's good friends as part of her flock.

He was sure Imani would help him ease Cora into their world, only to have her kidnapped and almost killed. He would never forget the terror and helplessness he'd felt watching Vincent bearing down on Cora, intent on murder. Only Kimble's timely arrival had saved her life. All their lives really.

Then Kimble had undone his good deed by shifting into a griffin and flying off with Cora clutched in his talons. It wasn't the first impression Pike wanted to make, but the damage was done.

There was nothing to do but try to talk Cora into giving him and Kimble another chance.

But where to begin?

He wanted to touch her so badly but worried she'd reject him so he greedily ran his gaze over her while waiting for inspiration to hit.

The purple highlights in her long black hair gleamed in the kitchen's harsh light. The dirt and dust covering most of her didn't detract from her beauty. She had an adorable button nose sitting in the center of her heart-shaped face, but Pike was most fascinated by her eyes. He hadn't known humans could have gray eyes until he met Cora.

He could gaze into her eyes for ages.

"Is that vampire your family?" Cora asked, breaking the silence and pulling Pike out of his admiring thoughts.

Pike blinked at her, unsure how to answer that question. "I'm his flock."

Now it was her turn to look confused. "Flock?"

Right, she knew Kimble was a vampire, but probably not much else. "Let me start at the beginning, okay?"

She picked up her bottle and leaned back in her chair. "Sure, go for it."

"Eight months ago, I got a flat tire down on 12th street, near Kimball Park," Pike started. "I was in naga territory at about three in the morning. I wasn't paying attention to where I was, so instead of leaving on foot and coming back for my car later, I got out and started changing the tire."

"What's a naga?" Cora asked.

"Snake shifters. Most of us shifters aren't very territorial, but nagas were almost hunted to extinction about a thousand years ago. They claim territories, mark clear boundaries, and get violent if you cross them."

Cora tilted her head. "What are you?"

"I'm a shifter too, black bear," he answered. "I come from a long line of West Coast black bear shifters."

She nodded her head. "And the snakes didn't want a bear in their territory?"

"It wasn't that I was a bear, it was that I was anything. The only species they don't care about are pure humans who don't smell like any magic."

Cora leaned forward with an intrigued look. "You can smell magic?"

"Um yeah," Pike said. It must be weird for humans who couldn't smell magic. "Even in my human form, I have almost as good a sense of smell as my bear. Vampires can't smell it, but they can see it. They can read what you are by looking at your aura."

"Does that mean you knew what Imani was the moment you met her?" Cora asked.

"It would've been hard to miss," Pike said. "The magic that comes off vampires is really distinct."

"I have more questions about that, but later. I need to know what happened after you got stranded in naga territory."

"I'd gotten as far as getting the flat tire off when a dozen shifted nagas showed up." He gave her a rueful smile. "I'm big and strong, but I'm not hold-off-twelve-adult-nagas strong."

"Don't stop there," she said, making a keep-going motion with her hand. "What happened?"

"Kimble," he said simply. "It was like he appeared out of nowhere, completely naked and covered in dirt. I thought he might be a golem at first. He killed two of the nagas and the rest ran away. Then he turned to me. By then, I knew he was a vampire, and I figured I was dead. My back was against the car and when he got close, I closed my eyes and asked him to make it fast."

"But he didn't kill you," Cora stated. "Why?"

"I'm his flock," Pike reminded her, then remembered she wouldn't know what that was. "A flock keeps a vampire sane. Vampires can live for a long time. Age makes them more powerful, but it can also cause them to lose their mind. Kimble can't tell me his name or anything about himself or his past. I named him after the park near where he saved me."

Cora glanced back at the closed bedroom door with a pitying look before returning her gaze to him. "This almost sounds like a soap opera plot line but for magical creatures."

"It's so much worse than some fictional daytime TV show," Pike pointed out. "When vampires get as bad as Kimble, they're declared feral and hunted down by other vampires. It's the only thing that vampires agree on. They worry a feral vampire with no control will expose their existence."

"Does this mean all vampires need shifters to keep them sane?" Cora asked.

"Eventually, yes. If a vampire can't find their flock, they will slowly lose their minds," Pike said. "But the flock doesn't need to be shifters. A vampire could pick a human, pixie, naga, or anything to be in their flock. Do you remember those two men with your friend Imani?"

"You mean her boyfriends, Mac and Lex?"

"Yeah, them. They aren't simply her boyfriends, they're her flock. She has shared a piece of her soul with them and taken a piece of their souls inside herself. They're bound for life. She'll keep them from aging, Mac and Lex will keep her sane, and they'll all get more powerful."

"That doesn't make sense," Cora said with a slight frown. "Why didn't Kimble pick someone to be in his flock before he went feral?"

Pike shook his head. "Finding your flock for a vampire is like finding your mate for a shifter. They're special and precious. They are the ones chosen by magic to match with you. It's one of the reasons why there are a surprising number of vampires in San Diego. There's a belief that it's a lucky place."

"It's like a fated mates thing?" Cora asked.

Pike startled. "How do you know that term?"

Cora gave him a wicked grin. "You don't read many romance novels, do you?"

Her relaxed posture and sexy smile made blood rush to his cock. The moment he'd stepped into the apartment, his inner bear had screamed at him to wrap his arms around her and rub his scent all over her. It was hard to constantly fight the urge to touch her, but this little exchange made it a thousand times worse.

Shifting uncomfortably, he cleared his throat. "Uh, I guess not. I don't know if the fated mates in your books are accurate, but it's a term we shifters use too."

"If you're his flock, then why isn't he getting better?" she asked.

Pike sighed. "He was. When he rescued me, he couldn't talk at all. Now he can say a few words."

Cora asked the next question in a rush of words. "Do you guys have sex?"

He'd been expecting a question along these lines. "We fool around a little, but he can't get an erection."

"Why?"

Pike shrugged. "Same reason he struggles to talk. Since he spent so much time being feral, it'll take time for him to recover." Suddenly, he felt tired. Slumping forward, he put his elbows on the table and rested his head in his hands. "I'm not enough. I've never been enough to bring Kimble back."

He felt a touch on the top of his head. Looking up, he found Cora stretched across the table, her expression full of kindness. "I know you're doing everything you can because that's who you are. Tell me what else is going on."

When he pulled her hand off his head to hold it in both of his, she didn't try to pull away. The touch felt good and made his inner bear stop screaming so loudly.

"I can't get him enough food," Pike admitted.

Instead of her features twisting into disgust, she looked intrigued. "You mean blood? Can't he take from you, or do vampires kill when they feed?"

"They don't need to kill. The evil ones might murder people, but that's because they like it," Pike said. "He won't feed from me because he's afraid he'll hurt me. There's a taboo among vampires about taking blood from their flock. They'll bite for pleasure, but not to feed."

"What about other people, or shifters?" she asked.

"Vampires have this ability called thrall that allows them to put people into a trance-like state. When someone's under thrall, they'll do anything the vampire wants. That way, the vampire can feed, and the victim doesn't remember anything. Kimble can't use his thrall so the victim might fight and end up getting seriously injured. We can't let that happen. He can't hunt for his food, so I have to buy it."

"You can buy blood?" Cora asked.

"Yeah, but it's expensive," Pike explained. "After rent, almost everything I earn goes to keeping Kimble fed, but it's never enough. Nothing I do is enough. I called in an order on my way here and that wiped out everything I had. My credit cards are all maxed out, and I don't even have enough to make rent next month. If I'm evicted, I don't know how I'll keep Kimble safe from the sun. I know my parents would be willing to help, but I don't want to burden them any more than I already have. They do well, but they aren't rich."

Cora nodded with sympathy, then glanced over at the closed bedroom door. Pike watched as her features hardened and she looked back at him.

"If you have Kimble, why'd you go out with me too? Was I someone to have fun with until your vampire boyfriend could get it up again?" her words sounded harsh, but her severe frown softened, and her lower lip quivered a little.

Pike shook his head violently, grasping her hand tighter. "You're my mate. My bear knew the moment we met."

"How can I be your mate if you're already with Kimble?"

"It means you're meant to be in his flock with me. It's really common for vampires to have a flock of two or three."

For a moment, Cora looked relieved, then schooled her features into skepticism. "So a flock is more than one person, and you think I'm both your mate and part of his flock?"

"Flocks are sacred to vampires. That's why he killed Vincent and carried you away. He probably wanted to carry both of us, but he wouldn't be able to fly with my weight yet. He only wants to protect both of us, but he's so weak and struggling with his mind that there isn't much he can do. You could be the key to bringing him back to his full self…" He let his sentence end in an implied question to see how Cora would take it.

"I'm not sure if I want to be in this flock, or even with you anymore."

Her words made him want to howl with pain. His distress must have shown on his face because she was quick to keep talking.

"Fuck, you look like I told you I killed your puppy. I'm not saying no, okay? This is a lot. I need time to process."

Pike tried to rein in his emotions. "I get that. It's overwhelming to find out about my world and almost be killed by it in one night."

Cora suddenly looked tired. The tough, angry woman was gone. In her place was a vulnerable human pushed beyond endurance. "I've seen more death today than I have in my entire life. I'm glad it was only the bad guys who died, but it was still a lot."

She shuddered and Pike couldn't stand it any longer. "Can I hold you, please? I might be a shifter, but I've never been involved in a situation like today either."

Cora wrinkled her eyebrows as she considered. "It's only hugging. It doesn't mean anything."

"Only hugging," he agreed.

"Then, yeah, I could use a hug."

Letting go of her hand, he popped up and leaned over the table to grab her. She made a little gasp as he lifted her small body and sat back down on his chair with her on his lap.

"Warn me next time," she grumbled even as she wiggled around and settled her right side against him as he wrapped his arms loosely around her. Her head fit perfectly under his chin, and he felt her relax into him with a small sigh.

Both he and his inner bear felt better now they were holding her. It settled something inside of them that had been unsettled for a long time. The only thing missing was Kimble, but hopefully Cora would let him in soon.

Cora was fiercely loyal. All he needed to do was prove to her that he and Kimble deserved her loyalty and love.

**Cora**

An insistent knocking woke Cora out of a sound sleep. Groggily, she started moving even before her eyes were completely open. Except she wasn't in her bed and when she tried to sit up, she found she was already sitting up.

Arms tightened around her, keeping her from falling flat on her face as a familiar voice murmured in her ear, "Easy, it's only the blood delivery."

Standing up, Pike placed her on the chair he'd been sitting on. She'd fallen asleep on his lap. Rubbing her face, she yawned and then watched Pike answer the door. A totally non-descript guy handed Pike a small cooler, then turned and walked away without saying a word.

Closing the door, Pike stood there, staring at the cooler that looked like it belonged to a child in his big hands. "I need to feed this to Kimble," he mumbled without looking up.

Cora was still half asleep and had a headache, probably from lack of food. It took her a few seconds to realize Pike was acting weird. He kept standing there, as if waiting for her to say something, but what? She asked a question instead.

"Did people have to die to get that blood?"

Pike looked up at her with wide eyes. "No! I swear that's not a thing. This is donated blood that blood banks can't use because it's got something wrong with it. Vampires are immune to everything, so they can drink it without an issue."

"That's efficient," Cora said with approval. "Do you need me to help or anything?"

Pike went back to looking uncomfortable. "I don't need help, but I thought you might want to watch. To see if you think it's gross or you can't stand it."

Oh, he was scared she'd turn and run after watching Kimble feed. Cora wasn't one to be soft on people, but Pike looked so worried she wanted to soothe him. "Yeah, I'll watch. I'm sure it's fine, though. It's not like he's ripping the heads off chickens or anything."

Pike managed a smile. "Nothing like that, I promise."

Tucking the cooler under one arm, he held out his hand, inviting her to take it. She felt a little wobbly getting up, so she was really going to need to eat soon, but at least her vision didn't have spots. Gray spots were a clear sign her blood sugar had tanked, and she was going to suffer some severe consequences very soon, but for now she still had a little time.

Tension went out of Pike's shoulders once she slid her hand into his. Leading her to the bedroom, he nudged the door open. Kimble looked sound asleep even though the lights were all on.

No, sound asleep was the wrong term. He looked dead, but he wasn't. Or maybe he was? Did they use the term undead or was that offensive to vampires?

Either way, Cora took a moment to really look at Kimble. He reminded her of Tom Hiddleston when he was playing Loki, except Kimble's hair was longer and unkept, and he might be a little paler than the English actor. Oh, and there were the red eyes too, hose weren't anything like Tom.

What would Kimble look like if he smiled? Would he appear adorable like the actor, or would his expression be more menacing? Cora found herself surprisingly curious about what the vampire would look like cleaned up and happy.

It had to be stress and low blood sugar, that's all.

Leading her to the bed, Pike stopped at the foot and looked down at her, his body tense. "If you need to look away or leave, that's okay. I, um, I don't want to scare you or anything."

"I think it's a little late to worry about that," she pointed out dryly.

Pike's lips twisted into a frown. "I couldn't control Vincent kidnapping you or Kimble whisking you away, but I can do my best to shield you from now on."

Relenting, she patted his arm with her free hand. "I know. I'm not pissed at you. I can see you were in a fucked-up position. It's not like you could say something like 'by the way, my soul is bound to a vampire who can't talk' during our first or second date."

He snorted, his body relaxing. "Yeah, that's a third date topic for sure."

Letting go of her hand, he opened the cooler and pulled out two bags of blood that wouldn't look out of place at a hospital. Tossing the cooler away, he moved to the side of the bed to sit on the edge, setting one of the bags next to him. Kimble didn't react until Pike eased a hand under his head.

Kimble's eyes shot open, then he pulled in a deep breath from his nose and smiled up at Pike. He opened his mouth, but only a wordless sound came out. Cora thought he might be trying to say hello.

"I'm sorry to wake you, but I have some blood," Pike murmured. He lifted Kimble's head a little and held the bag close to the vampire's lips. Cora expected Kimble to violently bite into the plastic, but his movements were careful and deliberate. He opened his mouth, exposing his lengthened fangs, and slid them delicately through the bag. She watched his throat work as he swallowed. His eyes fluttered closed as he emptied the bag.

"That's good," Pike said, leaning over to brush another kiss on the vampire's forehead. "You'll feel much better soon. I've got you, you're safe."

Even though both men were clothed, and one was covered in a blanket, the moment felt intimate. Cora wasn't sure how she felt as she watched something that felt private. Pike was a natural caregiver, and it showed with every word and gesture.

What would it be like to have Pike care for her like this?

Growing up with so many brothers, a dedicated but clueless father, and no mother made Cora tough and reluctant to let anyone see weakness. Any slight display of fragility was answered with harsh treatment as her father and brothers tried to "prepare her for the real world." Growing up, she'd learned young not to cry or show even a hint of fear.

All of it made her a successful business owner in a male dominated industry, but it also made her feel lonely and tired. It was exhausting always having to be on guard and never feeling like you could be honest with anyone, including her own family.

Cora had an overwhelming urge to snuggle up in the bed with Kimble so she'd be next in line for Pike's attention. Pushing her longings away, she watched Pike's murmured words of encouragement and affection as Kimble drank. The moment the first bag was done, Pike tossed it away and picked up the second one.

Kimble must have been feeling better because he took this bag from Pike and sat up. He fed himself with one hand and tangled his free hand with Pike's.

It was fascinating to watch Kimble's color come back. He was a pale guy, but with the infusion, his pale went from corpse-white to living-human-white. Vitality returned to his expression, and he was able to talk.

"Good. Yes, thanks," he said, nuzzling Pike's big hand.

Well, *talk* relative to Kimble.

"I know you need more," Pike said. "But could you please take some from me? I trust you, and I'm a big guy. You won't hurt me."

Kimble's expression was everything stubborn. "No."

Pike looked like was going to argue when Kimble let go of his hand and flowed out of the bed. With a blur of motion that should be familiar by now, he was suddenly in front of Cora, his brows furrowed in concern.

Startled, Cora took a half step back, but Kimble didn't try to grab her. He dropped to his knees in front of her and tilted his head. "Hunger?"

"You want some of my blood?" Cora asked, fear making her heart start to pound.

"No," Kimble denied. "You hunger."

Cora's worry diminished. Kimble must be confused. "I'm human. I don't drink blood."

Kimble's expression didn't change. "Human hunger."

Pike moved to stand next to her and pulled in a deep breath through his nose. "You don't smell right. What's going on? You smell a little like Corey at work when he's taken too much insulin for his diabetes."

Cora looked up at Pike. "You can smell that?"

"Of course," Pike answered. "And so can Kimble. Are you diabetic?"

Cora shook her head. "I'm not diabetic, but I do go hypoglycemic easily. I should really eat something."

Kimble peered up at Pike. "Human hunger!" he repeated triumphantly.

Pike gave the vampire a warm smile. "You were right. I get to feed Cora next!"

He looked so excited to fix her a meal that Cora found herself smiling as he walked out of the room. Kimble didn't follow him, instead he nodded his head, indicating he wanted her to go first. Stepping around his kneeling form, Cora followed Pike back to the kitchenette.

Pike had already set a pan on the stove and was busy pulling ingredients from the fridge. "How about an omelet?" he said. "I can make a mushroom cheese one."

Cora's mouth started watering. "Yeah, that sounds good."

She took a seat at the table, expecting Kimble to take the other one. Instead, he assumed the sentry spot in the middle of the living room he'd occupied earlier.

"How much blood should Kimble have?" Cora asked as the vampire's eyes bounced between her and Pike.

"At least double what I've been able to get him," Pike said as he cracked eggs into a bowl. "I think it's one of the reasons he's not getting better faster."

When he opened the fridge for another item, Cora realized he was using everything up except the few condiments he had in there. "Are you skimping on eating too?"

Pike turned to her with a small block of cheese in his hand. "Not really. I get a free meal each shift at one of my jobs, and I can buy discounted meals after I use up my free one. I usually eat there because it's cheaper and it can be hard to find time for anything but work and Kimble these days."

"Bar food every day can't be good for you," Cora said.

"I'm getting a little tired of it," Pike confessed. "If I was closer to the wild areas, I could shift into my bear form and forage, but all the good places are too far away."

"I can help. I've got enough money to buy you groceries and some meals for Kimble," Cora said, surprising herself with the offer.

"I can't ask you to do that," Pike argued. "We're not your responsibility."

Now that it was out there, she warmed to the idea. "Maybe you are, at least a little bit. You risked your life to try to rescue me, and you've been killing yourself trying to keep Kimble safe. I'm new to your world, but if it's one thing I understand, it's doing anything and everything for the important people in your life."

A painfully hopeful expression blossomed on Pike's face. "I'll pay you back, I swear."

"Don't worry about that right now," she said. "First feed me and then we need to figure out what happened to my purse. My keys, wallet, and phone are all there. So basically my life!"

Pike chuckled and went back to cooking. "I've got your purse. I found it in the alley behind the club."

Cora perked up. That was some very good news. "Where is it?"

"Down in my car. Once I finish here, I'll run down and get it," he said as he dumped items into the skillet. The smell of cooking food made her forget about her purse. Her hunger was so bad she felt nauseated. If she hadn't been dealing with hypoglycemia all her life, she'd think she was about to throw up.

Thankfully Pike was soon bringing two steaming plates to the table. There was a fork lying on her plate, so she wasted no time in digging in.

"Oh fuck, this is good," she moaned, then shoveled more food in. Pike ate more slowly and when she looked up, she found him watching her with a pleased expression. "What?"

"I've gotten to feed both my mates today," he explained. "It makes us happy."

She was about to ask what he meant by us, then remembered he referred to his bear side as a separate entity. "Is your bear a different personality than you?"

"Not a whole different personality, more like a strong part of my personality," he answered. "My bear is more about instinct and living in the moment. He doesn't understand having a job or stuff like that. He's always pressing me to go someplace remote so we can shift and do bear things."

Cora was intrigued. "What are bear things?"

"Forage, nap, wander around, and look at stuff. Real bears are naturally curious and problem-solving creatures, so bear shifters share those traits."

She could almost picture it. "I bet you're the cutest bear. Can I see you shifted, or is that a really intimate thing?"

Pike fumbled and almost dropped his fork. "I'd love for you to meet my bear. I know he's desperate to meet you."

She knew Pike meant that in a teasing way, but she felt slightly worried. "He wouldn't try to maul or eat me, would he?"

This time Pike did drop his fork. It went skittering off his plate and to the floor. "No! Never! The worse he might do is lick you all over. If you're really afraid, you can watch me from the inside of a running vehicle. You could leave if you're scared, but I promise my bear would only ever be violent to protect you." He looked crestfallen as he spoke. "You don't have to meet him."

Showing their animals must be important to shifters. She reached across to put her hand over his. "I don't think I'm scared, but let's hold off on making plans until everything around here is settled. Then I can meet your bear."

He looked relieved and turned his hand palm up so he could close his fingers round hers. The grip was loose, and she could've pulled away, but she didn't. Touching him felt good and settled some of the low-grade anxiety roiling in her belly.

"Finish your omelet before it gets cold," he urged. No longer in possession of a fork, he simply picked up the rest of his omelet and shoved it into his mouth. That's when Cora realized Pike could've easily eaten three or four omelets and still been hungry. The poor guy had to be starving!

Determined to fix what she could, she ate quickly. The sooner she finished, the sooner Pike would get her purse, and she could start ordering both the bear and vampire all the food they needed.

She didn't examine how happy it made her feel to think about providing for the guys. She certainly didn't want to think about how similar it must have been to how Pike felt earlier when he gave Kimble food and her an omelet.

Nope, it wasn't the same at all.

## Pike

Ignoring his complaining stomach, Pike rushed out of the apartment building and to his car. He almost plowed through Mrs. Jenson walking her dog Muggsie.

"Sorry, Mrs. J," he said, grabbing onto the elderly woman. He hadn't touched her, but she still looked unsteady.

"I'm fine, Pike," she said with a wheezy laugh. "I saw that vampire of yours fly in with a young woman. Is everything okay, or do I need to take care of him?"

If you made friends with Mrs. Jenson, it wouldn't be long before she'd offered to "take care" of something. Although she was trying to be sinister, she came off as sweet.

Pike moved in five years ago and made friends with Mrs. Jenson right away. At their second meeting, he'd learned all about Mr. Jenson's passing ten years ago, and Mrs. Jenson's reluctance to leave the apartment where they'd shared so many good years together. It was hard to feel sad when she was so relentlessly cheerful as she reminisced.

He'd never asked, but Mrs. Jenson smelled 100% human. From their talks, he knew she'd married a shifter, which was why she was able to get an apartment in the building back when the place had been new, elite, and didn't rent to humans.

Unfortunately, the building had changed ownership two years ago and gone downhill fast. Out of the original ten tenants, there was only him and Mrs. Jenson still living here.

"If Kimble has gone feral, he needs to be dealt with," Mrs. Jenson insisted. "I haven't read any reports of mangled bodies turning up, so I haven't asked before now. You'd tell me if Kimble is feral, wouldn't you?"

"I promise nothing's wrong, Mrs. J," Pike assured her as he leaned over to give Muggsie a pet. The ancient dog tolerated the touch for .00006 seconds before trying to nip him.

"Be nice, Muggsie," Mrs. Jenson admonished her dog. "We like Pike, remember."

As if trying to say sorry, Muggsie went quiet and moved his head to the side to invite Pike to pet him again. Pike didn't fall for the trap, withdrawing his hand and straightening up.

"It's always 50-50 if Muggsie will like me or not. I guess today wasn't in my favor," Pike said with a chuckle.

"Muggsie adores you, but he sure doesn't like your Kimble, I'm sorry to say," Mrs. Jenson said with a shake of her head. It was obvious Mrs. Jenson wasn't going to let the topic of Kimble go.

"What happened tonight was only a little misunderstanding, but Cora's fine, and Kimble won't do it again. He was only trying to protect her. You know how vampires can be."

"Cora?" Mrs. Jenson said, her eyes sparkling. "That's a pretty name. Is she your new girl? I've been saying all along that you two needed to add a woman. Flocks always need at least one female."

"That's probably true, but it's tough to find the right woman," Pike said with a grin. "Especially someone as perfect as you."

Mrs. Jenson laughed uproariously. "Go on, now. Your mates are waiting for you. Make sure to stop by with Cora so I can meet her. Remember, you can come to me if there's any trouble. I'll take care of it for you."

"Sure thing, Mrs. J," Pike agreed, then continued on his journey. It didn't take him long to get the purse out of his ancient, rust bucket Coupe DeVille Cadillac and jog back to the apartment.

He opened the front door to find Kimble and Cora staring at each other. His human mate looked determined, and his vampire mate had his usual inscrutable expression.

"Uh, what are you doing?" he asked Cora.

She turned to him with a shrug. "I have no idea."

Then she saw her purse and rushed at him, snatching it out of his hand and fumbling it open. She pulled out her phone with a sigh of immense relief. Dropping the purse, she tried to turn it on, but nothing happened. "Damn, I need a charger."

"Oh, that's easy!" Pike said and retrieved the box of random chargers he'd ended up with when he'd helped his sister move. Plunking the box on the table, he stepped aside to let her rummage around. She untangled one and headed to the nearest outlet over the kitchen counter.

He watched her face go through a lot of emotions as the phone came on and pinged over and over again. Some of those had to be from him, but the rest must be from family and friends.

"This is going to be so hard to explain," she grumbled as she started typing.

"Just say you lost your phone," Pike offered. "Or it broke."

"They probably won't believe me," she said without looking up. "I hate being without a phone. I have two backup phones and all my apps connected to my laptop and tablet for access. Losing my phone wouldn't put me out of contact. Being kidnapped would put me out of contact, and I'm sure that's the conclusion my family has jumped to."

Cora typed and sent several messages before she looked up at him. "I'm using you as an excuse, okay?"

"That's fine," Pike agreed. "Anything that'll make your life easier."

"You're officially my boyfriend now, or at least my boytoy, and I've spent the last forty-eight hours here with you doing unmentionable things."

"Except for leaving out the kidnapping part, that's mostly true," Pike offered with a wink.

Cora shook her head. "Damn, you're adorable when you're trying to flirt. Now, I'm sending you some money for blood. Go grab your phone and order for him."

Excited at the idea of Kimble finally being truly fed, Pike rushed to find his phone. The amount Cora sent him was enough for ten bags of blood and to have them delivered immediately instead of waiting. He felt some guilt at needing Cora's help, but relief outweighed it. Besides, he'd find some way to pay her back.

"It'll be here in about twenty minutes."

"Great," she answered as she tapped on her phone. "I'm putting in a grocery order. What's the address here? What stuff do you like to eat?"

He gave her the address. Trying to keep the bill low, he named ingredients he knew he could use to make large meals. "Ground beef, spaghetti noodles, spaghetti sauce, a block of sharp cheddar…"

She typed as he listed, but he must've gotten a little too eager because she held up her finger as he started listing spices. "I think that's good for tonight."

Kimble wasn't the only one who was going to get to eat his fill soon! He couldn't wait to see Kimble drink as much as he wanted and to fill his own belly with hot food that didn't come out of a fryer. "Thanks, Cora. I'll make this up to you, I promise."

She finished typing and slumped against the counter. Looking up at him with a dazed expression, she blew out a long breath. "Damn, I'm suddenly exhausted."

"A lot happened. You were attacked, you got kidnapped, and almost died. That's a good reason for anyone to be tired." He stepped closer, wanting to pick her up in his arms but unsure if his touch would be welcome.

She looked up at him, blinking slowly. "That's true."

Kimble appeared at her side and sank to his knees. It was something he'd done a lot when they were newly together, and his way of trying to appear unthreatening.

Cora didn't move or make a sound as Kimble slowly reached out to grasp her hand. Holding it in one hand, he started to rhythmically pet her knuckles with his other hand.

"What's he doing?" Cora asked. "Does he want me to order him something too?"

"I think he wants you to go to bed," Pike guessed. "You only got to sleep about twenty minutes earlier, before the blood delivery woke you up."

"Oh, yeah," Cora said. "Sleep sounds really good. Can I have the bed? Your couch is too gross. I don't want to catch whatever ecosystem is thriving there."

"And it's lumpy," Pike said, taking her free hand as Kimble stood up. "Let's put you to bed, okay?"

Cora nodded like a child and let both of them lead her into the bedroom. The covers were already pulled back, so Pike sat her on the edge of the bed to pull off her shoes. Kimble sat on the bed next to her, refusing to let go of her hand during the process.

Once her shoes and socks were off, Pike debated stripping her further. Her clothes were filthy, and it couldn't be comfortable to sleep in them.

"Would you like to sleep in one of my shirts?" he asked.

"What?" Cora asked, then looked down at herself with a grimace. "Ewww. Yeah, I'd like to wear something clean."

When Pike got up to get her a shirt, she stood also, causing Kimble to make a distressed sound. "I'm not leaving," she soothed him, patting the top of his head. "I need to change and use the bathroom."

Kimble's eyes closed in pleasure when she voluntarily touched him. Cora was probably too tired to notice his reaction, but Pike could see the vampire was thrilled. He remained on the bed as Cora pulled her hand free from his grip and accepted the shirt from Pike. Her movements were slow, but she wasn't stumbling.

Once he heard the door to the bathroom shut, Pike turned his attention to Kimble.

"She's my mate and your flock," he whispered to the vampire, unsure how good Cora's human hearing was. "If we want her to stay with us, we're going to have to prove ourselves. At some point, she's going to want to go home, you need to let her. Don't try to make her stay."

Kimble's mouth turned down into a mutinous frown. "Flock."

"I know she's flock, and we love her," Pike agreed, plopping down on the bed next to Kimble. "But if we push too hard, we're going to lose her. You need to trust me."

Kimble kept up the frown for a full two seconds before sadness overtook his expression, and his shoulders slumped. "Flock."

Pike wrapped both his arms around the vampire and held him tight. It was hard but both of them were going to have to control their natural instincts when it came to Cora.

— ❦ —

## Cora

Cora came halfway awake when she tried to roll over and found she couldn't. When she opened her eyes, all she could see was darkness. Wiggling her arms free, she felt around until she figured out that she was under the covers with Pike and Kimble on either side of her laying on top of the covers, trapping her.

She couldn't be upset at them wanting to sleep in the bed if the only alternatives were the couch or the floor. Pike's place was a total dump, but it was better than living in a car or on the street, especially since it kept Kimble safe from the sun. Cora could understand making tough choices to keep yourself and others safe.

Besides, after witnessing Pike and Kimble interact, she didn't view him as an intimidating vampire anymore.

After a minute or so, her vision adjusted to the dark, and she was able to make out Pike's hulking form on her right. Turning her head to the left, she found Kimble wide awake and watching her with intense red eyes.

"Um, hi," she whispered. She didn't want to wake Pike up, he had to be as exhausted, but she couldn't remain silent in the face of Kimble's relentless gaze. "Are you okay?"

"Fed," Kimble whispered back with a content expression. "Fed good."

The blood she ordered must have shown up after she'd gone to bed. Once they'd tucked her in, she half remembered Pike closing the bedroom door and then nothing.

"Need fed?" Kimble asked. "Human fed?"

It took Cora a moment to understand that he was asking if she was hungry. "No. Do vampires sleep?"

"Sleep," he agreed. "Sleep-night, dead-day."

"Oh, uh, okay," she responded. She was going to need Pike to interpret that one for her tomorrow. With the windows boarded up, she had no idea what time it was. She'd left her phone charging in the kitchen, and that was way too far away. One thing was certain: her body wasn't ready to get up yet.

"You sleep?" Kimble asked.

She yawned. "I was, but there are a lot of people in the bed."

He grinned, showing off canines that were only a little too long. "Perfect number."

He moved his face a little closer to nuzzle the top of her head. It should've been an innocent, comforting touch, but Cora's body didn't get the memo. She was suddenly very aware of Kimble's hard body pressed against her. The smell of smoky sage filled her nose, making her pull in a deep breath. Shouldn't he smell like death or something?

But no, he smelled earthy. She wanted to rub her cheek against him like a cat. Or more accurately, she had the urge to rub her entire body against him. It was the same kind of instant desire she'd felt for Pike. It made her heart start beating faster, and her body felt overly warm under the covers.

"Need me?" he asked

Need him? Could he sense her desire? Was he asking for sex, or was she reading the situation all wrong?

"Need you for what?" she asked cautiously.

"Comfort," he answered. His earnest expression made her smile; he sounded almost childlike as he spoke. "No bad sleep? No sleep images?"

She was pretty sure she knew what he was trying to say. "I wasn't having a nightmare. I woke up because I needed to roll over, that's all." Her heart slowed and her body cooled, almost as if responding to Kimble's desire to comfort her instead of becoming intimate.

When he moved off the bed, she thought he might be going to take his sentry position again, but instead, he stood next to the bed and lifted the covers, bunching them next to her before laying back down.

Settling on his side, he tugged at the comforter. "Can move."

"Thanks, Kimble," she said, rolling on her side to face him. She was forced to wiggle backwards, coming up against Pike's warm bulk. The shifter didn't move or change his quiet, rhythmic snoring during any of their conversation or movement. "You'd think Pike would be a lighter sleeper."

Kimble snorted, making Cora stifle a laugh. Looking up at the shaggy mass in desperate need of a haircut, she got the overwhelming urge to touch it.

Running her fingers through the long strands, she was mildly surprised to find it was clean and almost free of knots. She couldn't see Kimble taking care of it, so Pike must make sure the vampire remained well groomed.

"Good," Kimble purred. Going still, she moved her gaze to his face to find his eyes half closed, mouth slightly parted, and cheeks flushed. Continuing to watch his expression, she went back to running her fingers through his hair.

He moaned.

The way he was acting, someone would think her hand was between his legs, not on his head. His reaction was so over the top, she kept petting him until her arm was fatigued. When she withdrew, Kimble's eyes fluttered open. He looked half dazed with pleasure.

"Good," he repeated and leaned in close. She thought he was going to kiss her on the forehead again, but instead he brushed his lips across her. The touch was light and obviously a question, not a demand. Giving into curiosity, she opened her mouth to him.

By their second date, she and Pike had started making out like horny teenagers. She'd never felt so insanely and instantly attracted to anyone in her life. She certainly never expected anyone else's kiss to arouse her as much as Pike's had.

She was wrong.

Now it was her turn to moan. Kimble was an excellent kisser and while Pike had been eager and a little rough in a good way, the vampire was slow and sensual. Kimble and Pike couldn't be more different, but they turned her on equally well.

Just like when she'd kissed Pike, heat pooled in her belly and her clit throbbed. Her body started to feel too hot, so she pushed the covers off. She and Pike had probably been heading toward the bedroom by the end of their second date, but everything had gone to hell before that could happen.

Now she considered stripping naked and waking up Pike so the three of them could have some fun. This would be her first ménage à trois, and her partners weren't even human, but at the moment she couldn't think of anything she wanted more.

Images of getting to play with two dicks filled her head. Two sets of hands stroking her body. Two mouths on her skin. It was much too irresistible. She wanted it all.

Kimble ended the kiss. When she opened her eyes, it was to find him watching her closely, his expression cautious. "Good?"

"Fucking fantastic," she breathed.

A brilliant smile spread across Kimble's face. "More."

Ready for more kissing, Cora tilted her head up, except Kimble sat up. Confused, she watched him reach over her to shake Pike.

"Wake," Kimble said.

Ah, *more* meant adding Pike to their make-out session.

Pike didn't move. Kimble tried again, putting enough strength into the shake that the entire bed jostled. To Cora's surprise, Pike didn't even come half-awake to grumble at him. The man remained a motionless lump except for his soft snoring.

"No good," Kimble mumbled with a little smile as he settled back down next to Cora. "Very sleep."

"And here I thought you were the one who was supposed to sleep like the dead," Cora commented as she snuggled against Kimble. She pressed her face close to his, seeking more kisses, but he denied her. Tucking her head under his chin, he held her close and rubbed a hand up and down her back.

"Flock sleep." His words sounded like an order. "Wake together. Enjoy together. Sleep together. Nothing apart."

Pike's inability to wake up just caused Cora to lose out on amazing sex. Part of Cora wanted to be insulted that Kimble hadn't continued to make out with her, but the other part admired him. He wanted them to be together in all things. No one was going to be left out, even if she was sure Pike wouldn't be upset.

Was this what it meant to be in a flock?

She thought about it as she drifted off to sleep with Pike's solid body pressed against her back and Kimble's arms holding her.

**Kimble**

Kimble refused to sleep while his flock slumbered. It was his job to keep them safe and so far, he'd done a horrible job. His human had come close to dying, and his poor bear was run ragged. Everything was constantly going wrong, and it was all his fault. If only his mind would work as it should!

It was as if his memories before finding Pike were locked behind a wall. He knew they were there, a rich history of a long, successful life, but he couldn't make them come forward. The worst part was there had to be wealth somewhere that belonged to him, but if he couldn't even remember his name, how would he find it?

One thing vampires did very well was amass money. Within several decades, a vampire was often quite rich, allowing them to live a comfortable lifestyle and focus on finding their flock. If he was old enough to go feral from lack of a flock, he must be wealthy. He should've been able to solve all of Pike's money problems, but no, he was reduced to a simpleton instead. Young children could communicate better.

When his mind came back, he was probably going to die a second death from humiliation.

Not that his bear would ever be unkind to him about his feral state, and his new little human seemed tough but gentle. Still, it was humbling to be forced to rely on his flock to keep him fed and safe instead of the other way around.

The little human was curled up against, fast asleep. She was so much different from him or Pike. Small and delicate looking but possessing a will of iron. She hadn't frozen with fear when he'd flown away with her. The moment he landed and shifted back to his human form, she'd attacked him with all the force she possessed.

Her little fist had bounced off him as she cursed and screamed. He'd been scared to try speaking to her and making everything worse. He knew Pike would return soon and make the human understand that she wasn't in danger, but it was hard to listen to her curses and threats as he carried her inside the apartment.

As he expected, Pike arrived and calmed down the little human. It had all worked out and now they could be a flock! As soon as Cora agreed to exchange pieces of their souls, they'd all be stronger and safer. It was hard, but he forced himself to be patient. He couldn't force a soul exchange on her. If Cora didn't wholeheartedly agree to the exchange, it would poison the relationship. Vampires had few instincts but almost all of them revolved around creating and protecting a flock.

That meant Kimble planned to ignore Pike's insistence that they give Cora time *and space*. She could have the time, but she needed him close. She was the most vulnerable of the three of them; he couldn't let her go out in the world where anyone might hurt her. Especially now that she smelled of bear shifter and vampire.

Secure in the knowledge that everything was going to work out now, Kimble let his mind drift. If he was well fed and relaxed, sometimes a memory would float across the barrier. So far, they'd all been meaningless moments of enjoyment where he heard music or saw a work of art, nothing that would clue him in to who he was. Occasionally, there would be words in Russian, Ukrainian, Polish, or a language that felt ancient and without a modern country to tie it to. This led him to believe he might have been a human in eastern Europe before being turned.

*Kochanie.*

He knew it meant *my beloved* but wasn't entirely sure which language it was. Probably Ukrainian, as that seemed to be one of the languages he favored the most after English.

Yes, that was perfect for his little human. He had *sloneczko*, his sunshine bear, and *kochanie*, his beloved human.

An awareness of someone powerful nearby made him tense. It was faint and could be a vampire simply passing outside, but he thought that unlikely. He'd only sensed one vampire nearby the entire time he'd lived here with Pike and that had been brief.

No vampire would come near here except to put him down or steal his flock.

Getting out of the bed, Kimble paused to gaze at his flock. Without him holding her, Cora made a grumbly sound in her sleep and rolled over. When she found Pike's massive body, she snuggled up close and settled back down into sleep. The covers had fallen down to her hips, and he tugged them back up. It was too bad Pike was so far into sleep he couldn't embrace the human.

No sooner had he thought that than Pike came awake enough to roll on his side and wrap a beefy arm around Cora. The tiny human made a soft, content sound as she rubbed her face against Pike's broad chest. They were a perfect contrast both in bodies and temperaments, and he couldn't imagine having a more beautiful flock than these two.

He might not have words, but he could show them his love and devotion with actions instead.

Moving silently, he walked into the living room and closed his eyes, sending his magic out. He kept his touch soft and found a familiar young vampire getting much closer than he liked.

What was she doing here? He'd saved her life and the life of her flock, the least she could do was stay far away.

She must want his *kochanie*. Cora wasn't bound to him yet so another vampire could potentially steal her for their own flock. This young vampire was going to die due to her greed!

Stopping at the front door, he flung it open to find the vampire and her two flock members standing there. She looked surprised, but the shifters didn't.

"Mine!" he growled. When he'd rescued Cora from the collapsed building, he'd found her being sheltered by this young vampire, Imani. It was clear this vampire and his human were friends, that's why he hadn't hurt her earlier. She had pressed her luck too far by showing up at his domain!

He was well fed, and it was full night, so he'd easily destroy all three of these intruders if they tried anything.

Understanding the danger, Imani took a step back and held up both her hands, palms out. Her long magenta braids swung behind her shoulders, revealing the torn and dirty state of her clothing.

"I'm not here to steal or hurt anyone," she said in a calm, reasonable tone. "I only want to make sure Cora is safe."

"I warned you this was a bad idea," the chimera shifter muttered. His hand was behind his back, telling Kimble the male was probably hiding a weapon. If the chimera showed the weapon, he was going to lose that arm. Out of the three of them, this male was the deadliest. There was something about him that told Kimble he knew how to kill mercilessly and with great skill. If violence became unavoidable, the chimera was going to need to die first.

"Shut it, Lex. I'm not abandoning Cora," Imani retorted.

"The sun is going to be up soon," the bear shifter said. He was as big as Pike but looked far more dangerous. He didn't have the deadly air of the chimera, but the male had scars indicating he was used to conflict. "We don't have time to chit-chat. Let's go. We'll come back tomorrow night."

"Cora might be dead by tomorrow," Imani said to the bear. "I can't abandon her like that, Mac."

Kimble snarled, showing his fangs but none of them moved further away.

"I know you don't like another vampire close by, but I'm here as a friend," Imani said. "I have a flock I love; I don't need to add anyone to it."

Imani was showing concern for a friend. It could be a ploy to get close and steal Cora, or it could be honest worry. He didn't want to kill Cora's friend if he didn't have to, that might upset his human.

"Safe. Mine." There, that should convey everything important.

"I know you wouldn't mean to hurt her, but something might be wrong, and you didn't notice," Imani said. "She went through a lot, and she's a small human. Let me talk to her. I won't touch her, I promise."

"Imani?" a sleepy voice called out. Kimble half turned to see Cora stumbling out of the bedroom. Her hair was an adorable black and purple mess, and she was rubbing her eyes. The shirt Pike gave her to sleep in hung off one shoulder and the bottom hem dropped past her knees. She almost looked like a child.

"Cora?" Imani said and tried to step closer. Kimble let out a snarling roar, and she scrambled back against her flock. Unfortunately the sound woke Cora all the way up.

"Hey, don't roar at my friend," Cora reprimanded, stomping forward and pushing him to the side. She tried to slide past him, but he wrapped his arms around her and pulled her back against him.

"No!" he objected. "Flock!"

"Yeah, I know you want me to be your flock," Cora said, craning her neck to look up at him. "But if being your flock means I don't get to see my friend anymore, then it's a hard no."

Shock jolted through Kimble. She was saying no? He couldn't stand it. Letting go of her, he dropped to his knees and put his hands together in front of him.

"Flock?" Fear made his voice come out high and scared. He wasn't sure he'd survive if she rejected him. As long as there was hope that she'd accept a place in his flock, he felt mostly in control. If she refused, the madness might consume him.

"Fuck," she exclaimed, eyes going wide. She grabbed hold of his hands and tugged. "Get up. You're making me feel like I'm abusing you."

He didn't move. "Flock?"

"Are you asking me to be in your flock again?" Her frown deepened. "I can't wait for the day you can speak in whole sentences involving more than one or two words."

She wasn't the only one who wished he could communicate better. He had the urge to slam his forehead to the floor in an attempt to knock more words out of his stubborn head.

"He needs you to say you're not going to leave him," Imani said from behind Cora. "He's probably scared you're going to walk out because you're pissed."

Cora looked over her shoulder at Imani. "Thanks for interpreting vampire. Don't leave, okay?"

"I don't have much time," Imani warned her. "Sunrise is coming."

Cora nodded her head and turned her gaze back on him. "I'm not going to abandon you or Pike. I'm not sure what we are yet, but I'm willing to give us a chance. I can feel something here. Even when I was scared, I knew deep down you wouldn't hurt me."

Kimble slumped a little with relief at Cora's words, but when he reached out to hug her, she drew back.

"Hold on, I'm not done yet," she said. "I'm going to turn around and talk to Imani. I might even hug her because she's family to me. You're going to let me do that, understand? You can frown but no growling or starting a fight."

"No!" Kimble protested, getting to his feet. He had to ball up his hands into fists to keep from reaching for Cora. Instead, he stepped between her and the open door. "No!"

"What's going on out here?"

Looking past Cora, Kimble saw Pike clad only in his boxer briefs walking into the living room. Much like Cora, he looked sleepy and confused, but his eyes and senses adjusted much faster than hers did.

"Oh! Hi guys!" Much like an overly friendly dog, Pike hurried to the door to greet the intruders. Kimble was forced to hold his arms out to block Pike from stepping past him.

"These guys are friends," Pike said, his smile still in place. "That's Mac. He helped my sister once. And that's Lex. He's a great dancer. Imani's their vampire, and they're her flock. They'd never hurt me."

Kimble knew better. If it came down to a flock or an outsider, a vampire would do anything. Despite Pike's words, Kimble didn't move.

"No."

"That's his favorite word," Cora drawled, stepping up to stand next to Pike. Looking under Kimble's arm, Cora waved at Imani. "You better get home before the sun comes up. I've got my phone; we can talk tomorrow night."

Kimble looked over his shoulder to watch Imani and her flock. She was nodding her head at Cora while both her shifters had similar expressions of relief on their faces. They were eager to get their vampire to safety.

"If you don't call, I'm coming to get you," Imani warned. "And I wouldn't be just me. I'll call your family."

Cora grimaced. "Don't, I'm begging you! That's hellfire no one needs in their life."

"Then we better talk," Imani warned with a small grin. "Love you, Hellion."

Kimble watched Cora blink rapidly, as if trying not to cry. "Love you back, Dance Queen."

Pike called his goodbye to the guys as they tugged Imani down the hall to the stairwell. Kimble didn't move out from the doorway until they'd disappeared. He was about to retreat into the apartment when a door down the hall opened and a small figure wrapped in a bright yellow, fluffy bathrobe appeared.

"What's going on out here? It's nearly five in the morning!"

"Sorry about that, Mrs. J!" Pike called out over Kimble's shoulder. "Some friends stopped by unexpectedly."

Kimble didn't want this woman close to his flock. Snarling, he made sure to show his fangs and pushed power into his aura. He wanted to look big and scary because there was something odd about this woman's aura. Pike and Cora couldn't see it, but she wasn't what she appeared to be.

"Yes, yes," the woman said, waving a gnarled hand in the air. "You're a big scary vampire."

"Kimble's just a little upset," Pike said, tugging Kimble's arm. When he didn't move right away, Pike spoke firmly to Kimble. "Mrs. J couldn't hurt a fly. Stop growling at an old woman and come back to bed."

"Listen to your bear, vampire," Mrs. J said as she turned and shuffled back into her apartment, mumbling to herself. "Vampires, all of them stubborn as mules."

When her door closed, Kimble let Pike pull him into the apartment. It felt good to see the door close, shutting the world outside and his flock in with him.

"Cora, everything okay?" Pike asked.

Cora yawned. "I don't know. My emotions are all jumbled up, and my brain feels foggy. I need more sleep."

Eager to give his human comfort, Kimble took her hand and led her back to the bedroom. A small smile appeared on Cora's face.

"Are you going to tuck me in?" she asked.

"Flock," Kimble said as he pulled down the bedsheet.

"The word flock is starting to take on the same usage as fuck," Cora commented, confusing Kimble.

Pike barked out a laugh. "What?"

"You can put fuck in just about any context and it works," Cora explained, stifling another yawn. "Think about it. Flying fuck. My last fuck. Fucking great. We could fuck. Telling someone to get fucked. It can be a noun, adjective, adverb, or whatever. Kimble's using flock in a similar way, and we have to figure out what it means from the context."

Pike grinned as they reached the bed. Cora covered a yawn as he straightened out the covers. "So should we be saying flocking great or flying flock?"

Kimble hadn't understood what Cora and Pike were talking about until then. The humor hit him hard, and he laughed. He hadn't laughed in so long it was rusty at first, only a little chuckle. But the longer he chuckled, the stronger it got until he doubled over, having a hard time pulling enough air into his lungs between peals of laughter.

When the laughter finally abated, he straightened up to find Cora and Pike both staring at him with wide eyes. That's when an entire sentence finally made it to his lips.

"*Kockam cie.*"

I love you.

**Pike**

Pike woke up in the early afternoon starving. On his right, Cora was sleeping peacefully, and beyond her, Kimble lay with the unnatural stillness that came with his daytime sleep.

As he expected, Kimble's eyes shot open as he eased off the bed. The vampire's brow wrinkled as he watched Pike stand up and stretch. Circling the end of the bed, he leaned over and gave Kimble a gentle kiss on the forehead.

"I'll be in the kitchen cooking."

Kimble gave a slight nod and closed eyelids over bright red eyes. Pike had found out that the red wouldn't go away until Kimble completely came back to himself. Pike looked forward to finding out Kimble's natural eye color as Kimble healed from his feral state.

With Cora in their lives, it could be any day now.

Feeling buoyant, Pike pulled on a pair of sweats and headed into the kitchen. The only window in the apartment was the one boarded up in the bedroom and a tiny one in the bathroom. The ancient fixtures never provided enough light, making the apartment always seem gloomy except in the kitchen where the industrial fixture beamed light down in one spot, the kitchen table.

Looking at his place with Cora in mind, Pike shook his head.

He lived in a hovel. It wasn't messy, but everything was worn, poor quality, or both. He wished he had a nicer den to present to Cora. This must be how Kimble felt all the time, frustrated that he couldn't provide for his flock.

"It's fine," Pike muttered to himself as he started pulling out ingredients to make biscuits and gravy. "Cora understands."

If Cora rejected them, it wouldn't be because of his financial circumstances. It would be because she didn't want them on a personal level. The thought hurt, but he knew it was unlikely. He could already feel the bond between them growing.

Tossing some sausage into a pan, he set the burner on low, then pulled out a bowl to mix the biscuit dough. He wished he could put on some music to break up the silence, but he didn't want to wake Cora up before she was ready.

Hopefully, the smell of food would pull her from sleep, and he could present her with a hearty breakfast. There were even bags of blood in the fridge left over from the last delivery Cora paid for, so Kimble could be fed too.

Humming to himself, he jumped a little when Cora's phone started ringing. Rushing over, he grabbed it, pulled the short charging cable out, and answered it.

"Cora's phone," he whispered.

"Who the fuck is this?" a male voice asked.

He almost chuckled at hearing the word fuck used after their conversation before bed about fuck and flock. Clearing his throat, he answered.

"Uh, this is Pike, Cora's boyfriend." He liked the sound of that, so he repeated it. "Cora's boyfriend, David Pike."

"Cora doesn't have a boyfriend," the voice answered. "She has two-or-three night stands with guys that we never meet."

"I'm going to be more than a one-night stand," Pike answered. "We've only been dating about two weeks, but I already know she's the love of my life."

There was a moment of silence before the other person responded. "Love of your life after a couple of weeks? Oh shit, she's going to eat you alive. Look man, you might want to leave before she causes permanent damage."

Pike was an easy-going bear, but just like any bear, he could be possessive. He frowned, then made some demands of his own. "Who is this? Why do you want me to leave Cora? Do you want her?"

The man laughed. "Chill, she's my sister. I'm only warning you off for your own good. She can be mean."

If this man was Cora's brother, Pike needed to be nice to him. Even if he sounded like an asshole. "Cora isn't mean, she's loyal and tough. I'd never break up with her, unless it was to save her life."

Her brother snorted. "Save her life? That's a weird as shit thing to say. When are relationships ever life and death?"

That made it clear Cora wasn't the only one in the family who hadn't known about the magic world hidden in plain sight all around them. There was no equivalent of mates and flock to a human, so he didn't bother trying to explain.

"What's your name, or should I call you Cora's little brother?"

"Big brother," the guy answered quickly. "I'm her big brother, Ted. We're all her big brothers because she's the youngest."

"How many of you are there?" Pike asked.

"She hadn't even told you about us yet?" Ted said, sounding smug. "That means you're doomed."

"It means we're still getting to know each other," Pike argued. The sausages were starting to sizzle, so he shifted position, keeping the phone to his ear.

"Why don't you come to our next BBQ?" Ted suggested. "You can meet all six of us and Dad."

"I have to ask Cora," Pike answered. "I don't want to barge in on her family time."

"Yeah, you do that," Ted snickered. "Make sure to get permission to breathe while you're at it. Fuck dude, if you're this pussy-whipped, you might have a chance with her."

"I don't like that term," Pike said. "It's rude."

"Yeah, that's what a pussy-whipped beta would say," Ted answered. "I'll see you Sunday. Unless Cora says you can't come over to play." Laughing, Ted ended the call.

Pike carefully set the phone down, or he might have accidentally crushed it in his hand because he wanted to reach through it and wring Ted's neck. As eager as he was to meet

Cora's family, it was clear he wasn't going to like this brother at all. Hopefully, the others weren't such assholes.

"Was that Ted on the phone?" Cora asked from behind him.

He was surprised she was able to sneak up on him, even if he'd been distracted by the call. Looking over his shoulder, he gave her a smile. "Yeah, how did you know? Have you been there the whole time?"

Still wearing only his shirt, she took a seat at the table and shook her head. "I only caught the last bit, but I saw it was my phone, and Ted's superpower is the ability to piss anyone off in .4 seconds flat. It hasn't done his face any favors because he's gotten sucker punched for his comments so many times, his nose will never be straight again. Or at least not without major plastic surgery."

"Good to know I'm not special," Pike said, giving the sausages a last few rolls before going back to mixing the biscuit dough. "He said you have six brothers, all of them older than you."

"From oldest to youngest, they are: Caleb, Tim, Cooper, Ted, Carson, and Trevor."

"And then Cora," Pike said. "Cute."

"Only if you think growing up in a pack of feral dogs would be fun," Cora drawled. "I'm surprised Kimble didn't get up with me."

"He probably wanted to, but it's still daytime. It would be hard for him until he's had at least a week of meals like the one he had earlier," Pike explained, then turned the topic back to her brothers. "Are they mean to you?"

"They weren't deliberately abusive," she answered slowly. It was clear she'd thought about the topic a lot. "When we were young, they played a lot of pranks on me until I learned how to be even worse back to them. By the time I was nine, we had a ceasefire. They could do stuff to each other, but they had to leave me alone."

Pike couldn't imagine being the youngest and smallest among a bunch of rough boys without anyone to soften their behavior. His parents were immensely kind people who raised him to be gentle with anyone smaller, which was almost everyone.

"Where was your dad during all this?" Pike asked, sprinkling flour on the counter and dumping out the biscuit dough. "Did he ever step in to keep you safe?"

"Dad fell apart when Mom died," Cora said, her voice quiet. "I don't remember her. I was only a toddler."

Pike's heart hurt for child Cora. "Can I ask what happened?"

"Brain aneurysm," she said. "Caleb was twelve and was the one who called 911. He said she started asking weird questions and then fell over and started seizing. She died before they even got her to the hospital."

Hands covered in flour, Pike turned and took a half step toward her. He wanted to grab her in a hug, but worried that would be overstepping. She didn't look overwrought or upset; it was him who couldn't handle this story.

"I'm so sorry," he whispered, clutching his hands together and creating a little cloud of white powder.

Cora smiled at him, but it didn't reach her eyes. "It's okay, you don't need to be upset for me. It's hard to be sad about losing something I don't even remember. Dad's the one you should feel bad for. According to everyone, he was never the same. Mom's sister, Aunt Maria, ended up moving in to help take care of us, and his business partner took over everything else. Caleb says that Dad spent a lot of time hiding in his bedroom, crying or sleeping. Anyway, he managed to pull himself together and start taking care of us and working again, but it was a lot for one parent by themselves. He relied on Caleb and Tim to take care of the rest of us. Aunt Maria helped a lot too, bringing over food at least once a week and doing a lot of shopping."

The affection for the woman was evident in Cora's voice. "She was like a mother to you."

"Still is," Cora confirmed. "She's my favorite member of the family, including my siblings, and they know it."

Chuckling, Pike turned back to his dough. He could see Cora saying that to her brothers without hesitation. "After talking to Ted, I'd think the same way, and I haven't even met her."

"What about you?" Cora pressed. "What's your family look like?"

"My mom and dad live out in Bonita," Pike explained. "We talk every few days and get together for a meal once a week. I'd like to bring you to the next one."

"Have they met Kimble yet?" Cora asked.

"He comes with me for the weekly meals," Pike answered. "Mom and Dad have been great, talking to him as if he can respond and treating him like family."

Cora went silent, and Pike glanced back to see her blinking with shock. "They're okay with having a vampire in the family?"

Pike was confused by her question. "They want me to be happy, and Kimble makes me happy."

"Damn, I wish my family was like that," Cora muttered. "Tell me about you and Kimble meeting."

"I thought I did," Pike said, putting the biscuit disks on a tray, then popping them into the oven. The sausages looked done, and he had a good amount of grease to make the gravy, so he pulled them out and placed them aside.

"You told me he rescued you, but I want details," Cora pressed. "I feel like there's a lot of stuff you left out."

Pike felt his face getting hot. "Um, well, uh…"

Cora crowed out a laugh. "You're blushing! Oh, this has to be good. Spill everything, Pike!"

There shouldn't be secrets between mates. Reluctantly, Pike started talking.

**Kimble**

Unwilling to strain his body while the sun was out when he didn't need to, Kimble remained in the bed and listened as Cora and Pike talked in the other room. It was good that his flock was getting to know each other, but Cora's question about his rescue of Pike pulled him deep into that moment.

He let himself fall into the vivid memory as Pike described that night to Cora.

*Hunger. Always so much hunger.*

*The need to feed consumed him.*

*The driving hunger was so bad, he thought of himself as the personification of hunger. Since he couldn't think of what name he must have possessed before instinct took over, Hunger was as good a name as any.*

*In an attempt to satiate his driving need, he'd fed on several people, but one of them had died and that scared him. The man had been scum, smelling of drugs and talking on the phone and threatening someone. He hadn't meant to drain the human dry, but he couldn't stop once he started.*

*Somewhere in his chaotic brain, he knew causing too many unexplained or strange deaths would mean he'd be hunted down. He didn't want to die. He was feral, not suicidal*

*He'd decided that if he found someone big enough, he might be able to feed without accidentally killing them. He'd been flying high in the night sky, searching for the largest person he could find. That's when he'd spotted the massive shifter. It was clear from his bright aura that this was probably a type of bear shifter, giving Hunger hope for a good meal with no bad outcomes.*

*Dropping into a hidden spot not far away, he'd shifted to his human form. He planned to circle around the large male, but then a dozen angry nagas appeared, making him pause.*

*It wasn't that he couldn't easily defeat the nagas, but he didn't want anyone to know about his existence. He couldn't talk and had limited control. Slaughtering a dozen nagas would definitely be noticed.*

*Then the wind had shifted, and he caught the bear's scent at the same time he heard the large shifter pleading with the nagas to let him go. Something had snapped into place in his head, and he'd flown in to defend the bear.*

*It had taken no effort to scare the nagas off and then he was alone with the gorgeous, sweet-smelling shifter.*

*"Oh shit," the bear said, pressing his back hard against his car. He talked fast, his voice full of fear. "Thanks for the rescue, but please don't hurt me. My name is David Pike, and my parents would be really sad if I died. I have a lot of friends who call me Pike, and they'd be sad too. They might even try to avenge me, so you should probably keep yourself safe by leaving me alone."*

*As much as he loved to hear this male talk, the worry in Pike's voice was upsetting. He'd tried to speak soothing words, but only got one out.*

*"Flock," he whispered, stepping up close to Pike.*

*"Flock?" Pike repeated, his body relaxing a little, and the fear faded from his face. "You think I'm your flock?"*

*"Flock," he agreed.*

*Reaching out a hand, he cupped Pike's cheek. The bear didn't flinch, so he pressed his smaller body against the shifter. Pike's warmth helped chase away the cold that had seeped into his bones. Some of the chaos in his mind calmed.*

*Pike leaned in close and pressed his nose into Kimble's wild hair, breathing in deep. "Oh, you're my mate."*

*He knew that was important to shifters. It was rare for someone to refuse joining a vampire's flock, but it could happen. It was a relief that both Pike's human side and his inner bear were responding favorably to Hunger.*

*Pike wrapped his big arms around him, hugging lightly The embrace felt so good, he couldn't help the soft, content sound that came out of his mouth.*

*"Yeah, you feel good too," Pike murmured. They stood there embracing for several minutes before Pike spoke again, his voice full of wonder. "I can't believe I found my mate. Or I guess you found me."*

*"Flock," he repeated, agreeing with Pike. Desperate to say more, he focused on the swirling mass of thoughts and sensations. The right word finally popped into his head. "Sloneczko."*

*"I'm pretty sure that's not English or Spanish," Pike said with a little laugh. "I guess I'm going to be learning another language."*

*Hunger pulled away from Pike and placed a hand on the bear shifter's broad chest. "Sloneczko."*

*"Is that your word for me?" Pike asked. "I like it. What's your name?"*

*Hunger shook his head. He couldn't pull anymore words from his mind. He petted Pike's chest apologetically. "Hunger?"*

*"Is that your name or your state?" Pike asked with a frown. "Your eyes are red, and you're having a hard time talking. Will blood fix you or is there something else wrong?"*

*When Hunger didn't respond, Pike leaned over and bared his neck. "Take from me, my mate. Let me feed you."*

*Hunger violently shook his head. As much as he needed blood, he'd never feed on his flock! Never!*

*Pike made a soothing sound. "You don't want to take mine, that's okay. We'll find another way to get you blood."*

*Hunger smiled up at Pike, relieved he understood. Pike didn't see the smile; he was too busy taking in Hunger's appearance.*

*"You're a bit of a mess."*

*He probably was, but that didn't matter. He needed Pike to agree to a soul exchange, everything else could wait. Hunger moved in close and rose to his toes so he could press his lips to Pike's. The big shifter gasped and then parted his lips.*

*His bear tasted like a star-lit night after a rain. Pure and sparkling.*

*There was such an immediate and strong connection between them that the kiss felt like they were meeting after a long parting, not kissing for the first time.*

*A need even greater than his desire for blood rose up inside him. Pressing his body against Pike, he reveled in the feel of the bear's body. Shifters tended to be large and muscular, but Pike was even bigger and more muscled than average. The big shifter's body grew hot, and Hunger could feel Pike's massive cock getting hard in his jeans. Drawing his hands between them, he tugged at the closure of Pike's pants, requesting permission.*

*Without breaking the kiss, Pike made a whimpering noise that Hunger took as agreement. After tugging the button open and the zipper down, Hunger reached into his boxer briefs and palmed Pike's rapidly hardening cock. A pearl of precum smeared against his hand as he ran his finger up and down the length.*

*Shuddering, Pike moaned into his mouth. His hips moved a little as Hunger teased him with light touches and half strokes. Having Pike worked up and distracted would make the soul exchange easier. He wished he could make the bear shifter understand everything that was about to happen, but with his lack of language, it was impossible.*

*Pike had declared them mates, which meant their souls bonded the moment they touched. A soul exchange was only a small step beyond that.*

*When he tried to pull away and end the kiss, Pike made a sad sound and attempted to follow. A hand on his chest made the bear stop and straighten up.*

*"Please don't stop," Pike begged, his eyes glassy with need. Hunger made a comforting sound and reached up with his free hand to grip Pike's chin while still stroking the bear's massive cock with the other. Hunger held the man's head still, staring deep into his eyes as he sent his magic into the bear. Going slow so he wouldn't hurt the shifter, Hunger wrapped his power around Pike's soul and gently separated a piece. Pike didn't react until Hunger began pulling the piece into himself.*

*"What are you doing?" Pike asked, his eyes focused now, his erection deflating in Hunger's hand. "It feels like you're tugging something out of me that's pulling on my whole aura."*

*In an attempt to distract Pike, Hunger started stroking the bear again. Pike moaned and shivered from the touch, his eyes never leaving Hunger's.*

*Easing the piece of Pike's soul from his body, Hunger folded it into his own soul. Pike whimpered and shook, his body getting cold even as his cock stayed hard.*

*"I feel weird," he whispered.*

*If Hunger didn't act quickly, Pike would feel more than weird. Separating a piece of Pike's soul left a hole in his aura, causing him to bleed magic. Uncaring of his own discomfort, Hunger was far less gentle with himself. Ripping a piece of his own soul off, he ignored the agony and focused on feeding it gently into Pike. It was delicate work made harder by having to keep his hand moving on Pike's throbbing dick at the same time.*

*The moment that bit of soul touched Pike's, the bear's soul sucked it in, and his aura was whole. Their bond as vampire and flock snapped into place and power surged between them.*

*Pike threw back his head and cried out as he spurted hot jets of cum all over Hunger's hand. Hunger continued to stroke Pike through his orgasm until the shifter's head dropped, and his shoulders slumped.*

*"It's never been like that," Pike mumbled, moving Hunger's hand off his cock so he could wrap his long, thick arms around the vampire. He hugged Hunger tightly, breathing hard and covered in sweat. "What did you do to me? I feel different."*

*Hunger said nothing, only hugged Pike back and enjoyed the sense of peace that came with a successful soul bond.*

*"I guess you can't answer me," Pike murmured. "Whatever it was, I love it. I can feel you in the back of my head. Like a happy presence humming. I've never felt so loved before."*

*Joy exploded in Hunger. Yes, that was what he wanted, his flock to feel loved and safe. It was too bad that at this perfect moment, Hunger started to fade. He could feel the fatigue in his body threatening to drown him. He'd been starved before meeting Pike, but the energy he expended creating the soul bond had taken the last of his small reserve of energy.*

*"Flock," he whispered before he felt his body go limp.*

*"My mate!" Pike cried out, using the hug to awkwardly pick Hunger up. He held Hunger for several seconds, worry*

*coming across clearly in their link. Hunger tried to send him reassuring thoughts.*

*Pike shifted his body so the vampire was cradled in the bear's arms. He was staring at Hunger, his mouth turned down in a worried frown. Hunger tried to push thoughts of love through their link as he watched Pike through half-lidded eyes. His hunger might have made him weak, but he was content at the moment.*

*"I think you need blood. I can feel you in my head, happy but hungry." With Hunger still in his arms, he turned and managed to open the back door of the car. He gently laid Hunger across the long bench seat of the ancient Cadillac, bundling up a sweatshirt to act as a pillow.*

*"Rest, my mate. I'm going to change the tire and then I'll take us home."*

*That sounded good to Hunger. He'd been alone so long he'd forgotten what it was like to have someone in his life who cared if he lived or died. He tried to smile up at Pike, even as his eyes refused to remain open.*

*"You need a name," Pike murmured, using another sweatshirt as a blanket. "I guess I'll call you Kimble until you can tell me different."*

*Kimble. Hunger liked that. A new name for a new era.*

"Nine months later, and he still can only say a few words at a time, and his eyes are as red as the day we met," Pike concluded, pulling Kimble out of the memory. He heard the sadness in the bear's voice and wished he could make Pike understand that Kimble had come a long way because of Pike's hard work, dedication, and love. His mind was far less chaotic, and he could even think in clear sentences sometimes.

When he was completely back to himself, he'd shower Pike with words! He'd talk so much the shifter would wish he was mute again.

"It's romantic that he rescued you and then you rescued him," Cora commented. "But how can you be fated mates with more than one person?"

"It's uncommon," Pike said. "But not unheard of. And if I'm fated to a vampire, it would almost guarantee I'd have at least one more fated mate out there."

"Wouldn't you rather have another bear shifter?" Cora asked, the insecurity clear in her voice.

"Never," Pike answered without hesitation. "I couldn't ask for a more beautiful or fierce mate. I think you're tougher than a lot of shifters I know. When we were on our way to rescue you, Mac and Lex told me what happened in that alley. Did you really pepper spray a vampire?"

Cora chuckled. "Only after I kicked a guy in the balls. It didn't do any good though, Imani and I still ended up in Vincent's basement."

Pike shook his head. "You have the will to fight and with the right tools, you could be as deadly as any of us."

"I like tools," Cora murmured, sounding pleased.

Although he was determined to always be around to protect his human, he could hear the eagerness in her voice at the idea of owning weapons that would make her competitive in this new magical world she'd fallen into.

It would take some difficult trading, but Kimble knew exactly what he needed to get her.

## Pike

Pike was a naturally easygoing bear. He was slow to anger and quick to calm down. His mother often said he was born smiling and never stopped. While that was a gross exaggeration because he remembered bursting into tears plenty of times as a child, he understood what she was saying.

He was a happy bear who wanted nothing more than for those around him to be happy and content as well. The problem was that in order to make his new mate happy, he'd been forced to drive her to the club to get her car. He'd hoped she would agree to come back to his apartment, but she insisted she needed some time alone.

He'd followed her home and now he was parked across the street, staring at Cora's little house from inside the Coupe DeVille. It was a white, single-story home built in droves during the 1950s, with a single-car garage and a short driveway. The front yard was a collection of drought-resistant plants and an equal number of large ornaments.

There was even a white fence. It wasn't a picket fence, but it was white and only a few feet high. Her mailbox was a miniature replica of her house. It was all as adorable as the owner. She'd parked her car out front instead of the driveway or garage. Then she'd collected her mail and let herself into the house as if it was any average day.

But it wasn't! She was his mate and Kimble's flock. She'd almost died forty-eight hours earlier. He'd almost lost one of his mates.

What was he doing? If she found him sitting here staring at her house like a creepy stalker, it might make things worse. She'd asked for space and the first thing he'd done was ignore that request.

No matter how much he assured his bear that she was safe, he couldn't get himself to leave. In truth, it was hanging out with her friend Imani that had put her in the path of danger. Home alone, she probably wouldn't run into any more vampires or other creatures determined to hurt and or kill her.

Except that wasn't entirely true, was it? Anyone who watched the news knew that the average American woman was actually a common victim of human crime.

Why did he think that? Now that the thought of someone breaking into her home was in his head, he'd never get his bear to leave. He'd hoped to be back to his apartment before nightfall so Kimble wouldn't realize he'd been left alone. When the vampire rose from his daytime sleep, he was going to panic when he couldn't find Pike or Cora. That meant burning through the blood they'd fed him and setting back his recovery.

Frustration made Pike want to bash his head on the steering wheel. He either stayed here and watched over his human mate or rushed home to keep his vampire mate calm. Indecision kept him from moving. His bear side wanted to stay because Cora was the most vulnerable of the three of them. But his human side was more logical and wanted to hurry back to Kimble.

"If we go home, we can collect Kimble and come back here," he reasoned with his inner bear. Yes, that was an acceptable solution. Reaching for the keys, he was about to start the car when he saw a small pickup truck come to a screeching halt and park cattywampus in Cora's driveway.

As Pike watched, the man in the pickup got out and jogged around the back of the truck. Instead of taking the little path made of stepping-stones, he jumped over a planter to get to the front door fast. Pike was out of the car and sprinting across the street by the time the man opened the front door and boldly strode into Cora's house.

Fear for Cora and rage at this stranger made Pike's bear push to get out. It was hard, but Pike kept his inner beast locked down. When he got to the open door, he almost lost his hold on his bear. The stranger had Cora in his arms and was holding her in the air.

"Let go of me, you idiot!" she demanded, trying to kick her heels back into her attacker's shins.

With a roar, Pike grabbed the back of the guy's jacket and hauled him into the air. The attacker let out a surprised grunt and let go of Cora.

"What the fuck?" the guy screeched. Cora landed on her feet and only stumbled a step before she regained her balance.

"How dare you!" Pike shook the man violently. The guy lifted his arms and slipped out of his jacket, getting free of Pike's hold. With surprising speed for a human, the man twirled around and landed a solid punch to Pike's belly.

He barely felt it, but the man staggered back, yowling in pain. Holding his hand protectively against his chest, he backed up, herding Cora behind him.

"Run Cora!" the stranger said as he looked around, probably for a weapon. The man's actions were odd considering he'd attacked Cora first, but Pike was too enraged to think deeply about it.

"I'm going to break your legs first, then your arms," Pike said as he stalked forward. "Then I'm going to keep you alive in a basement until they all set crooked before I let you out!"

"Shit, that's dark," Cora said, neatly stepping around the stranger and standing between the two of them. "I think I might be turned on a little."

"Now isn't the time to be funny!" the stranger barked at Cora. "Get back behind me!"

Pike got the feeling Cora knew this man. Still unsure, Pike sounded a warning growl when the stranger reached for Cora. "Don't touch her!"

That made the man flinch back and stop trying to get a grip on her. She was within arm's length of Pike, so he reached for her. Her gaze intense, she held up a finger, and he stopped, hand in the air.

"That's one of my brothers," she said, gesturing behind her with a thumb. "Cooper, meet Pike, the guy I spent the night with. Pike, meet Cooper, my third oldest brother."

"Brother?" Pike's anger vanished and a healthy dose of worry set in. Looking beyond Cora, he tried to smile at her sibling. "Hi, uh, sorry about the hand. Want me to look at it?"

"I want you to stay the fuck over there," Cooper spat out, holding up a hand with one finger bent oddly. "Are you wearing some kind of armor or something? It felt like I punched a brick wall!"

Pike lifted his shirt to show his bare chest. "No armor, I'm, um, just naturally hard."

Cora snickered, and it took a moment to realize she was reacting to his *naturally hard* comment.

Cooper shoved her with his shoulder. "Shut up! I'm wounded here, and you're laughing."

Brother or not, Cooper didn't get to touch Cora like that. With a scowl, Pike moved Cora away from her sibling. "I'm sorry about that finger, but brother or not, I'll break more if you keep touching her like that. She's hum–small, so you need to be more careful."

"Calm down," Cooper said even as he backed away. "She's used to roughhousing. It's what we do. You know, it's how we show affection."

"Not any longer," Pike said as he drew her back against his front and wrapped his arms around her. His bear calmed considerably now that they were holding their human mate.

Shaking his head, Cooper frowned at Cora. "Tell him we do it all the time."

"And I tell you to stop every time," Cora answered. "Everyone else listens to me except you. I've even tased you, and you still pick me up. I don't like it now, and I've never liked it. I know you've hit your head a lot, but even you should've gotten the message by now."

"Cora, you're being mean," Cooper whined as he held up his hand again. "I was hurt trying to defend you."

"You got hurt punching my new boyfriend," Cora corrected, then smiled evilly. "But I could fix it for you. Come over here."

Cooper tucked his hand protectively against his chest at the same time Cora tried to step out of Pike's arms, but he tightened his hold. "Maybe Cooper should go to the hospital."

She made a disappointed sound. "You're spoiling my fun."

"This is really different," he muttered. Instead of leaving to find medical help, Cooper kept standing there, eyes bouncing back and forth between him and Cora. "You're never this nice to your boyfriends. If Andrew or Todd had tried to defend you, you'd have ripped into them."

"His name was Thomas, not Todd," Cora said. "And if they had ever tried to defend me from real danger, I wouldn't have said anything. All they wanted to protect me from was bullshit social situations."

"You can tell yourself that," Cooper said with a shake of his head. "But I've never seen you let anyone step in like this before. You trust this guy."

Cora stiffened and when she tried to pull away, Pike let her. It was obvious by her pensive expression that she didn't like what Cooper was saying, even if it was true. As fated mates, she'd instinctively trust Pike to protect her to the best of his ability. Maybe it would help if she understood it went both ways.

"I know you'd put yourself in danger to protect me," he murmured. "Even if I didn't want you to. That's how the bond between us works."

"Bond?" Cooper asked from behind her. "What kind of hippy-dippy shit are you talking about? Ted said you two had only been seeing each other for a few weeks."

"I swear you all gossip more than a bunch of old women at a church social," Cora muttered.

Pike leaned in close and whispered in Cora's ear. "Can we feed this brother to Kimble? You've got five others. Five is a good number."

Cora snorted. "He's not even the most annoying one."

Pike pretended to be shocked. "That can't be true."

"You sort of met the most annoying one over the phone," she reminded him. "Remember Ted? He invited you to our Sunday BBQ."

"Yeah, he totally needs to come," Cooper said, having sidled up close enough to hear that part of their conversation.

Cora took Pike's hand before turning to face her brother. "Why are you here anyway?"

"We were all worried," Cooper said. "Dad thought you might have joined a cult or something because you never go that long without answering your phone. Tim was sure you'd gotten kidnapped, and Caleb claimed you'd finally gotten fed up with all of us. I selflessly offered to check on you myself."

Cora narrowed her eyes at him. "Bullshit. You lost at arm-wrestling, so you're the one who had to make sure I wasn't dead or dying."

An unrepentant grin stretched across Cooper's face. "Yeah, but it wasn't just that. I was as worried about you as everyone else. I swear." He tried to hold up his right hand in a solemn promise, but winced and pushed it back against his chest.

"Idiot," Cora muttered.

Cooper ignored her and met Pike's gaze. "I'd like to formally invite you to our monthly BBQ this Sunday. Show up at four pm with the meat of your choice. Or fake meat of your choice if you swing that way. I think we'll probably be grilling some mushrooms and veggies too because Trevor's wife is a vegetarian."

Pike looked at Cora. "Do you want me to go?"

"Sure," Cora said with a resigned sigh. "Like I said when Ted invited you over the phone, you're going to have to meet them sometime. It's probably best to get it over with."

"You make us sound as fun as going to the dentist," Cooper complained.

Cora raised an eyebrow but didn't answer. The siblings stared at each other until Cooper broke eye contact with a wince.

"I'll tell the guys to be nice," Cooper said.

"I won't hesitate to fuck any of you up," Cora warned him. "Make sure they know that."

Cooper laughed. "I don't need to remind anyone of that. I still haven't gotten the dead fish smell out of my work truck."

Cora assumed an innocent expression. "I have no idea what you're talking about."

"Yeah, sure," Cooper answered. "Oh, and call Calab, he and Janet need help with the kids. And Dad wants you to pick up a few jobs that are too small for him. And…"

Cora shook her head. "Enough, I'll call everyone and figure it out."

"Good." Cooper turned his gaze to Pike, his expression turning mildly hostile. "I guess I'll see you around."

Before Pike could answer, Cooper walked by, deliberately hitting Pike with his shoulder. It didn't bother Pike, but Cooper ended up stumbling and almost ramming into the front door frame.

"Fuck me," Cooper muttered. "Built like a goddamn brick shithouse."

Then he was gone, and Cora strode past him to slam the front door shut. With a scowl on her face, she turned to face him. "Did I not say I needed some space?"

"Um, yeah," he said. Suddenly he was a three-foot-tall cub being reprimanded by his mom.

"Then what are you doing here?" To his surprise, her expression went from anger to concern. "Wait, where's Kimble? Did you leave him on his own?"

That's when Pike looked over at the large window at the front of the house to see the sun setting.

Oh, this was bad.

"Call me for anything!" Pike shouted as he barreled past Cora and out the door.

## Cora

Once she was alone, Cora locked her door, secured all the windows, then spent an hour in the shower. It felt like she had to remove all the grime and dirt in layers, but by the time she emerged, she felt much better. Another meal and a good night's sleep, and she'd be good as new.

Except there was a weird ache in her chest that wouldn't go away. It had started the moment she'd watched Pike drive away and only gotten worse over time. It was almost ten at night now and instead of feeling tired, she was wide awake and jittery, as if she'd downed an entire pot of coffee.

Lying in bed and staring into the dark wasn't going to do her any good, so she decided maybe a mug of tea and a boring documentary would do the trick. Throwing off the covers, she unplugged her cell and pulled on a comfy bathrobe. She didn't bother turning on any lights until she was in the living room, and then she only flipped the switch for the small set of recessed lights that illuminated her bookshelf covered wall.

That provided enough light for her to see the figure standing perfectly still in the living room, watching her with a blank expression.

Screaming in surprise, Cora grabbed the closest thing at hand, a brass bookend, and threw it with all her force. The person plucked it out of the air, tilted his head in confusion, then dropped to his knees and watched her with unblinking eyes.

By now, she realized it was Kimble standing there. Adrenaline was still coursing through her system, and her heart was pounding as she pressed a hand to her chest and sagged against a nearby bookshelf.

"Fuck, Kimble," she breathed. "You're lucky I didn't have a gun."

Kimble gave her a small, apologetic smile. "Flock. Safe."

Cora shook her head. Had she really been expecting more? Straightening away from the shelf, she gestured for Kimble to get up.

"Don't kneel like that. It makes me feel like I'm demanding weird things from you or something." She refused to acknowledge that she was glad he was here. If she called Pike, the bear would probably come over as well. By then, it would be too late for them to leave so they'd need to spend the night.

She might not have planned to invite them over, but she was ready to take advantage of the situation.

The vampire got to his feet slowly, keeping his hands clasped together in front of him. Holding out his hands, he smiled eagerly.

"Flock."

Cora watched as he opened his hands to reveal a piece of jewelry. It looked like a bronze disk with a garnet or ruby set in the center. The entire thing was about an inch in diameter and etched with symbols.

"What the flocking flock?" Cora asked with a laugh at her bad joke. "I hope you didn't steal that."

Kimble shook his head and moved his hands closer to her, offering her the necklace. "Tool-gift for human flock."

Cora blinked at him, impressed with the sentence. "That was a lot of words, good job!"

The compliment didn't affect Kimble; his focus never wavered from getting her to take the piece of jewelry.

"Tool-gift for human flock," he repeated and offered it again. He must've practiced those words to say to her.

"You don't have to give me gifts," Cora said. "Especially not jewelry. I'm not really a jewelry person."

Even as she said the words, she plucked the necklace from Kimble's hand. It was surprisingly cool to the touch considering Kimble had been grasping it in his hands.

"It looks old, like an antique," she murmured, examining the intricate carvings on the face of it, forming circles around the stone. It reminded her of the cuneiform writing she'd seen as a kid during a school trip to a museum.

The chain was made of the same metal as the disk with an unfamiliar clasp that took her a few tries to get undone. It didn't help that Kimble was intensely focused on her the entire time, as if he was trying to push her to move faster with the power of his gaze alone.

Getting the clasp closed was as hard as getting it open but when it locked in place, she felt a flash of static electricity wash over her skin. That wasn't the only weird thing, the disk got hot. Not warm but hot. It wasn't enough to be uncomfortable, but it was noticeable. Within seconds, the heat was gone. The disk hung down past her collarbone and felt so light it might as well have not been there.

Pressing a palm over it, she refused to think about the significance of the gift, and her eagerness to take it. She liked the idea of jewelry but had never worn it much. However, she couldn't imagine taking this piece off.

Pressing her palm over it, she smiled up at Kimble. "This is one of the nicest things anyone has ever given me."

Kimble beamed and lowered his face to hers. "Flock," he whispered, and she could hear the devotion and love behind those words.

The urge to say something stupid like *I love you too* pressed against the back of her throat, but she stifled the words. Swallowing hard, she pressed her lips against his.

A happy sigh came out of Kimble as he opened his mouth and invited her to deepen the kiss. Swept up in the moment, Cora slid her tongue in his mouth and found his fangs half descended.

Running the tip of her tongue over them, she shivered. The thought of him sinking those fangs into her made her want to press his face to her neck. She'd never understood why so many people swooned over vampires until now!

She had no idea how long they stood there kissing. She tangled her fingers into his messy black hair to hold his head still while they kissed. With a soft groan, Kimble wrapped his arms around her and pulled her tight against his body, then stood up. Her feet left the ground as he effortlessly held her.

She could feel his lean muscle through his thin t-shirt. She wanted to run her hands over his body and when she was done doing that, she wanted to go back and do it again with her tongue.

The first indication that Kimble wasn't feeling well was when he swayed a little. She wouldn't have noticed except when it happened again, he abruptly ended the kiss and set her down. Blinking rapidly, he opened his mouth to talk and then went corpse white.

"Sit down before you fall," Cora ordered, grabbing his hands from around her and leading him to her couch. They were nearly there when Kimble's legs gave out. He crashed painfully to his knees.

"Are you hurt?" Cora asked, dropping to one knee next to him. Kimble looked up and shook his head, but his gaze wasn't right. He didn't seem to be able to focus on her.

"You need blood," she realized. "Can you get on the couch if I push it closer? Once I've got you comfortable, I'll call Pike. He can tell me where to order the blood from. You're going to be fine, Kimble. I'll take care of you."

Kimble managed a half smile before his eyes rolled back and he slumped sideways. Cora wasn't fast enough to catch his head before it hit her hardwood floors.

"Damn," she muttered, staring at the unconscious vampire. "If this keeps up, I'm going to make you wear a helmet all the time."

Pike arrived less than a minute after the blood delivery guy dropped off a little cooler packed full of bags of blood. The moment Cora opened the door, he rushed to Kimble's side.

"Why do you keep doing this to me?" he whispered, picking up one of Kimble's limp hands. "I swear I'm going to be the first shifter in history that has a heart attack."

Carrying the cooler to them, Cora took a spot on Kimble's other side. "I got up to make myself some tea and found him in my living room. I don't know how long he's been here."

"He wasn't home when I got there, so your guess is as good as mine." Pike tried to smile, but the remnants of his earlier fear made the smile look forced. "Have you fed him yet?"

"No," Cora said, opening the cooler and handing one of the bags to Pike. "It just arrived."

Accepting the bag, Pike slipped his big hand under Kimble's head and lifted. Pressing the bag to Kimble's mouth, Pike whispered pleas for him to eat.

The vampire didn't move.

"Should we open the bag and pour it in his mouth?" Cora asked.

"That doesn't work," Pike said with a tired sigh. "He chokes on it. Would you talk to him too? It might help."

Putting her mouth close to Kimble's ear, she spoke in a calm but firm voice. "Kimble, I need you to open your mouth and bite into that bag right now. If you don't, I'm going to be pissed."

Kimble jerked slightly and opened his mouth. Pike was able to maneuver the bag between his lips and press it up onto his half-descended fangs.

"Drink it," Cora ordered. She grabbed one of his hands in hers and held tight. "Do it, Kimble. Drink!"

Her commanding tone worked, as Kimble's fangs fully descended, and he started to weakly suckle. Cora heard Pike breathe out a sigh of relief.

"Tough love," Pike murmured. "I like it."

Cora grinned. "We can't all be big softies like you."

When she straightened up, she found Pike regarding her with a longing expression. "It's going to be a rough night. He's not going to want to stay at my place. I don't know why he's so depleted from simply traveling from home to here, but it's going to be almost impossible to keep him contained until sunrise."

"I think he might have robbed a jewelry store on the way here," Cora said, tugging the disk out from under her shirt. "He gave me this before he collapsed. Even if it's stolen, I'm not kicking out the guy who brought me something pretty I actually like. With your help, we can board up the windows, and he'll be as safe here as he would be at your apartment."

Pike's expression turned ecstatic. "We can stay?"

"For tonight at least," Cora amended quickly.

"That's fine," Pike assured her. "I've been living one night at a time for nine months. I can keep doing it for as long as you want."

His eagerness made her feel guilty. "I might not be sure about being part of the flock, but I'm determined to help you two. You're important to me. I'm just not sure how important yet."

Pike nodded his head. "That's fair. More than fair. I bet a lot of other humans wouldn't be so accepting so quickly."

Noticing that Kimble had stopped drinking with the bag only half empty, Cora squeezed his hand again. "Keep going, Kimble. Finish this bag and then you can sleep."

"We're going to stay with you Kimble," Pike added. "We're all going to stay together all night."

Kimble made a weak, happy sound and started sucking again. It took another five minutes of their encouragement, but he finally finished the bag.

"Should we try for another?" she asked.

Plucking a pillow from the couch, Pike put it under Kimble and then lowered his head. "Not right away. Let's start getting the house vampire-safe and try feeding him another bag later. He's so depleted it's going to take most of tonight and tomorrow to bring him back."

Cora couldn't feel the weight of her necklace on her skin, but it weighed on her mind. "Do you think he did something bad for the necklace and that's why he's so weak?"

"Show it to me again," Pike requested and then leaned in close when she pulled it back out from under her shirt. "That's magic. I don't know what kind or what it does, but it smells powerful. However he got that, it probably wasn't by force. He must have traded for it and that's why he's like this."

"Should I take it off?" Cora asked. It felt wrong to remove it, but she shouldn't be playing around with magical items she didn't understand.

"Kimble wouldn't have given it to you if it was dangerous to any of us," Pike assured her.

"I wish I could've told him not to do whatever he did," Cora murmured. "I feel guilty as fuck."

Reaching across Kimble's supine body, Pike took one of her hands in his. "Don't. When Kimble gets an idea in his head, there is no stopping him."

Because she hated feeling guilty or helpless, Cora focused on practical matters. "Come on, I've got some sheets of plywood in the shed out back and all the tools we'll ever need in the work van. Let's play post-apocalypse and zombie proof this house!"

Pike laughed. "You're strange, and I love it!"

**Pike**

Sitting on Cora's couch watching TV while Kimble slept with his head in Pike's lap felt like the height of decadence. They'd managed to get three bags of blood into Kimble last night before Pike carried him into the guest room. He and Kimble slept there last night. He wished Cora had stayed with them, but it was enough to know that only a wall separated them.

When he'd woken up late the next morning, he found a note taped to his phone.

*I had to go into work or else I might not be able to keep you guys in blood and groceries! I should be home around five. Call if you need anything or if Kimble gets worse. Help yourself to anything in the kitchen.*

The note ended with a smiley face instead of a heart or I love you. For Cora, this was probably a pretty affectionate message. After talking to one brother over the phone and interacting with a second one, he was getting the impression her family didn't do normal displays of affection.

Or maybe he didn't know what was normal for humans. He'd grown up in a bear family that associated with mostly other bear and shifter families. His type didn't know how to be reserved.

Affection was freely given and received, there was no holding back.

Cora's family could be typical for humans, which made him feel bad for humans. Who wanted to live without hugs and words of love?

Pike was startled when his phone rang and didn't bother reading the screen before answering.

"Hello?"

"David, honey," his mother, Tina, said with a relieved little laugh. "It's good to hear your voice finally. It's been three days since the last time we talked!"

"Did you get a hold of him?" Pike's father asked in the background, his voice getting more frantic as he spoke. "Is he okay? Does he need us? Is it Kimble? What's going on?"

"I don't know yet, Mark," his mother said back. "All he said so far was hello."

"Tina, give me the phone," Mark demanded. "I want to talk to him."

"Mom, you should put me on speaker," Pike said. They always argued over the phone and rarely remembered that there was a speaker function.

"Oh, yes, I'll do that," Tina said, and then he got to listen to them argue about what to push. He laughed and muted the TV while they figured it out.

"Honey, can you hear me?" Tina practically yelled into the phone.

"Not so loud, Mom," Pike said with a slight wince. "You guys aren't that old, why do you have so much trouble with phones?"

"It's against nature," Mark grumbled. "I'm a man of words, not electrons."

Unwilling to get into a philosophical debate with his dad about modern technologies' effect on creativity, Pike was quick to change the subject.

"I'm sorry I didn't call back sooner; things got a little busy."

"I know you wouldn't make us worry on purpose," Mark said. "But three days is a long time."

"It's been a hectic three days," Pike said. "I found my mate."

There was absolute silence on the other end of the line before his mother spoke, her voice gentle. "We know, sweetheart. We've met Kimble many times."

Pike chuckled. "I meant another mate, Mom. Her name is Cora, and she's human."

"Does Kimble want her too?" Mark asked.

"He's desperate for her to join the flock," Pike assured them. "I can't wait for you to meet her. She's tiny but so very strong."

"Put her on the phone," Tina demanded.

"She's at work," Pike explained. "But I was thinking of bringing her over for dinner. Not this weekend because I'm going to a party to meet her family. Maybe next weekend?"

"Of course we can wait until next weekend," Tina said. "It'll give us time to make everything perfect." She made a sound of concern. "You're going to meet her family? Are they all human? Are you going to take Kimble?"

"They're all human and don't know about us," Pike began, but before he could answer any more questions, his father started talking.

"I teach mostly humans at the college; do you want us to come to help? I can bring my collection of winter poetry and do a reading," Mark said at the same time Tina gave instructions.

"You should bring them something humans enjoy, like Jell-O. It comes in all kinds of colors. Oh, and pudding. They like pudding too."

"That's a good idea!" Mark said. "We could both go and meet everyone too."

The thought of his gentle parents mixing with Cora's aggravating brothers made Pike wince. Better to wait until he'd met them and could get a feel for how to best introduce everyone.

"I love you guys so much," Pike murmured.

"We love you too, honey," Tina responded without hesitation.

"You're my favorite male child," Mark said.

"I'm your only male child," Pike responded. "I'll tell you guys all about Cora's family after I meet them, but we're probably going to need a little time to get you all together."

"That's fine," both of them said in unison. They did that a lot.

"I was thinking I'd bring something anyone could eat, like a bowl of cut-up fruit," he concluded.

"Fruit is good," Tina said with a sound of approval. "Don't put grubs in it though, even if they make it taste amazing. Humans don't eat grubs."

"Some humans do," Mark argued.

"Not many," Tina said. "But I guess he could put them on the side so people could add them if they wanted to."

"I think I'll leave all the grubs at home," Pike said.

"Has having Cora join the flock made Kimble any better?" Tina asked.

"They haven't shared souls yet," Pike explained. "Cora didn't know anything about our world until just before she met Kimble. Like I said, a lot's happened in the last few days."

"Oh, the poor thing," Mark said. "That had to be a shock. But if the magic picked her for you and Kimble, then she'll come around soon."

"You didn't really answer the question. Is Kimble any better yet?" Tina asked.

"A little better," Pike said, but didn't mention it was probably due to the blood Cora was buying him rather than her presence in his life.

"That's good," Tina said.

"If we have to wait to meet Cora, could you at least send us a picture?" Mark requested.

"Yes!" Tina agreed with a little cheer. "I want to see what she looks like."

That was when Pike realized he didn't have any pictures of Cora on his phone. Not even a single selfie of the two of them. "You guys will have to wait until she gets home."

He could feel their disapproval over the phone. His mother's phone was full of pictures of him, his sister and her husband, including pictures she'd taken of his baby pictures hanging in silver frames on the walls of her house. His father would have just as many pictures on his phone if he could work it half as well as Tina.

"Not even one of her face?" Tina asked.

"No, Mom. Not even one of her face," Pike admitted. "But I'll fix that tonight."

"Now tell us everything you know about Cora," Mark insisted. "No detail is too small."

Smiling with happiness, Pike started talking and the hours flew by.

## Cora

Parking her work van in her single car garage attached to the house was always a pain, but Cora refused to leave it parked in the driveway. If the van was stolen, she'd lose a lot of specialty tools and equipment. She didn't have a shop, just a small one room office she rented in an industrial building manned by Charlotte, her only full-time employee at the moment. The parking lot behind the building was secured by a tall fence and bright lights, but Cora still didn't trust her precious work van there. During his time off, Van Guts spent his nights safely tucked away in her small garage.

She was so eager to get inside to see the guys that parking was even more troublesome than normal. It took two tries and almost sideswiping the side of the garage door frame before she was successful. Once Van Guts was inside, she could get out and lock him up for the night.

She should be exhausted. She'd spent most of the night tossing and turning. Knowing the guys were sharing a bed on the other side of her bedroom wall made it hard to relax into sleep. She'd fought the urge to go to them the entire time and only fell asleep sometime around three in the morning.

It was unlikely she was going to be able to resist the impulse to go to them tonight. Even now, as she grabbed her purse and phone from the passenger seat, her chest felt tight from the need to at least set eyes on the two men.

These strong feelings should be freaking her out, but all she felt was impatience.

Going through the door from the garage into the house, she heard Pike laughing. Curious and maybe a little jealous, Cora dumped everything in her arms on the kitchen table and tiptoed to the open arch between the kitchen and the living room. At this angle, Pike wouldn't see her until she stepped through the opening.

Standing still, she listened to him talking.

"...that's it exactly," he said. "Fox shifter, I think you nailed it, Dad."

The jealousy fled. Of course he wasn't flirting with someone. This was Pike, he was incapable of cheating. He was so sweet and honest he wouldn't even watch series episodes without her.

"No, Mom, I don't think getting us all matching shirts is a good idea yet, maybe later," Pike said with another laugh, then he paused, listening before talking again. "Winter solstice is months away, Mom. Let's wait until November before we start planning for that."

There was another brief silence before Pike spoke again. "Mom, Dad, I need to go, Cora just got home."

Cora startled. How had he known she was there?

She stepped out from the kitchen as he was saying repeated goodbyes and finally took the phone away from his ear and tapped the screen. He looked up at her with a goofy-happy grin.

"It's so good to see you!"

Kimble was asleep on the couch with his head in Pike's lap. There were two empty family sized bags of chips on the coffee table in front of Pike along with half a dozen soda cans and a glass with a little water at the bottom.

Pike followed her gaze to the mess and grimaced. "I'm sorry. I was going to clean up but then my parents called, and I lost track of time."

Cora didn't respond as she drank in the sight of Pike and Kimble. Honestly, she didn't care about the mess, she was only looking at it to keep from jumping onto the two men on her couch.

When had she gotten so needy?

The sun had started setting as she'd hit her street and she watched as Kimble opened his eyes and sat up. He smiled at her and scooted away from Pike to pat the section of couch between them.

That got Pike moving.

"Oh, you're probably tired and hungry!" he exclaimed, jumping up from the couch. "Come sit!"

He pressed her to sit next to Kimble but didn't join them on the couch. "I prepped dinner, so it'll only take about twenty minutes to cook. Do you want a drink?"

Cora stared up at him, bemused. "This feels like Mad Men in reverse."

Pike looked confused as Kimble put an arm around her shoulders and cuddled close. "Mad Men?"

"It was a show set in the 1960s," she explained, noting Kimble's tidy appearance. She ran a hand over his smooth face. "Did you shave?"

"I bathed and shaved him today," Pike explained. "Your bathroom is surprisingly big for how small the house is. That made it easy to carry him in there for a bath."

When Cora dropped her hand away from Kimble's face, he leaned close and rubbed his smooth jaw against her cheek. Suddenly everything was better, and happiness bubbled up inside her.

She giggled and patted his head. "Yes, you feel very nice."

"Since you didn't answer on the drink, I'm going to bring you all the choices available," Pike announced, striding into the kitchen. He was soon back with several cans of soda, a glass of water, and a bottle of sparkling water. Setting them all out, he whisked away the empty chip bags and cans. When he returned again it was with a small bowl full of chips and another with dip.

"Here's something to snack on until dinner is ready."

Kimble snuggled against her as Pike rushed around to make her comfortable. A girl could get used to this.

**Pike**

Pike's bear was practically vibrating inside him with happiness as Cora finished every morsel on her plate. Kimble had already had several bags of blood and was sitting as close to Cora as he could get without inhibiting her movements at the kitchen table.

"Damn, that was good," Cora said, pushing the plate away. "You're hired, Pike. You can cook all my meals from now on."

"That's good because I found out I lost all my other jobs today." He meant the words to be playful, but they came out hurt instead.

"What?" Cora asked, outraged. "I'm sure you're the best employee they have. Why would they fire you?"

Her words helped soothe his wounded pride. "I guess that doesn't matter when you miss two shifts in a row without calling in."

"Did you tell them you were busy rescuing me?" Cora asked, eyes flashing with anger as she pounded her fist down on the table, making her plate jump. "I bet you didn't say anything about that. You didn't have to say anything about vampires or shifters, you could have just said some guys kidnapped me."

Pike's eyes went a little wide at Cora's vehemence. "There was no news about it or police report to show them. They'll think I made it all up."

Cora's expression turned hard. "I'm going to the Gas Lamp district tomorrow and getting your jobs back!"

Pike covered her clenched hand with his own. "I've had to call out sick a lot in the last nine months because of Kimble. All my bosses think I'm flaky. They were probably relieved to have an excuse to get rid of me."

"Still, it's not fair," Cora argued.

"Maybe it's a good thing," Pike insisted. "Kimble is steadier now that we have you. I could look for a better job."

Cora tugged her hand out from under his with a frown. "I'm not ready to do the soul thing yet."

Pike shook his head, upset that she misunderstood him. "I didn't mean it like that. Even if things stay as they are right now, you've made a huge difference in our lives. You're helping me keep him fed and accepting his affection. We'll do everything on your timeline, no rush or pressure."

"I feel pressured," Cora muttered, then held up a hand before Pike could apologize. "But the pressure is coming from inside me, not you or Kimble."

"That's the magic," Pike explained, wishing he could make Cora understand something that came naturally to him. "You know how water will always flow to the lowest point?"

Cora nodded.

"Magic is a little like that."

"Are you telling me I'm the lowest point?" Cora asked with a raised eyebrow.

Pike shook his head. "Magic likes balance, that's what water and magic have in common. They're constantly striving for equilibrium, and that's why you feel the magic pushing at you."

"Flock," Kimble added with a sage nod of his head.

Placing her hand flat on her sternum, Cora rubbed it back and forth a little. "I feel it right here when I'm away from you guys. Like there's a hand pushing here and making it hard to breathe."

Pike knew from talking to a few people that the pressure would only get worse over time. He didn't want her to feel like she had no choice, so he looked at Kimble.

"Our mate is uncomfortable during the day when she has to work. I'm going to go with her to help her feel better."

Kimble blinked a few times, as if he was translating Pike's words in his head. Then he looked hurt. "Flock stay."

"Damn it, he breaks my heart when he looks like that," Cora muttered, reaching for one of Kimble's hands and holding it in hers. "But I've got to work or we'll all starve."

Kimble leaned his body over until his forehead was resting on her shoulder and made a whining sound. Pike had never seen him do that before. When Pike tried to leave him during the day, the vampire would throw a tantrum and threaten to walk out into the sun. Now he was acting like a kicked puppy who only wanted to love his human.

"You're a lying liar who lies," Pike muttered under his breath knowing full well Kimble would be able to hear him, but Cora wouldn't.

Kimble didn't react, only whined again and snuggled his head closer to Cora's neck.

It turned out Cora was tougher than Pike.

"I'll try to make it so we can come back here between jobs and check on you," Cora said, petting Kimble's head. "But I'm not giving up my company. I've worked too damn hard to build it."

"You have a company?" Pike asked.

"Perfection Connection Electrics, PCE," she said, her eyes sparkling with pride. "I'm a licensed general electrician so I can do commercial and residential. I used to do new construction sites, but I'm starting to specialize in updating old houses instead. I don't make as much, but there's a lot less bullshit to deal with and women love to hire me. Business really picked up in the last six months, and I'm thinking of taking on another apprentice."

"You're an electrician?" Pike asked, easily picturing Cora wearing a tool belt and focused on running wires through homes and installing outlets.

Cora's eyes narrowed, and she stopped petting Kimble. "Is that surprising to you?"

"No! The opposite. You're so brave, it makes sense that you'd deal with something as scary as electricity."

"I think that's one of the sweetest things anyone has ever said to me," Cora said. Kimble made a soft protesting sound until she went back to stroking his head. "It's a good thing you're cute because you're the neediest guy I've ever dated."

Pike didn't comment on her use of the word dating but a little thrill went through him. He couldn't wait to meet her family and introduce himself to all of them as the boyfriend.

"How did you decide on being an electrician?" Pike asked.

"Family business," she explained. "Dad's an electrician too. He half-owns a business, Best Value Electrics. Three of my brothers are electricians too and work for him: Tim, Cooper, and Carson."

Although he had an idea what the answer would be, he asked anyway. "But not you?"

Cora snorted. "Work for my father? Never!"

Pike could understand Cora wanting to strike off on her own if the rest of her family was even remotely as irritating as Tim. "So you started your own business, that's amazing. I bet the reason women like to hire you is because they feel like they can trust you."

"That, and I don't talk down to them," Cora added. "About ten percent of my jobs are from women who've gotten multiple quotes, but the electricians wouldn't explain anything to them. By the time I show up, they're frustrated and full of questions."

"And you answer them all," Pike said with approval. "Was your dad upset that you didn't join his company like your brothers?" If his parents had a family business, he'd love to work for them, but his dad was an English professor, and his mom was a CPA who did forensic accounting. Pike had thought working side by side with his mom would be fun. After only one year of college, he realized he didn't have the patience for higher education. His parents were kind, but he knew they worried about his lack of career options.

Maybe he could be an electrician. He could learn anything under her guidance! Accompanying Cora on jobs was a perfect place to start.

Standing up, Pike gathered the empty plates and headed to the sink. "Then it's settled, I'll spend the day with you, and we'll come back and spend our evenings and nights together here."

"I don't remember agreeing to that," Cora muttered behind him. "Have you ever worked with electricity before?"

"Nope, but I can carry stuff for you better than anyone," he assured her as he returned to the table with the apple strudel he'd kept warming in the oven. Cora licked her lips as he set the pan on the table.

"I baked enough to take some with us to work tomorrow," Pike offered.

Cora looked up at him, her lips pursed. "Well played, Pike. I guess you get to be an electrician's assistant for the day."

Pike felt himself grinning like a fool at the same time Kimble made a disgruntled sound.

*Suck it up, vampire,* Pike thought. *Our human needs me more than you right now.*

After helping him clean up the kitchen, Cora demanded they all cuddle on the couch. Once she was situated between the two of them, she took control of the remote and flipped through a few streaming services.

"Do you guys mind watching this?" she asked. It was a mini-series drama about international politics. Pike normally liked romantic comedies or action movies, but he didn't care what was playing as long as he got to be close to Cora.

"That's fine," he agreed, snuggling down into the couch a little more. Kimble made a dismissive sound, probably indicating he didn't care what she chose. The moment the first episode started to play, Kimble leaned in close and began kissing Cora's neck.

"Stop that," Cora said with a laugh and pushed his face away without taking her eyes off the TV.

Kimble let her move him a few inches but once she let go, he went right back to kissing her. Pike was surprised at how forward the vampire was being with his advances. He'd never wanted more than cuddling from Pike.

Turning her head to face him, Cora tried to admonish him. "Kimble, you need to—"

Kimble ducked his head down and captured her lips in a kiss. That's when Pike realized what was going on. Kimble hadn't felt any physical desire during their relationship because he lacked enough blood to feed that part of his body and magic. Now that he'd had multiple days full of meals, he was ready to play.

Cora wasn't trying to pull away from Kimble or break the kiss. Her eyes were closed, and her hands were held out to her sides, curled into loose fists. Leaning close, Pike pulled her hair off to one side and kissed the back of her neck. He felt her tense before she moaned, the sound muffled by Kimble's mouth.

"We want you," Pike whispered before running his teeth over the delicate skin at the back of her neck. "But no matter how badly we desire you, we'd never force you, my mate. A single word from you, and we stop."

Cora pulled her face away from Kimble, breathing rapidly. He pulled back when she turned to look at him with dazed eyes.

"No!" Her voice was unsteady but firm.

Heartbroken that she didn't want them, Pike drew away. "As you—"

He didn't get a chance to finish his sentence because she was grabbing him by the back of the head and pulling his face close to hers.

"No, I mean yes. I want this. I want you. I want Kimble." She tangled her fingers in his hair and tugged. "Don't stop!"

"We won't." His relief was so strong he didn't care that she'd pulled a few strands of his hair out.

Kimble plucked at Cora's shirt, then said very clearly, "Need naked. Pleasure my flock."

"Kimble, you say the best things!" Pike declared.

**Cora**

She'd never felt so turned on in all her life, and she was still fully clothed! All they'd done was kiss and not even for that long, and she could already feel the need pooling in her belly.

"Let me help," Pike said and jumped off the couch. He grabbed her with those massive hands and lifted her to her feet.

Kimble flowed off the couch and joined him, each of them grabbing a long sleeve and tugging it over her hands. The moment she lifted her arms, the shirt came off. She felt a tug and the sound of fabric tearing, then her bra was gone too. Cool air hit her hot skin, making her shiver and nipples bead.

They didn't give her a moment to be uncomfortable. When she tried to cross her arms over her chest to cover herself from their hot gazes, Kimble put his lips to hers again.

"Perfect human," he whispered, then started kissing her again.

She felt Pike's hand settle on her shoulder blade and run down her back. "Goddess of the Hunt, you're gorgeous. I'm going to touch you everywhere with my hands and lips. Everywhere." He lowered his hand to her ass and squeezed. "But first I need these pants gone."

She heard him drop to his knees and then felt his hand snake around to her waistband. She heard the hiss of the zipper, then felt the fabric drawn down over her slim hips.

He took her panties also. Hands on her hips turned her until she was facing him. Kimble moved a little so she only had to keep her head to the side to continue kissing him as Pike kissed her mons and then the curls covering her sex. She gasped into Kimble's mouth when Pike flicked a tongue out, spearing between her feminine lips and briefly licking over her sensitive flesh.

Pike groaned as his hands tightened on her thighs where he still held her pants up. "Fuck, you taste good. I'm a starving man who needs to feast."

She made an eager sound, and Kimble ended the kiss to look down at what Pike was doing. He nodded in approval.

"Finish naked, all," Kimble ordered as he stepped back and made an encompassing gesture with one finger.

Dazed from lust, Cora didn't understand what he meant right away but Pike did. With one swift movement, Pike toppled her over his shoulder so he could untie and pull her work boots off.

"Pike!" Cora exclaimed, trying to straighten up. "I could've gotten those off!"

"This is faster," Pike responded as her shoes went flying and then her pants were gone. Before she could respond, he was standing up with her still on his shoulder and one beefy arm over her ass, holding her steady.

"Here or the bedroom?" Pike asked.

"Bed," Kimble answered.

"I agree," Pike said as he turned slowly, careful to keep her away from the nearby lamp.

"Do I get a say in this?" Cora asked with a laugh. She tried to reach down and touch Pike's ass, but the man was just too big. Even half dangling over his shoulder, she could only get her fingers in his belt loops. "This is so unfair."

"Of course you get a say," Pike said as he strode into her bedroom. "But only after the second or third orgasm."

Cora snorted. "That sounds like a brag."

"It's not a brag if you can back it up," Pike said with confidence as he gently pulled her off his shoulder, then dropped her on the bed below. Kimble was already kneeling on the bed, naked and eager.

Sitting up, she took a moment to admire Kimble while Pike stripped. Unlike the bulky and bulging Pike, her vampire was covered in beautiful lean muscles. He had black hair on his chest that narrowed to a band as it ran down his stomach. A narrow happy trail led her eyes to his half hard, uncut cock.

"I want to touch you," she whispered, unable to look away from Kimble's blossoming erection.

"You can touch either of us as much as you want, any time you want," Pike said, taking a kneeling position on the bed next to Kimble. The difference between the two was startling. Pike was so big and muscled that compared to him, Kimble almost looked delicate.

Except between the two of them, Kimble was capable of being a cold-blooded killer and Pike couldn't bring himself to kill the spider he found in the bathroom that morning. Unlike Kimble who wasn't quite there yet, Pike was fully hard and leaking pre-cum.

"This is killing me," Pike said, making her realize that she'd been sitting there staring at them for several minutes.

Leaning forward, she put a hand on each dick, grasping gently. Kimble was a handful, but Pike was large enough to be scary. She could wrap her fingers around him, but only barely, and she was sure there were at least nine inches there. Good god, it would be like trying to shove a baseball bat inside herself.

"I'm not sure I can handle this." She meant the words to be funny, but they came out sounding intimidated.

Pike put a finger under her chin and urged her to look up. When their gazes met, he smiled at her. "This is sex between mates, there are no expectations except pleasure. You don't have to sit on either of our cocks, you don't have to suck on us or even touch us if you don't want to. This is about enjoyment, not requirements. Let go of your human ideas about relationships and intimacy. Let Kimble and I show you what it's like to have magic in your life."

"You sound like a porno advertisement," Cora murmured.

Pike didn't take offense. "A very special porno only for you."

As they'd talked, Kimble had gotten harder and was now a solid, velvety rod in her hand. The foreskin was pulled back and a pearl of pre-cum dotted his slit.

"You're feeling better," she murmured.

"That's the first time I've ever seen him hard," Pike said in a husky voice. "How does he feel in your hand, my little human?"

"Strong," she answered, looking up to meet Kimble's red eyes. The vampire's expression had been needy but at her single word response his spine straightened, and his shoulders went back.

"Strong," he agreed.

She rubbed her fingers over their tips, smearing pre-cum and making both men suck in their breaths. With deliberately slow strokes, she moved her hands up and down a few times. Suddenly Pike moved away, pulling his cock out of her grip.

He stood next to the bed with his hands clenched. "Cora, it's been a long time, and I don't want to go off before we've even really begun."

It took her a moment to understand what he said but it was Kimble who commented. "Cub."

Pike snorted. "We're all cubs compared to you, old man. You're so damn old you can't even remember what century you were born in!"

Kimble laughed and Cora bit her lip. It was flattering that Pike almost came from only a few strokes of her hand. "Does this mean I can't touch you anymore?"

Pike put a single knee on the bed, his cock jutting out toward her. "You can touch me, but maybe not there."

She nodded her head and held out a hand. Taking it, he resumed his kneeling position next to Kimble.

"We touch?" Kimble asked.

"We want to touch you too," Pike explained.

"Yes," Cora agreed, but when she rose up on her knees to move closer, she got a clear view of all of them in the bedroom mirror and froze.

These two men were gorgeous specimens of male beauty and then there was her. She was flat chested with narrow hips. Tim always said she had the body of a twelve-year-old boy. Her pale skin didn't have the lovely alabaster glow Kimble had and there was nothing special about her hair or face.

What was she doing?

All desire fled, and she suddenly felt cold and vulnerable. Looking down at the bed cover, she started to retreat when Pike made a pained sound.

"What happened?" he asked, tightening his hold on her hand. "Why do you look so sad? And you're pulling away from me. What did I do?"

The thought that she'd accidentally hurt his feelings stopped her retreat. "You didn't do anything. It's, uh, me. I guess I'm not ready to be with you guys."

"But I could taste your desire," Pike protested. "Do you only want Kimble? I can leave the room."

Kimble made a negative sound, drawing both their gazes to him. He was regarding her with pursed lips and a shrewd expression. He pointed at the mirror. "Didn't like."

Pike made a confused sound. "Huh?"

Kimble continued. "Didn't like look. Didn't like image. Thinks ugly."

Cora felt her face get hot with embarrassment and tried an age-old distraction tactic. "It's nothing. How about I suck you guys off?"

Neither male took the bait. "You think you're ugly?" Pike asked.

"I'm not ugly," Cora answered, hunching her shoulders and crossing her arms over her breasts. "I'm just not anything special. I don't have the kind of body men go nuts for."

"Are you saying I'm not a man?" Pike asked, humor in his voice. "Because the last time I checked, I'm both male and hard as fuck for you."

She didn't expect Pike to swear. Looking up, she saw raw hunger in his eyes. Licking his lips, he swept his gaze over her body.

"I could tell you how sexy you are," he said. "But I'd rather show you. Can I?"

"We," Kimble interjected.

"Yeah," Pike agreed, never taking his intense focus off her. "Can *we* show you?"

Cora's attack of self-consciousness retreated under Pike and Kimble's admiring gazes.

"Yes," she sighed out and then Kimble was on her.

**Kimble**

If he couldn't tell his human how beautiful she was with eloquent words, then he'd show her with his hands, lips, and body. Uncoiling from his kneeling position, he pushed her backwards on the bed, covering her small body with his own. As he planned, he ended up on his hands and knees with his face looming over hers.

He didn't lower his head to join their lips, instead he nudged her head aside so he could kiss her neck. Vampire's fangs lowered due to hunger or arousal, and his had decided to the moment they'd started kissing. He scraped a fang across her delicate flesh and was rewarded when she shivered.

"Bite?" he whispered in her ear. "No drink, only play."

"Yes?" her answer didn't sound confident, but he heard the excitement along with the fear.

"Good human," he said. "Good flock."

He knew she expected him to sink his fangs in right away, but that wasn't how this worked. Fangs were like dicks, you had to ease the way with foreplay, or it wouldn't feel good. He tangled his fingers in her hair, holding her head still while he ran the sharp tips of his fangs against her skin.

Her skin was getting warm again, and her aura was lighting up with arousal. It filled him with relief to see her enjoying what he was doing.

"I can't reach Cora," Pike complained. "I want to touch our human too!"

Kimble looked over to see his bear pouting. With a smirk, Kimble let go of Cora's hair and rolled them over, so she ended up on top of him. It only took a little maneuvering as she floundered to have her legs on either side of his hips and his cock pressed against her belly.

He couldn't help the moan that came out of him. It'd been so long since he felt well enough to do this kind of activity.

Pike made an approving sound. "Oh, that's perfect."

The bed dipped as Pike moved. Then he did something that made Cora squeak with surprise, her hips jerked up, then she moaned, "Pike!"

Lifting his head, Kimble looked down Cora's back and saw Pike crouched at Cora's ass. His big hands were holding her cheeks apart, and his face was buried. Licking and sucking on her.

Cora shuddered and clutched Kimble's shoulder. "Fuck, that's… I've never…oh!"

It seemed Pike had found something Cora hadn't done before, but liked. It was going to be fun discovering all the things that drove her wild.

Focusing back on her neck, Kimble pulled her hair aside and licked the skin over her jugular. He would never bite her there, but he knew it was a sensitive spot and was a good place for nipping and nibbling.

With a hand on the back of her head, he held Cora still so he could run his fangs across the artery without worrying about accidentally puncturing her skin. When he sealed his lips against her to suck some of the skin into his mouth, she moaned and pressed against him. He sucked a little harder, enough to create a slight bruise but nothing else.

"Oh god!" Cora groaned, her entire body shaking a little.

He spaced out his sucks and nibbles so he didn't damage one area. Cora tilted her head away to give him more access. Moving up, he sucked her earlobe into his mouth. His free hand wrapped around her back to help hold her steady since the sensations he and Pike caused made her move uncontrollably. He could feel the tension in her body building and thought she might be close. How long had it been since his little human had been pleasured?

He'd never ask her that, but he knew without a doubt that she'd never felt so thoroughly worshiped as she did now.

**Cora**

Was this heaven or hell?

Pike was behind her, eating her ass. She'd never had anyone do that before. At best, lovers would reluctantly go down on her, but they always acted like they were doing her a big favor. Then there was Pike who was licking her asshole while fingering her pussy and clit.

It was no wonder gay guys raved about it, it felt fucking fantastic! When he'd promised that they didn't have to act like normal human couples, she had only thought he wouldn't bully her into sex. She'd never considered that he might dive face first into her ass.

As he speared his tongue inside her again and slipped a second finger in her pussy, Cora wanted to scream but was breathing too hard to do more than moan. On the other end of her, Kimble was teasing her neck and sucking on her ear. Every time he teased her with those fangs, she thought that was it, he was going to bite her. Then he'd move on to another patch of skin and start the process all over. He was probably leaving hickeys all over her neck, but damn it felt good!

"Kimble!" she gasped when he slid to another spot he hadn't teased yet. She tried to press her neck against his mouth, desperate to feel his fangs sink into her flesh. Using his grip on her hair to hold her back, he denied her the sensation and continued to tease her.

She was so turned on she could feel slick dripping down the inside of her thighs. Pike's fingers were making an audible squishing sound as they sunk inside her, pressing on her most intimate parts.

"I need more," she begged.

Pike lifted his face away from her. "What was that?"

His fingers never stopped moving, and she wanted to cry from need.

"You heard me!" Her words came out breathless and needy instead of sarcastic or forceful. She was a puddle of sensation and at this point, she wanted release so bad, she would've been willing to try and take Pike's behemoth dick up her ass if it meant she'd get to orgasm.

"But I haven't finished my meal yet." Pike said, licking a long swath across her lower back. "I haven't even gotten to eat my dessert."

"I can't… I…" She didn't know what she wanted to say, only that she needed more. She tried to press her hips back, but Kimble's hold on her hair kept her still. Instead, she wiggled them back and forth, causing Pike's fingers to slide over her flesh in an unexpected way. It felt good so she did it again.

"Poor Cora," Pike cooed even as he removed his hand from her pussy to place it on her lower back, forcing her to be still.

"No!" she wailed.

Kimble gave an evil chuckle as Pike licked and kissed his way up her spine. His bulk was lightly pressed against her ass, and Kimble's hard cock was trapped against her belly. So much touching and none of it was where she needed it the most!

Her legs were on either side of Kimble's thighs so she shifted her hips as she tried to rub her clit on Kimble but couldn't get the right angle. Kimble groaned a little because her movement pressed her stomach harder against his cock.

"Steady," he ground out and tightened his hold on her hair.

Finally, *finally he* set his fangs against her at an angle that would puncture instead of tease.

She was ready for a little pain, but there was none. Pulsing heat spread from the spot as his fangs slowly pierced her flesh. Electric tingling washed over her skin, making her squirm and whimper.

Pike's fingers returned to her pussy and clit as he pressed his lips to her ear, only inches away from where Kimble was biting her.

"How does it feel to be penetrated?" he whispered. "I've got my fingers in your hot pussy, and Kimble's got his fangs in your sweet flesh. Someday, we're going to fill you with our cocks, fingers, and fangs. There won't be a part of you we aren't inside."

Cora never liked sex talk. At least not before Kimble and Pike. The bear's dirty words shot through her mind, filling her with illicit ideas and positions at the same time as Pike's finger and Kimble's fangs were working magic on her body.

She didn't know much about magic, but it felt like there was heated power coming from both ends of her body and meeting in the middle. Pike's magic felt strong, and Kimble's was elegant and sharp. Combined, it was as if she was bathing in electrons, everything snapping and zapping through her body and along her skin.

If she could get her eyes open, she might even see sparks!

"Close!" was all she got out before she was overwhelmed. The most powerful orgasm of her life crashed through her, making her scream and jerk. Kimble's hold on her head tightened painfully but even that was interpreted as pleasure by her body.

Time stopped. She couldn't breathe. Couldn't think. There was nothing but a moment of bliss so pure it was agony.

When time started again, she was able to suck air into her starved lungs. Behind closed lids, her eyes rolled back in her head, and she went limp.

Pike withdrew his hand from her pussy and petted her sweaty back. Kimble carefully extracted his fangs and licked the spot, easing his hold on her hair. Boneless, she lay on top of Kimble and twitched as the orgasm echoed through her.

Kissing the shell of her ear, Pike whispered, "That was a good start."

**Pike**

The three of them together was everything Pike had imagined it would be, and he wasn't ready for their first time together to be over.

"Can't," Cora whimpered as he worked his arms under her torso.

"Don't worry, you don't have to do anything," he cooed, arranging her limp body into a sitting position on Kimble with her knees on either side of the vampire's thighs. No longer trapped by Cora's body, Kimble's weeping cock stood up straight and proud, begging for attention.

"More?" he asked. The vampire's red eyes were glowing with arousal as he watched Pike maneuver their human.

"Much more," Pike assured him, then dipped his head to put his lips to Cora's ear again. "I'm going to help you ride Kimble. You took my fingers so well, but he's going to feel so much better. He'll fill you, press on all the right places. Do you want that?"

She whimpered and gazed down at Kimble's cock though half open eyes. Her breathing was slowly returning to normal, but she seemed to be having a hard time speaking. It was a good thing she didn't need words to communicate. Pike could easily judge her arousal with the smell and taste of her.

Her slowing heartbeat began to speed up again as she focused on Kimble's dick. She wanted this, and he trusted her to give strong indications if they did anything she didn't like.

Wrapping one arm around Cora's chest, he lifted her a little then moved her forward until her sopping pussy hovered over Kimble. The vampire grabbed the base of his dick and held it steady for Pike.

"Look at him, waiting for you," Pike said. "Eager to be inside of you. Fangs and fucking."

His words made Cora suck in a breath and wiggle a little in his grip. She wasn't trying to get away, she was trying to drop herself down on Kimble.

"Slooooowly," Pike taunted as he lowered her a millimeter at a time. "I want you to feel every inch of him stretching you. He's getting you ready for me."

Cora stopped resisting Pike's hold and went still. Her head fell back onto his shoulder, and she gripped the arm around her chest.

"Pike!" she hissed in a long breath, as if Kimble's intrusion was pushing the air out of her lungs.

"More!" Kimble begged. Pike hadn't realized he was torturing both his mates, but Kimble's moan made him grin widely. It was only fair! He'd been horny as hell for the previous nine months while Kimble didn't have any sex drive. Then Cora showed up and gave Pike the worst case of blue balls ever after a heavy make out session.

Now it was his turn to drive his mates crazy with need, and he was going to enjoy every second of it!

"Do you want to come, Kimble?" Pike asked as he stopped lowering Cora.

Kimble opened his eyes and growled at Pike. In open defiance of Pike's obvious intentions, Kimble tried to lift his hips to fully impale Cora. Sensing his movement, Pike settled his weight on Kimble's thighs, trapping the vampire.

"No, no, bad mate," Pike teased, then laughed when both Kimble and Cora made sounds of frustration.

"I could do this all night," he warned them. Cora whimpered, and Kimble let his head flop back on the bed. Assured of their compliance, Pike started lowering Cora again.

She moaned and the hand on his arm tightened. Looking over her shoulder, he watched Kimble's cock disappear into her hot core. She was producing so much slick it was dripping down Kimble's dick and gathering in his dark pubic hair. The sight made Pike's cock throb. He wanted to be slathered in Cora's slick too.

Patience, he reminded himself. They had a lifetime to play.

Once Kimble was fully inside Cora, Pike paused so everyone could adjust. The vampire was breathing hard, and Cora's body was tense and twitching. Putting his nose to the skin at the back of her neck, Pike pulled her scent in through his nose, checking for the smell of pain or discomfort.

All he scented was arousal.

"I… I… need more!" Cora begged, her words disjointed, as if she was having to force them out of her mouth.

"Me," Kimble agreed. "Me me!"

Pike thought Kimble was trying to say *me too* but arousal was causing him to lose his language skills.

"More than this?" Pike asked, holding Cora still on Kimble. Now that he didn't need his right hand to guide Cora's hips, he brought it up to place it on her breasts. Her beaded nipples were irresistible. He plucked at one, making Cora gasp and thrust her chest out. That action made her hips move a little, which caused Kimble to groan.

"It's like playing an instrument," Pike said as he tugged again.

Kimble grumbled something, then schooled his features into a pleading expression. "*Sloneczko,* please!"

Pike loved the nickname, even if he didn't know what the word meant. The endearment tore away his resolve and suddenly he wanted to see his mates come together.

But they'd do it on his terms.

"Put your hands on Cora's hips," he ordered Kimble. The vampire was quick to obey, gripping Cora but keeping his eyes on Pike for further instruction. Rising up on his knees to give Kimble room, he issued another order. "Now lift her a little."

The vampire had no problem lifting Cora's slight weight. She gasped as Kimble's cock half slid out of her. With Kimble supporting Cora, Pike had both hands free. He ran one hand down her front until his fingers dipped between her legs. Her flesh felt different, pulled taut by Kimble's cock. When he ran his fingertips over her clit, she shuddered.

"Pike, p-p-please!" she moaned.

"Do you want to come again?" he asked, cupping a breast in his other hand. Under them, Kimble's glowing red eyes were focused on Cora's face. Her frustrated moan was her only answer.

"Beautiful," the vampire said, lowering Cora back onto his cock. His voice was low and husky and reminded Pike of his feral growls when they'd first met. "Hot, tight, perfect."

Cora put her hands over Kimble's, as if to urge him to go faster. Answering her need, Kimble started moving her up and down on his cock. Pike let his hand flow with the motion, rubbing Cora over her clit and plucking at her nipples. Because he didn't move his body to match theirs, Cora's back rubbed on his hard dick.

Fuck, he was going to come from that alone! He hadn't been this on edge since he was a teenager. The friction from the smooth skin of her back was almost painful but in a good way.

He was worried he'd blow his load before his mates did when Cora started rhythmically whimpering. Looking down, he saw her gripping Kimble's hands so hard her knuckles were white. Her shoulders were pulled back, her spine bowed, and she opened her mouth in a silent scream.

Pike could feel her flesh pulsing under his fingers and kept steady pressure even as he felt his own orgasm explode out of him. Grinding his groin against her back, he covered her flesh in his seed.

Under them, Kimble cried out and went rigid, every muscle in his abdomen and chest tightening as he strained to fill Cora. He pulsed himself in and out of her several more times before collapsing back and pulling Cora down with him.

She folded, laying on top of Kimble with an exhausted sob of pleasure.

Feeling a little dazed, Pike took in the picture his mates made. Cora's back was covered in his cum, and her legs were tucked under her and spread, showing off where Kimble was still buried deep inside of her wet core.

Wrapping a hand around his cock, Pike gave it a few pumps with the hand still covered in Cora's slick. Pleasure rocked through him as the last of his climax shot out, adding to the mess on his mate's back.

Even though he knew it wasn't something he should do without permission, he desperately wanted to take a picture. It was only because there were no phones within reach that he didn't.

"Next time," he whispered.

"Huh?" Cora mumbled, her eyes closed and hair covering most of her face.

"Nothing, my heart," Pike whispered, carefully maneuvering his large body off the bed.

"No go," Kimble grumbled, slitting his eyes open enough to glare at Pike. "No leave."

Pike gave him a reassuring smile. "I'm only going to the bathroom. I'll be right back."

Kimble made a grumping sound but let his eyes fall closed. It was tacit permission for Pike to leave the room. Before going to the bathroom, Pike double checked that the house was locked down for the night, gathered cell phones, and shut off the lights. Then he wet several washcloths and took them to the bedroom.

Setting the phones on a nightstand, he set about cleaning Cora's back. He liked her wearing him like a mark, but it would dry, and he didn't want her to become uncomfortable during the night.

After that was done, he gently untangled Cora and Kimble. The vampire had softened by then and pulled free of Cora's body with a soft pop and a small flood of cum and slick. Using the second washcloth he cleaned them up.

Cora was mostly asleep, and Kimble looked pale and exhausted, but content. Pike would need to make sure Kimble consumed a few bags of blood before he and Cora left for work in the morning. Setting his alarm for just before daybreak, Pike plugged his phone in and then tucked himself into bed with his mates. Cora mumbled something and snuggled against him while Kimble curled up against her back.

They were all fed, safe, and sated. Life couldn't get much better than this!

**Cora**

"I need to know exactly how long I won't have power," the tenant said to Pike while Cora gathered tools in the back of Van Guts. Today's job was to install 220 dryer outlets in both garages of a duplex. This was the third time she'd worked for the owner but the first time dealing with this tenant.

"I'm not sure," Pike answered.

"How can you not be sure?" the guy said, his voice getting more aggressive. If he got much worse, Cora would need to call the owner.

Leaving everything in the van, Cora jumped out and strode confidently to where Pike was standing with the tenant. He was a slim man with artfully mussed brown hair and a disgruntled sneer, wearing jeans and a cardigan over a graphic t-shirt. He looked a lot like someone trying to appear academic and elite, the young cool teacher, but instead looked like he'd spend an entire date talking about how smart he was.

The guy glared at Pike, undeterred by their size difference. "I want to talk to your manager or boss!"

"That would be me," she said as she stepped up to stand with Pike. Her bear gave her a grateful look.

"You're the manager?" the man said, clearly startled to be talking to a woman as he ran his gaze over her shorter form.

"I'm the manager, boss, and owner," she stated.

"That was all redundant," he sniffed. "Still, the question is the same, how long until I have power again?"

"I haven't even shut it off yet," Cora pointed out. "I'll be done within one to three hours, but that shouldn't be a problem. When Susan hired me to do the wiring and schedule, she assured me you'd been notified three times and reminded last night that we were coming."

"Leaving a note on my door hardly counts as notification," he protested. "And I missed her calls. Who even listens to messages anymore?"

Cora tilted her head down a little and rolled her eyes to look up at him. "Would it have been better by telegraph? Messenger pigeon? Message in a bottle?"

"I don't like your attitude." The guy stepped closer to her, trying to use his height to intimidate her. He was going to have to do a lot more than stare down at her if he wanted to have an effect.

Cora smirked. "That's weird because I think my attitude is great considering I'm dealing with you first thing in the morning."

"You work for me, and I expect—"

She cut him off by stepping into his personal space. "I work for Susan Green, the woman who owns this duplex and lives in the front unit. You're a renter who moved in two months ago and doesn't pay attention to anything, apparently. Susan is trying to be a good landlady by making it so you can have an outlet for the electric dryer you insisted you needed. Go find some coffee shop with WiFi or stand here and whine. I don't care either way."

The guy's expression went from surprise to absolutely livid, which surprised Cora. She hadn't even cussed at him. By her standards, she'd been downright pleasant.

He moved super close, almost touching her. She prepared herself to move out of the way if the dumbass decided to take a swing at her, but until he did, she wasn't backing down.

A big hand gripped her waist and lifted. A surprised sound came out of her mouth as her feet left the ground. She found herself being set down off to the side and Pike took her spot. He stepped close, putting his giant body only a hair's breadth from the tenant.

"Is there going to be a problem?" Pike's voice was low and dangerous. Bringing his hands up, he cracked his knuckles while tilting his head inquiringly at the guy.

She'd never seen him look so intimidating, damn this was hot!

"I, uh," the tenant visibly swallowed and stepped back. Catching Cora's smirk, the guy tried to recover. "Whatever, just get it done."

Turning, he rushed back into his house, slamming the door behind him.

The moment he was gone, Pike's entire demeanor changed. His shoulders dropped a little, and he shoved his hands in his pockets as he turned to face her.

"I'm sorry," he mumbled, staring at his shoes.

Confused, she stared at him, "What?"

When he didn't look up or answer, she moved closer and placed a hand on Pike's chest. "Why are you sorry?"

He placed one of his massive hands over hers, covering it completely. "I didn't ask before I acted. I should've waited for you to tell me you needed me. I'm really sorry, I just couldn't handle that guy being so close to you and acting like such a… a… dick!"

He spat the last word out, like it was the worst cuss word he could think of. When Cora chuckled, he looked up, finally meeting her eyes.

"If the situation was reversed, I'd want to protect you," she pointed out. "And it was fun to see that guy run off."

His features relaxed with relief. "You're not mad?"

"Hell no," she answered. "I know I'm a bad ass bitch who could take him down if I wanted to. I don't need to prove myself to anyone. Although ask before lifting me up, okay?"

Pike nodded his head. "I will. And that's true, you are amazing. Remember the night we met? You laid out Steve before I could get to you. You must've been fast with your knee to his balls because he was a wolf shifter. I think that's when I fell in love with you."

Cora grinned at the memory of the smarmy guy who was the catalyst of her and Pike's meet cute. "You say the sweetest things. That guy deserved more than what I did to him. Honestly, you throwing him out wasn't punishment enough. I couldn't be the first woman he harassed."

"Don't worry," Pike said, his grin matching hers. "After I threw him in the dumpster out back, I told Kimble he could make a snack out of the guy. Kimble didn't kill him, but he wasn't gentle either."

"Aww," Cora cooed. "He was a good vampire boyfriend even before he became my vampire boyfriend."

"And I'm a good bear boyfriend, right?" Pike pushed.

"The best," she agreed. Bunching up the shirt under her hand, she pulled him down to her level. He didn't resist and soon his lips were within easy reach. She meant for the kiss to be a quick reassuring one, but the moment her lips met his, sparks flew.

Moaning, he parted his lips and deepened the kiss. All thoughts of the job and decorum flew out of Cora's mind as Pike thrust his tongue into her mouth. The world disappeared, and she lost herself in the feel of Pike's mouth on hers.

She didn't realize Pike's hands were moving until she felt them cupping her ass. His hands were so much broader than her that when he straightened and lifted her up against his chest, she might as well have been sitting on a bench seat.

A bench seat that was massaging her butt through her jeans.

Without breaking the kiss, she wrapped her legs around his waist, and her arms around his neck, pressing her body hard against his. Heat pooled in her belly, and her core started throbbing. With a little whimper, she rubbed her sex against his muscled body, wishing there wasn't fabric between them.

Then his hands massaged her ass, pressing her lower body more firmly against him. She went still as pleasure shot up her spine. Could she climax by dry humping Pike while fully clothed? The thought excited her.

"I didn't realize you'd hired a new assistant," a voice said.

With a little gasp, Cora ended the kiss and looked over her shoulder to find Susan standing there with a bemused smile. Feeling her face get hot with embarrassment, she turned her head back to Pike. His eyes were big and slightly unfocused, his face was flushed, and his lips were wet and red from their kissing. She had an almost uncontrollable urge to nip at his plump lower lip.

But there was work to do and a friend watching.

"Put me down, Pike," she whispered, patting his cheek affectionately. This was probably one of the most compromising positions she'd ever been found in, but at least it was only Susan, and she stopped them before things had really gotten out of hand.

At her request, Pike blinked. "Down?"

"Yes, down," she said. "Tell your body to send some of the blood back up to your brain,  big guy. This was fun, but we need to do other stuff."

As she watched, Pike's face went through several phases. First was confusion, then disappointment, and finally realization and embarrassment at the same time.

"We're in a driveway," he hissed, setting her down on her feet. "It's not even your driveway, just a driveway. And there is a woman here staring at us. Why is she staring at us? Am I in trouble?"

Cora felt embarrassed, though not mortified, but Pike looked like he wanted to duck into Van Guts and hide, maybe even drive off without her.

"Everything's fine," Cora assured him before facing Susan. "Uh, I thought you were at work?"

"I was, then Mitch called me saying the electrician I hired was threatening to beat him up or even kill him. I took my lunch early to find out what was going on." Susan ran her eyes appreciatively over Pike. "Imagine my surprise to find you lip-locked with your assistant. Not that I blame you."

"Pike's my boyfriend, not my assistant," Cora said, moving to stand in front of Pike, as if she could hide him from the woman's admiring gaze.

Susan's smile widened. "And you brought him on a job with you? That's different."

Cora liked Susan but the woman was nosy beyond belief. Then she did something really odd. She sniffed, frowned, and addressed Pike. "Does she know?"

Pike moved to stand next to Cora instead of behind her. His earlier embarrassment was gone. Now he was matching Susan's frown. "Of course she knows. I'd never deceive my mate like that."

Cora eyed Susan suspiciously. This conversation could only mean one thing, Susan wasn't as she appeared. "What are you?

"Coyote shifter," Susan said. "This whole neighborhood is mostly coyotes. We don't have alphas or a strict pack structure like wolves, but we like to live close to each other."

Cora pointed to the tenant side of the duplex. "What about him?"

"Human and clueless," Susan said. "I wanted to rent to a coyote like last time, but no one needed a place. He seemed innocuous."

"You used the wrong word," Pike muttered. "I think you meant to say obnoxious."

Pike surprised a laugh out of Cora while Susan looked both amused and resigned.

"That Mitch guy was getting in my face, so Pike stepped in to make him back off. That's all," Cora told her. "No harm done except to Mitch's fragile ego."

"The moment I smelled black bear, I knew Mitch must have overstepped," Susan assured her, then looked at Pike. "You guys don't get aggressive except for when it comes to cubs and mates. Congratulations to both of you."

Pike beamed and thanked her, but it made Cora realize how much of a disadvantage she had in this world. Everyone could sense things she couldn't. Imani told her vampires could see auras, shifters could smell magic, and here she was with nothing but her plain human eyes and nose. It wasn't fair!

While she was thinking about the inequality, Pike and Susan were chatting. Looking down, she found Pike had tangled their fingers together and she hadn't even noticed. That must be what it's like to be in love—you don't know where you ended, and the other person began. It would be even worse if she agreed to a soul exchange.

The part that scared her the most was how much she wasn't scared.

**Pike**

The sun was starting to set by the time they finished the last job. Putting Cora's tools back in Van Guts, Pike marveled that she didn't murder more of her customers. They'd worked a long day, and it was shocking to find out that Mitch was the least annoying of all of them. He'd been the most threatening, but not the most obnoxious.

The other humans they dealt with insisted on talking to him, even after he'd pointed out that Cora was the one in charge, and he was only there to carry stuff. One elderly man even got upset when Pike couldn't answer any of his questions, despite Pike repeatedly explaining that he needed to ask Cora.

"Is it a human thing or a man thing?" he grumped as he slid a compartment box full of small components into its slot. Cora stuck her head into the open door of Van Guts and grinned at him.

"It's probably both," she answered, holding out another box.

He shook his head as he took the box and slid it in next to the other one. "How do you put up with it? They talk down to you, they demean you, and that one guy tried to get you to drop your price after you did the work. And that was with me standing there glaring at him. How much worse is it when you're by yourself?"

"You get used to it, but today was worse than normal," she said, stepping up into the van. "Don't worry, more often than not, I get even. I've done some stuff that I should probably feel guilty about after someone said shitty things to me."

Pike was intrigued. He dropped to a crossed knee sitting position on the van floor and pulled her into his lap. "Like what?"

She snuggled into him. "I think those are stories for another time, but I only did it to the really vile ones."

"Can we do something to this guy?" Pike asked. "Please!"

Cora laughed and kissed the side of his neck. "He wasn't bad enough to warrant a Cora Curse."

Ohhhh!" Pike murmured in her ear. "Cora Curse sounds kinda sexy."

"Stop it, care-bear." Pushing away from him, Cora got up with a grin and a shake of her head. "Let's get home before Kimble wakes up and comes looking for us."

Pike didn't know if Cora was developing a bond with Kimble despite not having shared souls yet or if she had amazing timing because he could suddenly feel the vampire in the back of his head. Before, it had been a soft presence in the background, like small waves rhythmically lapping against a tropical beach. Now it felt like storm winds pounding against a coastline.

"Kimble's awake," he whispered. "Something's wrong. We need to hurry!"

**Kimble**

Despite all the blood he'd consumed over the last few days, Kimble was still far weaker than he should be. It made fighting against the daytime induced sleep impossible. All he could do was listen as Pike whispered sweet loving words and promised he and Cora would be back before dark. Then they'd both left the safety of their new home.

He was forced to lay there helplessly as they went out into the dangerous world.

Pike's bear was large and strong. That alone would keep him safe from most predators. However, his human was tiny and helpless, and Pike didn't have the heart of a fighter. He would never strike first, and his hesitation could result in Cora's death.

Kimble wanted to fight the daytime sleep but forced himself to conserve his strength. If he was lucky, he'd be able to rise just before sunset. It wasn't much, but with the safety of his flock at risk, every second counted.

He was paying such close attention that he knew the exact moment the cursed sun had lost her grip on him.

Gripping the sheet covering him, he flung it off, or tried to. The simple blanket might as well have been made of woven steel for how heavy it seemed to his weakened state. He was shaking by the time he sat up and swung his legs over the edge of the bed.

Looking up, he focused on the bedroom doorway. It was wide open and the way the house was laid out, he could see across the living room and into the kitchen. There was blood in the fridge there, making that his first priority.

His body protested and urged him to lie back down and wait for the last vestiges of the sun's bright rays to descend past the horizon. He ignored it.

"Flock," he whispered to the empty room. The boarded-up windows allowed him to safely make his way from room to room without worry of being burned.

His unsteady gait caused him to stumble and lose his balance shortly after he passed through the bedroom doorway. He fell forward, all his normal speed and agility were absent. He landed on the coffee table, the delicate piece of furniture splintering and breaking under his weight.

Rage and embarrassment filled him in equal parts. Why was he still so weak? He could feel the tantalizing hint of power and strength he'd once possessed. In his past, he was a vampire of distinction.

He couldn't pull forward a single concrete memory to prove any of it, but in his heart, he knew his current state was a pitiful remnant of what he'd once been.

What was he doing, lying on broken furniture feeling sorry for himself? This was ridiculous. What if his flock walked in and saw him like this? They'd want to leave, and he wouldn't blame them.

It took several tries, but he finally got back to his feet. Crawling would've been easier, but his pride wouldn't allow it.

Once he was standing, he moved slowly to the kitchen, using furniture and the wall to keep himself steady. His human's home was quaint and tidy, but it was still far less opulent than she deserved.

Someday, he'd give both his flock everything they could ever desire, and they'd all live a happy and secure life where they never needed to be separated from each other again.

By the time he reached the refrigerator, he was having a difficult time keeping his eyes focused. Dropping to his knees, he opened the appliance door and fumbled around until he felt the familiar smooth bag.

He drank greedily. The bag emptied quickly so he found another. He continued until his fingertips felt nothing but glass shelving. Slumping down, he looked at all the discarded bags around him. There were so many that his belly should be full and his strength returning.

Fear tightened his chest. If anything, he felt weaker. As he stared at one of the empty blood bags, his vision narrowed, the edges eaten away with gray haze. He blinked rapidly and looked up. Everything looked dim.

Was he dying?

Memories of trading power with the bruja for Cora's necklace floated through his mind. Was that the problem? She'd pulled from his aura, but he'd been doing so much better. It should've healed instead of gotten thinner.

When the three of them had been making love the previous night, he'd felt powerful and complete, but his body had given out on him immediately after. That should've been a clue that he wasn't healing as fast as he thought.

He didn't have time to consider how to fix this further. A strange sensation of floating started as he lost all ability to see. He was unconscious before his head hit the kitchen tile.

**Pike**

Cora drove the top-heavy Van Guts as fast as she dared, but even as she turned corners at a speed that almost lifted the wheels, it wasn't fast enough for him. He'd felt nothing but rage and panic for twenty minutes and then nothing. He couldn't even feel the unconscious hum that was always there, even when Kimble slept.

There was a numb, blank spot in his mind, and it was one of the worst sensations he'd ever experienced.

"Are you okay, Pike?" Cora asked. "You're moaning."

"Sorry," he mumbled. He hadn't realized he was making any sounds. "I'll try to stop."

Cora made an exasperated sound. "I don't care about that. Are you in pain? Is Kimble in pain? Talk to me!"

"I think he's dead," Pike whispered, even though he didn't want to contemplate it. "He's gone from my head. There's nothing there. And I don't feel right. It feels like…"

His words trailed off. How did he describe the sensation of your soul dying while your body was still breathing? He might not be able to see auras like vampires could, but he knew Kimble's wasn't as vibrant or strong as it should be. Was this what happened to a flock when the vampire died?

"He's not dead!" Cora announced, aggressively dodging right to pass an SUV using the bicycle lane. Several cars honked at her, but she ignored them as she'd been ignoring all the angry drivers.

"Do you hear me, Pike?" Cora asked, her voice more a demand for obedience than a question. "He's not dead. Whatever's wrong, we're going to fix it. If he needs more blood, we'll get it. If he needs a vampire doctor, we'll find one. This is not how we end."

Pike tried to focus on Cora's commanding voice instead of his own fear and discomfort. "I'm so scared," he admitted. "If I lose Kimble then I'm gone too."

"All you have to do is listen to me," Cora said. "Because I'm not going to let either of you go!"

She kept talking to him, sometimes demanding that he respond. She helped keep his terror from overtaking him, so by the time she pulled into the driveway, he wasn't a sobbing, shaking mess.

Fear made him an uncoordinated mess as he fell from the van and stumbled several strides, almost going down face first before he caught his balance. He felt unsteady, as if suffering from vertigo. Cora flung open her door and rushed around the van to him.

"Lean on me," she urged, wrapping a steadying arm around his waist. She was surprisingly strong for such a small human. He was able to support himself, but Cora added a stabilizing effect. If he fell while Cora was helping him, they'd both end up on the ground, so he focused on putting one foot in front of the other.

Soon they were in the house and faced with broken furniture and a trail of blood across half the living room.

"This looks bad," Cora mumbled as she steered them into the kitchen, following the red trail. The sight that met his eyes made Pike go weak at the knees.

"Kimble!" he cried out. Pulling away from Cora, he made it the two strides to Kimble's side before he collapsed to the floor.

Kimble was lying unconscious in front of the open refrigerator. There was a massive piece of glass sticking out of his chest and several small pieces embedded in his arm and shoulder. Blood was seeping from the wounds and pooling on the floor.

With a shaking hand, Pike cupped Kimble's cheek. His skin was cold and felt lifeless.

"No," he moaned, hunching over as tears flowed down his cheeks. "No, you weren't supposed to leave me like this. We were going to live long happy lives."

"Pike, I don't think he's dead," Cora said. Pike looked up to see that Cora had peeled back one of Kimble's eyelids. "His eye is twitching a little. I think he's still alive. Or you know, undead. Whatever, he's still with us."

As he watched, Kimble's eye moved again before Cora let go of the lid. Sitting back, Pike rubbed his face and focused. "What do we do? How do we fix this?"

Cora blinked at him. "How would I know?"

"I, uh," Pike's mind blanked. He didn't know anyone he could call for advice that wouldn't take advantage of Kimble's weakened state. The people he trusted didn't know any more than he did.

"Imani!" Cora shouted and fumbled her phone out of her back pocket. "Imani's a vampire. She might know what to do."

Pike noticed her fingers shaking as she tapped on the screen. Even though he wanted to comfort her, he was too distressed to do anything but watch the phone as it started ringing.

"Hi, Hellion, what's up?" Imani answered cheerfully. They could hear murmured words in the background, then Imani's voice moved away from the phone. "If you're hungry go eat, I'll be down after I talk to Cora."

"It's Kimble," Cora cried out. "I think he fell on my coffee table and has a big shard of glass embedded in his chest and there's blood everywhere. He drank about ten bags that we had in the fridge, but he's not healing or moving. We don't have any more blood to give him. What do we do?"

"Have him drink from Pike, he's plenty big enough to handle some blood loss," Imani said.

Cora shook her head at the phone, even though Imani couldn't see it. "He's not conscious, Imani. We can't make him bite anything."

"Pike, you there?" Imani called out.

"Yeah," Pike croaked. His throat felt like it wanted to close up as tears pressed at the back of his eyes.

"Slit your wrist, put it to his mouth, and let the blood pour in. His body will know what to do," Imani ordered.

"What about the giant piece of glass sticking out of him?" Cora reminded her.

"Fuck, I'm not sure. Normally I'd say pull it out, but he should've been able to do that himself so there might be something else going wrong here. Let me call Briar and see if she and Tobias have any insights."

The call ended before he or Cora could say another word. Pike was already looking around for a knife. Reaching up, he grabbed one out of the holder on the counter. He moved to Kimble's head, then sliced his wrist and held the wound over Kimble's mouth. The first few drips splashed the vampire's lips, but Cora was quick to use her fingers to open Kimble's mouth wider to allow the rest to flow in.

Cora's phone rang. Picking it up with one hand, she tapped to answer. Pike didn't look. He remained focused on Kimble's face, watching for the slightest change.

"Who is this?" a male voice demanded.

"You called me, so who the fuck are you?" Cora answered back.

"I'm calling you on behalf of Imani Alexander, friend to my flock. If you don't wish my assistance then I can hang up, my duty fulfilled."

The voice sounded vaguely family, and Pike had to search his memory for a name to match it. "Tobias?"

"Ah, Pike, you remember me despite how brief our meeting was," Tobias answered, his tone warming.

A brief smile slid across Pike's face, even as another tear escaped to slide down his cheek. "It's hard to forget Briar. I've never known a human female so ready to pick a fight in my life, especially with a drunk troll shifter."

"Yes, you were the bouncer that night. You still have my thanks for intervening when my human's judgment was so flawed."

Pike could hear Briar in the background. "Hey, I could've taken him! I'm tough!"

If things weren't so dire, Pike might have laughed. "If you're thankful, could you help my vampire, Kimble?"

Tobias's voice turned all business. "Switch to a video call and let me see him."

Cora fumbled with the phone and then swept it slowly over Kimble's still form.

"Maksim!" Tobias said, clearly shocked. "That's Maksim Laske. I thought he'd died years ago."

Tobias knew who Kimble was? Later, Pike would consider how helpful this might be, but he was too scared to care about Kimble's past right now. He needed Kimble to have a future first!

"This is bad," Tobias continued. "His aura is weak and getting weaker. Did one of his flock die?"

"No, I'm perfectly healthy, but I left him alone today and didn't come back before he woke up," Pike wailed. "This is my fault!"

"Stop whining," Tobias barked across the phone.

"Dude, don't be mean," Briar snapped in the background. "He's scared!"

"Can you help us?" Cora asked.

"I believe I can, but all of you will owe me a favor," he warned them.

"Anything," Pike agreed.

"Wait I don't…" Cora started, but her words trailed off when Pike caught her eyes, begging with his own.

"Fine, I'll owe you a favor," she snarled, then rattled off her address. "If you can't save him, I'll kill you instead."

Instead of getting angry, Pike heard Tobias laugh. It wasn't a pleasant sound. "You're feisty, like my Briar. It's amusing in her, but if you threaten me again, I'll separate your soul from your body."

Pike heard Briar shouting angry words before Tobias ended the call.

"What an asshole," Cora muttered, dropping the phone to the floor. Her angry expression dissolved, and Pike saw tears gather in her eyes as she lifted her gaze to Kimble's face. "But I'll kiss his ass if he can fix you."

**Cora**

"How are you so calm?" Pike asked her, still pressing his bleeding wrist to Kimble's mouth. The vampire had swallowed a few times, but not enough to keep up with the sluggish flow of blood from the rapidly healing cut. Small drops of blood escaped the corners of his mouth, leaving trails of crimson down the sides of his jaw.

Cora blew out a harsh breath. "I promise I'm not."

She might not have gone as far as to twine her soul with Kimble and Pike yet, but it felt like she might as well have. She'd never felt so much fear and panic in her life, not even when Vincent was threatening to kill her and Imani. She wanted to collapse on top of Kimble and sob. She wanted to shake him and scream for him to wake up and say flock, or growl, or any sound!

These two men had only been in her life for a week, and it felt like she couldn't live without them. It was terrifying.

Pike tilted his head, as if listening to something. "You should open the front door."

Cora didn't hear what he was saying at first because she was caught by his eyes. They were glassy with tears, bringing out the green in his hazel eyes. His expression was open and vulnerable.

It occurred to her that Pike was everything nurturing and caring that she wasn't. He'd never voluntarily leave her, and he'd willingly live every day ready to be anything she needed. She knew with confidence he'd lay down his life to protect her and Kimble.

That's when she realized she felt the same. If that wasn't love, she didn't know what was.

"Cora?" Pike urged. "The door?"

Pulling in a sharp breath, she gave herself a hard shake. "On it."

She ran to the door on shaking legs, stumbling a little over the mess of her former coffee table. She flung open the door just in time for a red-tailed hawk to come flying through. The hawk flared his wings and tail, dramatically slowing its speed as he back winged. The bird's form blurred, and Cora thought her eyesight was getting as shaky as her legs.

"What the fuck?" she exclaimed as the bird morphed into a man wearing an immaculate three-piece suit. Coming to a stop in front of the mess that had been her coffee table, he looked around as he straightened his already perfectly aligned tie.

"What a quaint home," he said. It didn't sound like a compliment. This had to be Tobias.

"You're not here to critique my design choices," Cora growled, striding up to him and grabbing Tobias's arm. "You're here to save Kimble."

"Don't touch me," Tobias hissed, moving out of her reach with so much speed she couldn't track his movements. One moment he was within touching distance and the next he was on the other side of the couch. "Do that again, and I'll rip you apart, even if it would upset my Briar. No one touches me except my flock."

Surprised at his vehemence, Cora held up both hands palms out. "Sorry! I won't do it again." She pointed to the kitchen with one hand. "Dying vampire in there."

"Tobias?" Pike called out, leaning back so he could see into the living room. Fresh tears fell from his eyes. "Please, help him!"

Tobias seemed to disappear from Cora's sight. Suddenly she was alone in the living room with the front door wide open. After slamming the door shut, she rushed to the kitchen. Tobias was kneeling on the opposite side of Kimble from Pike, the spot where she'd been before getting up to open the door.

"Are you fixing him yet?" Cora asked as she took a position next to Pike. The bear shifter's wrist was still pressed against Kimble's mouth, but she didn't think the wound was even bleeding any longer.

Tobias didn't look up as he spoke. "There's an entire layer missing from his aura. Even in his diminished mental state no one could've simply taken it. He had to have given it away."

"Why would he do that?" Pike asked. "He had everything he needed."

Cora gasped and both men looked at her. "What do you know, human?" Tobias demanded.

Pike made a harsh sound, halfway between a bark and a growl. There were still tears coming from his eyes at irregular intervals, but the planes of his face had changed, and his teeth seemed bigger. At that moment, he looked like the deadly beast he could be.

"Don't talk to her like that. Her name is Cora."

"Don't waste my time," Tobias shot back then refocused on Cora. "What do you know?"

Feeling all kinds of guilt, Cora pulled the necklace out from under her shirt. "The night he showed up here, he gave this to me. I thought he must have stolen it or maybe found it."

Tobias leaned over Kimble's body to get a closer look at the piece of jewelry. "That's powerful bruja magic. He must have traded for it and that's what caused this."

Cora tried to find the clasp to take the necklace off. "Here, you can have it."

Tobias shook his head. "Giving it to me won't do Maksim any good."

"But that happened over a day ago, why is he hurting now?" Pike asked. When Cora looked at him, she noticed his face was fully human again.

"He's weak now but was powerful once. He had enough of his former self leftover  that he was able to last for some time before succumbing to the loss," Tobias explained, then raised an eyebrow at Cora. "If he had both his flock bound to him, he would've probably not been affected at all."

It was as if those words were a slap in the face, making Cora rear back and gasp. She opened her mouth, not sure what she was going to say, when Pike spoke.

"It has to be her choice," Pike bit out. "An unwilling soul poisons the flock."

Tobias's eyes started glowing with power. "Are you unwilling, human? Or is it something else?"

Cora fell into Tobias's gaze. All her worry vanished and the room around her disappeared.

"Tell me why," Tobias said, his voice wasn't harsh anymore. He sounded kind and understanding. Trust blossomed inside her and the words poured out of her mouth.

"I'm scared," she heard herself say. Why was she admitting this? Even more strange, why wasn't she upset? She should be furious at voicing any kind of weakness, but instead, she found herself wanting to tell him everything.

"What are you scared of?" Tobias asked.

She heard a faint choking noise but it barely registered as she explained.

"What if I can't leave? Binding souls is forever. I need to be able to leave. What about my family? I can't be vulnerable like that."

Tobias made a questioning sound. "Do you think your vampire wouldn't help your friends and family?"

Complicated scenarios filtered through her head, making it hard for her to speak even though she wanted to. Thankfully Tobias continued to speak.

"Your vampire will care deeply about everything and anything you care about," Tobias told her. There was another choking sound, then a gasp and a sharp intake of breath. Tobias looked away, and she followed his gaze to see Pike red faced, hunched over, and gasping. "Calm down, bear. She's perfectly fine. Don't make me hold you still again."

"Kimble's dying, and you decide to put Cora under thrall for questioning instead of fixing him?" Pike croaked out.

"I'm trying to gauge if I can bind her soul," Tobias said with a disdainful sniff. "It would be the best way to help him. Unfortunately that's not a viable option. She has too much doubt. It's something the three of you will have to address eventually."

"What can you do instead of binding Cora's soul?" Pike asked.

Cora felt herself coming out of whatever Tobias did to her. It was almost like waking from a dream. Shaking her head, she tried to understand what Tobias was saying.

"I can take from each of your auras and use them to repair his," Tobias explained.

"Did you hypnotize me?" Cora asked. She tried to feel outraged at the loss of control, but there was still a strange leftover calm from what Tobias had done.

"It's called thrall, human," Tobias answered. "Now catch up with the adults. I need to take some of your aura. It'll be painful and debilitating for a short time. Do you understand?"

Her calm didn't extend to Tobias's outright disdain. She smiled, showing all her teeth. "I might need to stab you later."

A smile flittered across the vampire's mouth, then he spoke in a dry tone. "Charming."

"Ditto," Cora answered then held out her hand, offering up her wrist. "Take whatever you need to fix Kimble."

Pike pulled in a sharp breath. "It's not going to feel good, Cora. I'll recover within a few hours, but you'll feel like you got hit by a truck."

"I'm tough," she assured Pike without looking away from Tobias. Her rapidly beating heart and sweat breaking out over her body belied her confident words.

Tobias pushed her hand away and tapped the floor. "Both of you need to lay on either side of him."

Pike flopped down and rolled on his side so his front was pressed against Kimble. Cora was slower to lay down. She didn't like Tobias looming over her.

Tobias shifted and raised both hands, hovering them over the three of them. He closed his eyes, humming to himself as he concentrated. Cora didn't feel anything and was about to open her mouth when she realized she had no control of her body at all.

"I've put both of you under thrall, so you don't scream," he told them. "Unfortunately, I can't block the pain. Brace yourselves"

That was all the warning she got and then it felt like someone was trying to rip her skin off.

Blood roared in her ears, and her lungs froze. She'd never experienced such pain in her life, and she couldn't even scream. Could someone survive something this horrible?

It was a relief when her vision grayed, and she passed out.

**Kimble**

Waking with a roar, Kimble shoved the vampire leaning over him and his flock with enough force to send the male sailing across the room. Scrambling to his feet, he found his flock unconscious on the floor. A quick assessment told him they were alive and asleep. He couldn't discern any wounds or damage to either of them, but he could smell and see his own blood on the floor where he'd been lying.

Turning to face the other vampire, he prepared to kill the intruder who attacked him and his flock.

In the short time he'd been assessing his flock, the intruder had gotten to his feet and closed the distance between them. When Kimble turned to face him, the male was already in his face. Their eyes met, and Kimble found himself unable to move.

Normally thrall didn't work on other vampires, but Kimble didn't have his full magic behind him yet.

"I'm not here to hurt you or your flock," a familiar voice said. Kimble was sure he'd known this vampire before he went feral. He got the impression of a cordial relationship. They hadn't been close, but they weren't enemies either.

"I don't know how it happened, but I've somehow found myself the caretaker of vampires in distress," Tobias said, sounding both amused and annoyed. "I'm unsure how I feel about all of it, but my helping others makes both my flock happy, so I'll continue until it proves too troublesome."

Tobias looked down at Kimble's unconscious flock, making Kimble want to growl and attack. He tried to fight the thrall and managed to move one arm, but that was it. Tobias looked back, easily subduing Kimble.

"The name you currently know me by is Tobias Becker, and you've been Maksim Laske for about sixty years now. Don't attack me, Maksim. It's my hope you'll come back to yourself before I'm forced to put you down."

The threat didn't surprise or shock Kimble. He'd thought the same thing, and Pike had lived in terror of Kimble being hunted. Kimble's only concern was keeping his flock safe and as long as Tobias was speaking to him, he wasn't doing anything to Cora or Pike.

He forced himself to calm down and wait for Tobias to release him.

Tobias gave him an approving nod. "That's better. I'm going to leave now. After I'm gone, put your flock to bed and care for them. Pike will be better quickly, but Cora will need a lot of attention. I'll have supplies delivered for all three of you. Even with more supply of human blood, you should drink from your bear after he's recovered. I know you think it will hurt him, but it won't. His blood will be powerful and help you come back to yourself faster."

He paused for a moment, as if debating his next words. "Your human needs you to understand her fears, or she won't agree to bind her soul with you."

Where was this statement coming from? What had happened to his flock while he'd been unconscious?!

As if he could read Kimble's mind, Tobias answered his question. "You traded some of your aura for a necklace and that weakened you. I was forced to pull aura from both of your flock to fix you. Even if the necklace granted Cora special powers, it wasn't worth it. Your actions put your flock in danger. Don't be that stupid again."

Shame washed over Kimble. When he'd traded with the bruja, he didn't think it would cause this much of an issue. Tobias's presence near his flock  while holding Kimble helpless was the reward for his idiocy.

He needed to do better.

He would do better!

"I see you're starting to understand the severity of the situation," Tobias said as he stepped back. "I'll leave now. Don't forget to pull the glass out of your chest, and don't attack the people delivering supplies, or I'll come back and put you down, even if it would make my Briar angry with me."

With those words, the vampire turned. The moment Tobias's back was to Kimble, the thrall broke, but Kimble didn't attack. He followed at a distance as Tobias casually strolled out of the kitchen, then flung open the front door. Taking several running steps, he leapt into the sky and shifted into his bird form, flying out of sight.

Once Tobias was gone, Kimble rushed up and slammed the door shut. Not that it would do any good if the vampire wanted back in, but it made him feel better. He imagined he could hear Tobias's mocking laughter as he rushed back to his flock in the kitchen.

He'd failed them in so many ways, but that ended now.

## Pike

Pike woke up with a new appreciation for anyone who'd ever had to deal with a hangover. As a bear shifter, it took a lot to get him drunk, and he'd never bothered drinking enough hard alcohol to get the job done. He'd heard his coworkers complain enough to know that his aching head, dry mouth, sore throat, and roiling stomach were all common symptoms.

Except he wasn't suffering from a hangover—it was part of his aura being stripped off! Hopefully, he'd never have to experience anything so painful again.

Sitting up with a moan he looked around, surprised to find that he was in Cora's bed and not the kitchen floor. How long had he been out? He only had long enough to notice Cora sound asleep next to him before a figure sat on the bed on his other side.

"Drink!" The demand was followed by a glass being pressed to his lips. Water splashed on his face before he could take the glass from Kimble's insistent hand. He downed all of it in a few swallows. The water made his mouth and throat feel better but didn't do any favors for his stomach.

The moment the glass was empty, Kimble snatched it back and got up, probably to refill it.

"Crackers," Pike croaked, closing his eyes and rubbing his face with both hands.

"Crack—" Kimble said, then grumbled and tried again. "Crack-crack… cracker. Crackers. Drink and eat. Yes."

He mumbled those words as he left, and Pike could hear him in the kitchen. Pike blamed how bad he felt as the reason he didn't realize that Kimble was talking until the vampire was back and holding a large plate piled high with crackers in one hand and the refilled glass of water in the other.

"Eat, eat, eat, and drink. More food, food."

Pike ignored the plate and glass as he dropped his hands to his lap and stared into Kimble's eyes. "You can talk now?"

"Talk," Kimble said with a frown. "Try. Try-try-trying."

Kimble's new speech pattern wasn't a stutter, it was more like a skipping sound bite. Pike didn't mind, Kimble had said more new words in the last few minutes than he had in months!

Discomfort forgotten, Pike beamed at Kimble. "You're doing great!"

To his surprise, Kimble didn't return the smile. If anything, his frown grew more severe.

"No good," he declared. "Very no-no-no good."

Pike didn't understand. "You're wrong. This is very good." Pike took the plate and glass from him. After setting them on the nightstand, he drew Kimble into his arms. The vampire collapsed against him with a sigh. Pike held him close and put his mouth near his ear.

"I'm so proud of you!" he whispered. "These new words make me very happy."

Kimble made an unhappy sound but didn't try to pull away. He might be frustrated with the slow progress, but Pike was overjoyed. Earlier that night, Pike thought he was going to lose Kimble and now he looked healed, healthy, and was even showing signs of coming back to himself.

"Best. Day. Ever," Pike said, with a happy sigh.

A moan from Cora broke the happy mood. Both men pulled away from the hug to look over at her. She was propped up on one elbow, her pale face scrunched up in pain, and looking up at them through squinted eyes.

"Fuck," she mumbled in a hoarse voice. "Did I drink or am I sick?"

"There wasn't any alcohol involved, but you are sick in a way," Pike said and grabbed the glass of water as Kimble rushed over to help sit her up. He took great pains to fluff several pillows before easing her back against the bed's headboard.

Pike waited until the vampire was done before offering the glass of water to Cora. She accepted it with a grateful expression and drank half of it before handing it back.

"I think my head's going to explode," she moaned, letting her head fall back against a pillow. "I need some Tylenol. What time is it anyway?"

"I think it's about three in the morning," Pike said. "Do you keep your medications in the bathroom?"

Cora didn't open her eyes when she answered. "Yeah, left-hand drawer."

Kimble had taken up a similar position with Cora as he'd had with Pike earlier, sitting on the edge of the bed with the plate of crackers. As Pike watched, he pressed one to Cora's mouth.

She tried to bat his hand away. "Stop it. I'm not hungry."

"Eat," Kimble insisted and tried again. "Please. Cora needs food."

Cora had a similar reaction as Pike to Kimble's expanded vocabulary. She didn't sit up, but her eyes opened wide, and she grabbed Kimble's hand to move it away from her mouth.

"You're talking," she said in a loud whisper. "You used my name. You've never said my name before!"

Kimble's pleading expression turned ashamed, and he looked down at his lap, his shoulders hunching. "Bad-bad-bad me. Sorry."

Cora looked at Pike, her expression confused and bordering on angry. "Has he been able to do this the whole time? Has he been faking being worse than he is?"

Pike shook his head. "No, he really was that bad. But whatever happened with sharing our auras must've not only healed him but gone a long way to helping him get better."

"Auras," Cora said with a grimace. "That's why I feel like shit. I remember some of it now, but it's all fuzzy. I haven't felt this bad since the last time I got sick and that was years ago."

"Cora eat, please?" Kimble begged, still looking down. He pulled her hand off his and turned it over to place the single cracker on her palm. "Please, please?"

Cora accepted the cracker and cupped Kimble's cheek with her free hand. "I'll eat, but you have to promise no more trading your aura for a necklace, no matter how pretty it is, okay?"

"Idiot," Kimble mumbled, looking close to tears. "Idiot and bad. Dumb-dumb-dumb. Will be better."

"Hey, easy there," Cora murmured. "No more guilt. Shit's hard enough. We're all just trying to do our best, and we're going to make mistakes. You wanted to give me a gift. I get that. It was sweet, and I love it, but what I want more is for you to be healthy. Yeah?"

It was obvious she was doing her best to keep the pain off her face as she spoke. That reminded Pike he was supposed to be getting her medicine. He heard Kimble say something and Cora responded as he searched the bathroom drawer. Once he found the bottle, he returned and shook out two tablets for Cora.

She managed to eat the cracker Kimble had given her and was now fending off a second one with a genuine smile.

"Let these take effect then I'll eat more," she promised, popping the pills in her mouth and swallowing them dry.

"Ewww," Pike said, his face contorted in disgust, making Cora chuckle.

"Whatever," she mumbled, letting her head rest back on the pillows. "I want matzo ball soup. I always have matzo ball soup when I'm sick."

"No problem," Pike answered without hesitation. He had no idea what "matzo" was, but he'd find out and make it into balls for her.

"Thanks," she whispered, then patted the bed next to her. "Kimble can cuddle me while you cook."

"Aren't we demanding," Pike teased as Kimble moved to snuggle next to her.

"I'm sick," she answered with a smirk. "That means that I'm a princess and get whatever I want. When you're sick, I'll do the same for you."

He didn't point out that shifters almost never get sick, and he was already feeling almost fully recovered from their earlier ordeal. Instead he bowed.

"Anything my queen wishes," he said, then swept out of the room with his nose in the air like a stiff-backed butler from an old movie. He was rewarded with a soft chuckle from Cora.

To his relief, it turned out matzo ball soup was easy to make because Cora had a jar of it in her pantry. According to the label it was even kosher, whatever that meant.

He didn't like that his mate felt ill, but he couldn't help but hum and dance a little as he heated up the soup on the stove. Kimble was getting better, Cora had already forgiven him, and everyone was alive.

Considering the year he'd had; this was as good as he could ever hope for!

**Cora**

The next morning, it only took one call to Charlotte to have the entire week of work either rescheduled or handed over to Glen Santos, a friend and fellow electrician with his own small company. With that done, Cora could concentrate on getting better. With two gorgeous men seeing to her every need, she was almost tempted to pretend to be sick for longer.

She'd slept for most of the last two days and on the rare occasion she was awake, Kimble, Pike, or both were trying to get her to drink and eat. It was the evening of the third day and although she was feeling better, she probably wasn't steady enough to take a shower. Even trips to the bathroom and back left her feeling exhausted.

Running a hand through her hair, she grimaced at how greasy it felt. Ugh!

"What's wrong?" Pike asked. She was snuggled between the two of them on the couch watching some emergency room drama that made Kimble laugh occasionally, probably from all the fake blood.

Pike's question drew Kimble's attention to her. "Tired? Do you need sleep again?"

Over the last few days, his language skills had improved immensely. His sentences might be simple and not always grammatically correct, but who cared when they could actually talk to him?

"I'm not tired," she lied because the truth was that she was always tired. Right now she was baseline tired, not extra tired. "I don't like being this dirty. Do you think you could put a chair in the shower so I could get clean?"

Pike frowned and shook his head. "That sounds super dangerous."

"No shower," Kimble agreed, but he was smiling. "Bath instead."

She hadn't thought of taking a bath. Not only would it get her clean, but she could relax into the hot water. That sounded wonderful.

"Yeah, let's do that," she agreed. "You guys chill here. I can do this by myself."

She planned to strip down, sit in the tub, and let it fill up around her. That way, she could take all the time she needed to wash herself and if she got too tired, she could lay back and rest.

However, it was obvious by their expressions that both Kimble and Pike didn't like her suggestion.

"No," Kimble said with a shake of his head. "You don't do bath alone. We do it for you."

She knew what he meant but couldn't resist teasing him. "If you and Pike take a bath for me, I'm not going to get clean."

Kimble burst out laughing, something he'd been doing a lot more lately. It seemed Kimble's brush with death had changed his attitude. He wasn't only trying hard to come back to himself, but he was enjoying life again.

He'd even started humming and swept Pike into an impromptu dance while the shifter was fixing dinner the other night. Poor Pike had looked awkward and confused but had tried to join in with Kimble's old time-y dance. By the end, all three of them were laughing, and Cora was gasping for air. It had been a little magical.

And now he was laughing again, making both her and Pike grin.

"You be in bath, Pike and I soap you," Kimble explained. He tilted his head thoughtfully. "With candles and wine."

Pike made a negative sound as he got to his feet. "Not wine. I bet you want a cold Coke instead."

"Yes to the bath, candles, and Coke," she agreed. "But do we have any in the glass bottles?"

"I picked some up this afternoon," Pike answered. "You guys cuddle here; I'll fill the tub."

Taking his job very seriously, Kimble picked Cora up and arranged her blanket-wrapped form on his lap. She was easily chilled since the night Tobias took some of her aura, so her men had made sure to keep her bundled. Kimble's well-fed body was always pleasantly warm, but Pike was a furnace, so she tended to cling to him in her sleep.

"Do you remember anything from your past?" Cora asked. She'd put off asking but with all of Kimble's good humor, she decided it was time.

"Jumbled images," he answered with a sigh. "Tobias knows me. Could ask him."

His reluctance was obvious. "But you don't want to, why?"

"Favors," he answered succinctly. "Nothing among vampires is free. Not to other vampires."

Kimble had a point. Cora vividly remembered Tobias demanding future favors for his assistance. Owing Tobias gave her an uneasy feeling. Whatever he eventually asked for probably wouldn't involve her skills as an electrician.

"Is he more powerful than you?" Cora asked.

"Yes and no," Kimble answered with a little grumble. When Cora craned her neck back to give him a look, he explained. "Me weakened. He is stronger. Now we are equal-ish. When you are a full flock member, I'll be stronger. Sup-sup-superior to almost all. I'm old."

He didn't glitch much anymore, but when he did, it was usually on bigger or less common words. Sometimes he'd mix in foreign words as he spoke. He wouldn't realize he'd done it until Cora or Pike pointed it out.

"I'm sorry I'm not ready yet," she whispered. He hadn't pushed her to exchange souls, but each day she felt a little guiltier for delaying.

Kimble pressed his lips to her forehead then urged her to relax against him. "No rush. I'm your vampire. I can wait a lifetime, only pick me before dying. Can't exchange souls with a ghost."

Cora snorted. "So I need to decide sometime in the next sixty years."

"Correct," Kimble answered, then chuckled. "Hopefully sooner, yes?"

"Maybe," she teased, making him huff out a laugh. "You know, you're so much happier now. It's nice."

He went silent for a moment, then spoke in a hushed tone. "I almost died for us, angry and anxious. That was bad. Better that I live for us instead, happy and loved."

Oh damn, that wasn't what she was expecting. Her philosopher vampire.

"Good choice," she murmured, tucking her head under his chin. "Very good choice."

While Pike helped Cora stand, Kimble stripped her out of her cotton pajamas and tossed them into the nearby hamper. The bathroom was cozy and warm, softly lit by a dozen candles and jazz music quietly playing from Pike's phone on the counter.

Cora had a moment where she felt mildly self-conscious, but it vanished when Kimble surveyed her body with lust sparkling in his eyes.

"Beautiful," he murmured as he ran his gaze over her.

She beamed at him, then let Pike lift her into the steaming tub. She moaned as hot water enveloped her. "Oh, this is nice."

Pike had brought in a stool that he sat on before reaching for a washcloth and a bottle of body wash. "You just wait, because it's going to get better."

She watched through half closed eyes as Kimble knelt next to Pike and reached for another washcloth, then accepted the bottle of wash from Pike. With soapy cloths in hand, the two of them went to work.

Cora didn't know what she expected, but the slow, sensuous rubbing wasn't it. Kimble started at her feet, running the cloth over her skin and then setting it aside to start massaging her.

She'd had a massage exactly one time in her life and hadn't been impressed. If the masseuse had been even half as good as Kimble, she would have gone back every other day.

"Very muscled," Kimble commented as he worked his way up to her calf. Pike was working on her shoulder and right arm, but she barely noticed as Kimble's magic fingers found all her knots.

"Sorry," she whispered. Then gave a little gasp and moaned, "Oh man, right there!"

"Muscled good," Kimble told her. "Strong survive."

"That was the truth in my household," Cora agreed with a grin, then opened her mouth and sucked in a breath. "Right there please, a little harder."

"If you didn't love him before, this might do it," Pike teased. "Could you scoot forward and dip your hair to get it wet?"

Kimble stopped massaging long enough for Cora to get her hair wet, then he went back to finding all her tense spots. She wasn't sure what felt better, Kimble's magic massage or Pike's fingers on her scalp as he worked in the shampoo.

"We need to make this a regular thing," Cora said. She meant the words to sound funny, but they came out needy instead.

"Any time you want," Pike promised with all seriousness. She opened her eyes in time to see him swoop down to lay a kiss on her lips before going back to washing her hair.

She didn't think it was possible for her to love these two any more, but as they cared for her body with the sole intent of making her feel clean and relaxed, she fell for them a little more.

By the time Kimble had washed and massaged most of her, Pike had finished with her hair. It had required getting a bowl from the kitchen as well as draining and refilling the tub once, but he'd been determined.

She barely felt the aches she'd been dealing with for the last few days, and her headache was completely gone. She felt clean, warm, and relaxed.

The relaxation was so complete that when Pike pulled her out of the tub and set her on her feet on the bathmat, her knees wouldn't lock, and she started to fall.

"You're not an equine shifter, so no falling asleep on your feet," Pike said after catching her and holding her to his body while Kimble dried her off.

"That was a first," she admitted, turning her head to rub her face against Pike's damp shirt. His muscles always needed to be worshiped. "I've never felt this relaxed."

But they weren't done there.

After she was dry, Kimble started applying lotion to her skin. As with his washing/massage, he took his time to rub every part of her, paying special attention to all the spots where he'd found knots. This time, his touch was everything gentle and soothing as if apologizing to all the muscles he'd worked on earlier.

Most guys would've taken advantage, especially when running their hands up the inside of her legs. He didn't ignore her sex, but he only gave the damp curls at the apex of her legs a quick kiss before concentrating on spreading lotion on her belly.

The kiss seemed like a promise for later. She was feeling well enough that maybe she'd be up to having some fun with the guys. After another nap.

Once he deemed her suitably moisturized, they wrapped her in a fuzzy blanket and carried her back out to the couch. Once again, she was arranged in Kimble's lap, and Pike went to work combing out her hair.

"How do you know how to do this?" she asked. "Did you have long hair once?"

"No, but I took care of my sister's hair when Mom didn't have time," he explained. "She had a sensitive scalp, so I learned to be gentle with the brush or comb. It got to the point where she'd ask me to do it instead of Mom."

He sounded so proud that it made Cora mildly jealous. "Sounds like you and your sister were close."

"When we were kids, we were best friends. I was Big Bear, and she was Little Bear. We did everything together. It was a lot of fun." He sounded wistful, and Cora went from feeling jealous to sympathetic.

"You're not close anymore?"

"Everything changed when she turned fourteen. She didn't have time for her brother anymore. It was all about her friends, boys, and having the latest of everything. I remember I saved up for months to buy her a phone she wanted, except by the time I got it, she already wanted a different one. I couldn't keep up so after that, I'd give her cash instead. That's a gift she always likes."

Kimble made a grumbly sound that Cora interpreted as disapproval. "Greedy."

Pike froze. "She's not greedy. I'm just a bad gift giver."

"You're perfect," Kimble answered. "Always."

It seemed Pike's sister was a sore point between the two of them. Pike was a sweetheart, and she'd known plenty of people who had blind spots when it came to their family.

"Kimble's right," Cora murmured, turning her head so she could see Pike. "I can't imagine you being a bad gift giver. Your sister is too picky."

Pike scrunched his forehead a little. "Can we talk about something else?"

Cora's phone rang shrilly, making her jump, Kimble growled, and Pike got up to retrieve it from the nightstand. She hadn't gotten many calls, but she'd made sure the guys knew it was important that she answered the phone. She'd been avoiding calls from her family and sending texts instead. So far, no one had any emergencies that required her help.

The call was from an unrecognized number so it might be work related.

The moment she answered, she wished she hadn't. "Perfection Connection Electrics, what—"

"You're so sick you canceled your entire week but didn't call me or any of your brothers?" her father yelled through the phone. Daniel might love her deeply, but one of the main ways he showed concern was with volume. Right now he was practically screaming.

"I'm not that sick," she answered but winced when his volume didn't decrease.

"You're like me, you'd have to be on the verge of dying to hand that many jobs over to Santos. Are you at the hospital? Did you crash that shit van? I warned you about that vehicle!" He talked too fast for her to answer any questions. Cora let him voice one horrible outcome after another until he paused long enough for her to speak.

"Are you tired yet?" Cora asked when he had to pull in a breath of air.

"Tired?" he asked, confused.

"Tired from leaping to all those conclusions," Cora explained, then snorted at her joke. She'd thought of it months ago and had been waiting for the perfect time to use it. Next to her on the couch, Pike laughed but Kimble didn't look happy at all. She gave him a reassuring smile before focusing back on the call.

"Dad, I'm at home and being taken care of," she rushed to say before he could start worrying at high volume again. "I'm sick but doing better. I took the whole week off because I wasn't sure how long it would take to get over whatever I caught."

"Did you even go to the doctor?" Daniel demanded. "I bet you didn't. I've never known a more stubborn person than you."

"Look in the mirror, you'll find one," she shot back.

"I'm coming over," he announced. "You shouldn't be alone. Do I need to bring groceries? Never mind, I'll stop by the store on my way."

"No." Her one-word sentence was everything final, and her dad heard it.

"Fine, then I'm sending Ted. He's a better choice anyway, he works at the hospital."

"As an x-ray tech!" Cora protested with a laugh. "What's he going to do here? There is an absolute lack of radiation equipment in my home."

"I still think—"

"No you don't, why start now?" Cora asked, making him sputter and Kimble and Pike laugh.

"Who's there with you?" he demanded. "Is it that guy Cooper met at your house?"

"Yes, Pike is here, and another guy named Kimble," Cora confirmed. She might as well get Kimble's name out there before Sunday's BBQ. She'd be fine by then, and if she didn't show up, her family would invade her home.

She knew all too well that she couldn't avoid them forever, unfortunately.

"Two men are there?" Daniel asked, as if he was making sure he'd heard correctly.

"Yes, two men. They're both mine, and I don't want to hear another word about it. We're all coming over on Sunday. If you visit here before then or send anyone by, I swear to God I'll move out of state," she warned him.

"First you drop the bombshell that you've got two guys and then you threaten me," her dad said. "These guys must be special."

"They are so don't test me," Cora said.

"Then I guess Sunday will have to do," he grumbled. "What did you say their full names were again?"

"I didn't," she answered, then hung up without saying goodbye. It was the price he paid for thinking he could run background checks on them.

Kimble plucked the phone from her hand and tossed it next to them on the couch. "Tense again," he grumbled.

"My family does that to me," she admitted. She felt weirdly awake but fatigued. Her body was tired, but her brain was whirling with thoughts and plans. "I hope you don't mind meeting my family, Kimble."

Kimble made a dismissive sound. "Don't care." Then he eased a hand under the fuzzy blanket and palmed her breast. "Want a happy ending?"

All thoughts of her irritating father and annoying brothers vanished. "Hell yes!"

## Pike

Pike's large size meant he had to hunch over to the point of almost resting his head on his knees if he tried to fit in Cora's small car. She wrinkled her nose at his Caddy but agreed to drive to the monthly BBQ in that instead, making Pike breathe out a sigh of relief.

She'd already called her dad to warn him they'd be late. Once the sun was down, they'd all gotten into Pike's rust spotted car. At least it wasn't hot because the car's air conditioner probably hadn't worked since 1982. It wasn't the car's only failing, but in the San Diego heat, it was a big one.

"I guess you can't argue with the room in here," Cora commented as they drove. The front seat couldn't accommodate all three of them, so Kimble had climbed in the back with Cora. Pike felt a little like a chauffeur. Or maybe the Wish version of an Uber.

"The room and price were the major selling points," Pike agreed.

"Did you bargain the guy down to a dollar or did you have to pay full price?" Cora teased.

"Hey, don't talk about the Caddy like that," Pike admonished with a chuckle. "To tell the truth, I didn't pay anything for it. I traded. It'd been sitting in his driveway for years. He lives in my parents' neighborhood and needed two trees cut down. I was able to do it in a weekend and he gave me the car."

"We'll have to see about getting you a better vehicle," Cora said. "Something you're comfortable in but that still has working shocks. I think my spine broke on that last pothole."

"And doesn't leak when it rains," Pike said wistfully, but then guilt hit him hard. "But I don't see that happening. I owe you so much money for all the blood you bought, and the coffee table Kimble destroyed. Finding your mate is supposed to be amazing, not destructive."

"Don't be silly," Cora responded, reaching forward to muss his hair. "You're not paying me back shit. Besides, we have an agreement, remember? You cook and clean, and I bring home the paycheck. We're in this together until Kimble's all better."

Pike hated it when she said things like that, as if the three of them were temporary. He knew she did it as a type of defense mechanism, but that didn't make it any less painful.

"I provide," Kimble announced, far louder than necessary in the confines of the car. He was probably feeling guilty too. "Not yet, but soon. Provide for my flock forever."

"Don't worry about it," Cora said. "I've got you. I'm not going to be buying Jaguars or mansions, but I can keep you two comfortable. I'll look around for something used that will fit all three of us comfortably and is in the budget."

Kimble grumbled but otherwise didn't argue with her. A glance in the rearview mirror showed the vampire cuddling up to the human. It didn't look sexual. It looked more like an apology.

As he drove, the two in the back murmured to each other, leaving him to his thoughts. That wasn't a good idea because one thing kept playing out in his head: the bad impression he'd made when he'd first met Cooper.

What if Cooper told Cora's family that Pike was a horrible person? They'd all hate him before they even got a chance to meet him!

The closer they got the more nervous Pike became. He was sweating by the time he drove onto a gravel drive that opened up to a gravel parking lot in front of a house.

"Dad doesn't believe in lawns," Cora said as Pike parked between a truck and a sporty compact. The two story, stucco house lacked a single decorative flourish anywhere. No pots of flowers, no curtains in the windows, and the color was a bland beige. It was completely different from his parents' small craftsman house with the colorful pollinator garden in the front that his mother was so proud of.

"It looks very, uh…" Pike was at a loss for a descriptor that wasn't as bland as the house.

"Practical," Cora finished for him. "That's my dad."

The moment he shut off the engine, he could hear people talking and laughing. The smell of roasting and burnt meat was heavy in the air, making him wrinkle his nose. Humans always insisted on ruining perfectly good meals with over cooking. Bracing himself, he decided that no matter how badly cooked the meat was, he'd choke it down.

Because the Caddy was a two door, Pike had to get out first and flip the seat forward to let Cora and Kimble out. He waited, his hand held out for her to take, but she didn't move. The look of reluctance on her face matched his internal struggle.

"I'm sure everything will be fine," he lied. "I'll be super friendly, and we'll say Kimble is learning English, so they won't expect much conversation from him."

"It's not them liking you I'm worried about," she admitted, taking his hand and climbing out of the car. "I'm worried they're going to make you mad. My family is really good at pissing people off and a few of my early relationships ended because I brought the guy to an event like this one."

"They must all know that you're in a relationship with two guys," Pike said, voicing one of his fears. "The most they could do is try to shame you into ending it, and we all know that won't work."

Cora snorted as she stepped away from the Caddy to give Kimble room. "I promise, that's not going to be an issue. Dad's bi. He was dating guys before he fell in love with Mom. In fact, when they met, he was living with two of his lovers. Cooper is married to a man, and Trevor and his wife are looking into the poly scene. My family would never give us a hard time about a non-traditional relationship."

That information made him feel a little better, but he was still nervous as hell. Kimble followed Cora out of the car, and Pike slammed the heavy door shut. The entire Caddy rocked and squeaked a little.

Standing next to it, Cora stared at the house. "Promise me something."

"Anything," Pike said without hesitation. Kimble grunted as if to say he agreed also.

"No matter what they say to you, come talk to me first," Cora said. "My family is really good at hurting people's feelings."

"They can try," Pike said. "But I'm confident in us, which makes me almost invulnerable to insults."

Cora didn't look convinced. "We'll see."

"You're fucking massive!" someone exclaimed as Cora led them around the side of the house.

"Nice welcome, Carson!" Cora yelled.

Pike stumbled to a stop when everyone at the gathering turned to stare at them with varying degrees of curiosity.

"There's a lot of people here," he mumbled. Kimble put a comforting hand on his back, and Cora tangled her fingers with his.

"They're all dumb, but nice," Cora said in a faux whisper.

"Hey!" Cooper yelled, holding up his beer. He had an arm around another man, probably his husband who stared at Pike with wide eyes. "Nice to see you again, Pike."

"Oh babe," the husband whispered, but Pike's bear hearing made it easy to overhear. "You said he was big, but you didn't say he was the size of a house! He could've killed you!"

Cooper looked down at his husband. "Nah, I'm a tough asshole."

The husband snorted. "You got the asshole part right."

Their little exchange helped Pike relax. It seemed everyone was hard on each other in this family.

"Pike!" a bunch of guys yelled together, holding up beers and then taking long drinks. Cora chuckled and waited until the drinking was over to start talking.

"This is Kimble," she said, pointing.

"Kimble!" the men yelled and drank again.

"You guys are idiots!" Cora announced, but she was smiling as she led him and Kimble deeper into the backyard yard. The place was large, bordered by tall, full trees. Just like with the front, there wasn't any lawn at all. At the center was a rectangular pool surrounded by lounge chairs, tables, and umbrellas. The back third of the space was a child's play area with swings, a climbing structure, and a wooden platform on squat springs. The ground was some kind of springy composite painted in bright colors.

About a dozen kids stopped playing long enough to look over at them, then went back to their activities. No one was in the pool, but by the looks of the wet footprints, there'd recently been children in there.

"Your timing is perfect!" a feminine voice said and stepped out from behind a smoking grill. "Dinner's finally ready."

"Hi Janet!" Cora said with a little wave of her free hand. "We ate earlier, but if you brought some of your peanut butter brownies, I'll have an entire plate of them."

"I'll grab you some," Janet said before bustling off into the house.

A silver-haired man with a graying beard stepped away from the grill with a large shiny spatula clutched in his hand.

"You already ate? What kind of bullshit is that?" he asked with a frown.

Cora didn't respond to the question, and her smile turned forced. She tightened her hold on him as they walked toward the man. This was clearly her father. Unlike all the brothers with their darker skin tones and long, thin faces, Cora's pale skin and round face resembled this man. Her siblings must take after her mother while she took after her father.

"Hi Dad, this is Pike and Kimble."

"I heard," he grunted, first eyeing Kimble, then turning his attention to Pike.

Cora ignored his grunt and finished the introduction. "Guys, this is my father, Daniel."

Pike tried to smile and held out a hand. "It's nice to meet you, sir."

Daniel eyed Pike's hand before accepting the handshake and then letting go as if he was afraid Pike would try to crush his hand. "Cooper wasn't exaggerating, you're a big motherfucker. Built like a brick shithouse!"

Pike winced and tried to figure out what to say. He wasn't used to all the casual cussing with so many children running around. Thankfully, Cora saved him, or maybe avenged him would be a better word.

"Watch your language Dad," Cora hissed.

"What?" Daniel feigned innocence. "These kids got to learn how to talk like men."

"Fuck yes they do," Cora agreed in a mock shout, then nodded her head toward the house. "Let me just grab Janet and tell her what you said."

Daniel looked momentarily scared. "She brought an extra pan of brownies for me. It's yours if you don't say anything."

Cora grinned. "Deal."

Daniel shook his head and turned his attention to Kimble. "Why are you wearing sunglasses at night? It's all kinds of suspicious, don't you think?"

"Sensitive eyes," Kimble answered, deliberately making his accent thick.

"He's got an issue with his vision and needs them," Cora added.

Daniel frowned at Kimble. "Where'd you come from?"

"Cora's home," Kimble answered.

Pike stifled a laugh as Daniel's frown turned to a scowl. Cora didn't bother hiding her amusement. "No more questions, Dad. It's been a rough few weeks for all of us, and I want to hang out and relax."

"Then you're going to need this," said a black-haired man as he swooped in with three bottles of beer clutched in his hands.

"Thanks," Pike said as he took one. They'd agreed earlier that Kimble should take whatever anyone offered, and Pike or Cora would consume it when no one was paying attention. That way, it would be less obvious Kimble wasn't drinking or eating.

"Thanks, Caleb," Cora said before taking a sip of her beer.

"No prob," Caleb said before moving his gaze between Kimble and Pike. "I'm the oldest of the siblings."

"And my greatest disappointment," Daniel grumbled.

"Go flip your burnt burgers, old man," Caleb said without any heat. "He's still holding a grudge because I went to law school instead of trade school. Anyway, let me point everyone out. Don't worry. There won't be a quiz later."

Three children ran past them and jumped into the pool as Caleb gave them a crash course on Cora's family. Pike tried to remember everyone but there were a lot of people. All the siblings except for Cora and Tim were married and most had children.

Caleb proudly pointed out his foster kids jumping into the pool along with his biological daughter.

It seemed the Walsh Clan was ready to include anyone whether they were born into the family or not. It made Pike feel better about Daniel's disapproval. He was simply protective of his large family.

It might take a little time, but the Walsh family would accept him and Kimble as permanent parts of Cora's life.

No one sat down to eat, everyone held plates in their hands and chatted as they consumed burgers, chips, and sliced up veggies. Unable to resist, Pike grabbed a plate and loaded it down with the veggies. The bear in him couldn't pass up fresh bite sized cucumbers, carrots, and broccoli. Oh, there were grapes and melon balls too!

Cora got called over to discuss zoning laws and Kimble followed, leaving Pike alone at the table to graze.

Everything was going great until he found himself alone with Trevor, Cooper, and Ted. The three of them boxed him in against a shed, mostly hidden from the rest of the backyard, and Pike prepared himself to take some hits. He'd let them get a few punches in before putting them on their butts, so it would make them less likely to be angry with him later.

Instead of hitting, the three of them leaned in close and started whispering.

"I'm only saying this to be kind," Cooper started. "But you should break up with her now before Cora gets a chance to stomp all over you."

Ted nodded his head, eyes wide and sincere. "She doesn't do long term, and you seem decent. That Kimble dude, not so much, but you have 'nice guy' written all over you."

"You don't deserve what she's going to do to you," Trevor said. "No guy does."

"Get out before she destroys you," Cooper added.

"Let me tell you a story," Ted said and the other brothers nodded their heads as if they knew what he was going to say. "It starts with a meet-cute between a tiny she-demon named Cora and a helpless, romantic guy named Seb."

"What the fuck is a meet-cute?" Trevor asked Cooper in a whisper. A glare from Ted had them both shutting up.

"As I was saying, this story starts out sweet, but turns dark and ugly fast. So begins the tragic tale of Seb and Cora."

**Cora**

Cora was so busy keeping an eye on Kimble that she didn't notice Pike's disappearance at first. He'd been chowing down at the table and now he was nowhere to be seen.

How long had he been missing and who was responsible?

Undaunted by his monosyllabic responses, Darcy, Trevor's wife, had been trying to converse with Kimble. She was doing most of the talking but then again, she usually did. She was the sweetest chatterbox Cora ever met.

It left Cora free to talk to Janet and Caleb about all their current challenges. Out of all her siblings, she was closest to Caleb, probably because Dad gave him as much shit as he gave Cora because both of them had refused to join the family business. As the first-born, Caleb should've been at Dad's side building the Walsh & Co. empire. Cora was the only electrician in the family that didn't work for Daniel.

It was a point of pride for both her and Caleb that Dad called them his biggest disappointments. It had cemented their bond as the oldest and youngest siblings. Daniel didn't like it when things were out of his control, and Cora and Caleb hadn't been under his control for a very long time.

It meant Dad was just as likely to run off a boyfriend as one of her brothers.

Far more observant than any of the other Walsh males, Caleb noticed her searching gaze. "Looking for Pike?"

"Yeah," Cora said, searching the surrounding area. "Dad's talking to Patrice, so I know Pike's not in danger of being forced into servitude for Walsh & Co."

"Dad would never talk him into free labor," Caleb said. "Not at the first meeting, anyway. He'd wait for at least a second or third meeting, then point out what a loser Pike is and how only Daniel can fix him." Caleb made air quotes around the word loser so Cora knew he didn't mean it.

"Daniel's a sweetheart!" Darcy exclaimed, shaking her head at Caleb as if he was being too cynical. It was amazing that she managed to be married to Trevor for over two years and still saw everyone as wonderful.

"Pike is perfect," Kimble interjected and bared his teeth in a threatening smile. "Anyone will be dead man if they insult Pike."

Cora felt the same way. "I should go find Pike before anyone says something they can't take back."

"I find him. You be here," he said.

"This is my family, I'm not in danger," Cora assured him, rubbing a hand up and down his arm. "Stick with me, and we'll rescue him together."

One of Caleb and Janet's kids ran up and distracted the group as she led Kimble away. There weren't many places someone Pike's size could be hidden from view, so Cora headed to the most likely spot; behind the large playhouse in the corner of the backyard.

Full of food, most of the kids had moved indoors to watch movies or play air hockey in the game room. It left the backyard far quieter, so she heard her brother talking long before she got to the playhouse.

"He was crying!" Trevor exclaimed dramatically. "Poor Seb didn't deserve that. She humiliated him in front of everyone and then acted like she was the one who was hurt."

At those words, Cora stopped and felt her skin flush. Trevor was telling Pike about the time Seb had proposed to her at one of these BBQs. It had been the height of summer, so the sun was still up at eight at night. Seb waited till everyone arrived then got everyone's attention, went down on one knee, and pulled a ring out of his pocket.

Cora still ranked that night as one of the worst of her life, but her family only saw the first part of it. They hadn't been there later, when Seb had cornered her at her old apartment or the horrible year that followed.

"That's an interesting story," Pike murmured in his familiar deep voice. "But it was his choice to propose in public without talking to Cora about it first."

"Of course he didn't talk to her!" Cooper exclaimed. "That's not how you're supposed to propose."

"He even had balloons and a cake waiting in the kitchen," Trevor said.

"So he goes down on one knee, holds up the ring, and Cora doesn't say anything except no," Ted said. "Then she turns and walks away, but she doesn't just leave the backyard. She walks to her car and leaves!"

"I don't think Seb had even gotten to his feet before we heard her tires slinging gravel around," Cooper added.

"You should've seen the expression on the guy's face," Tim said. "I've never seen anyone so devastated. Did I tell you there were tears? Big fat ones!"

It wasn't often that Cora had the urge to do something truly horrible to her family. She'd threaten them often and occasionally stop talking to them until they realized she meant it, but she almost never wanted to do them actual physical harm.

Tonight was an exception.

And it wasn't only Trevor, Cooper, and Ted she wanted to hurt. These three would've never thought to tell Pike this story if her father hadn't suggested it.

Furious and hurt, Cora stormed around the playhouse to see Pike shaking his head at her brothers and about to say something. When he saw her face, he pushed past them and rushed to her side.

"Cora?" he whispered, stopping short of touching her. "What's wrong?"

"I heard everything," she said loudly, her voice tight from suppressed emotions.

"You know I don't care about Seb or any man in your past," Pike said.

"I'm not angry with you," she whispered, then took one of his hands and tugged him to her. With Kimble on one side of her and Pike on the other, she faced her brothers.

"How dare you?" she hissed.

Trevor tried to look innocent while Cooper and Ted had identical expressions of surprise on their faces. The idiots didn't understand why she was reacting so badly.

Of course she'd never told them what happened, but maybe it was time her family found out.

"Seb wasn't the nice guy everyone thought he was," she spat out. "I'd already tried to break up with him several times before that night."

Cooper looked confused. "You had? He said you guys were happy and were even looking into buying a house together."

"Never," she answered. She could feel herself shaking. Telling her brothers this was hard, but she was determined to finish.

"Easy," Pike murmured. He pulled his hand from hers and stepped behind her to wrap his arms around her shoulders. The press of his big, strong body against her back made her feel better.

Kimble pushed gently against her side, lending his strength to her also. "We go?" he asked.

"When I'm finished," she whispered, thankful that he was willing to let her say her piece. She looked at her brothers and willed her eyes to stay dry.

"Each time I broke up with him, he raged and cajoled his way back into my life. He would call or come by my apartment at all hours of the night and demand I let him in. Then he'd keep me up all night talking until I didn't know what was up or down. I'd finally let him stay because I needed sleep and that was the only way to get him to stop."

"Why didn't you call the cops?" Ted asked as Cooper growled at the same time.

"Why didn't you tell us?"

"No one believed me!" she screamed at them. "Don't you remember when I told you he wasn't the sweet, sensitive man you guys all thought he was? I told you he had a violent temper. I did call the cops, but he'd charm them into leaving without doing anything."

"But he never hit you," Ted said, looking for reassurance. "You would've told us if he hit you, right?"

Cora shook her head at him, her features twisted in disgust. "No, he never hit me, so I guess it was okay when he threatened to go to all my clients, so I'd never work again. There was no physical abuse, so it was fine every time he made it impossible for me to hang out with my friends. He didn't lay hands on me, so the mind games and manipulation must not have been a big deal. Is that what you're trying to say, Ted?"

All three brothers grew pale as she spoke, and Cooper looked devastated. "Why didn't you do something?"

"I did!" she bit out. "I asked you to stop talking to him because he was using you to find out what I was doing." She focused her gaze on Ted. "I begged you to stop inviting him to our get-togethers, but you still made sure he was here, even on my birthday! Did you know he destroyed every gift you guys gave me the next day because he thought I liked those gifts better than what he'd given me?"

"But he seemed so happy for you," Cooper whispered.

"That was the year Dad and I gave you the welder," Tim said from behind her. She didn't look over at him. The welder had been expensive, and she couldn't bear to admit she hadn't been able to save it from Seb's retribution.

Trevor shook his head, as if he couldn't believe what Cora was saying. "He was so much fun. He helped build this playhouse."

"He knew how to make people like him. The first time I tried to break up with him, he said no one would believe me when I said how horrible he was," Cora said with a harsh laugh. "Turns out he was right. By the time he proposed, things were really bad. He'd find dead animals in the road and leave them on my car." She shuddered. "At least I hope they were animals he found and didn't kill himself."

"But you're Cora," Ted said, as if that should mean something.

"Yeah, I'm Cora," she agreed. "And I tried everything short of murder but he wouldn't leave me alone, no matter what I did. I changed my locks, changed my number, and carried around pepper spray and a taser. I even bought a house in secret. Why do you think I didn't tell any of you about the new place until almost a year later? I knew you all were talking to him. I couldn't get you to stop."

"Where is he?" Daniel growled as he stepped into sight. She didn't know how much he'd heard, but it must have been enough to make him angry. "I'll fucking kill him!"

"Why so angry, Dad?" Cora challenged him. "Aren't you the one who gave him my new cell number every time I changed it? Even though I asked you not to?"

Daniel's expression went from furious to shocked. "I didn't know. He said the two of you were working it out and that you were being huffy. You didn't—"

"Tell you?" Cora interrupted him. "But I did Dad, and you know what you said? I can tell you the exact words because that moment is burned into my memory. 'Cora, I'm sure Seb did wrong, but you've got a temper too. Please don't ask me to take sides in your couple's squabbles.'"

"How was I to know it was more serious?" Daniel said, the beginning of anger flushing his pale skin red.

"Maybe by believing me?" Cora suggested, as she looked at him and let all the hurt show on her face. "Couple's squabbles. That's what you called it. As if we were arguing over what color to paint the bedroom instead of me fighting to survive. At one point, he had me convinced that I'd never get a moment of peace if I didn't marry him and do everything he demanded. Do you know the most fucked up part of the whole thing? It took me years of therapy to realize it, but you set me up for the relationship, Dad."

Daniel's eyes went wide, and his mouth flattened in anger. "How can you say such a thing to me? I've always loved you!"

"But sometimes I wonder if you like me very much," Cora replied. "You call me your second greatest disappointment. Every time I come to one of these events, you always ask me if I've burned down a house yet. You ask when I'm going to get married and start having kids and in the next breath, you're demanding I come work for you so you can make me put in twelve-hour days for apprentice pay. You demanded I date, then tried to drive off every male except the only one you ever approved of, Seb."

Daniel opened his mouth, but nothing came out. For the first time in her life, she watched her father be shocked speechless. It felt good to unload everything on him, things she'd only ever spoken with her therapist about. Things she never thought she'd have the courage to say to her father.

She might regret all this later, but for now she was going to revel in the moment.

"Thanks for thinking you could beat Seb up for me, but that's not going to be possible," she taunted him. "He's in prison now. The only reason he finally left me alone was because he found his next victim, except when she tried to leave, he shot her. But don't worry, he didn't hit her first."

Adrenaline was surging through her system, making it impossible to stand still any longer. She needed to get out of there.

"Can we leave now?" Pike asked, his arms squeezing around her.

"Yes," she agreed. "And we might not be coming back."

"Good," Kimble spat out, casting an evil look over her father and brothers. "No men here, only selfish little boys."

With that, the three of them turned and left with Kimble and Pike pressing in close on either side of her. It was awkward, but she couldn't have stood on her own.

It wasn't until they were in Pike's car and leaving her father's property that she spoke again. "I don't want to go home. I don't want to be inside right now."

Kimble made a noise of agreement as Pike slowed the vehicle. The two-lane road was deserted so there was no one to get upset as he came to a stop. The Caddy's engine rumbled unsteadily and belched out a few plumes of smoke. The car wasn't a fan of idling.

"What do you want to do?"

"I don't know," she answered. "My skin feels thin. It's hard to describe, but it's like every sound or light around me is sandpaper to my nerves. Can we go somewhere outside but without people? I think I need to be somewhere quiet with a lot of open space."

Pike blew out a soft breath, as if she'd hurt him. "Can we be there?"

"I need you there," she responded quickly. "You guys and the quiet are what I want."

"Then I know the perfect place," Pike said and put the car in motion again. "I promise it's just what you need."

**Pike**

Pike knew the route to Otay Open Space Preserve by heart. He'd spent a lot of time there with his family as a cub. He also understood the need to be in the quiet. It was something most shifters craved from time to time, especially if they hadn't worn their fur for a while.

As he drove, he used the rearview mirror to keep an eye on Cora nestled in the back seat with Kimble. She reminded him of someone suffering from shock. Perhaps in a way she was.

They'd been driving for half an hour, and she hadn't said a word. He couldn't stop thinking about what she'd revealed. She'd suffered a major trauma that had left some emotional scars.

Her reluctance to join souls made much more sense now. It wasn't only a fear that they wouldn't let her prioritize her family, as she'd said under Tobias's thrall, it was the fear that her family would side with the outsider against her!

He couldn't understand family members not listening to each other. Maybe being dismissive of another's pain was a human thing. Being a bouncer and barback taught him that humans could be very callous to each other, but he didn't expect it to happen within a family.

It was a relief to find his usual parking spot and he eased the old Caddy in among a small cluster of trees. Beyond those trees was a narrow footpath leading into Otay preserve. No sooner had he shut off the engine than Cora made an animalistic noise and pulled away from Kimble. She scrambled over the front seat to claw at the passenger door handle.

"Cora?" Pike was startled by her feral action and froze in place. Kimble managed to flow over the seats as she got the door opened and spilled out of the car. He was right behind her, picking her up from the rough ground and cradling her to his chest.

"Safe," he murmured. Cora went still in his arms and started sobbing.

Shaking off his paralysis, Pike fumbled his way out of the car and around the back. He stood in front of Kimble, unsure what to do. The vampire had lost the sunglasses and when their eyes met, he saw his pain and helplessness mirrored in Kimble's eyes.

Getting in close, Pike wrapped his arms around Kimble and Cora. They stood like that, letting Cora cry. Neither of them tried to stop her, she'd probably been holding all this in for a very long time. It was hard to stand there and do nothing, but Pike reminded himself that giving Cora the time to release everything was important.

When her sobbing started to quiet, Kimble spoke again.

"Safe," Kimble repeated. "I'll drain Seb. No more Seb."

Pike latched onto that idea. "Yeah, we can make sure he never comes near you again."

Cora shook her head violently enough to send black and purple tendrils flying into Kimble's face.

"He's in jail, won't be out for at least ten years."

"We keep you safe from family too," Kimble said, surprising Pike. "Fuck them."

"I wish," Cora muttered, sniffling. At least she wasn't sobbing anymore. The tears had slowed to a trickle, but it was still heart wrenching to see his strong human crying.

"I agree with Kimble, fuck them!" Pike said. "My family can be your new family. My mom is great, and my dad is a big softy."

That made Cora meet his gaze. "What did they say when you went to work at the bars and clubs?"

Her question confused Pike. "Say?"

"It's not prestigious work," she whispered, as if afraid she'd piss him off. He only grinned at her, relieved to understand the question.

"They didn't care." She looked skeptical so he continued. "Honestly, they didn't. Mom wanted me to do what makes me happy. When Kimble came into my life, they were excited for me but worried because, well…"

He trailed off, he didn't have to explain Kimble to Cora, she'd experienced it.

"How is that possible?" Cora murmured. "Our families always want more from us. That's what it means to be a family."

"That's what it means to be in your family," Pike countered. "Being part of my family means cheering everyone on as long as they're happy with life."

"We decide," Kimble said. He grumbled a little in another language, then found the words he was looking for. "We make the family we want."

"Yeah, we'll make all the rules for our family!" Pike agreed, putting his cheek against hers for a nuzzle. The smell of her tears hit him hard and suddenly his bear was pressing hard to get out. He gasped and pulled away, fighting his shift.

"Pike?" Cora cried out, struggling in Kimble's arms. "What's wrong?"

Hugging himself tightly, Pike backed away. He didn't want to scare Cora by shifting without warning.

"His bear demands control," Kimble explained, setting her on her feet. All her earlier distress vanished, replaced by concern for him.

"Pike, what can we do?"

"Forgive me," he begged before giving up the battle with his bear. The inner beast roared to life, ripping through him and taking over the body they shared. He felt his clothes shred from his body as his shape changed.

As with most shifters, the change was quick and painless. One moment he was a man and the next he was a massive black bear standing on all fours among the remnants of human clothing. The shift took nothing out of him. If anything, he felt energized as the world around him came alive with smells and sounds he wasn't able to access while in his human form.

His bear was ecstatic to have control and intensely curious about their human mate. Pike tried to hold the bear back, screaming at his animal side that they could frighten Cora and drive away their mate.

Except Cora looked fascinated. His bear rumbled with pleasure at the curiosity on her face.

"Oh, wow, you're big!" she exclaimed, standing still as bear Pike ambled up to her. "I looked up black bears, and you're almost double the size of wild ones. That must be a shifter thing, right?" She looked to Kimble for confirmation.

Kimble grunted and stepped around her to sink his long fingers into Pike's fur. "Touch," he urged her. She moved up to run a hand over Pike's head right between his round fuzzy ears.

If Pike could purr, he would have as both Kimble and Cora petted him. Confident that Cora wasn't afraid and knowing his bear would never hurt their mate, Pike let his human side slide into the background so the bear could take full control.

"Pike, you're adorable," Cora cooed, no longer crying. "Can I hug you? Can you even understand me while you're a bear?"

To answer her question, Pike pressed his nose under her arm, in a clear invitation for a hug. She wrapped her arms around his neck and squeezed with a happy sigh.

"Oh god, it's like you're the biggest most wonderful plushy toy ever!"

Pike was content to let her hug him for as long as she wanted, but Kimble had other plans. With a squeak of surprise, Cora was pulled away from him. Pike bared his teeth at Kimble only to go perfectly still when the vampire settled Cora on his broad, furry back.

"Kimble?" Cora said, her tone close to being afraid. "I don't know if this is okay with Pike. He's a bear, not a horse."

"We should walk," Kimble said simply and strode off in the wrong direction. Pike grunted a few times to get Kimble's attention then pointed with his snout in the correct direction.

Kimble grinned, his red eyes flashing with amusement. "Then you lead. I follow like good pet."

Pike took a careful step, very aware of Cora's small form straddling his back. She laughed and clutched handfuls of his hair to steady herself. Her laugh convinced him Kimble was brilliant!

After another few steps, he was confident Cora wasn't going to tumble off him. As he led Kimble down the narrow path into the preserve, Cora chattered about the magnificence of Pike's bear.

If she kept this up, he might never shift back to human!

The preserve was mostly covered in scrub brush and native grasses with the occasional tree. The moon was only a sliver and didn't provide much light for Cora, but Pike didn't have any issues. He knew every inch of the preserve, especially all the tastiest places. He'd show Cora all his favorite areas, or at least the closest ones. Maybe he could even convince her to try a bite of sedge grass!

Her human palate probably wouldn't like it, but a bear could dream.

**Cora**

"I think I'd like being a bear," Cora mused as she leaned forward until her chest was flat on his back, her arms and legs dangling down his sides. Pike's gait was slow and steady, so she had no issue balancing.

Pike gave a little curious grunt. She took it as encouragement and continued talking. "I like the idea of being this big and ambling around searching for roots and berries. I'd get to be covered in fluffy fur like you. I'd never have to shave or wax again. Honestly, I'm not seeing a downside."

Kimble was a silent figure, walking next to them, keeping a watchful eye on the surroundings. Her cell phone was in her pocket, and she made a mental note to set an alarm so they could head back long before sunrise. The last thing she wanted was for Kimble to end up a crispy critter.

"Paws are another bonus. If I was a bear, I wouldn't be able to use a cell phone so no one could call me and demand anything. That sounds pretty great, doesn't it? No worries or cares, just doing bear things without people around."

Pike paused and started to run his claws over a patch of grass. She leaned to the side to get a better look at what he was doing. When he'd uprooted a patch, he grasped the end of it in his mouth and swung the bundle at her. Clouds of dirt smacked her in the face.

Laughing, she slid off the side of him and wiped the grime off. Pike crouched down at her feet and looked up at her with apologetic, puppy dog eyes.

"Were you trying to hand me the grass?" she asked, still laughing. Pike nodded his big head, the grass still clutched in his mouth. Crouching down, she planted a smacking kiss on his snout.

"Thanks, but I don't think I can eat that," she said and rolled back until she was sitting with her legs crossed. "This is edible though."

She pulled a stalk of sour grass out and started chewing on one end. Pike backed up until he was sitting on his haunches and started chewing the grass in his mouth, the dirt clumped at the roots swinging wildly.

"Truly eat?" Kimble asked, looking worried and a little disgusted. Cora patted the ground next to her, and he sat with his usual grace.

"I only chew on it," she admitted. "But I could eat those dandelion leaves if I was hungry, they're safe too."

"How know?" Kimble asked.

Cora debated about telling them the truth. Might as well, they'd seen the worst already. "When I was a kid, I dreamed about running away. When I was about ten or eleven, I read a book about a boy who ran away to live in the wilderness because he felt too crowded with all his siblings. I thought I could be like him if I learned all about the wilderness around here. Throughout middle school, I studied Southern California ecology and wilderness survival. I've forgotten a lot of it, but I remember some of the plants. I was endlessly planning my escape."

"Did you?" Kimble asked. Pike had stopped chewing and was staring intently, as if he was deeply invested in the answer.

She made a face at the memory. "I did but it only lasted three days. I bedded down next to a red ant colony and got bit to hell and then had a reaction to the bites. I dragged myself home the next day. It's funny, I didn't think they would realize I was gone because it hadn't been that long. When I turned on our street, I saw a ton of people at the house. At first, I thought they were having a party."

She'd almost turned around and gone to her friend's house instead when she'd seen all the cars. She didn't want everyone to see her covered in bite welts.

"It wasn't a party. They'd organized the neighborhood into a big search. Everyone was so busy organizing the volunteers and sending people out and keeping track of areas that had been searched that no one even noticed me at first. I was getting the calamine lotion when Dad found me. I'll never forget the look of absolute relief on his face when he rushed to me. He cried. It was the only time I've ever seen him do that."

Pike lowered his body and stretched his neck until his head was resting in her lap. He was so warm and soft she couldn't help but curl herself around his bear noggin.

"I know Dad loves me," she whispered. "But his love is very controlling and can be harsh. I think everything would've been different if Mom hadn't died. Maybe Dad wouldn't have been so worried about losing one of us or so determined about keeping me in line. I don't know. It's pointless to think about. Dad is what he is and except for Caleb, all my brothers pretty much do as he orders."

"No excuse," Kimble grumbled, flashing his fangs with anger. "Abusive control isn't love."

"Says the vampire who carried me off without asking permission," she pointed out. She couldn't see Kimble's face, but she could hear the contrition in his voice.

"Sorry. Doing better. No kill father or brother!"

She laughed, feeling much lighter than she had in years. Her eyes still hurt a little from all the crying, but she felt light. It was as if she'd shed a burden she hadn't realized she was carrying.

She reached over and patted Kimble's thigh. "You're totally right, you're improving and that's important. They aren't even trying."

Kimble moved so his front was to her back, and his legs were stretched out on either side of her. "Will do even gooder," he promised as he leaned forward and embraced her. "Much gooder."

With a bear head in her lap and a vampire at her back, Cora let the rest of the world fade away. Maybe this time she had successfully run away from home. Unlike the boy in the book, she didn't need a falcon and a weasel, she got a bear and a vampire instead.

**Cora**

"Don't need," Kimble grumbled as Cora handed him another shirt.

"We're meeting Pike's parents tomorrow. Don't you want to make a good impression?" she asked.

"He's already met them," Pike pointed out.

Cora's mouth tilted in a stubborn line. "Then we should be making an effort to make a good second impression because I'll be there too."

It had been a week since the disastrous evening with her family. She'd spoken to Caleb but blocked everyone else's number. It was the first time she'd ever done that, and she thought it would be painful and upsetting. It was surprisingly satisfying and everything had been a lot calmer.

She hadn't realized until then how much chaos her family added her to life on a daily basis.

Trevor had tried to visit. When she ignored his knocking, he'd let himself in with a copy of her key she didn't know he had. Kimble had picked him up and pitched him out onto the quiet neighborhood street. The next day, she'd changed all her locks because everyone probably had a key.

Turns out she didn't need to bother. There weren't any more visits. She was relieved. She didn't plan to go no contact with her family forever, but she needed some time off.

"Yellow?" Kimble grumbled, staring at the shirt.

"It's off white, not yellow," Cora corrected and urged him toward the fitting room. "Go try it on. You can't keep wearing the same two shirts and pants forever anyway. They don't even fit you. We might as well get you some new items now."

Kimble handed the shirt back. "Blue."

Now they were getting somewhere. "You could've said that earlier when I asked what color you liked." She put the off-white shirt back and pulled out one in navy blue and held it out to him. "Here, how about this one?"

Giving in, Kimble accepted the shirt and headed into the fitting room. The door was closing when Cora tossed several pairs of jeans at him. "Try these too!"

She heard a grumble as the door snicked shut. Pike smiled at her as they waited for Kimble to show them how the clothing fit.

"This is great," he said, wrapping his arms around her from behind. It was the default position both men assumed the moment they were still for more than a few seconds at a time. The one who didn't get the position behind her would take one of her hands. Other people gave them looks but no one said anything. This was Southern California. They were more likely to get offers for sex parties than condemnation from a passerby.

"You like shopping?" Cora asked.

"I'm not big into shopping, but it's great that we're getting Kimble new clothes. He really needed them," Pike answered, leaning over to nuzzle his face into her hair. "You smell good."

She relaxed into his embrace. "You always say that."

"That's because it's always true."

The door to the fitting room swung open revealing a scowling vampire wearing clothing that didn't look like it was going to disintegrate at any moment.

Cora pulled away from Pike to get a closer look at the fit of the jeans. "You look great. Does it feel good?"

Kimble grunted and shrugged. That was probably the best she was going to get. Noting the size on the jeans and shirt, she stepped back. "Go ahead and change back."

Kimble looked relieved but didn't close the door. "Done?"

"We're done with clothes shopping, but there's one more store I want to visit." She bit her lip to keep from smiling at the look of disappointment on Kimble's face. The vampire was definitely a homebody and wasn't fond of going out in public. He absolutely hated places crowded with people.

His favorite curse to mutter when he was annoyed at the humans around them was *peasant*. Sometimes it was *foolish peasant*. Thankfully, he hadn't started any fights yet, probably because Pike was with them. They needed to work on Kimble's lack of public politeness, or he'd have to stay home on the evenings when Cora and Pike went out.

"One more stop, then home?" he asked.

"Yes, one more stop and then we'll go home," she agreed and heard Pike chuckle behind her when Kimble slammed the door shut.

After buying six of the same shirts in shades of blue and three pairs of jeans, they all piled back into Pike's car. She really needed to take Pike car shopping because the Caddy had been reluctant to start for the last few days. Pike promised he'd service the carburetor that weekend and it would run like new, but Cora had doubts.

Judging by the way the Caddy shuddered and clunked every time Pike put it in drive, it was clear the car also had doubts.

It didn't take long to arrive at their next destination, and Cora was delighted by the look of absolute joy on Kimble's face.

"Books!" he breathed, pressing his face to the window like a kid as Pike pulled into a parking spot.

"I noticed you'd read the few physical books I had," Cora commented as Pike got out and flipped the seat forward for them. "I thought about getting you an e-reader but decided you might like this instead. There are a few used bookstores we can visit some other time. Imani reads a lot too, and she's always swapping books with people. I bet she's got a collection we could—oh!"

Her words were cut off by Kimble picking her up and sprinting across the parking lot and into the building. Pike laughed and chased after them.

Cora liked to read the occasional book but nothing like Imani, or Kimble apparently! He made his way to the nearest row of books labeled fiction and started looking while still holding her. When he wanted to pull a book off a shelf, he turned to Pike and handed her over.

"You could've put me down," she laughed as Pike cuddled her to his chest.

"I like this better," Pike said.

Catching some side eye from one of the employees, Cora tapped his arm. "Put me down so I can look at the magazines. You stay with Kimble and keep him to one armload, okay?"

Pike put her down with obvious reluctance. "I can't promise anything."

Chuckling, she headed to the racks of shiny magazines and found the section on fashion. She'd flipped through several by the time Kimble and Pike appeared at her side, both of them loaded down with books.

Eyeing their burdens, she did a quick calculation in her head. "I think doing drugs would've been cheaper!"

Ignoring her words, Kimble set his books down on a nearby table and took the magazine out of her hands. "Fancy clothing?"

Embarrassed, she snatched it back. "I like pretty dresses and shiny outfits."

"Don't be defensive," Pike said, setting down the stack he was holding. "He was surprised. You are so practical, and you don't have any showy clothing at home. I don't think you own a dress or skirt. I didn't think you were interested in fashion."

"Sorry," Cora mumbled, rolling the magazine into a tight tube. "I want to wear gorgeous things like Imani does, but I'm not as pretty as her. I'd look like an idiot."

Kimble growled. "You beautiful."

Pike looked upset. "Both you and Imani are beautiful women."

Cora snorted. "Imani is tall and curvy, I'm short and built like a plank of wood. I don't have breasts, hips, or an ass, not to mention I'm ungodly pale. I could never pull off any of these dresses."

When Kimble scowled and Pike looked like he was going to protest more, Cora held up her hand to stop them. "I'm not putting myself down. I'm stating facts."

"The facts as you see them," Pike responded, sliding in closer to her and taking the magazine from her grip. "Kimble and I see very different facts."

Cora tried very hard not to be charmed. "You can't possibly tell me that I'm prettier than Imani."

Pike tilted his head. "Why do you think beauty is a zero-sum game? There is no winner or loser."

She blinked, surprised by Pike's words. "That's an enlightened view."

Pike gave her a shy smile. "I never found anyone beautiful before Kimble and you. For a long time, I thought there was something wrong with me and then someone suggested I was demisexual. That made so much sense to me and also made me realize that beauty, lust, and love can be different for everyone."

Cora put a hand on Pike's arm. "Have you had sex before us?"

Pike snorted out a laugh. "Of course I have! I haven't had many partners because I had a hard time coming, but I'm not totally inexperienced."

Cora let out a relieved sigh. "Thank fuck."

"Don't worry, you didn't corrupt an innocent virgin," he teased. Holding up the magazine, Pike's expression turned serious. "Cora, you're as beautiful as any of these women."

"Sure." Cora tried to look like she believed him then moved to distraction. "Are all these books for Kimble?"

"Except for that one," Pike said, pointing to a book on drawing.

"You draw?" Cora asked.

"Not yet," Pike answered with a boyish grin. "That's why I need the book."

"That's fair," Cora said with a chuckle. "If you boys are ready, then let's check out before Kimble has me buying the entire store!"

"There's one more place I want to stop at," Pike said as he gathered up all the books he'd set down. He was still holding the magazine and pulled it out of her reach when she tried to take it to put back. "I want that too."

He'd dropped the subject of beauty, so she let him include the magazine in the purchases. Loaded down with bags of books, they piled back into the Caddy, then held their breath while Pike finessed it into starting. Once it was clunked into drive, Pike drove the vehicle to a trendy outlet mall.

"My sister shops here a lot," he said after he'd parked and urged everyone to follow him. "She says they have the best selection."

Cora started feeling uneasy as Pike walked past several boutiques full of the latest fashions. "What are we shopping for?"

"Sparkles!" Pike declared as he opened a door and gestured for her and Kimble to follow. Cora went still in the doorway, blocking traffic and getting some curious glances.

"I don't want to go in there." She sounded like a petulant child, but that was better than sounding half panicked, which was how she felt.

"We don't have to," Pike agreed, but didn't move. "I'd like to point out that Kimble tried on outfits when you asked him to. It's only fair that you return the favor."

Kimble stepped up behind her. "I pick something," he whispered in her ear, his warm breath sending shivers down her spine. "I pick something for us. You wear it for us."

Cora's resistance melted. The idea that anything from this store would only be seen by Pike and Kimble made it sexy and fun instead of intimidating and potentially humiliating.

"Fine, but only one outfit," she agreed and let Kimble lead her into the store with Pike right behind them.

Cora was impressed with Kimble's ability to pick out items that fit her. She was in the third dress he'd insisted she try on and it fit her body as if it was made for her.

The one she was currently wearing was made of sparkly gold material that shimmered as she moved. The spaghetti straps left her shoulders and arms bare, drawing attention to her lean muscles. Far from looking flat chested and pale, the fabric draped over her to make her appear lithe and elegant.

This was the type of dress she'd always wanted to buy but never did.

The lighting in the dressing room was soft and flattering and helped Cora imagine what the dress would look like in a public setting. This was the kind of dress you wore to dance the night away at a club. Add a black shawl and it was perfect for a romantic dinner at a fancy restaurant. The necklace Kimble had given her matched the dress perfectly, almost as if the two had been designed for each other.

"Can we see?" Pike called out from the other side of the dressing room door. Cora looked at the door and clutched her hands together.

"Um, maybe," she whispered.

"Please?" Pike responded. She'd forgotten about his amazing hearing. "Kimble looks like he's ready to pull the door off to get to you."

Pike's warning made her smile and relax a little. These were her men; they'd never hurt her feelings. Opening the door slowly, she stared at the floor and waited for their reactions. When no one spoke, she looked up to find both men gazing at her intensely. Kimble with raw hunger, and Pike with admiration.

"You're perfect," Pike murmured, stepping inside the small room. He took both her hands in his and pulled her out of the fitting room. Letting go of one hand, he raised the other above her head and guided her in a slow pirouette. "You make this dress look amazing."

Kimble grunted in agreement. "Shiny is you."

Cora flushed from all the compliments. "It's not practical."

"Oh hun, you've got to get it," a woman standing next to a nearby rack said. She had a soft Texas accent and flawless ebony skin with tightly curled hair styled in a small afro around her head. She had several items draped over one arm and a massive purse hanging off the opposite shoulder. Her dark, friendly eyes sparkled with appreciation. "If I didn't know my wife would object, I'd talk you into joining us."

A wide grin unfurled across Cora's face. "Thanks."

"I'm only speaking God's honest truth. Now you get that dress and let these boys take you out for a nice evening. And if either of them makes you unhappy, you come find me." She fished around in her purse then produced a business card. "My name's Mama Monroe, and I'll give this bear and vampire a piece of my mind if they don't treat you right. You hear me, sweetie?"

Kimble glared at her. "Go away."

Mama Monroe wasn't intimidated by Kimble at all. "What are you, about 2500 years old? Don't get fussy with me, young man. I've dealt with tissue paper tougher than you."

Cora felt her mouth drop at the woman's bold words. Then Monroe raised an eyebrow, and her skin glowed slightly.

Pike looked wary as he tucked Cora under his arm and reached out to pull Kimble behind him. "Are you a cupid?"

"Well spotted," she said. "What gave it away?"

"Silver glow," Pike murmured. He didn't stop moving until they were several steps away. Cora noticed Kimble didn't resist

Pike's movement. That told her very clearly that Mama Monroe was a powerful creature. "Cora hasn't agreed to be part of Kimble's flock yet, but she loves us. Please don't take her away."

Mama Monroe frowned. "Why y'all always thinking we're going to steal your love? That's not how it works. We break bonds that were never meant to be, that's all. Your Cora is safe. And I don't like that cupid nonsense. We were around before that word, and we'll be around long after it's gone out of fashion."

"Yes, ma'am," Pike answered quickly. "I didn't mean to offend you. It's all I know you by."

"That's fair," she agreed, then turned her gaze on Cora. Monroe's expression didn't change, but Cora felt as if some weight was being pressed down on her. She sucked in a breath and found she couldn't look away from the woman's eyes. The way Pike and Kimble tensed told her they were experiencing something similar.

"Ah, that's good," Monroe cooed. "Not only is this a good match, but all of your souls have matched before."

Another woman appeared next to Monroe. She had long, light brown hair pulled up in a high ponytail. Her tank top and tight jeans showed off her heavily muscled body as she held up a shirt and shorts combo. "Honey, what do you think?"

Then she noticed the three of them basically huddled together in the dressing room. "M, are you scaring people again? We've talked about this!"

Monroe laughed and pulled the woman into her embrace. "I didn't mean to, Ellie. I was only making sure that sweet child knew she looked great in that dress. Then I gave her my card and the bear got a little fearful. That's all."

Ellie turned in Monroe's arms and took in Cora's dress. "Damn girl! You've got some nice muscle definition, you work out?"

The moment Monroe hugged Ellie, Cora was released from whatever magic had been weighing her down. She cleared her throat before answering. "Not deliberately, like at a gym or anything. My job's really physical."

"Nice!" Ellie said, then turned to look at Monroe over her shoulder. "If we're going to make dinner with Jo, we need to buy this stuff and get going."

"Oh, yes," Monroe agreed, letting Ellie go and snatching the shirt and shorts from her. "I'll get these for you and meet you out front. Tell these three they're safe, will you?"

Monroe bustled off, grabbing one more item off the rack as she moved to the cashier's station.

Ellie gave them a little shrug. "She means well, I promise. It's only that she can get a little enthusiastic when she sees soul mates. She's had to lose and find me so many times that it makes her sensitive to others."

"Uh, find you?" Cora asked.

"Her kind are immortal but only have one soul mate. Every time I die, she has to wait for me to be reborn and then hope she can find me before I die again. It's cruel but also beautiful in a way. I've gotten to fall in love with her thousands of times, and she swears every incarnation is new and different. She says the pain makes our time together all that much sweeter."

"That's nice for you two," Cora said, then winced once the words were out of her mouth. That was by far the stupidest thing she could have possibly said!

Ellie's smile didn't waver. She was probably used to people responding in odd ways. "You really need to get that dress. Then you guys should visit Sanguine over in the Gas Lamp district. They have the best drinks and all three of you will be able to enjoy something. Have fun! Please do everything I'd do!"

With a laugh, she turned and rushed off. Monroe was standing at the open door of the boutique with an indulgent smile on her face. The two of them linked arms and strode out of the store. Cora could've sworn that the moment they touched, both were glowing faintly.

"Woah," she whispered, relaxing against Pike. "I've had more interesting experiences after meeting you guys than I have my entire life, and that includes the time I almost accidentally joined a cult."

Before either of them could respond, the clerk came up to them. "Your friend paid for your dress," she explained, handing Cora a receipt and then handing her a soft pashmina shawl with jet black beading on the ends. "And this. You can wear it out or you can change."

Cora accepted the piece of paper and shawl. She wasn't about to chase down some immortal and demand to pay her back. It looked like she was getting a fancy dress today.

"I should probably change," she said, and the clerk started to nod, but Pike spoke up.

"Or you could keep it on," he said. "You know, the Gas Lamp district isn't very far, and I've been wanting to see inside Sanguine. Kimble could change into one of the outfits you bought him, and I've got a nicer shirt in the car. We could finish this date night in style."

Kimble nodded with enough enthusiasm to send his untidy hair flopping in his face. "Yes. Must agree."

Cora wasn't about to argue because she really didn't want to take the dress off. She looked at the clerk with a smile. "Got any shoes to match this?"

Pike and Kimble cheered.

**Pike**

Pike paused at the sign outside the exclusive bar.

*Sanguine*
We have the perfect drink
for every client

He'd never been here, but he'd heard about it from several other shifters. It had an enchantment on it so only creatures with magic could see it, which was why Cora was staring at the windows of the place with a frown.

"Cool name, but it looks abandoned."

Kimble chuckled and took her hand in his to lead the way inside, Pike following behind. Once she was inside, the enchantment no longer affected her. She came to a dead stop, her eyes wide as she took everything in.

The place had an old-world elegant feel to it with dark wood tables and plush overstuffed chairs everywhere. Pike made out everything despite the dim lighting, but Cora was probably unable to see much beyond the pools of light at each table and the bar itself. Almost all the tables were occupied and about half the seats at the bar. Pike could smell all kinds of creatures including at least one silkie. This was a popular place.

"Fancy," she murmured.

"We are," a masculine voice agreed cheerfully. They all looked at the man behind the bar. He was wearing a blood red button up shirt with black slacks. His loose, shoulder length hair was curled around his head in artful disarray.

It was the type of styling Pike had tried once in his teens and gave up within a few weeks. He didn't have the patience to put that much effort into his hair. He pulled in a deep breath  and smelled cat shifter, probably a mountain lion. That made sense, cats were all about grooming.

"You must be the throuple Ellie sent over," he said, waving them over to a small table at their right. "Have a seat, and I'll bring you some drinks."

"Wow, Monroe buys you a dress, and Ellie buys you drinks," Pike said. "I'd be jealous if I didn't know better."

Kimble moved over to hold a seat out for Cora. She blushed and demurely sat down. He could tell she felt a little self-conscious in the dress. By the end of the night, he was determined that she would understand how beautiful she was, in this dress or out of it!

Cora looked out the nearby window. "Why can I see everything now but when I was outside this place looked empty?"

"That's because I paid a lot of money to an entire coven to help keep this place hidden from the average human," the man said as he carried over a tray with drinks. "Welcome to the Sanguine. My name is Zan, owner and master mixologist. I've taken the liberty to bring our vampire friend a nice fresh vintage of 0+. For the bear, I got a hefeweizen with a hint of orange."

As he spoke, he set the drinks down. Kimble's blood was in an ornate crystal wine glass while Pike's beer was in the largest glass mug he'd ever seen.

So far, Zan had gotten their orders spot on, but a bear shifter and vampire weren't hard to guess. What would he choose for Cora?

"For the lovely human, I've brought a magic concoction of my own creation," he announced as he set her drink down. Cora's drink was some kind of colorful cocktail topped with several vivid ornaments.

Cora stared at it warily. "Magic?"

Zan laughed. "Magic because I make great cocktails, love. There's nothing but regular ingredients in that. Not a single speck of the supernatural, I promise."

Cora looked at him expectantly, so Pike leaned in and took a sniff. He smelled a lot of things, but none of it was magic.

"It's safe, but there is alcohol in there," he warned her.

"I can do one drink without falling asleep," she murmured, picking up the glass and holding it high over the table. "Cheers!"

He and Kimble quickly clinked their glasses with hers and took sips of their drinks. His beer was cold, crisp and refreshing and by the expression on Kimble's face, the blood was palatable.

After a small experimental sip, Cora made an appreciative sound and took a longer swallow. "Oh damn, this is good!"

Pike watched the drink disappear way too fast for the amount of alcohol he'd smelled. Oh well, he could carry her back to the car if necessary.

Zan brought over a bowl of mixed nuts, giving Pike a sly grin as he set it down. "Sorry, I don't stock roots or berries. I hope this will work."

He was gone before Pike could take a swipe at him. Damn cheeky cats!

Cora laughed and picked a Spanish almond out of the bowl, making Pike look closer and realize this wasn't average bar fair. In that bowl was a mix of expensive nuts including macadamia and pine!

It took some effort, but he kept himself from picking up the bowl and tipping the whole thing into his mouth. Instead, he was a well-behaved bear and pulled out a single Brazil nut and popped it in his mouth.

"Are we ever going to talk about Maksim Laske?" she asked. "Or are we going to pretend Tobias didn't know who you are?"

Cora's questions were so unexpected that Pike choked on his Brazil nut, and Kimble snorted into the blood he'd been about to sip.

"You remember that?" Pike asked after he'd cleared his throat.

"It took a while," she admitted. "Lots about that night are still fuzzy, but I clearly remember Tobias calling Kimble by that name. I didn't say anything before because we were so busy after missing work and then the fallout from the BBQ."

"We've had a couple of rough weeks," Pike agreed.

Cora didn't take her eyes off Kimble. "Things have calmed down, so I think we should talk about it."

"Not my name," he declared, staring at his glass.

"It's not your name?" Cora clarified. "Because Tobias is wrong or because you don't want to talk about it?"

"Not my name anymore," he amended. "Long life, lots of names. Maksim Laske was before. Kimble is name now."

"Vampires live long lives," Pike explained. "They often go through several name changes."

Cora nodded her head, but her brow was still furrowed. "Does that mean you don't want to remember who you were?"

Kimble set his glass down and sat back. He rubbed a hand over his face and sighed. "Yes and no. Want to remember but worried. What if no resources? What if no wealth?"

He mumbled more words, but they were an unintelligible mix of other languages and English.

"Hey," Pike said, reaching across the small table to put his hand on Kimble's arm. "I'm not with you for money. I love you. That doesn't come with a price tag."

Pike was shocked to see tears forming in Kimble's eyes. "Love you, *sloneczko*."

Cora leaned in close and wrapped an arm around Kimble's waist. "We can figure everything out, I promise. If the situation were reversed, would you abandon us because we weren't rich?"

"You won't share souls," Kimble pointed out. One tear fell from his left eye, leaving a sparkling, iridescent black trail down his face.

"That's because of my issues, not you," Cora said as she reached up with her free hand to touch his face. "Your tears are beautiful, but don't cry. I think I might almost be ready."

Pike felt excitement rolling off Kimble in waves at Cora's words. Pike was excited too, but cautious. "What changed your mind? Or started to?"

"I'm not sure," she admitted, resting her head against Kimble. The vampire shifted a little so Cora could nestle against his side. Pike resisted the urge to move his chair so he could be part of the cuddling. He didn't want to disrupt Cora's thought process.

If anyone deserved the time and space to talk out their thoughts and feelings, it was Cora.

"Talk to us," Pike urged. "You don't have to make sense, just put the thoughts out there."

"I never expected to get married," she admitted, her voice turning hard as she spoke. "I didn't want to be tied to another male. I already had so many wanting my attention. I never even let a guy move in with me. I think that was one of the reasons Seb fixated on me, I was a challenge. The truth is my family makes so many demands that I couldn't handle the idea of adding anyone else to my life."

"We are your mates," Pike said. "That means we'll feel when you're upset or unhappy. We won't add to your burden. We had a rough start, but there was a lot going on. Everything's getting better now."

"I know." Her simple statement was spoken in a flat tone, devoid of any reassurance. Pike wanted to press her to say more but wasn't sure that was the best idea.

Without moving her body away from Kimble, she picked up her drink and took another sip. It was almost empty, and Pike looked up thinking to order her some water, but Zan appeared at his side with another round of drinks. Before Pike could protest, he plopped them down on the table and left.

Cora looked at the fresh drink with appreciation and was quick to finish off the first one. "Tasty," she murmured after the first sip of the second drink. "Maybe even better than before."

"Alcohol makes everything taste better," Pike pointed out dryly. "It enhances all things except common sense."

Cora laughed. "Isn't that the truth. I remember when Dad got super drunk once and insisted on telling me all these stories about his wild days before meeting Mom. I think he scarred me for life!"

Pike chuckled, letting her change the subject. "I know the feeling. I walked in on my mom and dad once. They were fully naked and having sex in the garden shed."

Cora gasped. "No! How old were you?"

"It was last year!" Pike said, dramatically covering his eyes. Cora gasped, then laughed uproariously.

"Do you have any funny stories?" Cora asked Kimble, her eyes half open, and her body relaxed against the vampire.

"Many," Kimble answered with a mischievous smile. "But can't remember."

"Bad vampire!" Cora pulled away long enough to smack his shoulder before snuggling back up against him. "Such a tease."

They chatted, sharing funny stories and commenting on the unsuspecting humans passing by the bar's windows. Cora consumed her second drink slower than the first, but it was still too fast for Pike. He did get Zan to bring over some water but only got half a glass into Cora before she was closing her eyes and using Kimble to prop her up.

"I think it's time to head home," Pike murmured. The vampire nodded and easily pulled Cora into his lap. She mumbled something, giggled, then rubbed her cheek against Kimble's chest without opening her eyes.

"Are you all leaving my fine establishment?" Zan asked, stepping up and holding something out to Pike. He assumed it would be a bill but instead it was a small envelope. "That's for the little human. Druid magic cure for hangovers. I keep a few on hand for the rare occasion a human overindulges here."

Pike accepted the envelope and tucked it into his pocket. He had a little bit of cash from his last paycheck so he pulled that out and offered it to Zan. The shifter tucked his hands into his pockets and stepped out of reach.

"Nope! Ellie said to bill her for the drinks, and I would never go against her orders. Upsetting Ellie means making Mama Monroe angry. People who piss off Monroe don't get to live long lives."

There was no arguing with that.

"Thanks," Pike said, putting his money away. "Next time we pay though."

"Of course," Zan agreed. "Unless some other immortal with deity-like powers tells me not to take your money."

Chuckling at his own joke, Zan returned to his spot behind the bar. Kimble stood with Cora cradled against his chest. Pike moved to open the door for him, but Cora spoke up, freezing them both in place.

"I promise, I'm really thinking about it, every day," she said, without opening her eyes. "I only need my fear to listen to my heart because I want to be joined to you guys more than I've ever wanted anything."

It was the sweetest words he'd ever heard.

**Cora**

Rubbing her sweaty hands on her jeans, Cora took in the California ranch style house with a long front yard full of planters overflowing with blooming flowers. There was a gravel path from the sidewalk to the light blue front door. The color of the house and front yard set the property apart from all the other houses on the street with their almost uniform lawns and white, or off white, painted stucco.

Pike's parents had bought a house that looked like everyone else's and with a little paint and a lot of love had transformed it into a colorful oasis in a sea of uniformity.

In the dim evening light she could just make out the hillside beyond the house. It was a typical Southern California hillside covered in cacti and scrub brush. Being backed up to a wild area must have made the house expensive to buy and difficult to insure. Wildfires were a yearly problem, and Cora bet the fire a few years ago got close to this property.

"Everything okay?" Pike asked. His question made her realize she'd been standing there staring at the house for several minutes.

"Yup," she said, popping the P sound. "I'm great."

Pike raised an eyebrow. "You sound constipated."

Cora rolled her eyes as Kimble chuckled. "I might be a little nervous about meeting your family."

Pike took her hand in his. "Don't be, they're going to love you."

"Because you love me," Cora murmured.

Pike kissed the top of her head. "Exactly! Now you're getting it."

"Good bears," Kimble told her, then frowned. "Pike's parents are good bears."

Was Kimble implying someone wasn't a good bear, perhaps the sister? Before Cora could question him, Pike took Kimble's hand in his and pulled them up the gravel path to the front door.

He let go long enough to open the door then shouted, "We're here!" Then he pulled them inside and kicked the door shut with his heel. Unlike her father's place where all the furniture was on its last leg, sometimes literally, this living room had nice matching furniture but wasn't stuffy or pretentious. Unlike a few houses she'd been in, nothing felt "too nice" to sit on. It was the perfect combination of decorative and comfortable.

"David!" a deep feminine voice called out, then a woman who had to be Pike's mom appeared through an open door.

She was tall, at least six feet, with a solid build and shoulder length brown hair liberally streaked with gray. Her size would've been intimidating if not for the wide, welcoming smile on her face. She and Pike had the same kind eyes and open expressions that made you want to trust them immediately.

"Hi Mom! Cora, this is my mom, Christina, but everyone calls her Tina. And—"

Before Pike could finish his sentence, Tina rushed forward and swept Cora up in a bear hug. "I'm so happy to meet you!"

"Mom!" Pike shouted and pulled Cora away from her. "Cora's human, you can't just grab her like that!"

Tina clasped her hands together and took a big step back. "Oh dear, I'm so terribly sorry! Are you upset? I have a wonderful collection of honey in the pantry. And I'm fixing salmon for dinner with a lovely herb sauce."

"You mean I'm fixing salmon for dinner with an herb sauce," an immensely tall man said, stepping up behind Tina. He smiled at Cora and extended a hand over Tina's shoulder. "I'm Mark, but you can call me dad. We're so pleased you're here."

"Yes, you should call me mom," Tina said with an eager nod. She unclasped her hands to reach behind her and touch Mark.

Cora stepped close enough to give Mark a quick handshake before retreating to press herself against Pike. "It's nice to meet both of you."

"You're so tiny and cute," Tina murmured with a happy little smile. "The three of you will make the most adorable babies!"

"Mooom," Pike moaned. "What did I tell you on the phone?"

"It was a long list; do you want me to repeat it all?" she teased.

"Among the top two were no touching and no baby talk," Pike growled. It was obvious he was fighting a smile at his mom's antics. He looked down at her with a shrug. "I'm sorry, my parents are, um…"

Cora supplied the only word that fit. "Enthusiastic."

"The traffic getting here was a bitch. Do you guys have any cold beer? And I need a shot of something to go with it!"

They all turned to the door in time to see a woman dressed in cut off jean shorts, sandals, and a cropped tank top slam into the small house. Compared to the rest of the beefy Pike family, Lucy was strangely thin and lacked muscle.

As Cora watched, she dumped several bags on the floor, then ran her hand through her damp hair. Her top was damp too, and it looked like she'd been sweating. Maybe her car was like Pike's and the AC didn't work, but it was still strange because it was a cool evening.

Tina made an aggravated sound. "Lucy, what have I said about dropping your things wherever you feel like it?"

"Not to do it," Lucy drawled as she stepped forward, leaving the bags where they were. She wasn't as tall as Pike, but she was taller than her mother with her father's bright blue eyes, and her mother's generous mouth. But that's where the similarities ended. This woman had a hardness that put Cora on edge.

"Lucy!" Pike gushed and grabbed the woman in a hug before presenting her to Cora. "This is my twin. Lucy, this is my mate."

Lucy tried to smile, but it was tinged with disgust. "A human?"

Either Pike didn't hear the tone or chose to ignore it because he never lost his smile. "The most perfect human!"

Lucy gave her a smile that wasn't friendly and held out her hand. "Hello, Cora. Welcome to the family."

Cora slid her hand in Lucy's, then worked on not showing pain when the woman clamped down with far more force than necessary. This wasn't the first time Cora had played this game, and she had a trick of her own. Bringing up her other hand to cover Lucy's, she smiled widely and showed off her teeth.

"Nice to meet you," she said, using all the strength in her free hand to pinch a nerve in the back of Lucy's hand. With a little gasp of outrage, Lucy let go and tucked her injured hand against her chest.

"What the hell? That hurt!"

Cora pretended to frown in confusion. "Did I grip you too tight? I'm sorry, I didn't mean to. Sometimes I don't know my own strength."

With a growl, Lucy stepped into her personal space and loomed over her threateningly. Cora didn't back down. She was ready to duck and dodge a blow from the woman and answer back with one of her own. You don't grow up with six brothers without learning a thing or two about fighting.

What Lucy didn't know was that Cora's specialty was fighting dirty.

Strangely, Cora noticed the necklace Kimble gave her felt unnaturally warm against her skin. Most times, she wasn't even aware of the jewelry, but now it felt as if it was being heated from the inside.

She ignored it, unwilling to be distracted from her opponent. She shouldn't have been worried because Kimble was suddenly in front of her, shoving Lucy away.

"Son of a bitch!" Lucy cried out as she stumbled back, saved from falling on her ass by Pike's solid body.

"Easy," Pike said, pushing Lucy behind him while keeping his eyes on Kimble. "Lucy would never hurt Cora."

Cora doubted that. Lucy had fully intended to do some damage and it didn't matter that Cora was smaller and human. Pike's sister was the kind of person you didn't turn your back on.

Kimble let out a hiss and then picked Cora up and stalked into the kitchen.

"I could've handled it," Cora whispered to Kimble as he sat at the kitchen table and settled her on his lap. "But thanks for white knighting for me."

Kimble made a grumbly sound and pressed her head under his chin. "Trouble."

"Yeah, she is," Cora agreed, relaxing into his hold as the sounds of Pike, Lucy, Tina, and Mark talking in angry, hushed tones filtered in though the semi shut door.

"Both of you," Kimble said.

Cora ignored that and straightened up with alarm as the voices got louder, especially Lucy.

"I'm your fucking daughter! That human should leave, not me!"

There was the sound of something crashing and then Pike's soothing voice. "No one needs to leave, Lucy. If you'd calm down, we could all still have a nice dinner."

"I'm behind on my rent, my credit card is maxed out, your human tried to hurt me, and you want me to calm down!" Lucy screeched. "Fuck this, I'm out!"

The sound of a door slamming shut echoed through the small house and then silence.

"I guess that's one way to get her to pick up her things," Tina said in a tone so dry it could be born in the Sahara. "Now that the drama is over, let's see about dinner."

Cora eyed the honey jars Tina was setting on the table. They'd finished dinner, and Mark was putting together a tray of fruit for dessert. Tina going back for more jars of honey reminded Cora that she'd offered honey earlier in the evening when they'd first arrived.

Reaching over, she grasped Pike's shirt and drew him down so she could whisper in his ear. "What's with the honey?"

"We're bears," his mother answered, her back turned while she pulled out another dozen jars. "Any good dessert should have honey on it."

"I forgot you guys have really good hearing," Cora mumbled, letting go of Pike's shirt and focusing on one of the jars. She'd never seen so many types of honey and never knew they could come in a variety of colors.

"Most of these are local, but a few are from out of state," Tina said as she set down more jars, then took a seat herself. Mark followed with a massive tray of fruit all cut into bite-sized pieces. Unsure what to do, Cora watched as the family took up forks, speared pieces of fruit and dipped them in honey before eating.

"Huh," she said before trying it herself. "Woah!"

"Good?" Tina asked around a mouthful of honey slathered apple.

"Yeah," she agreed. She didn't plunge the entire piece of fruit into the honey like the rest of the bears did, but she tried several different jars by dipping only the tip of apple slices. It was a refreshing dessert she wouldn't mind having again.

"Do you guys do this with strawberries?" she asked.

Tina nodded her head. "When they're in season."

Throughout the meal, Kimble had sipped at the glass of blood Pike's parents had given him. They had a few bags of it tucked in the back of their fridge. They asked him several times if the blood was good or if they needed to heat it or add anything. The way Kimble responded with a smile and kind word told Cora this was a common routine for all of them.

When the platter was empty and their hands were sticky, everyone sat back with full bellies. No one seemed interested in moving any time soon, so Cora leaned against Kimble and debated about trying to undo the top button of her jeans because it was digging into her painfully full stomach.

Tina focused her gaze on Cora. "I can't tell you how wonderful it is to see Kimble doing better. I'm sure it's thanks to you."

Cora was quick to deny her assertion. "It's entirely Kimble, I swear. I'm only human, no magic here."

Tina chuckled as Mark spoke up. "I think she means that your influence is pushing Kimble to work on himself. Pike was too easy on him. My son is many wonderful things, but a hard taskmaster isn't one of them."

"Hey, Kimble needed love and kindness, not bullying," Pike protested.

"You're a pushover, David," Tina said with a loving smile. "If you ever have children, you're the parent they'll always go to when they've done something naughty."

Standing up, Pike grabbed the empty platter. "We will not talk about babies."

As Pike put the platter next to the sink and started doing dishes, Tina leaned over to whisper to Cora. "It's so easy to get a rise out of him."

Cora laughed, and Pike spoke up without turning around. "Mom, you should show Cora the backyard. Us manly-men will clean up the kitchen."

Tina gave Pike's back a fond look then nodded her head to Cora. "Pike helped me design and build the backyard. He's a genius when it comes to backyard or small space horticulture!"

Her enthusiasm was infectious and soon Cora was following Tina from plant to plant and nodding along as she explained all the intricacies of the garden. Cora didn't know much about gardening, but she knew enough to be impressed.

There were lantern style lights hung throughout the long and narrow backyard, allowing Cora to see everything despite the late hour. The first two thirds of the area was full of fruit trees, mostly citrus, with raised planters scattered among them. The last third was bare without even a weed growing. All around the perimeter of the yard were blackberries and raspberries growing up trellises.

"Is that fence ten feet tall?" Cora asked, eyeing the very sturdy cinderblock wall that enclosed the backyard. There was an equally tall and heavy wood garden door at the very back.

Tina straightened up from where she'd been checking an herb bed. "It sure is."

"It seems, um, tall," Cora commented.

Tina chuckled. "When we first moved in, there were humans on either side of us. We like to shift and forage in the backyard but couldn't risk anyone seeing us. We might have overdone it with the cinderblock but when David was little, he liked to rub his back on everything while he was shifted. We worried he'd knock down a regular wooden fence and go spilling into someone else's backyard!"

Cora could appreciate her concern. Even when he was young, Pike must've been a big kid.

"Then the high fence makes a lot more sense," Cora agreed.

"We have wolf shifters on one side and an adorable fox shifter family on the other, so it's not an issue anymore. Most of the neighborhood is made up of shifters now. It's nice."

That made Cora wonder how many of her own neighbors weren't what they appeared to be. She'd have to ask Pike to use his nose to sniff around and give her the tea on the people in her neighborhood.

Tina led her to the bare dirt area and explained all the things they planned to do there. Cora's mouth watered at some of the fruit producing trees and shrubs Tina named.

"You can really grow cherimoya here?" Cora asked.

"I'm part of a gardening group that focuses on all kinds of fruits that grow well here," Tina said. "In a few years, we'll have cherimoya, bananas, kiwi, and persimmons."

"I'm willing to help if I get to eat my fill later!" Cora offered.

"You're so tiny, could you even finish an entire kiwi by yourself?" Tina teased.

Cora almost answered with *I've managed to get your son's giant banana dick down my throat* but remembered just in time that this wasn't her family. The Pike's probably didn't make crude jokes like that.

Still, she'd have to remember to tell Pike later, he'd laugh!

Assuming the tour was over, Cora turned to head back inside when Tina put a hand on her arm to stop her. The woman's expression was pained, and Cora tensed. Was this when the real Tina showed herself and warned Cora away from her precious son?

"David is the most generous and kindhearted person I know," Tina began. "I'm not saying that because he's my son, I'm saying it because it's true. It's his best and worst quality. He'll refuse to see the bad in anyone unless they actually attempt to murder someone in front of him."

Cora pulled her arm away from Tina's light hold and braced herself for cruel words. "What are you trying to tell me?"

"I love my daughter, but she isn't always a good person. The way she acted tonight was typical and, I'm afraid, on the mild side for her. She's selfish and can be horrible when she doesn't get her way. David makes excuses for her, but the truth is she's manipulative and…" Tina's voice trailed off as she held up her hands and shrugged her shoulders.

If anyone understood dealing with a difficult family, it was Cora. She could empathize with Tina's sense of guilt even as she admired her for the honesty.

"Consider me warned," she said, stepping into Tina's personal space and holding out her arms for an embrace. Tina's face lit up, and she picked Cora up in a giant hug.

Cora felt her feet leave the ground at the same time she heard Kimble's warning growl. "Gentle."

It wasn't a surprise to find Kimble had silently followed them into the garden. Tina probably knew he was there all along.

Tina made a *pfft* sound. "Calm yourself, Kimble. I'm always gentle. Besides, I can tell our Cora here is a damn tough human."

"True words," Kimble commented as he stepped up and pulled Cora from Tina's embrace. "We go home now?"

After he set her down, she patted him on the chest. "Let's go in and talk to Mark and Pike first."

"You did very well on this visit, Kimble," Tina praised before looking down at Cora. "Don't worry about leaving early, meeting new people can be exhausting! We'll see all of you again next week, yes?"

"I'd like that," Cora said without thinking, then realized it was the truth. She was looking forward to spending more time with Tina and Mark. Their calm, easygoing life was a sharp and welcome contrast to the chaos of her family.

Something inside her clicked, and her mind felt peaceful and calm. Something about this night and meeting the people who'd raised Pike helped quash the last of her fears.

She was ready to be flock.

**Kimble**

Cora had a far off look on her face and was silent the entire ride home. Pike tried to get her to talk several times, but she would hum or nod instead of answering. Kimble didn't like it. What was she thinking about that had her basically ignoring Pike, especially after visiting his family?

It wasn't possible that Cora didn't like Pike's parents. They were incredibly generous and loving people, even by black bear shifter standards.

Was it Lucy?

Cora hadn't seemed intimidated by Pike's volatile sister, but then again, Pike hadn't reprimanded Lucy either. Maybe Cora feared Lucy would hurt her when Pike wasn't around. Kimble would have no problem popping the woman's head from her body.

She used to call Pike all the time, demanding money or asking him to call in favors. He'd burned a lot of bridges to get her jobs or out of trouble and only stopped giving her all his cash when Kimble's life was at stake.

Cora might not realize Kimble had no problem with ending Lucy's life to protect his flock, even if it would upset Pike. He needed her to know she was safe from Lucy but couldn't say those words within Pike's hearing.

"You're safe, always," Kimble murmured, hoping she'd get the hidden meaning.

She hummed again and snuggled closer to him but didn't take her eyes off the passing scenery. She probably hadn't even heard what he'd said. Should he try again?

No, he'd wait until Pike wasn't within hearing range and then bluntly tell her Lucy wasn't a problem.

Maybe he should slip out one night and take care of her. It would be days or even weeks before anyone realized she was missing, and he could make sure there wasn't a body left to find.

It would be impossible to lie if Pike asked him directly, but it was unlikely sweet Pike would think to ask out right if Kimble had killed his sister. Their bond allowed for lies of omission.

The idea was gaining traction in his head when Pike pulled up to Cora's little house. Kimble was pleased to see the place. Pike's apartment had been a shelter but not a home. Cora's house felt like a home to him.

As Cora slowly climbed from the car with an oddly serene expression on her face, Pike exchanged a confused look with Kimble. It was good to know Pike noticed Cora's strange mood also.

"Anyone interested in an evening stroll?" Pike asked. "It's a pretty night."

Cora didn't say anything. She took their hands in hers and led the two of them into the house. Normally, she liked a short walk in the evenings, so what was going on?

Once inside, she walked them to the middle of the living room. They still hadn't replaced the coffee table he'd broken so there was a good amount of room for the three of them to stand in a small circle.

Finally her expression changed. A slow, confident smile curled her lips as she looked from one to the other. "I'm ready."

"Ready?" Pike repeated, as puzzled as Kimble was.

Before Cora could answer, it dawned on Kimble what she was saying. "Souls?" he questioned.

She looked at him, her gaze bold and confident. "Yes."

On the rare occasions he'd thought about this moment, he'd expected to feel jubilant. Instead he felt cautious and even a little insecure.

"Because of Pike's family?"

She tilted her head and regarded him curiously. "They're part of it, but also you."

A small hint of excitement filtered through his worry. "Me?"

"You got better without me," she explained. "I mean, I was here helping to keep you alive when you did something dumb, but after that, you focused hard on remembering how to talk and keeping control of your protective instincts. I don't need jewelry or shit like that. I need people I can depend on. People who aren't going to use me to prop them up."

Pike made a pained sound. "No, never."

"Meeting your family made me realize how dysfunctional my family is," she whispered, a frown breaking through her serene happiness. "It was the final piece I needed. Eventually, I'm going to start talking to my dad and brothers again, but you can help me keep perspective when they start spewing crap. At some point, or many points, they're going to need my help, and I'll have to help because they're family. With Kimble getting so much better, I can trust him not to massacre one of my brothers when he acts like a colossal dick."

"Still might bite them," Kimble murmured, relief at Cora's words making him feel lighthearted.

"A few bites are fine," Cora agreed, then an evil grin took over her face. "Hell, some blood loss might make them easier to deal with."

A bark of laughter came out of him. Cora and Pike chuckled at his laugh, then she spoke again.

"My fear is gone, and my heart wants this. I promise I'm ready."

"No pain," Kimble promised. He was far more controlled now than when he'd first found Pike and knew he could do this exchange without causing her any discomfort. He let go of their hands and moved Pike and Cora until they were facing each other, hands clasped between them.

"Be still and focus on Pike. Breathe together."

Kimble could see a little worry in Cora's face, but also confidence. Kimble moved to stand behind Cora and drape his arms over her shoulders so he could join his hands to theirs but also press his front to her back.

Closing his eyes, he focused on finding her soul. It was bright and lively, full of yellow, orange, and red hues. She was so beautiful it took his breath away. Slowly and with great care, he tugged a piece free but didn't pull it from her body. He left it there and focused on his soul.

"I feel weird," Cora murmured. "Like something is loose inside me."

"It's part of the process," Pike assured her. Kimble ignored their conversation as he separated a piece from his soul and moved it into Cora. The moment it was near her pulsing soul, his piece sped ahead of him, like a magnet near another magnet. It hit with a little more force than he wanted, but Cora didn't wince or cry out in pain.

Pulling in a sharp breath, she looked around the room. "Oh, wow, everything seems brighter."

Pike explained that the process gave the flock some advantages they didn't have before. He helped distract Cora as Kimble did the most dangerous part of the process: pulling the piece of Cora's soul out. Like their bodies, human souls were more fragile than vampires or shifters.

He took his time teasing her soul from her body and into his own. When he pressed it into the pulsing red of his soul, the colors mixed and melted until his entire soul was a slightly lighter shade.

He only got a moment to enjoy the feeling of being whole with both his flock's souls secured to him when a tidal wave of memories hit him. He was pulled under. Unable to speak, he felt his entire body jerk, then go numb. He lost all control of his body, and the last thing he was aware of was Cora screaming and the sensation of falling.

"You exchanged souls and then he fainted?" a familiar voice asked. Kimble lay still, unsure how long he'd been unconscious. His brain was a mess of memories that weren't layering themselves in any specific order. The screaming face of a woman dressed in clothing three centuries out of date felt as fresh as the memory of Cora wearing the glittering gold dress Mama Monroe bought for her.

He heard Cora make an aggressive sound and then declare loudly, "I said that already!"

"Then there's nothing I can do," Tobias answered. The way his voice sounded off told Kimble he wasn't in the room but on speaker phone.

"Are you sure?" Pike asked. "This isn't like when he passed out exchanging souls with me. He's fed and strong now. Shouldn't he be able to do this without going limp?"

"Theoretically, yes," Tobias agreed. Then he sighed, long and heavy. "Most vampires don't recover from going feral, so I don't know what is or isn't common."

"But he isn't feral anymore," Cora argued. "He talks and everything now."

"Don't lie to yourself, Cora," Tobias cautioned. "He's still in the recovery phase. Until he has his memories back, he's considered feral. At least now that he's got a flock, it's unlikely anyone would bother hunting him down. Flocks stabilize even feral vampires."

Kimble listened with half an ear as he let the jumble of memories settle into a semblance of order. When he had a basic time frame for them, he opened his eyes to find Cora and Pike kneeling on either side of him. It was both a familiar and disheartening position. He hated that he'd caused them worry again.

"I'm fine," he said, sitting up and rubbing his face.

"Kimble!" Cora cried and launched into him. She wrapped her arms and legs around his body and squeezed tightly. "Fuck, I thought you were dying again. Don't ever scare me like that! *Ever!*"

Kimble hugged her back and looked up at Pike. The bear's face was pale, and his eyes were round with worry. "Are you still you?"

"I'm fully me," he assured the shifter and let go of Cora with one hand, holding it out to Pike. His bear grasped his hand with both of his large ones and pressed it to his cheek. Pike's slight stubble felt good against his palm.

"I'm sorry I scared you," Kimble whispered. He regretted the way everything came back to him, but it felt good to no longer need to hunt down every word he wanted to say. There were so many languages he knew, modern English being the most current one he'd learned, so it was the hardest to remember while he was feral. Now all the words simply flowed to his mouth without the need to concentrate. "I didn't know that was going to happen."

"What happened?" Pike asked. "Why did you fall down like that?"

"I know who I am," Kimble said and felt Cora jolt in his arms at the same time Pike's eyes blinked in surprise.

"Your memories are back?" Pike asked.

"They are, *sloneczko*. If it's not too late, there's a place I'd like to go," Kimble said. "Would both of you please take me there?"

As both Pike and Cora made sounds of agreement, he noticed a phone still lit up with an active call.

"It seems I'm no longer needed," the dry voice of Tobias commented.

"No my friend, you're not," Kimble agreed.

"Good luck to you," Tobias said, and the phone went blank.

Kimble didn't think he needed luck anymore, which was probably a good thing. He must have used up his allotment of luck while he'd been feral. Now it was time to rely on his cunning and power as a good vampire should.

**Pike**

Of all the places he expected Kimble to direct him, the east side of Palomar Mountain wasn't it. As he drove the dark, winding, rural road, Pike watched for wildlife or shifters out having a good time. This was the kind of area both could be found in large numbers.

Behind him, Cora continued to quiz Kimble on his past. She'd started asking questions the moment they'd gotten in the car and hadn't stopped since.

"What's the earliest thing you can remember?" she asked.

"You've already voiced that question," Kimble reminded her. He'd been patiently answering everything to the best of his ability while hugging Cora to him. "I'm not sure which memory is the oldest, they're still forming themselves into a cohesive timeline."

"Right. But give me an example of a really old memory," Cora pressed.

"I have a vivid image of my maker," Kimble answered. "She was beautiful, but the moment you spent any time with her, you'd realize the beauty covered a rotting core."

Words poured out of Cora. "What did she look like? Why did she decide to turn you? When was this? Do you remember anything before being turned? Do you remember what it was like to eat food? What—"

"Cora!" Pike exclaimed, feeling pressured even though Kimble didn't seem to mind. "You're acting like you're in grade school! Pick one question and give him a chance to answer it."

Kimble laughed. "I don't mind Cora's questions. Both of you spent so much time without any knowledge of my past that it's only fair that I answer everything to the best of my ability."

"Pike's right," Cora said with a wry smile. "I'm acting like a kid. How about we sit down one evening, and you start telling us about your life when you're ready? I can be patient if I know the story's coming."

"I would enjoy that immensely," Kimble agreed. "If possible, I'd rather not talk about my maker. She was a deeply unpleasant person who hurt me badly."

Cora made a pained sound, and Pike wished he could reach back and embrace Kimble. "When we get to where we're going, I want to hug you."

"I'll accept every kiss, hug, or touch you wish to bestow on me," Kimble agreed.

They'd been driving for over an hour, and Pike still couldn't get over the change in Kimble. Not only was he speaking normally, but his speech pattern and vocabulary was that of a well-traveled and educated person. Pike hadn't met that many vampires, but he'd been told that it was common for the older ones to sound like college professors.

Kimble's improved language skills wasn't the only thing that had changed. He carried himself differently now. Before, he'd always seemed uneasy, even when they were inside his apartment or Cora's house. When they'd go out, he would watch the world around them as if an attack was imminent. Pike never saw him relax apart from when the sun forced him to.

Except maybe after sex, but even then, he wouldn't rest easy for long.

Now Kimble was practically lounging in the back seat of the Caddy, back resting against the side of the car, one leg stretched out across the bench seat and Cora tucked securely against his body.

It made Pike think Kimble was used to being chauffeured around. For the first time, Pike got a slightly uneasy feeling. It hadn't bothered him that Kimble had a life before because the vampire couldn't remember it. Now that he knew who he was, Pike worried he wouldn't fit into Kimble's world.

Pike hadn't even attended the last year of high school. He'd hated the way the other kids teased him for his size, and some would even try to pick fights to show how tough they were. His mom helped him test out early so he didn't have to do his senior year.

He wasn't a big reader, like Kimble, and he wasn't a skilled tradesperson with his own business like Cora. Despite his tall stature, Pike felt small compared to his lovers.

A warm hand landed on his shoulder and squeezed. "I can feel you fretting, but don't. You're perfect, *sloneczko*. You were perfect when I found you, and you're perfect now."

As Kimble said the words, Pike felt a warm rush of love push through their bond. Before, the best Kimble could do was press his anxiety on Pike. Now he could share all kinds of emotions including the one Pike needed the most.

"Were those Pike's feelings?" Cora asked.

Kimble kept his hand on Pike's shoulder, massaging the muscle there as he spoke to Cora. "What did you feel?"

"I got suddenly worried about being good enough and felt like I wasn't worthy."

Mortification made him glad he was alone in the front seat. "Sorry. I'll try not to bleed my emotions onto you over our connection."

"That isn't what you should be apologizing for," Kimble admonished.

"It's still there, maybe even a little stronger now," Cora said. "Pike, how can you feel embarrassed or as if you're less than either of us? You're the best of us. Anyone can learn shit; you are naturally kind and caring. That's damn near impossible to learn!"

"She's correct," Kimble said, sending him another wave of tender emotions. "You've proven to both of us over and over again that you have no end of patience and love. Someone as pure in heart as you are is rare. You're a treasure."

Cora's hand landed on his other shoulder. "You're the best bear a girl could have."

His worry didn't completely vanish with their words, but most of it dissipated as he felt Cora and Kimble's honest adoration of him come through their link.

"Here," Kimble called out suddenly, startling Pike into slamming on the brakes. The Caddy screeched to a halt with groans from the frame and ancient suspension. A glance over his shoulder showed that Kimble had kept Cora secure against him during the sudden stop.

"Damn, we can always turn around, no need to make Pike park in the road!" Cora grumbled.

"Now it is I who is embarrassed," Kimble said, giving Pike's shoulder one more squeeze before letting go to point out the window. "I'm sorry. My excitement at being home got the better of me. Please turn into that drive on your left."

Pike slowly nosed the car around until he was on the road Kimble indicated. There were several signs declaring the place private property and warning people not to trespass. No sooner had he passed the second set of signs than he started smelling wolf shifters. Lots of wolf shifters!

"Are you sure we're in the right place?" Pike asked. "I don't want to upset a wolf pack by entering their territory without permission."

"Are we talking about real wolves?" Cora asked.

"Shifters," Pike answered.

"They won't hurt either of you," Kimble promised.

"Should we call someone?" Pike asked, slowing the car to single digit speeds. "We should really contact the pack's alpha. Good alphas are protective of their people."

"I know the alpha," Kimble said, then his voice lost a little confidence. "Or I knew the alpha of this pack. I've been feral for a few years; I hope she's still in charge."

That didn't give Pike any confidence at all. The car was going so slow that when he lifted his foot off the gas pedal, it rolled to a stop almost before he touched the brake.

"I won't go any further," Pike declared. He didn't want to go against Kimble, but he couldn't risk getting attacked by a large wolf pack in their own territory. The drive had trees on one side and large rocks on the other, making it impossible to turn the large car around. He was going to have to back up. Finessing the Caddy into reverse, Pike put an arm on the seat to help look through the back window and almost yelped in surprise.

Standing right at the Caddy's rear bumper were half a dozen people, their angry expressions well-lit by the bright reverse lights.

"Oh shit!" Cora cursed, giving voice to Pike's startlement. "Where did they come from?"

"What are you doing in our territory, bear?" a person shouted from the front of the car. They looked forward to see seven more people gathered there. A round woman glared at Pike through the windshield, her eyes glowing with power. This had to be the alpha.

"Annette!" Kimble called out, a wide smile on his face.

Annette's mouth dropped open, and she put both hands on the hood to lean forward. "Maksim?"

"Yes," Kimble said. "I've returned."

"Is it really you?" Annette cried out as whispered conversations broke out among the other shifters.

She marched around the car and rapped on the window insistently. Pike rolled it down and then was forced to lean away as Annette pushed most of her body into the car. She took a few deep breaths while staring at Kimble intensely, as if searching his face for answers.

"It is you," she whispered. Her face rapidly went through a bunch of emotions: surprise, pain, relief, and finally impatience. "It's about fucking time you got back!"

**Cora**

Cora's first impression of the wolf pack, once they got the Caddy parked and everyone inside, was friendliness.

There were roughly fifty people in the pack and about half of them lived on the Palomar Mountain compound with the rest visiting on a regular basis. The building Annette led them into reminded Cora of Caleb's dorm. The first floor was mostly an open floor plan with a large industrial-looking kitchen at one end and the rest of the space full of tables, chairs, couches, and TVs in various configurations. Unlike Caleb's dorm, this place was tidy with the only mess confined to a small area scattered with children's toys.

Kimble radiated happiness as he took it all in. "I remember all this."

"Half the rooms are empty because we've sent the last of the teenagers to college," Annette explained with a wave of her hand to indicate the upstairs. "All the cabins are full, and two of our families are expecting cubs soon."

"The pack is healthy under your leadership, Annette," Kimble praised.

Annette blushed. "As our benefactor, you're responsible for our prosperity as well. We were a struggling pack of ten when you first took us under your griffin wing."

"That was many years ago," Kimble said with a dismissive gesture. "The pack has paid me back tenfold over the last century. Besides, I probably wouldn't even have a home right now if it wasn't for this pack. You have my deepest gratitude and a promise to reward all of you properly."

"Did he say century?" Cora asked Pike. She tried to whisper but realized too late that everyone was going to hear her no matter how quietly she spoke.

All eyes turned to her, and she pressed back against Pike. "Um, I'm sorry if my question wasn't appropriate or something. This is all kind of new to me."

"We're happy to help you learn," Annette said without a trace of mockery. "Maksim and my great-grandfather made a Blood Pact. He let the pack live on his land and provided shelter for our human forms. In exchange, we kept him safe during the day. It used to be a common exchange between packs and vampires, but unlike other vampires, Maksim never took advantage of us. He paid us wages, paid for our children to attend the schools of their choice, encouraged us to open businesses, and even wished anyone well if they wanted to leave. I remember the day my beloved uncle, the old alpha, died."

Annette turned to face Kimble. "You cried for him."

"He's cried for all of us," someone else said. "He's been at the bedside of almost every dying wolf."

"I've loved all of you as family," Kimble said, his voice thick with emotions. Cora felt a little jealous of all the history these people had with the man she'd always seen as alone in the world except for her and Pike. The addition of this wolf pack was going to take some getting used to.

Annette looked like she was ready to shed some happy tears. "How could we not love the vampire who mourns like a wolf?"

Then she flung herself at him in a hug. Kimble started to hug her back but to Cora's absolute shock, Pike growled and moved past Cora to pull the alpha off Kimble.

"My vampire!" Pike said, stepping between her and Kimble. Seeing Pike's blatant possessiveness made Cora feel a little better about her own insecurity.

Kimble wrapped his arms around Pike's middle and hugged him tightly. "Be at ease, *sloneczko*. This pack is like a family to me. As with your parents, they want me to be happy and that means adding you to their lives."

Annette's eyes moved from Pike to Cora before settling on Kimble. "Are they your flock then?"

"Yes," Kimble answered, and there was no mistaking his pride. He stepped around Pike and held out his arm to Cora. Once they were standing on either side of him, Kimble addressed the gathering crowd.

"Meet Cora Walsh and David Pike. My human and my bear. My flock. Treat them as you would treat me."

Everyone clapped and cheered. Annette smiled and greeted Cora and then Pike with the same words.

"Welcome to the Laske Pack. It's good to have you home."

**Kimble**

Annette insisted that he walk the grounds and greet everyone who hadn't been in the room. It was how a wolf would treat the return of a long absent pack member, and Kimble couldn't refuse. Memory after memory piled on top of each other of every birth and death in this pack over the last hundred plus years. He couldn't refuse a request as simple as letting everyone see that he was alive and well.

By the time they finished greeting everyone, Cora looked exhausted, and Pike seemed overwhelmed. Kimble didn't think it was because of the walk itself.

No, it was more likely that his human and bear hadn't been prepared for any of this. He hadn't warned them because he'd been afraid that they'd arrive to find the place abandoned. He'd been so scared that he couldn't bring himself to even say the name of the pack.

Now that he saw the pack thriving, he wished he'd told his flock more about what they were getting themselves into. Honestly, he should've put off the reunion for a day or two, so he could make sure Cora and Pike had no cause to be jealous or insecure about his relationship with the wolves.

"I'm going to inform everyone who isn't living here that you're back," Annette said. "They'll probably rush here as soon as they can, maybe even tonight. Some might already be on their way; I saw a lot of texting going on."

As he watched, Cora blinked several times as if she was trying to clear her vision. It was a sign that she needed to rest. Cheerful, gregarious Pike hadn't said a word since the introductions had started. He needed to get his flock alone.

"Can you ask them to wait until tomorrow night?" Kimble asked. "I promise I won't disappear again."

Annette chuckled. "They won't like it, but I'm sure they'll listen to me."

He didn't want to drive all the way back down the mountain to get back to Cora's house. Hopefully, the pack hadn't given his place away to one of the families. "Do I still have a house here?"

"Of course, Maksim!" Annette exclaimed. "Right this way."

She pointed down a path, and Cora and Pike started walking. Kimble and Annette fell in-step behind them. Several other wolves took up lead positions in front of their group, falling into a familiar pattern Kimble remembered fondly. His pack had always been so protective of him, even though he was the most powerful creature most of them had ever met.

A wolf stepped up next to Annette to address him. "We've kept your house clean and even re-treated the windows last month. I called in an order for blood, so we'll be able to fill the fridge for you."

"Thank you, Dylon," Kimble said, making the young man beam with pride.

Annette touched Dylon's arm to get his attention. "Pike and Cora will need real food. Can you see that the kitchen is stocked for them?"

"Sure!" he said and sprinted off. The last time he'd seen the young man, he'd been a teenager. How many years did he spend feral?

"You disappeared five and half years ago," Annette murmured. She'd always been good at answering questions that hadn't been asked yet. Moving his eyes from the man's retreating back to Annette, he noticed more gray in her hair and fine wrinkles around her eyes. She'd always been wise beyond her years, but now she had an air of calm resilience. It must have been a struggle while he was gone.

"I'm sorry," he said. Cora and Pike joined hands as they walked ahead of them. Cora's movements were slowing, and he could see that Pike was resisting the urge to pick her up. "After these two have settled into life here, I'll make a formal apology to everyone. I let the pack down."

Annette snorted out a derisive sound. "There's nothing to apologize for. You didn't abandon us. You went feral."

"The result was the same," Kimble pointed out.

"No, it wasn't. As a feral vampire, you managed to find your flock and come back to us. Now we get to have you and Cora and Pike as part of the pack. It was hard without you, but five and half years is nothing. I'd rather you go missing for triple that and come back than die because we kept you from searching for your flock."

Kimble went quiet as he digested her words. Had he needed to go feral to find Pike and Cora? Was it being in a state of almost pure instinct that allowed him to home in on Pike and then rescue Cora?

He'd never know, but he'd be forever grateful that fate worked in his favor.

**Cora**

The last time Cora had felt this overwhelmed was when she'd started Perfection Connection Electrics. Every night she'd fall into bed exhausted both physically and mentally. Today was worse.

Stumbling over her own feet, Pike's hand on her kept her from a painful fall to her knees. That was the third time it happened. She didn't normally have such trouble simply putting one foot in front of the other.

"Thanks," she mumbled, giving Pike's hand a squeeze once she was steady on her feet again.

"Cora?" Kimble asked from behind her. Before she could say she was fine, Pike picked her up.

"I can walk." Even to her ears her words lacked any conviction. It felt good to be held by the bear. For some reason, she felt cold even though the night wasn't that chilly, and she was wearing a jacket. Being cradled against Pike's warm, muscled chest was immensely comforting even if it made her look like a weak human in front of Laske Pack.

"Please let me carry you," Pike whispered, nuzzling his face against the side of her head. "Suddenly Kimble doesn't need me anymore, and you never needed me. I need to feel useful."

Kimble appeared at their side. His vampire speed had been fast before but now he seemed to appear out of thin air like magic.

"Are you well, *kochanie*?"

"I think Cora needs a break," Pike said. "All of this is a lot to take in."

She could feel Pike's need to be alone also. She let him use her as an excuse, this time.

"Of course," Annette said. "We're almost to Maksim's house, it's right over there," she said, pointing past an old-fashioned barn. "Once all of you are inside, we'll leave you alone until tomorrow night."

"If you would please call me by my new name," Kimble requested as he curled an arm around Pike's lower back and walked with them. "Pike gifted me the name, and I like it. It's fitting I have a new name for a new era."

Annette didn't blink at the request. "Of course. I'll let everyone know. Will you keep your current last name?"

"I don't know yet," Kimble said, putting a hand on Cora's leg so he was touching both her and Pike. "I might take the name of my flock, but we haven't decided that yet."

It was a sweet thing to say, but Cora didn't have it in her to care at the moment. The three of them were surrounded by about twenty people, all friendly but also loud and noisy. It was like being at one of her family's BBQs but surrounded by strangers.

"Here we are," Annette announced as they rounded the barn. Cora had expected a grand chateau or at least some kind of large, opulent house. Instead, she was faced with a medium sized, single story Spanish style house. It was nice, but nothing like what she expected.

"Come, my flock," Kimble said, urging them up the short flight of stairs to the porch. A wolf was already there, opening the door for them and shutting it as soon as they were inside. The change in sound was notable. The house must have amazing soundproofing because the moment the door shut; she couldn't hear anyone outside.

"The house has four bedrooms so each of you can have your own personal space," he explained as he guided them toward the back of the house. "My bed is only a king, but I'm sure Annette is already rushing home to search for a larger, custom-made bed for all of us to share. We'll probably have something new within a few days."

Cora could feel the tension in Pike's body ease now that they were alone. Neither of them talked as Kimble told them the history of the property and why he decided to settle the wolf pack here instead of somewhere else in San Diego county. Honestly, she wasn't listening to Kimble's words but focused on the pulses of emotions she was feeling through the bond.

Their vampire was nothing but love and enthusiasm, but Pike felt unsteady, like her.

They followed Kimble into the main bedroom which seemed to take up about a quarter of the house. Like the rest of the place, it was nicely furnished but nothing was as fancy as she expected.

Where were the Persian rugs, esoteric artwork, and bookshelves full of weighty tomes? No, the books wouldn't be in the bedroom. He should have a library full of dark wood shelves, lit by a large fireplace bracketed by leather wingback chairs.

"There is no place like you're picturing in your head," Kimble said with a slight frown. "But I could build it if you desire."

Cora patted Pike's arm to indicate she wanted to be set down. She could feel his reluctance, but he gently set her on her feet anyway.

"Can you read my mind?" she asked.

"Only when you project that strongly," Kimble said with a smile. He stepped close so Cora was the meat in a vampire/shifter sandwich. "I can teach you how to keep your thoughts secure in your head so I don't pick up anything you don't want me to. Will that make you feel better?"

She nodded her head, enjoying the warmth of being snuggled between the two of them, their heat seeping into her, chasing away the earlier chill.

"Are we staying here tonight?" Pike asked.

It was obvious by the way Kimble stiffened that he heard Pike's reluctance. Or maybe he felt it. "We don't have to stay in my home. We can return to Cora's house or your apartment."

"Not the apartment," Cora said quickly in case Pike didn't realize that wasn't an option. Her adamant words make both men laugh and hug her a little tighter.

"I need to go back some time to get the rest of my stuff," Pike said. "But we never have to spend another night there."

"We can split our nights between here and Cora's house," Kimble offered. "Or spend the week there and weekends here. I have to spend some time here or the pack will feel neglected, but how much time is negotiable."

"Bears don't have packs," Pike said, his tone shifting to uncertainty. "What if the Laske Pack decides they don't want a bear in their territory?"

"A healthy wolf pack often has members that aren't wolf shifters," Kimble explained. Cora felt movement and looked up to see Kimble rubbing his hand up and down Pike's back. "I think there are a few humans in this pack and of course there's me, a vampire. Adding a bear won't be a problem for any of them."

Cora caught a hint of emotion from Pike. It took her a moment to sort it out, but finally she realized he was intimidated. His family was small and mostly calm, he wasn't prepared for the type of controlled chaos that came from a large family-like organization.

She might not know wolf packs, but she did know what it was like to have a family you loved and avoided, sometimes in equal measures.

"Don't worry," she said, snuggling down between the two of them. "The first time anyone does something mean to you, I'll show you how to set up booby traps. They'll live in fear of putting their shoes on for the rest of their life."

There was a brief pause before the guys roared with laughter. Pike's emotions calmed and started moving back to their normal happy state.

Seeing that Kimble's house wasn't some fancy mansion with servants helped her feel less intimidated by the whole thing. It was going to take some time to get used to all this, but at least she didn't have to worry about dressing for dinner or which fork to use.

Still, she was mentally and physically exhausted. "Can we go to bed now? I know you've got hours of night still left, but my body is done."

"Anything you wish," Kimble agreed, pulling away from them to start stripping her of clothing. Pike hurried to get naked, and they all climbed into the bed.

Cora was asleep before Pike even finished wrapping his big body around her and Kimble.

**Pike**

Pike woke up horny. That wasn't unusual, sleeping next to both his mates often gave him stiffies. This time was different because the sensation of neediness wasn't only his, but he was getting it from both Kimble and Cora.

Opening his eyes, he rolled over to find Cora on her back, hands gripping the headboard, legs spread, and Kimble feasting on her sex.

Goddess of the Hunt, his mates were sexy!

Cora and Kimble seemed to notice he was awake. Cora opened her eyes and rolled her head sideways on the pillow, at the same time Kimble lifted his head and grinned at him.

Then the vampire looked at Cora's face. "I told you this would wake him up."

Pike flushed with embarrassment. Shifters were usually quick to wake at the slightest change in their environment, but not Pike. He'd always been a heavy sleeper and was teased mercilessly about it when he was young.

"Wanna join us?" Cora asked. She was trying for wicked, but it came out more breathless.

His discomfort vanished at Cora's invitation. These were his mates. There was never a reason to be ashamed.

"Yes, please!" he agreed. After their first night of sexual exploration, they'd fallen into a pattern where he was in charge of this aspect of their relationship. It was the only place he felt truly confident.

It was obvious by the way they not only let him take over but encouraged it that they enjoyed everything he did. It was a small thing, but it made him feel necessary and adored. By the eager anticipation he was feeling through their link, tonight was no different.

Pike threw off the covers and stood up to strip off his boxers. "You should probably keep doing what you're doing, Kimble."

At his order, Kimble dove back between Cora's thighs. She gasped and gripped the headboard tightly. "Oh damn, he's good at that."

Now that the three of them were fully bonded, Pike noticed something different. He could feel Kimble's mouth sucking on Cora's clit almost like the vampire had his mouth around the tip of Pike's cock. It wasn't a strong sensation, but it was enough to make him jerk a little.

"I can feel that," he murmured, putting a knee on the bed behind where Kimble was crouched. Reaching forward, he put a hand on the back of Kimble's head and put a little pressure down. "Suck harder."

Cora cried out at the same time Pike felt the sensation on his dick get stronger. "I didn't know this could happen."

Knowledge filtered into his mind from Kimble telling him that this wasn't common among flocks and that the three of them were special. Could it be because Kimble was so damn old and powerful? With his feral mind no longer hampering his power, the link between them was so strong, they might even be able to talk to each other in the future.

A mental shrug came to him from Kimble, then a slight feeling of exasperation. The vampire didn't want to contemplate their bond. He wanted to play!

"Sorry," Pike murmured, lifting his hand from Kimble's head.

Cora whined and thrashed a little. "I want to come!"

"Patience," Pike said as he moved to her head. "Let me give you something to do while Kimble enjoys his meal."

Maneuvering carefully so as not to accidentally put a knee on Cora, Pike moved into position. Cora watched him with eager eyes as he wrapped his hand around the base of his cock. The moment his cock was close enough, she sucked the tip of it into her mouth. The first time she gave him a blow job, she pushed herself too hard and choked badly enough that they stopped the whole session.

Pike had been reluctant to do it again, but Cora convinced him she'd be more careful. He was going to make sure she didn't get the chance to hurt herself by keeping his hand on his dick as a limiter.

Her hot mouth worked his tip, making him want to roll his hips forward. When she reached for his balls and rolled them gently in one hand, Pike moaned.

"How are you so good at that?" he asked, letting her take a little more in her mouth. She looked up at him and ran her tongue over his slit. Through his bond with Kimble, he could taste Cora's pussy in his mouth at the same time he felt like his mouth was full of cock.

The sensations the three of them experienced were all jumbled up. When Kimble eased a finger into Cora's hot pussy while sucking on her clit, Pike felt it, a phantom intrusion that made him groan with pleasure.

What would it be like to fuck someone and be fucked at the same time while the bond was open? He had to know!

**Kimble**

Having his face buried in Cora's sex was heavenly. He'd been worried that Cora would have to orgasm before Pike woke up to join them. Thankfully, the bond had pushed the shifter into waking before that happened.

It was no surprise to him that the bond let them feel each other's pleasure. It was something every vampire hoped for but not all got. Not only was he blessed with a flock, but they had the type of bond that allowed for shared sensations.

It was going to be a lot of fun to explore!

Even now, as he licked and sucked Cora, it felt like his dick was in her mouth instead of Pike's. When she tugged at Pike's balls, he felt it on his own. Experimentally, he pushed a finger inside her and heard Pike gasp. Yes, this was perfect!

Then Pike was pulling out of Cora's mouth and moving away from them.

"Pike?" Cora protested, reaching for him. "Where are you going?"

"There's something I need to do in the bathroom really quick," he explained. Kimble could feel his excitement but not his intentions.

Kimble looked up to frown at Pike. "Right now?"

Pike winked at him as he stood up, his thick cock thrust out in front of him. "Trust me, you'll love it."

Kimble's eyes dropped to the bear's meat, and his mouth watered. "Whatever you're thinking, let's do it next time."

"Oh no, I really want it," Pike answered, then leaned over the bed and grabbed Kimble. With the ease of a giant bear shifter, Pike moved Kimble until he was kneeling between Cora's legs. Reaching between Kimble's legs, Pike gripped his dick and guided it to the entrance of Cora's sex.

"You need to get her ready for me," Pike explained. "You're going to sink yourself inside Cora, nice and slow. Let her feel every inch. Then when you're inside, you have to stop moving. You can play with her titties and kiss her, but you can't fuck. Got it?"

"Who says you're in charge?" Cora challenged.

"No one," Pike admitted with a wicked grin. He gave Kimble's dick a squeeze, making Kimble drop his head back and moan. Then he used the head of Kimble's cock to rub Cora's clit, making both of them gasp. "But I make everything so good, right?"

"Right," Cora agreed in a shaky voice. "Hurry, okay?"

"I will," he promised. Moving Kimble's dick again, Pike pressed the head into Cora. He let go but gave Kimble's balls a few gentle tugs before withdrawing his hand entirely. "You two are so pretty," he murmured, putting a hand on Kimble's ass and pushing.

Kimble moved his hips forward, slowly entering Cora until his entire tip was inside her. Pike made a sound and stopped.

"There, perfect. Now go super slow. No cheating." Pike gave his ass a slap that sent pleasure shooting up Kimble's spine. Pausing, Pike tilted his head at Kimble. "You liked that. You liked that a lot." Pike brought his hand down several more times on each cheek, making Kimble shake a little. It wasn't because of pain; it was because it felt too good!

The skin of his ass was hot and throbbing, similar to his dick. Even with only the tip inside Cora's hot, wet body, Kimble thought there was a good chance he could come if Pike kept spanking him.

This was a new aspect to Kimble's sexuality that he was as eager to explore as Pike and Cora!

"Our vampire is kinky!" Cora said. Kimble could tell she wanted the words to come out bold and teasing, but they were breathless instead.

"I'm trying it on you next time," Pike warned her. "Your ass will look especially adorable with my red handprint!

"I might let you," Cora agreed. "Or at least do it more to Kimble!"

With a chuckle, Pike straightened up. "Later," he promised. After a quick search of the nightstand drawer for something, Pike marched determinedly into the bathroom.

For a brief second, Kimble felt bereft. Why would his *sloneczko* leave them like this? Then Cora's legs wrapped around his waist, and she tried to impale herself on him. He was quick enough to grab her hips and keep it from happening.

"Kimble!" she whined. "Come on!"

Fully engaged with his human, Kimble lowered his face to her ear. "We're to go slow, *kochanie,* remember?"

Before she could try to talk him into letting her orgasm while Pike was distracted, he let his fangs extend and pressed them against the flesh below her ear. Gasping, she wrapped her arms around his neck.

"Why does that feel so good?" she moaned. "Please, bite me again, like you did the first time. Please!"

She'd taken weeks to fully heal after he'd gnawed on her neck during their first foray into sex. After realizing she was so easily hurt and slow to recover, Kimble refused to do it again, no matter how much she begged.

"Shouldn't I heal faster now that we shared souls?" Cora asked. "And the bond means you can tell if it's too much. There's no downside here!"

She was correct, but he still hesitated. Then he felt the longing for his bite through their bond. It wasn't only sexual, she'd felt intimately connected to him when he'd bitten her before and was desperate to feel it again.

He couldn't deny her any longer. Pressing his fangs into her flesh, he shuddered as a few drops of her exquisite blood hit his tongue.

As he bit down, the sensation of being bitten zinged from his neck and down his spine. They moaned together as both his teeth and cock sank deep inside of her.

"Please fuck me," Cora begged, her legs tight around his waist. "I'm going to die if you don't."

It took every molecule of willpower he possessed, but he didn't move his hips. Cora's tight heat surrounded him, squeezing his cock and urging him to move. He wanted to pull out and thrust into her again, but he refused to disappoint his *sloneczko*!

He had Cora pinned to the bed so there was no way she could shift him enough to start moving her hips on her own. If Pike wanted both of them to be wild with need by the time he got back, then that's what Kimble would do.

Slowly, he pulled his fangs free of Cora's neck. She whimpered and tried to keep his head in place with her arms around his neck. His little human was strong, but no match for him. Reaching back, he captured both her wrists and pulled them off his neck as he finished pulling his teeth from her skin.

"No!" Cora protested. "That's not fair!"

"Life isn't fair." He transferred both her wrists to one hand and pressed them to the pillow over her head. She struggled briefly but went still when he cupped her jaw with his free hand and forced her head to the side.

"I'm going to bite you again," he warned her. "I'm going to push my fangs into your flesh just like my dick is pressed deep into your pussy. I'm going to taste your blood on my tongue and there's nothing you can do about any of it."

A violent shiver racked Cora, and he felt a wave of lust wash across their bond. It was strong enough to make him suck in a breath. He was vaguely aware of a crash from the bathroom, probably Pike startled by the strength of Cora's reaction.

He licked across the virgin skin on the other side of her neck, enjoying the feel of gooseflesh breaking out all over her neck and shoulders. Sucking a section of skin into his mouth, he held it there even as Cora tried to thrash against him.

"I'm… I'm… Kimble!" Cora stuttered. He could feel her pleasure crashing back and forth between her pussy and her neck.

"One," she begged. "Give me one. I can have more, but I need one now!"

Feeling naughty, Kimble pressed his pelvis harder against Cora and ground down. It created friction against her clit, making her breathe out a surprised sound. Technically, he wasn't breaking Pike's order, but he was definitely skirting around it.

"Like that," she moaned, tilting her hips to increase the pressure. Just as he felt her ready to crest, he bit down, breaching her flesh again. He felt the pleasure from her clit shoot up her spine at the same time his bite caused sensation to shoot down. They exploded together, making her convulse and scream.

Her climax was intense. Not only did her feminine muscles clamp down on him, squeezing his dick like a hand, but her pleasure rocked through his body, a strong echo of what she was feeling.

It almost made him come, and he had to focus on blocking some of their bond so he wasn't feeling everything.

"What the hell?" Pike said as he came bursting out the bathroom door. "I can't trust either of my mates for even a few minutes!"

Kimble could feel the humor behind his outrage and answered by biting down a little harder, causing Cora's climax to reignite. Kimble could just see Pike over Cora's wild hair, his bear's enormous cock jumped and leaked pre-cum as they felt Cora's pleasure.

"Damn, this is amazing," Pike muttered, rushing to the bed. "My turn!"

**Pike**

It was a risk leaving his mates alone but as long as Kimble didn't come, he was ready to reward them. Cora might end up wrecked, but only in the best way because he expected her to have at least one more orgasm, maybe two.

Actually, he intended to leave them all wrecked!

"Okay, you guys finish each other off. I'm done for the night," Cora mumbled, going limp under Kimble.

Carefully extracting himself from Cora at both ends, Kimble sat up and hissed. Pike could feel all his pent-up need as if it was his own. Well, it was his own because he hadn't even gotten to sink balls deep in Cora yet.

"I guess you could fuck me if you wanted," Cora offered with a lazy grin.

"You're a bad girl," Pike said. "And bad girls get punished."

She raised an eyebrow. "Yes, please?"

Her answer made Pike chuckle even as he pulled Kimble entirely off their human. "Lay down next to Cora," he instructed.

Kimble rolled onto his back, his thick cock slapping against this muscled belly. Pike took a moment to stare at it. Kimble wasn't as big as he was, but he wasn't small by any means. This was the first time Pike was going to try this, and he hoped it would be as enjoyable as it was when he'd experimented with a dildo.

Time to give the real thing a try!

Cora made a little surprised sound when Pike straddled Kimble, hoovering his ass over Kimble's hips.

"I'm going to take you inside me," he warned the vampire. "I'm going to ride you until I come. You only get to climax when I say, understood?"

Kimble nodded, blinking rapidly as if he couldn't believe this was happening. "Are you sure? There could be pain and—"

Pike shook his head. "I went to the bathroom to make sure I was clean and ready for you. Judging by what I was feeling while I was there, you'll know if I'm enjoying it or not. Our bond is strong despite being brand new."

Kimble shrugged. "I'm old and powerful. The bonds reflect that."

Reaching between his legs, Pike grabbed hold of Kimble's erection and held it in place. "Then let's get to riding powerful vampire dick!"

Cora rolled on her side and wiggled closer so she could watch. "Damn, this is hot."

Pike had to work on not holding his breath as the tip of Kimble's cock breached his hole. It didn't hurt or even sting, probably because all the toys he'd played with were as big or slightly bigger.

Kimble was covered in Cora's slick and Pike was full of lube, so between the two, Kimble slid in easily once the thickest part of his head passed Pike's tight ring of muscles. They both sighed out a long, pleasured sound as Pike let go of Kimble and slid all the way down.

"I can feel it," Cora said, rolling on her back and spreading her legs. Slick coated the inside of her thighs as she reached down and started stroking her clit. "I can feel you inside my ass and it feels so good. Like I have another clit in there, and Kimble's pressing right on it."

"My prostate," Pike grunted. Talking was hard right now. There were so many sensations he wasn't expecting, including feeling Kimble's dick inside of his own ass! It was strange and wonderful all at the same time.

Lifting slightly before pressing back down, Pike made all three of them moan. "Do it again!" Cora demanded, rubbing herself more fiercely. "Keep doing that!"

"I will," Pike ground out, his voice deeper and huskier than normal. "But I need something first."

It was a little awkward, but he managed to grab Cora and lift her up. She squeaked in surprise as he arranged her so her legs were around his hips and the head of his dick was pressing at the entrance to her pussy.

"I dreamed this," he admitted.

"Make all your dreams come true," Cora urged, gripping his shoulders with her hands.

Cora was small, making him cautious as he pressed his length into her. She'd taken him before, but only after several orgasms and a good fucking from Kimble. He wasn't sure she'd done enough yet to be ready for his beast.

He was wrong.

Slick, hot heat enveloped his cock as he slid inside her. Cora's eyes closed, her head flopped back, and her mouth opened in a loud moan. Her body welcomed him inside, enveloping him in heat. Freezing, Pike took a moment to let all the different sensations swirl through his body, some from him and some from his partners.

His dick in Cora.

Cora full of him, stretched in all the right ways.

His back hole filled with Kimble's dick.

Kimble's dick held tightly by his ass.

There was no pain, only electric sparks of pleasure coming from everywhere. He went totally still because the moment he moved, he was going to start thrusting, and he wouldn't be able to stop until they all crested.

He'd thought he was ready for this, but he wasn't because he might drown in all the sensations.

"This is everything," Kimble gritted out from under him. The vampire's fingers were digging into his hips while Cora's blunt nails scored his shoulders. He wished both his mates had claws to dig into his flesh and mark him as theirs. He hadn't realized he wanted a little pain with his pleasure too until he could feel how good it felt through Cora and Kimble.

"I can give that to you," Kimble said.

"Huh?" Pike mumbled, looking down in time to see Kimble's fingernails grow long and darken. They became pointed and curved as the vampire moved his hand from Pike's hips to his thighs.

"Talons!" Pike whispered. Even as he said the word, Kimble's griffin talons dug into his flesh, dragging shallow furrows down his thighs. Pain and pleasure mixed together, shooting up his spine and making his entire body tighten.

Kimble gasped as Pike's ass clamped down on his shaft, and Cora ground her hips onto him with a low, "Fuck!"

"Again," Pike begged, lifting his body a little to slam back down on Kimble. The vampire cried out at the same time he reached up and dragged his claws down again.

"Me too," Cora said and put her mouth to the meaty muscle connecting Pike's neck to his shoulders. Opening her mouth, she bit down viciously, and Pike could taste a hint of his own blood in her mouth. Kimble must taste it too because he gasped and arched under Pike.

"Fuck yourself on me," Kimble demanded and extended his arms to grab Pike's ass, urging him to move.

Unable to resist the direct order, Pike started to move his hips. As he rose and fell on Kimble's cock, he held Cora so he could move her up and down his rock-hard shaft. With her teeth still locked on Pike's neck, Cora whimpered, sending vibrations through the tender bite.

"Do I taste good?" Pike asked. Her response was to tighten her jaw.

**Cora**

Every guy Cora ever slept with wanted anal sex. The one time she gave it a try was a disaster. It hurt like hell, making her punch the guy until he got off her. That incident made her swear it off forever.

But the amount of pleasure rolling off Pike and into her changed her mind!

There'd been a few occasions growing up when she wished to know what it was like to have a dick, and now she almost felt like she did! The way she could feel what it was like to sink deep inside a body and having that body squeezing you tightly was amazing. Never in her wildest dreams did she think she'd get to experience sex from both sides at once.

She also never thought she'd bite a guy to the point of drawing blood, but she could feel how much pleasure it was giving Pike.

"Do I taste good?" His voice was a low, sexy rumble that shivered over her skin. It made her tighten her jaw. Pike moaned, and under them, Kimble hissed.

She wasn't sure if it was her tasting blood or Kimble because she was flooded with the vampire's desire. It was similar to the way she'd felt when he bit her, and his pleasure at the feel of her flesh under his fangs.

Her lovers had a different feel to the pleasures bounding between them through the bond. The feelings coming from Pike felt hot, like electricity skittering over her skin. Kimble felt deliciously cool, like water caressing over her body. It was almost too much and not enough at the same time!

Her jaw was aching from holding onto Pike's flesh. Letting go of him, she licked over the area she'd abused. When she pulled her head back, she could clearly see teeth marks and a little blood welling from the two spots where she'd punctured his skin.

Something primitive welled up from deep inside of her. "I've marked you."

Pike's arms tightened around her at the same time his massive shaft twitched within her. "Mark me every day," he growled. "I need my mates to mark me inside and out."

He'd been moving slowly up until that point, but that changed with his words. He started moving with purpose, slamming himself down on Kimble over and over again.

Pike was able to hold her in such a way that as he dropped himself down on Kimble, he was pulled from Cora's body. As he rose up, he thrust into Cora and pulled himself up Kimble's cock. He was fucking himself on Kimble while fucking into Cora.

This was something straight out of a porno, but real!

As he moved, Cora felt like her clit was a dick, being pushed in and out of a tight, hot body. Pressure squeezed up and down, as good as any mouth had ever done for her.

"Faster!" she demanded, feeling herself on the edge of climaxing. She just needed a little more, just a—

Kimble roared as he came, clamping his hands on Pike's hips and forcing the big male to sit down hard and stay there.

Kimble caused a chain reaction because as she felt Kimble filling Pike with cum, she felt Pike fill her passage.

He gasped and hugged her tight to his body, tears rolling down his face from the intensity of the pleasure.

Their orgasms flooded her, sending her cascading over into bliss that whited out her vision. She clung to Pike, unsure what was up or down. The sensations swirled through the three of them to the point that Cora thought she was under Pike, penetrating him. But no, she was Pike with his dick in her, and she was herself with the faint taste of his blood still on her tongue.

The three of them shuddered, jerked, and panted. It was only after she was sure she knew which was her body that she opened her eyes to find they were all glowing. The dim room was awash in the faint blue glow coming off them.

"Damn," she whispered. "We're fucking radioactive!"

**Pike**

Several days later, Pike quietly eased the front door of Kimble's house shut, then stood on the porch. It was five in the morning, the pre-dawn light weakly illuminating the heavy mist that had formed during the night. If his life was a horror movie it would be creepy, but because the loves of his life were asleep in the house behind him, the mist was romantic instead.

Opening his mouth wide, he exhaled to watch his warm breath turn white as it met the cold air. His inner bear wanted to shift and forage on the new land, but he held the beast back. The last thing he wanted to do was upset the pack by shifting without giving them proper warning.

Not that they'd indicated it would be an issue. Everyone had taken great pains in the last few days to tell him how welcome he was and that they had his scent so he could shift at any time, and no one would attack him. It was nice, but he was still cautious.

The real question now was what the hell was he going to do with his life?

Kimble had his life back, Cora had her company, but what did Pike have? He wasn't even employed anymore. He felt adrift and redundant. He didn't even need to cook for Cora any longer. If they weren't joining one of the wolf families for dinner, then food was delivered to the house. When he'd tried to politely object, they'd only smiled and pushed the containers at him anyway. The Laske Pack was determined to feed Kimble's flock.

They were all so nice but made Pike feel obsolete.

Needing to move, he took all three porch steps in one stride and headed to the path he'd seen yesterday. Someone said it circled the fenced-in portion of the compound and was about two and half miles all the way around. That sounded like a nice walk to help clear his head.

"Pike?" He turned to find Annette watching him with a worried expression. How had she snuck up on him?

"Hi, Annette. I thought I'd hike the path around the property," he said, pointing to where he was going.

She nodded her head, but her eyebrows didn't smooth out. "Your mates are tucked away in bed, and you decided to go for a walk? Are you feeling ok?"

Guilt hit him. A good bear wouldn't leave his mates' sides while they slept. On the heels of his guilt was aggravation. Who was Annette to ask him questions like that?

Feeling annoyed at Annette, who'd been nothing but nice to him, caused the guilt to come back even worse. What was wrong with him?

As if sensing his turmoil, Annette stepped back a few feet and tried to smile at him. "I'm not judging you. I only wanted to see if you needed anything."

Pike blew out a long sigh and felt his shoulders slump. Shoving his hands in his pants pockets, he stared down at his shoes. "I'm a bear, mated to a vampire and a human, and now I live with a bunch of wolves. Life feels weird."

Annette made a sympathetic sound and stepped up next to him. "It seems like you need to talk. Let's walk the path, and you can tell me everything going on in your head."

"It's a mess," Pike admitted, falling into step with the alpha.

"I've raised three cubs. I'm good at cleaning up messes," she offered, making him chuckle.

Annette was a good listener and let Pike pour out all his thoughts and feelings. His love for Kimble and Cora, his worry about being good enough for them, his concern over Cora's family, and his worry about his own place in the world.

The wolf didn't give advice, only asked questions and sometimes helped him express his thoughts when he was struggling. She reminded him a lot of his dad; he was a good listener too.

Before he knew it, an hour had passed, and they'd done a full circuit and were starting on the second one. Feeling calmer, Pike stopped at the section where three paths intersected with the circuit. One would lead off to a cluster of houses, one would lead to Kimble's house, and the third to the barn.

He was hungry and ready to make a hearty breakfast for himself and Cora before she left for work. If he was quick, he could get it done before anyone delivered food. "Thanks for the walk. I think I'll head back to Kimble's house."

"Can I say something before we part?" Annette asked.

Pike braced himself. "What?"

"It's not Kimble's house; it's your house. The three of you might be in different bodies, but you share souls now, that makes you almost a single entity. What belongs to Kimble belongs to you and vice versa. You need to start thinking of this place as your home. And most importantly, they bonded with you, not someone else. You are who they want, that means you could never be a disappointment to them."

"I feel so useless," he admitted. "I want to do more than keep house for them."

"You do," Annette argued. "You love them."

Pike rubbed a hand over his head. "It doesn't feel like enough. They're both so successful, and I'm just me. I can't even fight. The only reason I can act as a bouncer is because most of the clients are human, and they're easy to pick up and carry out of the club. The shifters tend to go because they smell bear, but if any of them challenged me, I wouldn't know what to do."

Annette blew out a long breath then said very quickly, "I've never been in a fight."

Pike blinked in surprise. "I thought you have to fight to be alpha."

She snorted. "Alphas that have to fight for their position are shit leaders. Healthy, well-adjusted packs are formed when wolves want to follow an alpha because they know they'll be cared for. Most packs are small, basically extended families, and rarely have any issues. When they get as big as ours, it's common for outside wolves to challenge the alpha. If they win, then they can claim all the pack's wealth for themselves. But I've never been challenged. No one has ever even looked at me sideways. Do you know why?"

"I don't know that much about wolf pack dynamics," Pike said with a shrug.

"I'll let you in on a little secret. It's not because of my powerful build," she said with a twist of her lips as she stepped back and held out her arms. She was a lovely woman who looked to be in her mid-forties, but nothing Pike would call menacing. "It's because of Kimble. None of our leaders have ever been challenged because we have a vampire. While he was gone, I lived in constant fear that someone would find out and our pack would face challenges. We're fiercely loyal to Kimble, not because he bought this property and has all kinds of funds and trusts set up for us, but because he's always made it a priority to keep us safe. That means we want you and Cora happy also."

Stepping up to him, Annette grabbed his hands in hers. "I will do anything to make you feel better. If you want to spend an hour walking and talking every morning, I'll set my alarm. If you want to go to college, I'll help you apply. If you want to start a business, I'll walk you through the paperwork. Do you understand me, Pike? You are as precious to me as any other member of my pack because you're part of Kimble."

Uncomfortable with her intensity, Pike tried to make a joke. "Be careful, I might ask for a blood sacrifice!"

"I know you're trying to be funny, but I'm going to answer the unasked question: what if you ask for too much, and we come to resent you?"

Pike's eyes went a little wide. He was impressed at Annette's level of intuition. "I don't want to upset anyone."

"I doubt you could," Annette said, letting go of Pike's hands. "If Kimble picked you to be in his flock, then you must have the same sense of kindness and duty as he does. I don't fear the requests because I know they'll all be reasonable and even tame." Turning, she pointed at the bare patch of earth behind the barn. "I have a suggestion for you. A project to think about. You should turn that into a garden fit for a bear to forage in."

It took him a moment to realize she was referencing the garden he was helping his mother create. It was one of the many topics he'd mentioned during their conversation.

"I don't know," he hedged, but he could already see the way he'd organize the space.

"We had a kitchen garden there once, but the couple who created and maintained it got too old, and no one else wanted to take over the duty," she explained. "It would be nice to have one again. I can get you a pack credit card."

Pike wasn't surprised by the offer, but he was startled at how badly he wanted to accept. "I'll think about it."

No sooner were the words out of his mouth than he wanted to call them back. There was no thinking. There was only want. The area was calling to him, just like his parents' backyard. He was desperate to start working in the soil with the knowledge that he'd eventually coax a fabulous garden to grow.

"If it would help the pack, I could probably find the time," he said before Annette could respond to his lukewarm response. "I'll have to see when I can borrow my parents' truck though. I'm going to need a lot of supplies."

Annette smiled broadly and pointed to the barn. "All the tools and the utility vehicle are in there to use, no one has touched them in years." she frowned thoughtfully. "The vehicle might need to be serviced so I'll talk to Kell about it."

Pike had to keep himself from rushing off to the barn to start looking at what they had. "Thanks, Annette."

"Don't thank me yet," she warned. "I have a feeling the pack will start putting in requests as soon as they find out what you're doing. As far as borrowing a truck, you can use one of the pack vehicles. I'll send Kell over with keys. We have plenty of cars and trucks, so don't feel like you have to return the keys. Use it as you need to."

Then she said something under her breath about the sorry state of his Caddy. He ignored the accurate comment and started for the barn.

"Thanks, Annette," he called back. Maybe being part of a wolf pack wasn't so bad after all.

**Cora**

Waking up to the smell of food wasn't unusual for Cora anymore. Pike was an early riser and often hurried to cook her something fabulous for breakfast. She'd never eaten so well in her life and if she wasn't careful, she was going to need to buy bigger sized jeans.

Sitting up, she looked down at Kimble. His eyes were open but with the out-of-focus aspect she'd gotten used to seeing when it was daytime. With his returning strength, he could get up and move around during the day, but only for a limited time. Each day he could stay awake a little longer, so she expected he'd be able to resist day sleeping within a few months.

"I'm getting up," she warned him. Sometimes he'd get up with her and other times, he'd wait until after breakfast so he could help her shower and get dressed for the day before going back to bed.

His bedroom en suite boasted a massive shower stall with two shower heads so they could all get clean together. Well, mostly clean. Shower sex seemed to be Kimble's new favorite thing, and Cora wasn't about to talk him out of it!

"Later," Kimble mumbled, then let his eyelids drop closed.

"Okay, I'll come back after breakfast," Cora promised and dropped a kiss on his cheek. He smiled before his features relaxed back into unconsciousness.

Pulling on a robe, Cora shuffled out into the kitchen just as Pike was about to place two heaping plates of food in the oven to keep them warm.

"You're up!" he said with way more excitement than a Thursday morning warranted. "I made French toast the way you like it with extra cinnamon."

Cora stopped dead in the large opening to the kitchen and blinked at him. "I need coffee."

Pike's expression turned sympathetic, and he lowered his voice a little. "Sorry, I forgot about the sleepy Cora rule." He set the plates on the kitchen table and pulled out a chair. "Come sit, mate. I'll fix you a cup of coffee."

It took at least two cups of coffee before Cora could carry on a conversation. In sharp contrast, Pike was ready to start his day the moment he opened his eyes and had to learn to keep his chatty nature in check until Cora had a little time to finish the painful process of waking up.

No sooner did she sit down than Pike was plunking a mug of coffee with the perfect amount of cream in front of her. She ignored the food and slurped down half the mug in one go.

Holding the warm mug in both hands, she let a contented sigh ease out of her.

"That's better," she murmured. Pike brought the coffee pot and creamer to the table, then took his own seat and started shoveling food in his mouth.

Considering he'd seemed a little depressed the last few days, this change in mood was startling. First, she finished her coffee, then broke the silence with a question.

"What's going on?"

Pike straightened in his chair and lowered his fork full of food as joy and enthusiasm radiated off him. "I'm going to design and plant a giant garden for the pack!"

His declaration wasn't anything she expected. "That's great?"

"Isn't it!" he said, obviously not hearing the question in her words. "Kell gave me the keys to a truck and said I can use it every day if I need to. I'm going to spend the day clearing the old garden area and breaking up the soil. I promise I'll have dinner ready for you when you get back."

Cora latched on to the last part. "You don't have to cook for me. You're not my house-spouse. Spend your days doing anything you want."

"House-spouse!" Pike chortled. His phone chimed, and his laughter disappeared as he looked at the screen. Dropping his fork on his plate with a clink, he picked the device up and typed. The happiness of earlier was gone, replaced by a furrowed brow and tightly pressed lips.

Cora poured a second cup of coffee and added cream while Pike sent a message to whoever took his smile away. She heard the whoosh sound of a sent message just after taking a sip of another perfect cup of coffee.

Pike sat the phone down and looked at her, trying to smile. "So I was thinking—hey!"

Cora swiped the phone to see who'd made him unhappy.

The identity at the top of the window said Sis and the three dots were moving, telling Cora there was probably a rude message incoming.

Before she did anything, she looked up to warn Pike of her intentions. "I'm going to message your sister. If she needs money for rent, I'll pay the manager directly, but we won't be handing her cash anymore."

She expected Pike to get upset at her for being controlling, instead, the large man's shoulders slumped in relief and a real smile tentatively formed on his face.

"I'm sorry," he whispered as several chimes indicated the arrival of Lucy's response.

She waved the phone in the air. "You don't ever have to deal with her again. Kimble and I will take care of her finances until she can handle them herself."

"Then she and I can go back to the way we were," Pike agreed. Cora had a bad feeling he didn't realize Lucy wasn't the adult he wanted her to be. But you couldn't fix family, so she simply nodded her head.

"Be prepared for the fireworks until she gets used to it," Cora warned as she read the messages from Lucy, all of them demanding Pike get her money right away.

> Hello Lucy, this is Cora, the human. From now on I'm in charge of your finances. I'm going to text you my number so you can send me the contact info for your apartment manager. I'll pay him directly. You will no longer be receiving cash from Pike.

After she hit send, she pulled her phone from the robe pocket and copied Lucy's number, then sent the same message again. Lucy's response was rapid and full of vitriol. It was easy for Cora to remain calm in this situation. She had all the power.

> Cussing at me won't help you. I'm going to block you on your brother's phone until you agree to be civil. You're free to complain to your parents, but I think we both know they won't advocate for you. It's time to

Cora quickly blocked Lucy's number on Pike's cell and turned hers to silent. She was sure that Lucy would only send abuse until she realized two things: Cora was serious, and there was no one left to manipulate.

Satisfied with her morning work, Cora handed Pike back his phone. "Lucy's blocked. I'll tell you when you can unblock her."

Again, Pike only looked relieved. "She's a good person. It's just that she's dealing with a bad break up and having a hard time holding down a job."

Cora made a sympathetic sound. "I'm not going to let your sister go homeless or starve, but she can't treat you like this, okay?"

Pike nodded. "She really tries to be responsible with her money though, I swear."

Cora didn't argue with him. That wasn't what he needed right now. "We'll help her, but no more cash, got it? She'll find some way to talk to you. That means you need to stay strong."

"That's easy to do when you don't really have money," Pike tried to joke.

"I'm sure you'd sell a kidney if she pressured you enough," Cora said. Unlike Pike, she wasn't joking. Pike was much too good for this world, and it was Cora's job to keep him safe despite himself.

She knew Kimble would agree.

**Cora**

Now that she was fully bonded, she could spend an entire day away from Pike and Kimble and not feel any ill effects. Pike had been coming to work with her anyway, probably because he didn't have anything else to do, but not today. Nothing was going to distract him from the new garden!

It was nice to have Pike with her, but she didn't mind working alone. With their bond humming in the back of her head, she felt secure and happy no matter how far away she was.

Before heading to her first job, Cora stopped by the office. Charlotte had everything so ruthlessly organized that Cora only needed to stop by to sign things. Today was one of those days.

"Heya sweetie!" Charlotte called out as Cora entered. The office came with a small industrial space in the back that Cora used for storage.

Looking around, she noticed Charlotte had made some changes. The small office looked better with a few pieces of art on the walls and new matching chairs.

"Please tell me you didn't pay for any of this," Cora begged, flopping down into one of the chairs.

"Nope, it came out of the office supply account," Charlotte said as she got up and poured them both cups of coffee. The woman loved her coffee and had a nice little coffee bar set up behind her desk. After handing Cora a cup of perfectly prepared java, Charlotte retook her seat and started pulling out paperwork.

"I need you to go over this contract for the Johnson house and make sure all the numbers are correct. Then you need to approve these."

Cora leaned forward and started going over the paperwork. She gave up halfway through, sat back, and rubbed her hands over her face. "No more!"

Charlotte chuckled. "This is what happens when you don't come by often enough. I send you emails and texts, but you never respond. I'm forced to print out actual paper!"

An idea hit Cora. Dropping her hands from her face, she pointed a finger at Charlotte. "You!"

Charlotte tilted her head, her short, curly hair bouncing a little. "Me?"

"Yes, you," Cora said. "I want you to become a partner. Then you can sign all this shit, and I'll only need to stop by to get something out of storage."

The woman's eyes went wide, and she sat back, obviously stunned. "I'm sorry, what?"

Cora put her forearms on the desk and leaned in close. "You buy into the company, and we become partners."

"But I'm not an electrician," Charlotte protested.

"Who cares?" Cora answered. "You know how to type up the bids. You do all the scheduling and customer service. Some things have changed in my life right now, and I don't want to spend any more time doing the stuff I don't like."

"Do the changes have anything to do with you having a vampire and a bear shifter clinging to your aura?" Charlotte asked.

"What the hell?" Cora said, throwing her hands up. "Did everyone know but me?"

"Probably," Charlotte said with a chuckle. She stood up and stretched a hand over the desk. "Nice to meet you. I'm Charlotte Davis, member of the Ember Druid Clan."

Cora grabbed her hand to shake. "Druid, huh? Would that stop you from being a partner? Like would the other druids not want you to do business with me?"

Charlotte shook her head and sat back down. "We aren't a conservative clan like the Foundation Druids. Even if someone said something, I'd ignore them."

"Then let's talk to a lawyer about getting you on board," Cora said.

"Are you sure about this?" Charlotte asked. She looked both excited and intimidated.

Cora gave her one, slow, emphatic nod. "I've never been more sure. Don't worry about the money. We can figure that out. The important thing is that I never have to deal with paperwork again!"

Assured that Charlotte was going to make her life even easier; Cora left the office with a spring in her step. The rest of the day flowed quickly, and the next thing she knew, she was packing up and ready for a shower.

After belting herself into Van Guts, she stared at the vehicle's dashboard. "Should we go to the Cedar Street house first and pack up clothes or drive straight home?"

The moment the words were out of her mouth, she went still.

*Home?* How had the Palomar Mountain compound become home to her unconscious mind so fast?

Apparently, it only took her several days to start thinking of Kimble's place as home instead of her little house. He'd repeatedly offered to split their time between locations, but it seemed like there was no point. As much as she loved the house on Cedar, it didn't feel right anymore. She should pack as much as she could in the van and come back for the rest later.

She debated selling versus renting her little house the rest of the drive. She was so deep in thought that she didn't notice the car parked in front of her house or the person sitting in it. Hitting the automatic opener, she eased Van Guts into the crowded garage. Getting out, she was surprised and wary to see a familiar figure striding up the short driveway.

"You bitch!" Lucy hissed, stopping at the back of Van Guts and effectively blocking Cora. The door from the garage to the kitchen was between them, and she knew the bear shifter would be faster than her.

There would be no retreating from this conflict.

"I told you I'd pay your rent," Cora reminded her, blindly tapping her phone with her thumb, hoping she hit the right spot. "But no one in the family is giving you cash anymore."

Lucy bared her teeth at Cora and made an inhuman sound. "Just because you're fucking my brother doesn't give you control over me!"

"I'm in love with your brother," Cora said as she looked around for a good weapon. "And the two of us are part of Kimble's flock. You know that's a deep connection."

"Kimble is the most useless vampire to ever exist," Lucy declared, dramatically throwing up her arms in frustration. "The one thing you can count on with vampires is that they're rich as hell. Pike should've had more money after Kimble claimed him, not less. Every month he was poorer and poorer. That's not how it's supposed to work. Being with Kimble should've meant I got everything I wanted."

She sounded like a child having a tantrum. How was Pike so blind to his sister's true nature?

Really, she shouldn't judge. How long had she put up with her family?

Welp, all of that changed now!

Spotting something that would work as an excellent weapon, Cora edged toward it while bringing both hands up, palm out. The move made her accidentally drop her phone but that was fine, she needed her hands free anyway. "I don't carry cash and hurting me isn't going to get you anything."

"You have a bank account, right?" Lucy said, advancing a step. "Send me money with your phone. Send me a lot, or I'll fuck you up."

Cora pretended to shy back against a set of metal shop shelves, the bottles and cans clinking with her impact. "I won't, and your brother won't be happy if you hurt me."

Lucy's expression was nothing but absolute confidence. "He won't believe you."

She reached out to grab Cora's arm at the same time Cora raised the spray can and covered Lucy's face in flat white.

Lucy screeched with surprise and frantically wiped her face. "What the—"

Cora thought that would give her time to skirt around Lucy and away, but the bear blindly lunged, her massive body leaving no room for Cora to duck away. The impact drove Cora into the shelves and knocked the air out of her.

"You stupid, useless human!" Lucy screamed as she grabbed hold of Cora. One hand balled up in her shirt and the other wrapped around her bicep. The grip on her bicep was painfully tight, making clawing at Lucy's hand ineffective. The necklace under her work shirt felt hot and tingles radiated from it. Suddenly, Lucy's grip didn't hurt as much, but she was still working on pulling air into her lungs.

"I could squeeze your throat," Lucy hissed. "I could put my fingers around your tiny, scrawny throat and keep you from breathing. Then we'd both get to die!"

They'd both get to die? That didn't make any sense! "I'll get you the money," Cora wheezed out. "I need my phone."

Lucy was blinking rapidly, but her watery eyes couldn't focus as she looked around. "Where is it?"

"At my feet," Cora said, pointing.

"Get it!" Lucy let go of her shirt and arm, then shoved her roughly. "Send me everything you have. I need everything!"

Dropping to her knees, Cora swept up a length of lead pipe that had fallen over during their struggles. Using both hands, she drove it up with all the power in her small, muscled body. She might be human, but that didn't make her weak!

The impact made Lucy gasp and double over. Even a bear shifter couldn't withstand a solid blow to the solar plexus. Cora was able to scramble out of the way before Lucy dropped to her knees and started heaving.

"You do not get to come into my house and threaten me," Cora growled, feeling strangely strong and energized. The pipe felt light in her grip, and she could sense both Pike and Kimble in the back of her mind, worried and scared.

She pushed assurance at them as she backed away from the bear shifter. She didn't know how long it took for them to recover, so she kept moving until she was all the way out of the garage with plenty of exit points and in full view of her neighbors and any passing cars.

"I won't be bullied, harassed, or threatened ever again," she declared. Memories of Seb floated through her head. All the things she let him get away with because no one believed her. Now she had people who wouldn't question what happened. Even Pike, who'd let Lucy walk all over him, would draw the line at Lucy's actions today.

She watched Lucy painfully get back to her feet. Her face was scrunched in pain, and her skin flushed. "You're dead, human."

She opened her mouth to speak but two things happened at once. The necklace got super-hot and a heavy hand landed on her shoulder and swung her around. She looked up and up to find a guy almost as tall as Pike glaring down at her.

"What's going on, Luc?" the stranger asked. "Is this the human with the money?"

"Damn it!" Lucy wailed. "Look what you've done! Why couldn't you have just given it to me?"

Oh damn, Cora hadn't thought Lucy would have a partner. She didn't hesitate to swing the pipe again, but there wasn't much room between the two of them. Without the proper momentum, the blow wasn't substantial. The guy didn't even flinch when it landed against his torso.

Wrenching the pipe away from Cora, he tossed it aside and raised a hand, knuckles out. He was going to back hand her and because he was so damn big, the blow might kill her. His other hand was only gripping the shoulder of her shirt.

Thinking fast, she dropped to her knees and slid out of the shirt. Before he could reach down to grab ahold of her, Cora punched his groin. She hoped to at least startle him, but what happened next was as much of a surprise for her as him.

She felt the warmth from the necklace flow over her entire body. She'd felt strong since bonding with Kimble and Pike, but at the moment, she felt like a superhero. The blow was so solid, she knocked the guy off his feet. Curled up on his side with both hands covering his crotch, the stranger whimpered and moaned.

"She punched my dick! The human punched my dick!"

Shakily getting to her feet, Cora moved so she could see both shifters. The guy was still clutching her shirt, but she didn't want to get close enough to get it back. Should she run? Hit both of them again?

"Oh damn, that's impressive Cora." Looking over her shoulder, Cora found Luis from three houses down standing at the end of her driveway, eyeing the man with lifted eyebrows.

That's when Cora remembered she was standing there in nothing but her bra. As if reading her mind, Luis pulled off his overshirt and tossed it to her, leaving him in a white ribbed tank top.

"Thanks," she muttered while pulling it on over her head.

"Why did this bear attack you?" Luis asked as he stepped a little closer to the growling stranger. "Where is your vampire? It's well past dark, he should be here protecting you."

Cora gaped at him. "What?"

"Oh, you didn't know?" Luis asked. His eyebrow moved from surprise to scrunched up. "Weird, I thought you'd know since Mikey told me to keep an eye on you and your mates."

"Mikey?"

"Yeah, Mikey," Luis said with a little nod. "Alpha of the Lobos Gris Pack and friend of just about everyone including Imani."

"You're a wolf?" Cora guessed, relieved to hear one familiar name in the mix. Luis nodded his head; then his expression turned worried as he focused on something behind her. Cora pivoted to see what caused the reaction. Even as she turned her body, she heard Luis start sprinting up the drive while shouting for her to run.

Lucy had gotten to her feet and was rushing at her.

Without thinking, she dodged to the left at the same time she used her entire upper body to throw a jab to Lucy's throat with her right. She wasn't playing nice with these bear shifters; they were just too damn big and tough.

Again her entire body went warm, and the punch was strong enough to send Lucy flying back. She landed hard on her back just as Luis reached them and stuttered to a stop. They both stood over the gagging and gasping Lucy.

He cast her an admiring glance. "Woah! I didn't think humans could do that."

"I'm stronger than I was," she murmured, shaking out her right hand. Her knuckles hurt from delivering two powerful blows, but that was better than the alternative. She raised her left hand to grasp the necklace through her shirt. "I think I might have had a little power boost."

"What do we do with these two?" Luis asked. "I think Imani's flock knows a guy who could take care of them."

Lucy whimpered at Luis's implied threat, but the strange man only cursed and moaned. Neither shifter was getting up any time soon.

"I'm not sure," Cora said. "Watch them for me, 'kay?" Luis nodded and skirted around them to find her phone in the garage. It had ended up under the van and was still working.

She knelt next to Lucy to show her the screen. The woman started crying fat tears when she saw the phone had been connected to Pike the entire time.

Tapping the speaker, Cora spoke into the phone. "Pike?"

There was the loud sound of wind and then Pike spoke. "Kimble is in his griffin form, and we're flying to you. We'll be there soon!"

"Take your time, guys," Cora drawled. "None of us are going anywhere."

While they'd waited, Luis dragged the shifters into the backyard. Then he'd stood over them, glaring. Neither tried to get up. It wasn't long before a griffin appeared with Pike clutched in his front talons.

There was a rush of wind as Kimble set Pike down, then landed while shifting. Cora didn't think anything of it since she'd seen him do it before, but Luis let out a low whistle of admiration.

"Damn, vampires have all the cool magic."

Cora ignored him and focused on her bear. As relieved as she felt to have them there, it was still hard to see the devastation on Pike's face as he took in the sobbing Lucy.

The moment Pike got close enough, Lucy lunged for his leg and hugged it tight. "They were going to kill me!"

Pike crouched down and gently pried her off his leg. "Look at me, Lucy."

"You have to save me," Lucy begged. "Cora's jealous of our relationship. She wants me dead because she doesn't want competition for your attention."

He shook his head slowly, his face tight with pain. "I heard everything Lucy. We both know you came here to hurt my mate. Even though I won't let them take your life, you're dead to me now. I have no sister."

Lucy cried out and for the first time, Cora thought she saw real panic and regret on the shifter's face. Pike stood up and turned his back on Lucy to face Kimble. "I need you to take them both somewhere away from here. I don't want them dead, but can you use your thrall so they won't come near me or Cora again?"

Kimble looked heartbroken for Pike. "Of course, *sloneczko*. Consider it done."

Shifting again, Kimble grabbed one of them in each claw, then pumped his wings hard to lift his burden into the air. No sooner was he above the house than Cora noticed his shape shimmer and seemed to distort and disappear.

"Huh," she muttered. Now she understood why there weren't pictures of Kimble as a griffin all over the place.

"It's glamor. It's kind of an extension on their ability to thrall people," Luis explained as Pike pulled her into a full body hug. "Looks like it's time for me to head home to my mate. Have a better evening."

Pike didn't respond, and Cora gave a small wave as Luis left through the gate at the side of the garage. She focused on Pike, his body shaking, and his breathing uneven.

Feeling for their link, she pressed love and reassurance at him. She didn't talk. What would she even say? I'm sorry your sister tried to kill me? Yeah, no, better to be silent and let Pike talk when he was ready.

"How did I not see what she'd become?" Pike whispered, his voice breaking as he spoke.

The answer was as simple as it was complex. "Because she's your sister, and family is complicated."

Pike clutched her a little tighter. "I need to tell Mom and Dad what happened."

"Later," Cora urged. "I came over to pack up some of my things before heading back to the mountain. Let's do that. If we hurry, we'll get there before Kimble."

"Yeah, I want to go home," Pike agreed with a sniff.

"Home," she echoed. The word sounded perfect and right. A place for all of them to heal.

## Kimble

Hours later, Kimble landed in front of his house. It seemed like every light inside and outside was on, and he absolutely knew his flock had done it on purpose. As much as he wanted to rush in, he paused outside to gather his thoughts.

He'd been forced to kill Lucy's companion. The man had been vile and while under thrall admitted he would do anything to kill Cora after she humiliated him. Vampires could create strong compulsion using thrall, but it wore off over time. If he'd left the shifter alive, Cora would never be safe.

He'd drained the man dry and left his body out in the desert for the buzzards to eat. A fitting end for a male who admitted he enjoyed hurting humans who couldn't fight back.

Lucy had been different. She'd stopped crying by the time he landed. She remained passive and quiet as he'd interrogated the male and watched with dead eyes as the life had drained from the man's body.

After rolling the body down into a dry creek bed, Kimble had turned to her. Lucy's next words had shocked him.

*"I'm ready to die,"* she said, watching him with resignation. *"Please make it painless. I know you can do that."*

*"I promised your brother I wouldn't kill you,"* he reminded her.

*"I'm sure you lied," she said, her head dropping. Her greasy hair fell forward, obscuring her face. "I threatened to kill a member of your flock. I think I wanted to. It didn't matter that she was Pike's mate, all I could think about was getting money. She made me so angry when she said no and fought back. Humans aren't supposed to fight back like that."*

*He took in her thin appearance and splotchy skin. Most shifters tended toward muscled bodies, but she resembled the unhealthy human models that starved themselves. It wasn't a natural state for a bear.*

*Leaning in close, he breathed her in, but smelled nothing unusual. "Why can't I smell drugs on you?"*

*Her entire body shuddered as if she was cold. Wrapping her arms around herself, she looked up at him through her hair. "Ash," she whispered. "It's called ash. No one can smell it, but it makes you feel invincible. For a while."*

*He'd never heard of the drug, but he hadn't been on speaking terms with the world for over five years. During his life, he'd seen illicit substances rise and fall in popularity and abundance. Ash was only the newest in an unending parade of powders and pills that would cure any illness by creating a new one.*

*"Do you want to die?" he asked. "If you see death as a mercy, I'll go to Pike and make a case for ending your life."*

*She shook her head. "I want to live, but I've destroyed everything." She laughed humorlessly. "Even now I want more. After everything I did and the people I betrayed, all I can think about is getting more ash. The guy you killed was my dealer. I know he has a packet on him. Probably a dozen. Enough to keep me high for weeks."*

*She looked at the lip of the ravine he'd tossed the body into, as if gauging how hard the descent would be if she tried to climb down. Kimble got the feeling she'd mostly dismissed him now that she was sure he wasn't going to kill her.*

*Kimble had dealt with addiction before but only as one person among an entire supportive pack. He wasn't sure how someone without a pack came back from this.*

*Crouching down, he waited until she looked at him. He pointed southeast. "There is a housing tract fifteen miles that way."*

*She glanced to where he pointed then back at him. "You expect me to walk fifteen miles?"*

*He nodded his head and then pulled a business card from of his pocket and held it out. She stared at it like it might be a cursed object. "Take it," he ordered. "If you make it the fifteen miles, you can call for someone to pick you up."*

*Her fingers trembled as she accepted the card. "Whose number is this?"*

*"It's a main phone line for the Laske Pack. I'm going to warn them that they're not to get you unless you're at that housing tract or close to it, understand?"*

*She clutched the card tightly. "Why would a wolf pack want to help me?"*

*"Because they are family to me, and Pike is my flock, so he is pack to them," he explained.*

*Dropping her gaze to the ground at his feet, she shook her head. "What's keeping me from taking everything Danno has on him all at once and ending it right here?"*

*"Absolutely nothing," Kimble answered, his tone calm and even. Anything he felt regarding her passing would be a second-degree agony felt through Pike, not a direct pain. That made it hard for him to summon much sympathy.*

*"You should volunteer for a suicide hotline," she muttered. The sarcasm was the first time she'd shown any emotion beside desolation.*

*"I'm here to give you options, not hold your hand," Kimble said. "You can die here in the desert either by overdose or dehydration. You can start walking and find your way to whatever hovel you've been living at. Or you can walk and call the number I gave you. I'll warn you, if you choose the third option, there will be rules and boundaries. You will live on my property, and you'll do as the pack and I demand. We'll help you get clean and start your life over again. It will be hard, but in the end, you'll have a future and your family back. The other two options mean death. One will just take longer than the other."*

*Tossing her head back, she looked up at him with a pleading expression but calculation in her eyes. "If you could give me—"*

*"No," he said, standing and stepping back so he could shift. "You have your options."*

*Then he reached for the magic that let him turn into his griffin form and took to the air. He heard her crying out and begging for him to come back, but he ignored her.*

As he stood staring at his front door, he couldn't decide which option he hoped she would choose. All of them would cause Pike pain, but would her quick death be easier on him than a long fight with addiction?

Kimble wished there were easy answers. As he gathered the courage to enter his home and explain to the gentlest member of his flock that his sister might be dead by morning, the door swung open to reveal Pike's hulking silhouette.

"Why are you standing out here?" Pike asked.

"We've been waiting for you," Cora said, pushing past Pike to rush at him. Holding out his arms, he let the little human barrel into him and wrap her arms around him in a fierce hug. "It took you a long time. I hope you flew them way the hell out into the east county desert."

"Not that far," he murmured to her. "But far enough."

Pike made a pained sound as he stepped closer. "Is she… was she…"

Seeing one of his flock close to tears was unbearable. He reached out and pulled Pike to him. "She was alive when I left her. I gave her the number to call if she was ready to get clean."

"Clean?" Pike asked as he pressed close to Kimble.

"She's been taking something called ash," Kimble explained.

Pike sagged a little. "That explains so much. It wasn't her; it was the drugs." There was pain and relief in his voice.

Cora pulled away from him and grabbed hold of Pike's shirt. "Come on, let's go inside. I need cuddle time and that blue couch is calling."

"Cuddling sounds good," Pike agreed. He hooked an arm around Kimble's shoulders and pulled him against his side, so they walked together with Cora leading the way.

Relieved to be with his beautiful flock, Kimble fell in step with Pike. "Anything my flock desires is also what I want."

⸎————————⸏

It wasn't until almost dawn that Kimble's brand-new phone pinged several times in a row. Cora and Pike were snuggled on either side of him. It had taken several hours, a lot of edging, and an orgasm so powerful it almost made him pass out before Pike was finally able to fall into a restful sleep.

Worried that the phone would wake Pike, Kimble carefully reached across Cora to silence it but was captured by the messages on the screen, the first was from Annette.

> We have Lucy. We put in the cabin with Stan and Enrico. They'll help her get settled and keep an eye on her.

The next several were from an unknown number, but he guessed it was Enrico.

> Lucy is sleeping right now. Stan volunteered at a rehab for years, he knows what to do. Stan says that by noon tomorrow, she's going to be sick as a dog from withdrawal. I would keep Pike away for now.

> Annette is going to make sure we have the resources we need to help Lucy. Tell Pike we'll be doing everything we can for her.

Kimble responded to Annette with gratitude and then to Enrico with a warning that he couldn't control Pike. The best he could do was make sure Pike spoke to Stan before venturing over. Stan responded with a thumbs up emoji.

Perhaps Pike would be content to know Lucy was safe and being looked after. Kimble wasn't sure if he was happy about this outcome, but it was done, and he couldn't take it back.

Time would tell if he'd made a wise direction. One thing was certain—if Lucy ever threatened his flock again, not even Pike's love would save her.

**Pike**

Standing in the living room of his old apartment, Pike took in all the nasty things that he'd ignored but found unacceptable now that he lived with Kimble. The mold all over the ceiling, the crumbling sheetrock, and soft spots on the floor were only the visible issues. The lack of water pressure and getting lukewarm water for his showers, if the water warmed up at all, were constant problems.

Worst of all was the damp, rotting smell permeating the whole place. How had he ignored it for so long?

Next to him, Cora made a quiet, disgusted sound. "Sad to say that this place is as bad as I remember. I can't believe you paid rent for this dump."

Pike looked down at her. "Funny you should say that. I missed paying last month and this month and nothing happened. No call, no text, no email. I wonder if this place even has a manager anymore."

Cora grinned. "Too bad you didn't know that sooner, you could've stopped paying rent months ago." She hooked an arm through his and led him to the bedroom. "Let's get your stuff and get out of here. I want to be home before Kimble wakes up. If we don't get time with him right away, we might not see him until bedtime!"

Kimble was busier than Pike and Cora combined. Between his businesses and the pack, he spent a good deal of his night on a computer or phone. Annette had kept everything running while he was gone, but it was really a two-person job. Without Kimble, things had been missed and pushed aside. Not that it bothered Kimble. The vampire absolutely jumped into a hectic nightly work schedule.

It almost made Pike miss the old days just a little, when Kimble's whole focus was only him. Coming to his old apartment felt like saying goodbye to the last part of Kimble's time being feral. Now that he was breathing in the mold and looking at the nastiness, Pike could say with confidence that he had no regrets.

"We can leave all the furniture behind, but I want my clothes and some personal stuff," Pike explained.

"Whatever can fit into the truck," Cora agreed. They'd driven the pack truck that had basically become Pike's vehicle. "Grab anything and everything this time because we aren't making a second trip."

Pike chuckled and rubbed his irritated nose. "Agreed!" He handed her one of the trash bags he had in his hand. "Can you get everything in my dresser?"

"Sure," she agreed and shook open the bag. Pike opened a second bag and started on the contents of his closet. They worked in silence for a few minutes before Cora spoke. "I talked to Stan today."

Stan and Enrico kept Cora and Kimble apprised of Lucy's progress and condition, but Pike had asked not to talk about it. Cora's statement was to see if he wanted to know. Every time he'd say *that's good,* or something equally hollow, she'd drop the subject.

This time, he didn't immediately respond. Trash bag half full, Pike went still debating whether he wanted to know more.

He hadn't seen Lucy since the night she'd attacked Cora. She was living on pack lands now, but at Stan and Enrico's place. Their cabin was on the far edge of the property, away from the main fenced-in area. They even had a separate driveway so the likelihood of running into his sister was slim.

The separation was good. It gave him time to figure out how he felt about her abuse and betrayal. He was going to forgive her, but he needed to decide what kind of forgiveness he was going to extend. Would he try to rebuild the close relationship they'd had as kids or was he going to forgive but keep her at a distance?

Either way, maybe it was time to start *talking about her* before he started *talking to her* again.

"How is she?" he asked.

Cora jerked straight with a slightly surprised expression on her face. "She's uh, doing well."

"I know I didn't seem interested before," Pike admitted, feeling guilt creep up again. He ducked his upper body back into the closet, so he didn't need to face Cora. "But I wasn't ready. I think I'm ready now."

Cora dropped the bag and rushed to his side, climbing up and clinging to his back like a monkey.

"Nope," she declared firmly. "We aren't doing that. No guilt allowed. You did your best, and now it's Lucy's turn to do her best."

His mate's firm tone and warm body made the guilt ease. "I should've known."

"Or she should've told you. There are a lot of *should'ves* in this world."

Reaching his arms back, he cupped Cora's ass, making her wiggle against him. "No sex here," she admonished. "It's too gross."

She was right, and honestly, he didn't want sex at the moment. He wanted comfort. When he withdrew his arms, she slid down and turned him to face her. He hoped for a hug, but he got a sincere expression instead.

"I know you've got all kinds of mixed feelings about Lucy. If you don't feel comfortable talking to me, then talk to Kimble. Or you can talk to Annette. She's an amazing listener. I blabbered at her for hours yesterday before I realized how much of her time I took up. When I tried to apologize, she got that sweet earth mother look on her face and said, *you can talk to me anytime and know that everything you say was heard and understood.* I think I love her!"

Pike nodded in agreement. "Did you know she's a trained therapist? She closed her practice when she took over running the pack."

"That makes so much sense. She might have closed her practice, but she's still practicing," Cora quipped.

"Very true," Pike agreed. "I'm not surprised a therapist is a pack alpha. Packs love nurturing leadership. What did Stan say about Lucy?"

"The worst of the withdrawals are over, but she's still sick. She'd been taking ash for years, and it's going to take some time for her body to come back from that."

The thought of Lucy suffering made Pike feel like a monster. "Should I be there to help?"

Cora shook her head. "She needs to be around people she can't manipulate or terrorize. Stan and Enrico are taking turns staying with her so she's never alone, and Annette is going over to talk every day. Although now that I know she's a therapist, I guess she's having sessions with Lucy. Annette told me it could be years before Lucy's really back to herself."

The unspoken *if she comes back to herself* hung between them.

"Stan and Enrico are amazing," Pike murmured. "I should talk to them."

That made him realize he should call his mom and dad and tell them what was going on. As far as they knew, Lucy was simply not talking to them. She'd done it before. Pike had wanted to wait until she was well enough to see them before saying anything about the drugs and attack on Cora. If Lucy's recovery was going to take months more, he should tell them, so they didn't worry.

"We can tell your parents together, if that's what you're worried about," Cora offered. Like Kimble, Cora had gotten good at guessing thoughts based on the feelings coming through their bond. She was right more often than not, and it made Pike feel loved to know Cora cared enough to offer help.

"Yeah, I'd like that. Thanks," he agreed. "I think—"

His words were cut off by the sound of the apartment door crashing open and a voice yelling, "Where the fuck is my cousin!"

**Cora**

Pike's face mirrored the surprise Cora was feeling. When he rushed to the bedroom door, she was right behind him and almost bumped into his back when he came to an abrupt stop.

"Who are you, wolf?" Pike asked with a fierce scowl. He straightened up his spine, pulled back his shoulders and cracked his knuckles. She'd seen him do this before back when he'd been a bouncer. It made him appear intimidating and more often than not ended a fight before it even began.

The expressions on the faces of the dozen men crowded into the apartment's living room told Cora that Pike's tactic wasn't working this time.

"I'm Danno's cousin and alpha," the guy in front said. "The last I heard; he was with your sister Lucy. She begged us to give her one more chance and because Danno's such a soft wolf, he agreed. This was the address she gave me for you. Tell me where Danno is, and I might make your death a painless one."

There wouldn't be any rescue from Kimble. It was still at least two hours until sunset. As she'd done her entire life, Cora looked around for viable weapons. There wasn't anything more in the apartment since Kimble had rescued/kidnapped her so many months ago. She hadn't found weapons then and doubted any would magically appear.

Tugging at Pike's shirt, she tried to get him to move back into the bedroom. Barricading the door would give them a little time.

They were on the third floor. Could Pike shift and climb down?

This time, it was Pike's turn to read her mind.

"They'll be through the door before you can blink," he murmured while keeping a wary eye on the men. "When I move, you need to run for the door. Don't stop. I'll survive but only if you run."

She hated the idea but promised herself that she'd only run until she found a weapon. Then she'd be back to bash some faces in.

"I don't know where your cousin is," Pike said in a reasonable tone. "Lucy showed up a week ago, and I gave her all the money I had. I haven't seen her since."

Cora winced; she should've been the one to lie. Pike sounded like he was reading lines from cue cards.

The leader shook his head. "I'm pretty sure you're not telling me the truth," he drawled.

"We could play with the little human," one of them said, licking his lips as he stared at Cora. "That might make the bear be more honest with us."

Without warning, Pike roared and charged. Cora was startled enough to freeze in place as he shifted mid-stride, his clothes turning to shreds and falling from his body. He bowled over three of the wolves and ripped his claws down a third and forth.

Belatedly, Cora realized this was when she was supposed to run, but the melee was between her and the front door. There wasn't enough room around them, and she wasn't going to make it if she tried to go through.

Suddenly, one of the wolves was next to her, his eyes full of malice. "I know a quick way to end this!"

Scrambling sideways, she barely stayed out of his reach, and it was only because he got shoved from behind by a flying body that she managed to make it into the bathroom.

"Where do you think you're going?" he asked, easily catching up with her. She felt an arm go around her waist at the same time her hands found the heavy ceramic top to the toilet tank. Gripping it in both hands, she lifted and swung with all the muscles in her small frame. It impacted the guy's head with a satisfying sound and cracked in half. Just like when she'd fought Danno and Lucy, the necklace got warm and sent electric sparks over her skin. She swung and sent the guy flying.

To her disappointment, the guy wasn't knocked out. He hit a wall, blood gushing from his nose but was still focused on her.

"You bitch!" he shouted. Shaking his head like a dog, he sprayed blood on the nearby walls, then looked at her with murder in his eyes. Getting up, he easily dodged her attempt to hit him again and was equally fast with a backhand to her face. She lost hold of the remnants of the lid and went to her knees. For a few blessed seconds, her face was numb and then the pain came, making her sweat.

She tasted blood in her mouth and felt something dripping down her chin. When a hand grabbed hold of her upper arm and hauled her to her feet, she tried to resist but was having trouble getting her vision to focus.

It seemed the necklace couldn't make her fast enough to beat this wolf shifter.

"That's only the beginning," the man hissed in her ear, then shook her a little. That didn't help her brain re-orientate her vision.

When he dragged her back into the living room, she saw Pike had knocked out a few of the wolves but was bleeding from wounds on his face and hind quarters. Half the remaining wolves had shifted and were taking turns baiting him so the others could rush in and bite him before dancing back. The ones that hadn't shifted were standing there yelling encouragement as if this was a sporting match.

There was howling and roaring but considering the empty state of the apartment building and most of the area, Cora knew help wasn't coming.

Was this it? Had Lucy managed to kill them after all?

The man holding her up pressed his hand to her throat. She felt his finger shift and sharp claw-like nails dug into her skin. She went perfectly still, scared that any movement would cause him to puncture her vulnerable throat.

"Bear! I have your human!" the guy called out. Pike turned and roared when he saw them. He started to move but the wolf holding her tightened his grip, and she felt his claws slide into her flesh. She couldn't help the cry of pain that came out of her.

Ashamed by her weakness, she yelled as best she could. "Fuck him up, Pike! Don't worry about me!"

Her words were more of a croak than a bellow, but either way, they were ignored by all parties.

"You know I'll kill her," the wolf warned.

She needed to distract him so Pike could take him out. She didn't have anything on her person but maybe her nerve pinching trick would work.

Or make him squeeze down and kill her.

Everything was worth a try.

"Please don't kill me," she begged as she brought her hand up and placed it on the back of his. She stroked as if trying to soothe him, hoping he'd relax just a little. "I have money. Lucy asked for it, but I refused. It's at my house in a safe. You can have everything."

The alpha shifted from wolf to human and stared at her. "You have the money?"

Seeing hope, Cora put her hand in place to pinch but waited. Maybe they could buy their way out of this. "Tons of it. Hundreds of thousands of dollars. In cash."

He eyed her, as if gauging her words, then scoffed. "You're lying."

"What if I'm not?" she asked. "If you kill me, you'll never find the safe."

The alpha nodded his head. "Sure, I'm willing to listen to you." Cora saw a possible escape until the man continued talking. "I'll keep the bear with me. Quick and Bagger will take you on a little road trip. If I lose contact with them or there's no money, your bear becomes a rug." He looked at Pike. "You try to maul my men, and Quick will ventilate the human's neck. Do we all understand each other?"

Cora wanted to cry. This wasn't what she wanted to happen. There wasn't money back at her place. She was going to have to come up with another plan during the car ride there.

"What's going on here?"

Horrified, Cora watched Mrs. J hobble into the apartment with her little dog at her side. Muggsie blinked milky white eyes at the strangers and gave a yipping bark while Mrs. J frowned at everyone.

She raised her cane and pointed it around the room at the wolves. "Cora and Pike are friends of mine, so all of you should go."

Pike shifted back to his human form and faced the old woman. "Please, Mrs. J, you need to leave."

With his back turned, Cora could see dozens of deep puncture wounds all over his thighs, buttocks, and back. Those were bad enough, but there were several deep gashes across his left side. Blood streamed down his skin and even in the short time he stood there, puddles had formed at his feet.

He was hurt so much worse than she thought. Now Mrs. J was in danger. Could this get any worse?

**Pike**

There wasn't a part of his body that didn't hurt, but the pain was nothing compared to his terror at losing Cora. He was ready to keep fighting, push every wolf into the bedroom so Cora could escape. He was ready to die, but once one of the wolves got a hand around her throat, he didn't know what to do.

Dying seemed inevitable, but he didn't want Cora going with him, and the addition of Mrs. J meant another innocent life would be lost.

"Please, Mrs. J, you need to leave!" He begged even as the elderly woman brought her cane down with a thump on the floor. Muggsie barked again and pulled on his leash.

"I heard you the first time," Mrs. J said as she slowly leaned down to pet Muggsie. "But I think you need me here, Pike. This is too many wolves for one bear to handle and poor Cora is over there bleeding."

When she straightened up, Pike could see Muggsie's leash wasn't attached to the dog anymore. What was Mrs. J thinking? She'd never seemed confused or suffering from dementia before. Why wasn't she running, or rather hobbling, for her life?

"Fucking old bitch," the alpha grumbled. "You should've minded your own business."

Mrs. J tilted her head as she looked at him, her deep brown eyes curious. "That wasn't very kind of you. Are you the alpha of this pack?"

Nodding his head, the man pushed a limping pack member out of the way so he could loom over the old woman. "I'm the alpha. Why? You think I'll give you time to call for help? Who would come help you anyway? More humans?"

He laughed at his own joke and the wolves that were still conscious laughed with him. The ones in wolf form yipped and howled mockingly.

Pike was puzzled. These guys might not realize it, but this was odd behavior for an elderly human. By the time they reached Mrs. J's age, they were usually far more cautious around strangers and quick to leave at any hint of violence. Why was Mrs. J acting like a pack of violent wolf shifters wasn't a big deal?

Mrs. J looked sad for a moment. "You're correct. I have no one to call for help. They all died long ago, but I'm still here in the same place. Perhaps it's time to start living again instead of hiding. When my sweet Harry died, I fell into a deep mourning. That was a long time ago. I've mourned enough."

"Ain't that the saddest damn story," the alpha mocked. "But if you want to keep living, you're going to have to give me something." He turned to another wolf. "Take her to her place and clean out anything of value."

When the wolf jumped to do the alpha's bidding, Mrs. J put up her cane to ward off the wolf. "Stay right there, pup. Before any of you try anything, I'd like to give you a chance to leave."

The wolves laughed again and the one slapped Mrs. J's cane out of the way and reached for her arm. "Don't make me hurt you, lady. All I want is money and jewelry, yah?"

"You've made your decision then," Mrs. J said with a sad little shake of her head. "I warned you."

Pike blinked rapidly and hoped he hadn't sustained brain damage because Mrs. J seemed to be shrinking!

"What the hell?" the alpha cursed. "Is she a vole shifter or something?"

The wolves laughed again, but their humor was cut off when the shrinking reversed and she seemed to explode out into a brand-new body.

This new Mrs. J was far taller than her earlier diminutive shape, with a round, voluptuous build. The clothes that had been oversized and baggy before were tight and barely holding in her generous breasts. Thick tendrils of long black hair flowed around her shoulders and head as if she was in water.

No, that wasn't hair, those were snakes!

"Fuck, fuck, fuck!" the alpha screamed as he staggered back. "It's a gorgon!"

"Those don't exist," the wolf holding Cora captive said, his voice high with fear. "Right? It's got to be an illusion!"

Mrs. J pursed her full lips at the wolves. "You think I'm an illusion? How amusing!"

Pike couldn't see auras like vampires and druids could, but Mrs. J was glowing with enough power to light up her tan skin. She was so powerful he could feel her magic even though he was half a room away.

This wasn't an illusion.

"She can't be a gorgon. We're all still breathing and talking," another wolf said. "None of us are turned to stone or nothing."

Mrs. J's hair moved and writhed around her head as she turned her neck to look at the wolf who spoke. "Oh, silly pup, that's not how my power works. If everyone I saw turned to stone, I'd never be able to go grocery shopping or get another manicure."

The wolf who'd spoken so confidently shied away from her until his back hit a wall. "Please don't hurt me."

"I'm afraid you didn't give me a choice," she answered. Her eyes flashed a bright amber for a moment, and the wolf shrieked and then froze in place. Pike watched his skin change color starting with his face and then going down the rest of him until he was a uniform gray with the texture of rough stone.

"You bitch!' the alpha screamed, then shifted and lunged at Mrs. J. He was close to her, but she didn't flinch. Color flashed from her eyes again, and he fell mid-leap, his stone body breaking into dozens of pieces when it hit the floor.

When she looked away from the alpha's body, the rest of the men in the room flinched and all but one started begging for their lives.

She ignored all of them and focused on the one still holding Cora hostage. "Let the human go."

The wolf hesitated. "You're going to kill me if I do."

Mrs. J put her hands on her hips and smiled at him. "You're dying either way but turning to stone will be a lot less painful than what Muggsie will do to you."

Everyone looked down at the little dog, and the wolf holding Cora barked out a high pitched, nervous laugh. "Your rat doesn't scare me, gorgon. I'll kill it with a stomp."

"This pack contains some of the stupidest wolves I've ever met," Mrs. J murmured. Looking down at her dog, she gestured to the pet. "Make sure the human doesn't get hurt. She's Pike's mate and remember, you like Pike. Well, you like him most days."

Muggsie gave a single yip and trotted across the room. As he moved, he got bigger and bigger until he was the size of one of the shifted wolves.

He wasn't a wolf though, or a dog. He was something Pike had never seen or heard of. The closest Pike could think of was that this thing looked like an alligator with long legs and fur!

As Muggsie opened his giant mouth, Pike wasn't surprised to see row after row of teeth, but he was very shocked when tendrils shot out and wrapped around the wolf holding Cora.

The wolf screamed and let go of Cora to fight the tentacles. As he was drawn closer, Muggsie's mouth seemed to get even bigger!

Worried about Cora, Pike jumped over Muggsie and got his arms around her as her legs gave out. He lowered both of them to the ground and watched Muggsie pull the fighting and screaming wolf down his throat whole.

They could still hear the man's muffled cries even after Muggsie's jaw slammed shut.

"I think I can see him moving inside," Cora whispered hoarsely. Pike shifted his gaze and noticed that there was faint movement rippling on Muggsie's sides.

Mrs. J gave a cheerful, airy laugh. "I wish you'd at least bit him in two before swallowing."

Muggsie turned to Mrs. J and made a whistling sound that reminded Pike of a bird. Mrs. J answered his whistle with another laugh. "I know, I know. You like the way they thrash around while you digest them." She looked around at the rest of the stunned and pale pack and shrugged. "I warned him turning to stone would be less painful."

The remaining wolves went back to begging her for mercy. Holding Cora tightly to his chest, Pike watched as Mrs. J surveyed them with a considering expression. Finally she pointed to one and spoke.

"You aren't truly corrupted yet," she announced. "Your soul is salvageable. I'll let you serve me as penance. It won't be easy, do you accept?"

"Yes, ma'am!" the wolf said and rushed to kneel in front of her.

One of the other wolves tried to join him. "I want to serve—"

Mrs. J's eyes flashed, and the wolf fell over mid-step, the pieces of his stone body scattering among his alpha's.

"None of the rest of you can be saved," she declared and between one breath and the next, Pike watched all of them turn to stone. Most fell over and shattered but two remained on their knees, faces frozen in expressions of fear and horror.

When she turned to face them, Pike flinched. Pushing to his feet, he rushed to use his body to shield Cora. "Please don't hurt the human!"

Mrs. J rolled her eyes and laughed. "I let Muggsie eat the wolf holding her, remember?"

Pike relaxed a little, realizing they probably weren't in danger from the gorgon. "Thank you for saving us."

Cora moved to his side and stumbled. Looking down, he saw blood dripping from her mouth and nose, and her complexion was pale. She had to be in pain.

They were quite the pair. With the danger gone, Pike noticed there wasn't a part of his body that hadn't been bit, slashed, or hit. He hurt everywhere.

As damaged as they both were, he'd hate to think how much worse it would've been without Kimble's bond making them stronger and tougher.

"You two look like you've been in a car wreck," Mrs. J murmured. Muggsie made one of his bird sounds, and she looked down at him. "Do you think I should?"

He whistled again, then looked at the remaining wolf. Moving in close, he nosed the young man. The wolf was still on his hands and knees in front of Mrs. J and when Muggsie touched him, the wolf curled into himself and whimpered.

"He's not going to eat you," Mrs. J assured the wolf as she stepped around him and made her way to Pike and Cora. "He's still digesting your friend."

It took all of Pike's willpower to remain still as Mrs. J got close. She gave him an approving grin before reaching out and cupping his cheek. Her touch felt warm, and he could smell strong magic wafting off her.

"You've got one of the purest souls I've ever seen," she told him. Her hand got warmer, and his entire body started to heat up like he had a fever. "After my sweet Harry died, I almost wanted to join him. It's hard for us to die, but we can do it. I let myself grow old to make it easier, and then you moved into the building. You made me realize that there's still kindness and joy in the world, even if Harry wasn't here. I'd been thinking of resurrecting myself when you brought Kimble home. I was so worried for you. Soul bonds are strong, and Kimble wouldn't mean to hurt you, but feral vampires are unpredictable. I decided to stay in my elder form, in case you needed me. No one can sense us when we don't want to be known, not even ancient vampires."

Pike had a hard time paying attention to Mrs. J's words because he was distracted by the pain fading. Where her warmth spread through his body, the early discomfort eased and then disappeared. Her gentle grip on his face kept him from looking down, but he'd bet anything his wounds were rapidly healing.

"Now that you're safe with your vampire and human mates, it seems you don't need me to watch over you any longer." One of the snakes slid against his face, tasting his skin with a long, forked tongue. "I'm going to take my new pet wolf, and my beast and find a new place to live before this building falls down around us."

She laughed, the sound of it washing over Pike and making him want to laugh with her. There was no fear any longer and not even the snake touching him felt weird.

"Mrs. J, um Mrs. Gorgon person?" Cora said. "I'm not trying to disrespect you or anything, but I'm going to have to sit down now."

Pike saw Mrs. J's eyes go wide at the same time he felt Cora's grip on him loosen. Mrs. J let go of his face and reached for Cora. She was able to hold his little human up long enough for Pike to shake off the effects of her calming/healing magic and grab Cora up in his arms.

"I don't feel good," Cora mumbled. "My head really hurts."

"Oh, you poor thing," Mrs. J cooed, moving in close to press both hands to either side of Cora's face. "I should've started with you. Muggsie wanted Pike healed first because Pike gave him bacon a few times. That beast's affections are easily bought!"

She chuckled at her own joke while several of her snakes moved to taste Cora's skin. Pike could feel Cora's body getting hot and while he watched, her swollen nose went back to normal size and the bruising on her face faded. Those were only the visible injuries though. Mrs. J was probably healing a lot of internal damage that might have killed Cora if left much longer.

"There now, aren't you feeling better?" Mrs. J asked.

"Yeah," Cora agreed. To Pike's horror, Cora reached up and touched one of the snakes. "Pretty."

The snake weaved through Cora's fingers before retreating back to the rest of the writhing mass. "They are pretty, aren't they?" Mrs. J said, letting go of Cora's face to touch her snake hair.

Taking a step back, Mrs. J turned to regard the wolf on the floor. He was sitting back on his knees now, with Muggsie rolled on his back in front of him. The wolf was scratching the creature's belly while Muggsie moaned and shook a paw in the air from pleasure.

Mrs. J snapped her fingers. "To me, wolf," she ordered.

The young man scrambled to his feet and rushed to her side, head bowed, and arms wrapped around his chest.

"Yes?" he squeaked.

"You're going to help me pack and then we're leaving here," she explained. "Do you have a vehicle?"

He shook his head, then nodded. "I don't have one, but my alpha's car is here. We can take that. Except, uh, you might have turned the key to stone."

Mrs. J examined the pieces of stone that had been the alpha, her eyes flashing as she looked them over. "Here they are," she said and reached down to one chunk the size of her fist. The moment she touched it, the stone turned into a piece of bloody pant leg.

A moment later, she pulled a key fob free of the cloth, which had been the pocket of the alpha's pants. She held it out and the young man took the fob with a shaking hand.

"What are you called?" she asked.

"James Dean, but everyone calls me JD," he whispered.

"Very well," Mrs. J said. "I'd like to be called Ysabel. It's such a lovely name, and I haven't used it before."

Now that she was healed, Cora was coming out of her gorgon induced daze and looking around the room with a critical eye. "Why does it feel like I dreamed all this?"

"Brain trauma," Ysabel said airily. "Your brain was swelling a bit, but you're fine now. Off you two go. I'm sure Kimble is eager to set eyes on the two of you after feeling everything through the link. Poor vampires. I'd never trade eternal life for the sun. We gorgons thrive in the light."

"Thanks for not letting me die," Cora said.

"I'll take payment in drinks. I like fruity cocktails the best," Ysabel said, then turned her attention to JD. She pointed to the apartment's empty front door frame. "My apartment is the one with the open door. Go in there and find something to eat. I can hear your empty stomach complaining from here. Eat fast. We have a lot to accomplish tonight. I'm impatient to begin my new life after putting it off for so long."

JD rushed out the door as if she'd screamed at him to move instead of giving her order in a reasonable, even affectionate tone. They heard his feet pound down the hall and then cut off as he got to her apartment.

"That one is going to be an eager disciple," Ysabel commented.

"Well, you inspire eagerness with that whole turning-people-to-stone thing," Cora quipped.

Pike stiffened but Ysabel didn't take offense to Cora's sass. Instead, she threw back her head and laughed. Wiping a tear from her eye, she headed to the door. "I'll be in touch, little human. We'll have a girl's night. I haven't been young for a long time. This'll be fun."

Then she was gone, and the room seemed to dim a little. Pike remained still, surrounded by bits and pieces of stone wolves, staring at the door and still holding Cora.

"Is any of your stuff that important?" Cora asked after several seconds of silence.

"Not a damn thing," he agreed and carried her out of the building and to his truck. He was still naked but didn't care. There were extra clothes in the truck, and he couldn't stand to be in that place a moment longer. "I'm never leaving the compound again."

**Kimble**

Cora frowned at her phone again, then deliberately set it on the kitchen table face down. Kimble didn't need to see the message to know it was from her Aunt Maria. She was desperate to broker peace between Cora and the rest of her family. As time went on, Maria's pleas became demands, and Cora stopped responding.

It bothered Kimble that he couldn't simply fix the problem of Cora's family for her. It had been several months since the revealing confrontation at Daniel's house, and Cora's anxiety about talking to them had only gotten worse. Pike noticed also but had no more clue how to fix it than Kimble.

"Want to talk about those texts?" he whispered in Cora's ear.

"Never," Cora answered, then spoke up to Pike. "What are you going to plant in the southeast corner, near the barn?"

"I was thinking of planting rhubarb there," Pike answered, his arms elbow deep in soapy water.

It was early evening. Cora and Pike had finished dinner, and Cora was sitting crosswise in his lap while Pike cleaned up. At first, it'd bothered Kimble that Pike wouldn't let him help; then he'd realized it was because the bear was possessive of the kitchen. Although he might have a laid-back personality, Pike had very strict rules about how everything was done in his domain.

"Have you thought about pomegranates?" Cora suggested. Along with the kitchen, Pike's other domain was his garden. Cora and the wolves had tried to help him in the early days but had been gently rebuffed. It was his place to be king and caretaker, and it was obvious he loved it.

"Pomegranates," Pike repeated, pausing with a skillet in one hand and a soapy sponge in the other while nodding his head. "That's a good idea. It's a winter fruit, and I'm trying to put in more winter and fall plants."

Cora's phone buzzed repeatedly, making her tense. Kimble worried that she might have a nervous breakdown if she kept putting off dealing with her family.

When he looked up, it was to see Pike drying his hands off and staring at Cora's phone with a frown. "Is it Imani or Aunt Maria?"

"Maria," Cora admitted, slumping against Kimble.

"Tea?" Pike asked, reaching for the pot of tea he'd prepared earlier. He harvested and dried the herbs himself and every evening, he brewed a small pot for them to share. Even when Cora said no, he'd poured her a mug, and she drank it.

"Sure," Cora answered, her half grin telling Kimble that she might grumble about having to drink "hot herb water," but she still found the ritual soothing.

Pike joined them at the table with two mugs of tea. "I have an idea about your family."

Cora held the hot mug between her hands and stared at the steam. Her answer was a lackluster, "What?"

Kimble could feel her reluctance and apprehension and rubbed a soothing hand over her back. As interested as he was to hear Pike's plan, his first concern was keeping Cora happy.

"We would never force you to do anything," he reminded her.

"I know," she responded, still staring at the cup. "I don't mean to take my problems out on you guys."

Pike held up his left hand to show off the ring he wore on his third finger. "They're officially our family too, remember?"

The three of them had an Alighting Ceremony several weeks ago. It had been a massive party with several wolf packs in attendance along with Pike's family, Imani with her flock, and Tobias and his flock. Kimble had hated every moment of it, but

Pike and Cora had enjoyed it immensely. Their joy made the crowds tolerable. They might even be able to talk him into doing it again at some distant future point.

Cora looked at his ring then to the one on her hand holding the mug. "I've met your family; I think you got the worst part of the deal here."

"What's your idea?" Kimble asked before Cora could start a fight about why her family was "the worst."

"I think we should have a family board meeting," Pike answered.

Cora wrinkled her brow in confusion. "Board meeting?"

Pike leaned closer, eager to explain. "Yeah, board meeting. Treat it like you're negotiating a contract."

"What do you mean by contract?" she asked.

"I think you're anxious because you feel trapped," Pike explained. "You think it's all or nothing. If you have a relationship with them in any way, they'll go back to treating you the way they have been, or you'll have to go no-contact and give up on the people you love."

Cora's eyes narrowed. "Did Annette talk to you?"

Pike shook his head. "Of course she didn't, but I can feel your thoughts sometimes coming through our link, and I can feel all your heavy emotions. With all that, it's not hard to figure out what's going on in your head." His expression changed to one of hurt. "I love you and want to help so I've thought a lot about your situation. And I'm not a dumb bear, even if I didn't go to college or trade school."

"Oh Pike, I'm sorry," Cora said.

Sensing her intentions, Kimble was quick to take the mug from her hand so she could scramble from his lap to Pike. Cora hugged Pike around the neck before kissing his cheek and sitting up with her back against the table.

"Tell me about having a family board meeting, please."

For the first time in a while, Kimble felt Cora opening up to let them help with her family. It had taken time, but she was finally realizing that Pike and Kimble were impossible to scare off.

Kimble had made sure the family board meeting was as formal as possible. Several members of the pack had volunteered to escort the family to a small office building on the compound where he, Pike, and Cora would already be waiting.

Normally, the largest room in the building was full of workstations. For tonight's gathering, the wolves had shoved everything into other rooms. Gone were all the colorful pictures and notes on the walls or the mismatched chairs, yoga balls, and standing desks.

In their place, the wolves brought in a single, rectangular table and matching chairs. Someone had even set up a small platter of pastries and a carafe of coffee in the center. It was a little late in the evening for most humans to drink coffee, but it set the right tone. This room could be located in any non-descript corporate office in America. It was sterile, inhospitable, and exactly what Kimble had wanted.

The three of them were sitting on one side of the table with Cora between them when Daniel walked into the room followed closely by his five sons. The three of them stood up but didn't move to physically greet them.

"Welcome," Kimble said. "Thank you for coming. Please be seated."

"It's been months, and I don't even get a hug?" Daniel asked. He was smiling, but it didn't reach his eyes, and his tone was full of censure.

"Not yet," Cora said. She dropped back down to her seat. Her expression was focused, but Kimble could feel the emotions rioting inside of her at the sight of her family.

Placing a hand on her thigh, he put his mouth to her ear. "We have a plan."

Her mind calmed a little at that reminder. The three of them had spent days pre-gaming this meeting. They'd even called Annette to help them strategize. All that effort was reflected in the three-page document Pike was currently handing out.

"Before we begin, we'd like you to read through this," Pike said.

"What the hell is it?" Daniel asked as he accepted his copy and scowled at the first page.

Now it was Kimble's turn to speak. "That will become self-evident once you finish reading it. Please be aware that the moment even one of you raises your voice or starts using insulting language, everyone will be escorted off the property. This is nonnegotiable and will result in a delay of reconciliation between all of you and Cora."

"Jesus Christ, you sound like a damn lawyer," Caleb said with a grin. "I like it."

Cora laughed, and Kimble felt some of her tension ease. "You would."

"Is this what you want, Cora?" Daniel asked, his brows furrowed in confusion this time. He used the paper to indicate the setting. "You want to treat us like some kind of business thing?"

Kimble felt a spike of hurt and anger come from Cora. Pike must've felt it too because both of them leaned in close to lend Cora their support. Cora placed one hand over Kimble's on her thigh and tangled her fingers with Pike's hand on the table.

She pulled in a deep breath before she spoke in an even, reasonable voice. "Read the paper, Dad. Then we'll talk."

Daniel and the brothers seemed to realize she wasn't going to be baited, cajoled, or teased out of this. All of them bent their heads and started reading.

**Cora**

Predictably, Caleb was done first, and he smiled broadly as he set down his copy. "I accept all terms of this contract without reservation."

Cora felt something ease inside of her. Caleb was only one of seven men sitting across the table from her, but it felt good to know someone else was on her side. She hadn't really worried about her brothers accepting the contract. It was her dad that was going to be the biggest issue.

She honestly didn't know how he was going to react to the contract the three of them had labored over for hours. So many family injustices were addressed in those three pages that Cora was surprised the paper didn't weigh hundreds of pounds.

As she watched her father read, she was impressed the paper didn't catch fire from the way he was glaring at it. His reading glasses were perched on the end of his nose, and his mouth was settled into a severe frown. When he got to the last page, the paper crumpled under his tightening grip until he realized what he was doing and set it on the table to finish reading.

By the time her father was done, the rest of the brothers had long since set their copies down. Everyone remained silent, waiting to see how the patriarch of the Walsh family would react.

Sitting back, Daniel took his glasses off and gently folded them up before tucking them in the front pocket of his shirt.

"It seems you think I don't love you," he said, breaking the silence.

Cora had been ready for the ploy, but it still hurt. She employed the tactic Annette had taught her. "If that was the case, why would I go to so much effort to bring you back into my life?"

It was obvious Daniel didn't like his question being answered with another question. He kept his tone even, but his motion was violent as he pushed the paper across the table. "It's obvious, isn't it? It says it right there, in black and white, I'm a shitty father."

"It does?" Kimble asked, pretending to examine his copy. "I don't remember using those words anywhere."

"The words aren't there, but I can read what you meant," Daniel sneered. "I'm not allowed to say mean things even if I'm doing it in a," he raised his hands to make air quotes, "a teasing way. That's because I call Cora my second biggest disappointment, isn't it? She knows I don't mean it."

Cora took a deep breath. It was time. Her next words would cause Daniel to either blow up or stay and hash this out.

To her surprise, Caleb spoke up before she could get a word out.

"I want the same contract as Cora." Everyone looked at him in surprise as he stood up and walked around the table to sit next to Pike. "I'm done being called your greatest disappointment. I have a career I enjoy, a wife I love, and children I can't imagine living without."

"You know I don't mean it like that," Daniel blustered.

"Maybe," Caleb responded. "The thing is, Dad, I love my kids so damn much. I want them to be happy and succeed in anything they find joyful. I'd never look at either of them and say the things you've repeated to me over and over again through the years. It would hurt me inside to do that to my children. How can you keep saying that to me? I'm with Cora. I'm not sure you love us."

Daniel looked stunned. "I'm just giving you a hard time. You know I'm proud of what you've accomplished."

"No, I don't know that," Caleb bit out. "You didn't even come to my graduation from law school! Everyone else was there except you."

With a determined frown, Tim stood up and sat next to Caleb. He didn't meet Daniel's eyes and spoke quietly but firmly. "I never wanted to be an electrician. I wanted to go to college and study history."

"What were you going to do with a history degree? Teach?" Daniel scoffed.

Tim looked up, hurt clear on his face. "What's wrong with teaching?"

Cora leaned forward to address Tim. "It's not too late. I'll help you pay for college. You can still be a teacher or historian or whatever the fuck you want. I promise."

Caleb, Kimble, and Pike all echoed her sentiment. Their support helped Tim sit up a little straighter. "Thanks guys," he said. "I'll think about it."

Cooper stood up and took the chair next to Kimble. "I still want to be an electrician, but I don't want to be your slave anymore. I'm good, and you treat me like I'm still an apprentice who doesn't know shit. I'm done with that, Dad. Consider this my resignation."

It seemed Cora wasn't the only one who felt mistreated by their father.

Daniel shook his head, incredulous at what was happening. "I raised you, clothed you, cared for you even after your mother died, and this is how you treat me?"

"There's more to raising children than seeing to their physical needs," Cora stated.

"Children need to be loved," Caleb said with clear condemnation.

"We needed someone to build us up, not tear us down," Cooper added. "I'm tired of being called a dipshit every time I make a mistake. You're not perfect either, Dad. I've fixed plenty of things you've done wrong."

Daniel made a disgusted sound and shoved away from the table. He stood so quickly his chair toppled over behind him.

"When did my boys turn into such pussies? I'd expect this emotional overanalyzing from Cora but not my boys. When you all come to your senses, you can call me." He looked down at the brothers still seated at his end of the table. "Let's go."

Ted, Carson, and Trevor stood up, but they didn't move to the door. Instead, they all silently shuffled over to Cora's side of the table. A deep love for her siblings filled her at the same time she fought against the anger making her want to scream at her father. He was losing all of them due to his stubbornness.

He pointed a shaking finger at Cora. "This is all your fault. I knew you'd be trouble the moment you were born, and I was right!"

"I believe it's time you leave now," Kimble said. "I'll have the terms emailed to you. If you ever want to interact with Cora again, you'll have to sign the contract and abide by its rules."

For the first time, Daniel raised his voice. "I'm in charge here! I'm the one who decides what's what. It's all of you that will have to come begging me."

He turned to storm out, but Cora had one last thing to say. "Dad?"

When he looked at her, there was triumph on his face. He thought she was about to give in, but he was dead wrong.

"Yes?"

"If Mom was alive, what would she say about everything you've done since she died?"

The question hit Daniel like a blow. He staggered back, his expression going from triumph to disbelief. "I can't believe you asked me something like that."

"Think about it, Dad," Cora urged. "I don't remember her, but Aunt Maria always told me she was everything loving and kind. When she was alive, did she stay silent if you bullied us?"

Daniel's mouth opened and closed, but no words came out. It struck Cora that he suddenly looked far older than his years. His shoulders were hunched a little, and he appeared worn and tired, as if he'd been so busy trying to control everything in his life that he'd aged himself prematurely. It struck her that he'd traumatized his children because his wife's death had left him deeply wounded.

Cora's next words came from a place of peace and acceptance as she realized Daniel was as fucked up as the rest of them.

"I think you lost your way, Dad. It's up to you to find it again. We'll be waiting."

**Pike**

Worried that Daniel would start hurling abuse at Cora, Pike was quick to stand up and forcefully guide the human out of the building. Waiting outside the front door were the wolves who'd escorted the Walsh men in.

"He's ready to leave now," Pike explained. "The rest of them will be staying for a while longer."

The wolves nodded and took positions on either side of Daniel. "This way, sir."

"I didn't drive," Daniel mumbled, staring straight ahead and looking shell shocked. "I rode with Cooper."

"We'll get you home," one of the wolves said with a nod at Pike, then they guided him away.

Confident that Daniel was taken care of, Pike made his way back into the room to find Cora sitting on Kimble's lap and laughing. In fact, all the siblings were laughing. It was the type of laugh you heard after living through something that should've been deadly. The relieved merriment of survivors.

"I didn't think this would ever happen," Tim said softly after the laughter had died down.

Pike made his way to Cora and put a hand on her shoulder. She relaxed back against him, some of the tension going out of her body. Grabbing the hand on her shoulder, she pulled it down and hugged his arm to her chest.

"You didn't think anyone would ever stand up to Dad?" Caleb asked, giving Cora an admiring look. "Of course it would be Short Stop who did it."

"That too," Tim agreed, giving Cora a hopeful look. "I didn't think I'd ever be free. Can I come work for you now?"

Cora shook her head. "No way."

Tim's jaw dropped. "What?"

"You're going to college," she stated firmly. "No more electrical work for you."

His face flushed. "I can work for you until the semester starts. Oh shit, what am I going to do about a place to live? I was renting from Dad."

"You're going to move into my house," Cora stated firmly. "I haven't rented it out yet so you can stay there for as long as you need to. No rent."

"Careful, with that kind of sweet deal, he might get to college and decide to never finish!" Cooper teased.

Tim pretended to punch Cooper in the gut. "Says the guy who moved in with a guy after the first date because he got himself evicted."

Cooper grabbed Tim around the waist and lifted him into the air. "You promised to never bring that up again after I covered you on the Stell Street job!"

The brothers started wrestling in earnest, and Pike debated about pulling them apart. Then Caleb nudged the two out of the way so the rest of them could keep talking. It seemed this was common with those two.

"I'm out of a job too," Carson said with a hopeful look at Cora.

"Of course you're going to come to work for me," she said. "You and Cooper both. I only refused Tim because it's not the life he wants."

"I guess no more monthly BBQ," Caleb commented. "Looks like this is the end of an era."

"We could try going to a park or something," Carson suggested. "Other big families do that. And a park means playgrounds for the kids. It could be even better. There's a great one by my office."

"Sure, I guess that could work," Caleb said without an ounce of enthusiasm.

"If the old era is ending, then a new one must begin," Kimble said. "There's plenty of room here and a small playground. As long as my people are invited, we could host your monthly parties."

"Yeah!" Cooper shouted from the floor as he and Tim wrestled. "Let's do that! Cora's in charge of the family now!"

Cora jolted against him, her hold tightening around his arm. "Uh, no, I don't think—"

"I second Cooper's suggestion," Trevor said, cutting Cora's protest off. "I second the idea of Cora as head of the family. Everyone who agrees, say aye!"

There was a chorus of "ayes" from the assembled siblings.

Pike could feel both pleasure and apprehension coming from Cora. "All of you are so dumb," she said, fighting a smile. "Didn't we just rebel so no one was in charge of the family?"

"We staged a revolution to oust the dictator. Now we want to elect a president," Caleb quipped.

Cora hung her head with a sigh. "Is there any way I can say no?"

"None," Caleb answered with a chuckle, then looked at Kimble. "Are you sure about this? We're a rowdy bunch."

"So I've witnessed," Kimble answered. "But you haven't seen my people when alcohol is abundant. I think you'll find your wildness is well matched here."

Carson tilted his head and stared at Kimble. "What happened to your super thick accent? The last time I saw you, it was all one-word sentences and grunts. Now you sound like Caleb, all slick as snot with those fancy words."

"Hey," Cora said, mock glaring at Carson.

"Let me handle this," Caleb said, then spoke with a soft conciliatory tone. "Which word confused you, Carson? I can explain it, or maybe give you other words you already know. Alcohol is a term for drinks like beer. You know what beer is, right?"

Carson rolled his eyes. "You sound like you're talking to one of your kids."

"Might as well be," Caleb said, making Carson laugh.

"Whatever," Carson said, returning his attention back to Kimble. "My question still stands, what happened with your accent? Were you testing us before by acting all dumb and shit?"

"Perhaps," Kimble said with a little shrug.

"I bet he was trying to get us to say stuff in front of him so he could get intel," Trevor suggested.

They argued amicably about Kimble's accent with Cora adding in some outrageous conspiracy theories making them all laugh. As the friendly conversation went on, the food was eaten, coffee drank, and eventually everyone started to look at their phones.

It was clear to Pike no one wanted to leave the little bubble of family camaraderie they'd created. Tomorrow they'd have to face the reality of standing strong against an angry family patriarch.

Pike spoke up before he could consider the wisdom of his words. "Any of you can call me if you need some help, or someone to talk to."

All the brothers looked over at him with surprised expressions.

"That's nice?" Caleb said, making it more of a question than a compliment.

Pike felt his face get hot with embarrassment, but he forged on. "Cora and Kimble both tend to work long hours and can be hard to get a hold of, but I have a lot of free time. All of you are family to me now so if you need some help, I'm here. It doesn't matter whether it's moving furniture or letting you spill your guts over a beer, I've got your back."

The siblings blinked at him, and he felt Cora's pleasure at his sincere offer. "You're the sweetest bear ever," she whispered.

Kimble pushed a feeling of warmth and support at him, clearly stating the vampire was proud of his courage to speak up.

It was Cooper who broke the silence. "Thanks, man. You can never have too many brothers."

The others murmured their agreement, and Pike saw real acceptance in their eyes. They all talked a little longer before they walked the brothers back to their cars. The three of them stood there in silence and watched the cars' lights disappear down the dark driveway.

"It really is the beginning of a new era," Cora murmured. The three of them pressed close together, enjoying the feeling of love flowing through their bond.

Cora turned slightly so she could look up at him and Pike. Her eyes looked bright and luminous, and her lips were curved in a soft smile as she spoke. "I'm really glad I didn't try hard to kill you, Kimble. Turns out you and Pike are the loves of my life."

Kimble laughed and grabbed her around the waist to throw her over his shoulder. He slung his free arm around Pike's shoulders and guided him into the house.

"Let's reenact the kidnapping as it should've been!" he suggested. Pike felt a shot of lust come from both his mates, making him instantly and painfully hard in his pants.

"Can I be kidnapped too?" Pike teased.

"Of course, *sloneczko*." Kimble tightened his arm around Pike's shoulders and pretended to drag him through the wide-open front door. "Come with me, my flock! It's time to ravish you both!"

"Save me, Cora," Pike called out, putting the back of his hand to his forehead. Cora's peals of laughter echoed into the night until Kimble kicked the front door shut and proceeded to ravish them both repeatedly.

## THREE MONTHS LATER, THE FIRST WALSH FAMILY BBQ AT THE LASKE PACK COMPOUND

**Cora**

Julie and Hailey cackled with laughter as they ran by Cora, Caleb, Tim, and Kimble. Right behind the two eight-year-olds was Pike, waving his arms in the air and pretending to roar. The three of them disappeared behind a small cluster of leafy avocado trees.

"It looks like Pike is having a fun time," Cora commented as the three reappeared on the other side with the girls now chasing Pike. The big shifter was smiling as he begged for mercy and pretended to trip. Julie and Hailey were on him and started tickling him mercilessly.

Julie was one of Caleb's kids, and Hailey was the oldest child of one of the pack's families. Cora had worried about letting all the kids play together, not that she thought the wolf shifter children would deliberately hurt the human kids, but accidents happen. Even though they couldn't shift yet, the shifter children were bigger and stronger than most humans their age.

Kimble and Annette assured her that pack children were taught to be gentle with other species at a young age and this party was proof. Not only were all the kids getting along, but it was obvious there were a few best friend situations brewing.

"It seems we've successfully created a Walsh family BBQ," Kimble said. "I see nothing but happy faces and hear nothing but laughter."

Cora nodded and pressed in close. Kimble slung an arm around her shoulders, his other hand holding a beer he was pretending to drink.

"You were right, this place is perfect," Cora agreed. She'd been sure no one would drive all the way out to the compound. Then family members started arriving, and on time too! A rare occurrence within her family.

"All you need is a pool, and this place would be way better than Dad's," Trevor said as he joined their group.

"I'll look into it," Kimble said. Translation: *I'll have a pool installed before the next party.*

"I can't believe your friends roasted a whole pig," Janet said, looking over to the empty fire pit where they'd dug up a perfectly roasted animal hours earlier.

Cora watched several of the pack families expertly prepare the pit yesterday. Around noon they'd lit the fire and buried the animal. That was when she found out that the Laske Pack looked for any excuse to roast a pig.

Every member of her family had raved about the food and made the wolves promise to do it again. Cora suspected that a few brothers might ask to be part of it next time so they could learn how to do it themselves. Too bad it looked like it required a tractor. Her siblings were going to be disappointed!

"I can't believe you made napoleons," Cora said to Janet. They were standing near the dessert table and although Cora already ate two, she was eyeing the last one sitting on a platter.

"You'll make your belly hurt," Kimble warned her.

"Worth it," Cora decided and reached for it. She felt Kimble's amusement through their link.

"I can teach you how to make them," Janet offered.

"No way," Cora said around a mouthful of food. "I'd end up the size of a house."

"Speaking of houses," Tim said, sidling closer to her. "I was wondering if I could do a little renovation at your place. Just a few things, nothing major."

Cora raised an eyebrow. "We can talk, but I'm not giving you permission to build a dungeon."

"Hey, that was uncalled for," Tim protested.

"But was it?" Cora responded.

"I put a collar on once to spice things up, and you guys never let me forget it!" Tim whined, turning red.

"You answered the door wearing it and nothing else!" Cora reminded him.

"I told you; I thought you were Rachel!" Tim said. "It's your fault for not warning me you were coming over."

"The front door has a ring camera for a reason," Cora pointed out. "I gave you the log on and everything."

Tim looked to Caleb with a pleading expression. "Change of subject, please?"

"Sure," Caleb agreed. "How are classes?"

Tim groaned and hid his face in his hands. "Never mind, let's go back to my sex life."

To keep costs down, Tim was doing his first two years at a local community college before transferring to a university. High school had been years ago, and Tim was finding out that college was harder than he expected.

"That bad?" Cora asked.

"Why do I need to take a biology class?" Tim moaned. "I want to study history, not dissect a fish!"

"I remember thinking the same thing in an Eastern Philosophy class," Tina said as both she and Mark joined their little group. "I like numbers. Why did I have to learn about Taoism?"

Tim pointed at her and nodded his head at the rest of the group. "She gets it!"

"I don't know what you guys are complaining about, I loved every class I took," Caleb said.

Cora gave him some side eye. "Really? So that wasn't you who complained bitterly about economics class?"

"I was complaining about the professor, not the subject," Caleb answered. "He could've made the study of pornography boring!"

"Personally, I'm very grateful for the Eastern Philosophy class you took," Mark said. "If you hadn't needed a study partner for the class, we might never have gotten together."

"Yes, we would've," Tina countered. "I'd been stalking you since the first semester of school. You just didn't notice."

As they laughed, Pike appeared, soaking wet and smiling. "Beer me!" he shouted to one of the wolves near a cooler as he nudged his way between Cora and Kimble.

The wolf picked up a can and tossed it to Pike. Plucking it out of the air, Pike popped it open, took a long swallow, and sighed with happiness.

"You're wet!" Cora protested and tried to move away from him. Pike put an arm around her and snuggled closer, squishing his wet clothes between them.

"I got caught in the crossfire of a water balloon war," he explained. "I've been mortally wounded; don't you want to comfort me as a die?"

She was lucky it was an unseasonably warm night because one side of her was soon as wet as Pike. "Bad bear!" she admonished.

Kimble moved them apart and tutted at Pike. "You know better. She could get sick from being outside and damp at night."

The vampire's worry over her "fragile" human body was the only thing they fought over on a regular basis. He was sure she was only one cough away from dying of consumption even though the bond made her far stronger than a regular human.

Along with being strong, she would stay young for as long as Kimble lived. Eventually, she'd need to explain to her family why she wasn't aging, but she could put that off for years, or even decades.

"I'm damp, not dying," she assured Kimble. Pike had grabbed a blanket from a nearby seat and wordlessly handed it to Kimble so he could wrap her up tight. She rolled her eyes and let him.

"You call him bear?" Caleb asked, eyeing the dripping Pike. "Fitting."

Cora grinned. "You have no idea."

"Was that sexual innuendo?" Trevor asked, pretending to cover his ears. "Because I'm young and impressionable."

"Pike, we need you!" a young voice yelled out. "Our position is taking heavy fire!"

Pike chugged back the last of the beer and tossed the can over his shoulder. "Duty calls!" Then he sprinted off with a battle yell that sounded like something from a cartoon.

"He's so great with them," Tina said. "Just think—"

Cora pulled a hand free from the blanket and held up a single finger to cut her off. "First warning."

Tina laughed and pretended to zip her mouth shut. Cora had learned quickly to stop the wistful baby talk before it got started. So far, they hadn't had to get to a second or third warning let alone any true threat. Cora having a baby wasn't on the table yet. Maybe someday, but not now.

"I've had a great time, but Sammy managed to make himself sick by eating too much," Caleb said as he moved in close to give Cora a hug. "We're going to head home so he can recover without further temptation."

She leaned into his hug, then smiled at his wife. "Drive safe."

Standing next to her, Tim asked, "Have you heard from Dad?"

Cora shook her head. "Not a word."

"None of us have," Caleb said. "He's not even talking to Maria."

"He had to hire three guys to take over for all the work I was doing," Tim commented. "And a lot of the guys are quitting because he's taking his temper out on them because we're not there to yell at."

"He's going to have to adapt or die alone," Cora said, feeling both sad and angry at her father.

"I'm sorry he's proven to be so stubborn," Kimble murmured in her ear as Caleb and his family said their last goodbyes and headed to their car.

Cora snuggled against him. "This is real life, not a Hallmark movie. You don't always get everything tied up in a neat bow, but I'll settle for my happy ending with you guys."

**Pike**

Shucking off his waterlogged shoes, Pike calculated the best way over the chair barrier on the other side of their "battlefield." Picking up the bucket full of water balloons, he readied for a sprint across no-man's-land only to see something that made him freeze in place.

Half a dozen water balloons all hit him in the chest and face at the same time he dropped the bucket and formed a T with both hands.

"Time out, everyone!" he shouted. There were groans from all the kids and adults he'd been playing with, but the moment he called time out, a bunch of parents and partners swooped in to start drying off the warriors and urging them to stand next to the bonfire.

He was only peripherally aware of everything going on around him, his focus was on the tall, gaunt, pale woman walking between two wolf shifters. This was the first time he'd seen Lucy since Kimble had carried her away in griffin form, and she looked like a hollowed-out shell of herself. After Kimble got back and told him about her addiction and his offer to help, Pike had thanked him and spent every day after trying not to think about her.

Swallowing hard, he walked toward her, and worked on keeping his emotions in check. There was so much anger and hurt but at the same time relief that she was alive. Shifters addicted to ash could die while trying to go off the drug. During the early days, he'd half expected a call telling him Lucy hadn't made it.

But that call never came and now she was up and walking under her own power, even if both wolves looked ready to grab hold if she stumbled.

Crossing the distance between them, Pike tried to figure out what to say. He'd rehearsed all kinds of conversations between him and Lucy, but now he couldn't think of anything.

"You're too thin." He winced the moment the words were out of his mouth, but it was probably the most shocking part of her appearance. She'd been skinny before, but now she looked almost skeletal.

Lucy didn't take offense to his thoughtless comment. She looked down at herself and shrugged. "You won't believe it, but I've put on some weight."

Her appearance wasn't the only thing that had changed. Gone was the high, shrill voice of the past, now she spoke in a deep husky tone.

"Don't worry, we'll get some meat on her bones," Stan said. He placed a hand on Lucy's lower back. At the same time, Enrico moved until his side was touching hers. It reminded Pike of the way he and Kimble would bracket Cora.

If nothing was going on between these three yet, then it was only a matter of time.

"There's food," he said, pointing with his thumb over his shoulder. The way Lucy blanched and put a hand over her stomach told Pike that his suggestion didn't go over well.

"Thanks, but she's on a special diet right now," Enrico said, then took a long pull of air through his nose. "Smells good though. No one told us they were roasting a pig!"

Feeling awkward, Pike rubbed the back of his neck and looked up at the night sky, trying to come up with something to say.

Lucy spoke before he could think of anything. "I wasn't going to join the party," she explained, pulling his eyes from the heavens back down to her. She tucked a strand of hair behind her ear and tried to smile again. "We walk in the evenings and this time I wanted to walk this way. I only wanted to see you. We, uh, I mean you and me, we're gonna need to talk. Like, a lot of talking, but not yet, okay? I'm not ready yet."

Pike blinked rapidly and nodded his head. "Sure, when you're ready."

Sliding her eyes away, she leaned heavily on Enrico. Stan moved his hand from resting on her lower back to around her waist. It was hard to tell, but Pike thought she'd gotten even paler.

"That was a long walk for you," Stan murmured. "We should head back home now."

Lucy didn't answer Stan. Instead, she looked back at Pike. "Annette is helping me understand everything I did and why. It's a lot. I have so much I need to make up for, but right now, I need to focus on fixing myself before I can fix us."

There were tears in his eyes, and Pike had the urge to hug her and tell her they were fine. But that impulse wasn't as strong as his remaining animosity over her actions regarding Cora.

"I might not be able to forgive you," he whispered, pain lancing through his heart as he said the words, but he felt she should know.

Lucy flinched and both Stan and Enrico glared at him, but their hold on Lucy remained gentle.

"Annette said I shouldn't talk to you yet, so this is my fault," she mumbled, rubbing a fist over her eyes. "Once again, I fucked everything up."

Stan made soothing sounds while Enrico leaned in close and whispered something in her ear. She nodded her head and started to turn but paused and looked back at him.

"Just so you know, I'll live the rest of my life with the weight of having hurt the people who loved me the most. Every moment I breathe, I'm filled with guilt and regret. I won't ever force you to talk to me, but I want you to know I'd do anything you ask. Anything, even ending my own life."

Enrico growled and forcefully turned her to face him. "Did you forget your promise already?"

Pike watched Lucy stare into Enrico's eyes without a hint of fear. "That promise only counts if I want to do it from my own pain. If he asks me, then it's a cure for someone else's pain."

"I don't want you dead," Pike whispered. "I would never want you dead. Even if you'd killed my mate, I don't think I could've taken your life. If I wouldn't take it, then you're not allowed to."

Lucy gave him a watery smile. "You're too good for this world, David. I hope your mates appreciate how wonderful you are."

"We do," Kimble said, appearing at Pike's side with Cora in his arms. He set Cora down, and she unwrapped a towel from around her shoulders and put it on him.

"You're soaked!" she exclaimed cheerfully, pointedly ignoring Lucy.

"Enjoy the love you very much deserve," Lucy said and let the men walk her away. With his emotions in a turmoil, Pike was relieved to see them go.

"I'm safe. Kimble's not feral," Cora said, letting go of the towel to reach up high and cup his cheeks. "And we love you."

Their love coming through the bond warmed him from the inside out, chasing away the pain seeing Lucy had caused. Putting an arm around both his mates, he pulled them close.

No words needed to be spoken, the bond between them said it all.

⸺⬥⸺

**Kimble**

It wasn't until they were all in the house, clean, dry, and snuggled in bed that Kimble relaxed. He'd tolerated the party, especially after realizing that Cora's siblings were on their best behavior, and Pike was enjoying himself immensely. The prospect of holding one of these gatherings once a month no longer seemed so heinous.

Could he have a pool built before the next one? It would be difficult but he could get it done with enough money. It was going to start getting cold soon, so he'd need to make sure the pool was heated. They'd require a small building for the swimmers to use when they needed to clean off the pool water and dry. The building would require several showers at least, and perhaps....

He was so involved in his thoughts he didn't realize his flock was sound asleep until Cora mumbled something and accidentally smacked him on the chest as she shifted position. Usually Cora read a little, and Pike would scroll on his phone before they fell asleep but not tonight.

Reaching across Cora, Kimble petted Pike's side and at the same time buried his face in Cora's hair. Pike made a soft, content sound, and rolled over to spoon Cora, trapping Kimble's arm between the two of them. Even though she was sound asleep, Cora turned her head and nuzzled Kimble's chest. Smiling, he closed his eyes and soaked in the happiness.

It was official, he was the luckiest vampire to have ever unlived.

<h1 style="text-align:center">Bonus Chapter: New Besties!<br>One and a Half Years Later</h1>

**Cora**

The thumping beat of Club Gaudium was almost completely muted as the door softly clicked shut behind Cora, Kimble, and Pike. Blinking at the sudden quiet, she looked around at the people gathered in the room. For a brief moment, she thought about turning around and leaving but then Imani was suddenly in front of her, thrusting a cold glass bottle of Coke into her hand.

"You made it!" she said.

Cora gave a single nod, still unsure what was going on. "Yep, and Kimble even brought a book!"

Imani gave her an approving smile, then nodded her head. "Perfect. This way."

As they followed Imani through the room, Cora noticed almost every person there was holding a book in one hand and a drink in the other. She saw a few faces she knew, but most weren't familiar to her.

Then Imani walked them the short distance to where Briar, Memphis, and Tobias were sitting.

"Sister!" Cora shouted in a dramatic voice. "It's been ages since we saw each other last!"

"Sister!" Briar repeated and stood so the two could embrace. "In truth, a lifetime has passed! My heart is overjoyed to be in your presence once more!"

"Didn't they hang out last night?" Memphis asked Tobias.

"They need to stop watching Bridgerton," Tobias grumbled. "It's making them both positively histrionic."

Cora met Briar at Imani's club opening and the two had instantly bonded. They were both the youngest in large, dysfunctional families—it was a lot to have in common. Tobias and Kimble hadn't been thrilled at their friendship, but both put up with it. Cora and Briar ignored their grumbling.

"If I knew you would be here, I wouldn't have debated about coming for so long that I was late," Cora said, making Briar laugh.

"You're really going to do me like that?" Imani asked, her hands on her hips. "You could've just said you didn't want to come instead of telling me there was a last-minute job, and you might not make it."

Cora grinned at her long-time friend. "I didn't lie exactly. There was a last-minute job."

"Yeah, a blowjob!" Briar cackled.

Giving up on her frown, Imani rolled her eyes and then noticed more new arrivals. "Tag, you came!"

She rushed to greet the three people standing just inside the door. Ignoring the heavily muscled man and woman, probably shifters, Cora watched Imani wrap her arms around a slim, anxious-looking young man with big, dark eyes.

"Uh, hi Imani. I'm sorry we're late," Tag said, returning the hug, then letting go and pressing close to the couple behind him as soon as he could.

"We might not stay long," the woman warned Imani without giving any reason.

Imani wasn't fazed. "Of course, Harper. You guys stay for as long or little as you like."

Tag looked past Imani, and his features lit up. "Sopek!"

Cora followed his gaze to see a large, overstuffed copper colored, wingback chair that didn't match the rest of the club's sleek furniture at all. There were stacks of books piled high enough that the person in the chair could easily reach the top over the arm and grab the one on the top.

She would have sworn that spot was empty when she first walked in. Even more startling was the occupant of the chair.

The creature wasn't something Cora had ever seen before. He was small, maybe three feet tall if he stood up, covered in greenish gray skin, and with small horns on his head and stubby spikes scattered over his body. He had a book open on his lap but was regarding the room instead of reading it.

The way Kimble let out a startled sound and dragged her tightly against him clearly declared this creature as something formidable.

Tag wasn't scared at all. He moved toward the chair with confidence, the two people he came with following close behind. Once he got to the chair, he leaned over and gave the small guy a hug.

"It's good to see you, Sopek."

"Why must you always embrace me?" Sopek grumbled, even as he returned the hug.

"That's a hobgoblin," Kimble whispered in her ear.

"Oh shit," Pike muttered. Everyone in the room was staring at the exchange between Sopek and Tag, some with expressions of surprise and others of horror.

"Uh, guys, clue me in here," Cora whispered.

"Hobgoblins are formidable creatures," Kimble explained. "They can pull magic directly from the void. I'd heard that's how Imani and her flock became covered in void magic, but I didn't believe it."

"So that means these guys are really powerful," Cora said. "But he's so small and cute."

Kimble looked down at her with a raised eyebrow. "You should be the last person to judge strength based on size."

She had to give him that. "Point taken. How powerful are we talking?"

"Only creatures like demi-gods and gorg—"

Before he could finish his sentence, a familiar woman strode through the door. This time it was Cora's turn to shout out a greeting. "Ysabel!"

Ysabel was dressed in a sleek white pantsuit, matching heels, and a purse so tiny, Cora wasn't sure anything but a single tube of lipstick could fit in there.

"I was going to say gorgons," Kimble finished dryly.

"Cora!" Ysabel yelled back and made her way across the room.

Briar made an admiring sound. "I wouldn't wear it, but I like her style, and she's loud. I think we need to be friends."

Cora glanced over her shoulder and caught a look of commiseration between Kimble and Tobias. Poor vampires, forever lamenting all the inappropriately dangerous people their humans wanted to be friends with.

Then Ysabel was on her, giving her a warm hug. Muggsie was right at her side, back in his little dog form disguise but no longer looking old.

"It's been foooooorever!" Ysabel declared. "When are we getting together for drinks again?"

"It's been two weeks," Cora said with a laugh. "We're having a party at the compound this Saturday. Want to come?"

"Wouldn't miss it," Ysabel purred, her eyes taking in the room of people. "Will there be singles there? Everyone here is attached."

"A few," Cora said. Since revitalizing, Ysabel had been partying hard and enjoying herself. Cora suspected she was also sleeping her way through most of the population of San Diego. "Probably mostly human or wolf shifters, though."

Ysabel's grin turned predatory. "Sounds perfect. I do love a good dog pile."

Briar barked out a laugh. "Fuck, that was funny!"

Cora was quick to make introductions and the three of them were soon comparing notes on sex with shifters vs vampires vs humans. They were talking about dick shapes and sizes when Sopek spoke up.

"If everyone could be seated," Sopek called out. "We'll begin."

"Thank whatever gods are listening," Kimble muttered. "I don't think I could listen to another description of a dick."

"I'll send pictures next time," Ysabel said with a chuckle.

Kimble grumbled something under his breath as all eyes turned to look at the hobgoblin. So far, only Tag and his two mates were sitting next to the powerful creature, looking happy and at ease. Everyone else was keeping space between themselves and the hobgoblin.

"Begin what?" Kimble asked as Pike pulled chairs out for the three of them.

"I didn't tell you?" Cora asked, looking at him with a mischievous grin as she pulled the book he was currently reading out of her purse and handed it to him. "This is a book club. We're here so you can talk about books."

Kimble saw through her subterfuge. "I think we're here so you can hang out with Imani."

"That's a bonus," Cora assured him.

"What about the gorgon? She didn't even bring a book," Kimble pointed out.

Ysabel hummed happily. "I'm another bonus. I bring joy and light everywhere I go."

"That's only because everyone's scared you'll turn them to stone if they don't laugh at your jokes," Cora teased.

"How did my life come to this?" Kimble asked the ceiling. "For a long time, I was the most powerful creature I knew. Now I'm in a room where I'm third on the list."

"Fourth," Pike said and pointed. Walking through the door was Mama Monroe and Ellie linked arm and arm. They were wearing matching shirts that had an image of a book and said *Sorry, I can't make it. I'm booked.*

"Are we too late?" Monroe asked.

"Not at all!" Imani said and rushed over to sort out drink orders.

After the two women had drinks and found seats, Sopek started speaking. "As it seems everyone has arrived, I'll begin the first meeting of this book club. First and most important, if I ever catch any of you doing this, I'll eat you myself."

Holding up a book, he pretended to dog-ear a page, then brought the book down and petted it as if to apologize for almost folding a page.

Looking back up, he gave an expression that Cora thought was his version of a smile. "Now that is out of the way, let's talk about books."

A mug of steaming tea appeared in his hand, and he held the book up again. "Who's read this one?"

"Sopek, we talked about this," Imani said, taking a seat on her mate Mac's lap. The large sloth bear shifter brushed a kiss on her cheek before turning his attention back to Sopek.

"I wasn't being rude," Sopek objected.

"You need to let people talk about the books they're reading, not the one you're currently focused on," she reminded him.

"Oh, yes, that's right," Sopek said with a nod of his squat head. "Someone tell me about their book, right now!"

Cora couldn't help it she laughed. Then Briar joined her, followed by Monroe, Ellie, and Ysabel. No one else laughed, but

Cora could tell the tension in the room eased. Still, no one spoke up.

It was Tag who got everyone talking by pointing at the book Lex was holding. "Have you finished that one yet?"

Lex nodded his head. "It was good."

"As good as the first one in the series?" Tag asked. "I felt like the action was good in the first one, but the plot lagged a little."

"It's better than the first."

Lex's answers might have been short but that little exchange helped other people start talking. Soon there were lively discussions going on about authors, books, and series in all different genres.

To Cora's delight, even Kimble ended up engaged with several people about historical fiction. Imani moved from group to group making sure everyone had drinks and having a good time.

The only scary part of the evening was when Monroe and Ysabel got close enough to almost touch and a few sparks flew. Lex was quick to put out the smoldering carpet, and Kimble reminded the ladies that they were far too powerful to even shake hands or risk setting everyone on fire.

Laughing, Ysabel moved a chair away, and Monroe linked her hands with Ellie's. It wasn't subtle when almost everyone moved their chairs further away from the demi-god and gorgon.

"You know, if I was to give a gathering of readers a name," Briar mused as she wiggled around a little in Memphis's lap before taking another sip of her beer. "Before Tobias, I would've called them a Silence of Readers."

"And now?" Cora asked as she leaned back against Pike's chest. "No, wait, let me guess, a Binding of Readers?"

Briar laughed. "That's a good one, but no. I think it should be a Binge of Readers."

"That's fitting," Pike agreed. "Even when Kimble wasn't talking well, he'd read an entire book in a few hours. It was intense!"

Pike and Briar talked, exchanging stories about the trials and tribulations of caring for sick vampires while Cora let her eyes wander the room. Life was a crazy ride and it had plunked her down in the middle of a world she never knew existed. The story of her meeting Pike and Kimble would make a great book.

Maybe she should start writing books. The story of Briar, Memphis, and Tobias was an adventure tale, Then there was Imani and her amazing strength in surviving a world set on destroying her only to find love with Lex and Mac.

Looking around her, Cora realized there were a lot of good books in this room waiting to be written. Perhaps it was time for her to try her hand at being an author. She had enough source material, and she bet Briar and Imani would love to help.

*Watch out world,* she thought. *You're about to get some badass stories you'll never believe were true!*

Dear Readers,

Thank you for reading *Kidnapping Their Third*. If you want more Ours Evermore series the next book is ready for pre-order: *Pastries on a Plate and Blood in a Mug*. Also keep and eye out for a holiday novella I hope to release this winter: *Deck the Skulls*.

I hope you enjoyed *Kidnapping Their Third* enough to leave a review! As an indie writer without the support of a publishing company, I need all the help I can get. Your good reviews keep me writing.

If you have any questions, comments, or suggestions feel free to contact me via email: author@rk-munin.com

I'm on Instagram, Facebook and I have some free novellas available. You'll find all the links of my website:

www.rk-munin.com

Thanks for reading!

Cheers,
Rye

## Other books by RK Munin

### -Science Fiction-

### Hissa Warrior Series
Rescuing Halin (Mian and Halin)
Buying Tiran (Mara and Tiran)
Tempting Selon (Lara and Selon)
Defying Kilan (Deena and Kilan)
Healing Mavito (Raleen and Mavito)
Claiming Yopin (Mouse and Yopin)
Teasing Woken (Safena and Woken)
Defending Revin (Kamaril and Revin)
Trusting Warik – Coming soon


### Human Pets of Talin Series
Loving Captivity (Sora and Searin)
Escaping Captivity (Lakin and Dalt)
Negotiating Captivity (Nalia and Derani)
Fighting Captivity (Zia and Palforma)
Tender Captivity (Jinna and Holian - This is a novella you can get for
free by signing up for my newsletter)
Craving Captivity (Lasha and Tamerin)
The Twelve Nights of Halloheen: A holiday mashup novella (Isla and
Tisuran)
Stealing Captivity (Kasi and Ignatias)
Redeeming Captivity – Coming soon


### Origins (A Human Pets of Talin Series)
Creating Captivity (Ari and Bazium)
Gossamer Chains (Rain and Hesarium)
Golden Cages – Coming soon
Purring, Presents, and Parties – Coming soon


### -Paranormal /Urban Fantasy-

### Ours Evermore Series
Two Wolves for Soren (Soren, Kalli, and Quinn)
A Hacker, Vampire, and Chimera Walk into a Bar… (Tobias, Briar, and
Memphis)
When Darkness Meets Dawn (Imani, Lex, and Mac)
Tag, You're It (Novella)
Kidnapping Their Third (Cora, Pike, and Kimble)

Pastries on a Plate and Blood in a Mug – Coming soon

**Alpha Series**
Alpha Mage (Emma and Kade)
His Alpha Mage (Avery and Jason – Novella)
Alpha King (Cathleen and Lazlo)

**New Clan Series**
Stray Wolf (Steph and Eli)
Lost Lion (Maeve and Cyrus)
Reluctant Cervid (Tavi and Donovan)
Broken Thorn (Sabina and Theodosius)

www.ingramcontent.com/pod-product-compliance
Lightning Source LLC
Chambersburg PA
CBHW060431310726
48977CB00001B/142